Robert Fordyce Aickman was born in 1914 in London. He was married to Edith Ray Gregorson from 1941 to 1957. In 1946 the couple, along with Tom and Angela Rolt, set up the Inland Waterways Association to preserve the canals of Britain. It was in 1951 that Aickman, in collaboration with Elizabeth Jane Howard, published his first ghost stories in a volume entitled *We Are for the Dark*. Aickman went on to publish seven more volumes of 'strange stories' as well as two novels and two volumes of autobiography. He also edited the first eight volumes of *The Fontana Book of Great Ghost Stories*. He died in February 1981.

T0160613

The Unsettled Dust

ROBERT AICKMAN

FABER & FABER

First published in this edition in 2014
by Faber and Faber Limited
The Bindery
51 Hatton Garden, London ECIN 8HN

Printed and bound by CPI Group (UK) Ltd, Croydon, CRO 4YY

A CIP record for this book is available from the British Library

ISBN 978-0-571-31173-6

Printed and bound in the UK on FSC® certified paper in line with our continuing
commitment to ethical business practices, sustainability and the environment.
For further information see faber.co.uk/environmental-policy

Contents

Robert Aickman: An Introduction

by Richard T. Kelly

Is Robert Fordyce Aickman (1914–81) the twentieth century's 'most profound writer of what we call horror stories and he, with greater accuracy, preferred to call strange stories'? Such was the view of Peter Straub, voiced in a discerning introduction to *The Wine-Dark Sea*, a collection which, like *The Unsettled Dust*, gathered together some of Aickman's finest pieces posthumously. If you grant Aickman his characteristic insistence on self-classification within this genre of 'strange', then you might say he was in a league of his own (rather as Edgar Allan Poe is the lone and undisputed heavyweight in the field of 'tales of mystery and imagination'). 'Horror', though, is clearly the most compelling genre label that exists on the dark side of literary endeavour. So it might be simplest and most useful to the cause of extending Aickman's fame if we agree that, yes, he was the finest horror writer of the last hundred years.

So elegantly and comprehensively does Aickman encompass all the traditional strengths and available complexities of the supernatural story that, at times, it's hard to see how any subsequent practitioner could stand anywhere but in his shadow. True, there is perhaps a typical Aickman protagonist – usually but not always a man, and one who does not fit so well with others, temperamentally inclined to his own company. But Aickman has a considerable gift for putting us stealthily behind the eyes of said protagonist. Having established such identification, the way in which he then builds up a sense of dread is masterly. His construction of sentences and of narrative is patient and finical. He seems always to proceed from a rather grey-toned realism where detail accumulates without fuss, and the recognisable material world appears wholly four-square – until you realise that the narrative has been built as a cage, a kind of personal hell, and our protagonist is walking towards death as if in a dream.

This effect is especially pronounced – Aickman, as it were, preordains the final black flourish – in stories such as 'Never Visit Venice' (the title gives the nod) and 'The Fetch', whose confessional protagonist rightly judges himself 'a haunted man', his pursuer a grim and faceless wraith who emerges from the sea periodically to augur a death in the family. Sometimes, though, to paraphrase John Donne, the Aickman protagonist runs to death just as fast as death can meet him: as in 'The Stains', an account of a scholarly widower's falling in love with – and plunging to his undoing through – a winsome young woman who is, in fact, some kind of dryad.

On this latter score it should be said that, for all Aickman's seeming astringency, many of his stories possess a powerful erotic charge. There is, again, something dreamlike to how quickly in Aickman an attraction can proceed to a physical expression; and yet he also creates a deep unease whenever skin touches skin – as if desire (and the feminine) are forms of snare, varieties of doom. If such a tendency smacks rather of neurosis, one has to say that this is where a great deal of horror comes from; and Aickman carries off his version of it with great panache, always.

On the flipside of the coin one should also acknowledge Aickman's refined facility for writing female protagonists, and that the ambience of such tales – the world they conjure, the character's relations to people and things in that world – is highly distinctive and noteworthy within his *oeuvre*. Aickman's women are generally spared the sort of grisly fates he reserves for his men, and yet still he routinely leaves us to wonder if they are headed to heaven or hell, if not confined to some purgatory. Among his most admired stories in this line are 'The Inner Room' and 'Into the Wood', works in which the mystery deepens upon the final sentence.

And lest we forget: Aickman can be very witty, too, even in the midst of mounting horrors, and even if it's laughter in the dark. English readers in particular tend to chuckle over 'The Hospice', the story of a travelling salesman trapped in his worst nightmare of a guest-house, where the guests are kept in ankle-fetters and the evening meal is served in mountainous indigestible heaps ('It's turkey tonight . . .'). In the aforementioned 'The Fetch', when our haunted man finally finds himself caged in his Scottish family home, watching the wraith watching him from a perch outdoors up high on a broken wall, he still has time to reflect that 'such levitations are said to be not uncommon in the remoter parts of Scotland'. This is the sound of a refined intellect, an author amusing both himself and us.

2014 is the centenary of Aickman's birth and sees him honoured at the annual World Fantasy Convention, the forum where, in 1975, his story 'Pages from a Young Girl's Journal' received the award for short fiction. His cult has been secure since then, and yet those who have newly discovered his rare brilliance have quite often wondered why he is not better known outside the supernatural cognoscenti.

One likely reason is that his body of work is so modestly sized: there are only forty-eight extant 'strange stories', and there was never a novel – or, to be precise, the two longer-form Aickmans that have been published – *The Late Breakfasters* in 1964 and *The Model*, posthumously, in 1987 – were fantastical (the latter especially), not to say exquisite, but had nothing overtly eerie or blood-freezing about them. Aickman simply refused to cash in on his most marketable skills as a writer (somewhat to the chagrin of the literary agents who represented him).

He was also a relatively late starter. *We Are for the Dark*, his co-publication with Elizabeth Jane Howard to which they contributed three tales apiece, appeared from Jonathan Cape in 1951; but nothing followed until 1964, with his first discrete collection, *Dark Entries*. By the turn of the 1980s he was a significant figure in the landscape, and from there his renown might have widened. It was then, however, that he developed the cancer from which he would die, on 26 February 1981, having refused chemotherapy in favour of homeopathic treatments.

Aickman's name would surely enjoy a wider currency today if any of his works had been adapted for cinema, a medium of which he was a discerning fan. And yet, to date, no such adaptation has come about. If we agree that a masterpiece is an idea expressed in its perfect creative form then it may be fair to say that the perfection Aickman achieved in the short story would not suffer to be stretched to ninety minutes or more across a movie screen. But the possibility still exists, for sure. If Aickman made a frightening world all of his own on the page, he also took on some of the great and familiar horror tropes, and treated them superbly.

To wit: the classic second piece in *Dark Entries*, 'Ringing the Changes', is a zombie story, immeasurably more ghastly and nerve-straining than *The Walking Dead*. And the aforementioned 'Pages from a Young Girl's Journal' is a vampire story, concerning a pubescent girl bored rigid by her family's Grand Tour of Italy in 1815, until she is pleasurably transformed by an encounter with a tall, dark, sharp-toothed stranger. In other words it is about the empowering effects of blood-sucking upon adolescent girls; and worth ten of the *Twilight*s of this world. On the strength of such accomplishments one can see that, while Aickman remains for the moment a cult figure, his stories retain the potential to reach many more new admirers far and wide – rather like the vampirised Jonathan Harker at the end of Werner Herzog's *Nosferatu the Vampyre* (1979), riding out on his steed to infect the world.

Had Aickman never written a word of fiction of his own he would still have a place in the annals of horror: a footnote, perhaps, to observe that he was the maternal grandson of Richard Marsh, bestselling sensational/supernatural novelist of the late-Victorian and Edwardian eras; but an extensive entry for his endeavours as an anthologist, who helped to define a canon of supernatural fiction through his editing of the first eight volumes of the *Fontana Book of Great Ghost Stories* between 1964 and 1972.

His enduring reputation, though, would have been based on his co-founding in 1944 of the Inland Waterways Association, dedicated to the preservation and restoration of England's inland canals. Such a passionate calling might be considered perfect for an author of 'strange stories' – also for a man who was, in some profound way, out of step with or apart from his own time. By all accounts Aickman gave the IWA highly energetic leadership and built up its profile and activities with rigour and zeal. His insistent style, however, did not delight everyone: in 1951 he argued and fell out definitively with L. T. C. (Tom) Rolt, fellow conservationist and author, whose seminal book *Narrow Boat* (1944) had inspired the organisation's founding in the first place.

When we admire a writer we naturally wish to know

more of what they were like as a person. Aickman's admirers have sometimes found what they have heard of him to be a shade forbidding. Culturally he was a connoisseur who had highly finessing tastes in theatre, ballet, opera and classical music. Socially he was punctilious and fastidious, unabashedly erudite, an autodidact not shy about airing his education. His political instincts were conservative, his outlook elitist. The late Elizabeth Jane Howard – first secretary of the Inland Waterways Association, with whom Aickman fell in love and for whom he carried a torch years after her ending of their brief relationship – would tell an interviewer some years later that there were at least two sides to the man: 'He could be very prickly and difficult, or he could be very charming.'

Nonetheless, those whom Aickman allowed to know him well and whom he liked and trusted in turn clearly found him to be the most marvellous company – for a night at the theatre, say, or a visit to a rural stately home, or at a catered dinner *à deux*, after which he would be inclined to read aloud from whichever strange story he was then working on. The reader will learn more in this line from the afterwords to this series of Faber reissues, which have been written by admiring friends who had just such a privileged insight into the author.

These reissues are in honour of Aickman's 2014 centenary. Along with the present volume, readers may choose from *Dark Entries*, *Cold Hand in Mine*, *The Wine-Dark Sea*, and (as Faber Finds) *The Late Breakfasters* and *The Model*. Whether these works are already known to you or you are about to discover them, the injunction is the same – prepare to be entranced, compelled, seduced, petrified.

RICHARD T. KELLY *is the author of the novels* Crusaders *and* The Possessions of Doctor Forrest.

The Unsettled Dust

During the period of my work as Special Duties Officer for the Historic Structures Fund, I have inevitably come upon many strange and unexpected things in all fields; but only three times that I can recollect have I so far encountered anything that might be thought to involve an element of the paranormal.

Since interest in paranormal phenomena appears to be growing steadily, partly no doubt as an escape from a way of life that seems every day to grow more uniform, regulated, and unambitious, I have thought for some time that it might be worth while to set out at least one of these cases, the most striking, I think, of the three, in an orderly though completely frank narrative; separated from the many other documents connected with my employment. It is not a matter of struggling for half-lost memories, since for the most part the task consists in adapting extracts from my Diary for the period of time concerned. I have now been Special Duties Officer for just over ten years, and I think the moment has come to set about the task.

It so happens that it has been during those ten years that the Fund has set up a Psychic and Occult Research Committee. As is well known, the Council hesitated for many years before taking this step, having in mind the extreme undesirability of the Fund involving itself in controversy of any kind, and also the constant danger of its being charged with crankiness or reaction; but in the end the pressure became so great that a response could no longer be avoided. I think it was inevitable. The link between an interest in old buildings (often ruinous and sometimes ecclesiastical), and an interest in what are popularly called 'ghosts', is obvious. Also the Fund, like most established voluntary societies, is supported mainly by the elderly. A Psychic Committee was and is as inescapable as the Animals Committee that has been with us almost from the start.

The P. and O. Research Committee has undoubtedly done much good work, but I have hesitated to deliver to them a report of my own, despite the fact that I am possibly in a position to deliver three. The Fund is a very conservative organisation (not in the party sense, of course), and my dilemma is that of the civil servant. If a civil servant takes an initiative and things go right with it, he cannot, in the nature of his employment, look for much in the way of reward; whereas if his initiative goes wrong, he can expect all kinds of trouble, everything from a reprimand to blocked promotion, and a permanent black mark against his name in the files. It is accepted, therefore, that the way to advance in the civil service, or in any field where civil service conditions prevail, is never to take an initiative and never to support anyone else's. It is inevitable that this should be so, as long as we base all our administration on the bureaucratic model. The Fund is not as hard a master as the civil service, of course, if only because no one had to answer to Parliament for its actions; but caution is compelled upon it by its sheer size, and by its obligation to offend no one, if this can possibly be avoided, not even its direct critics. A report, even if carefully edited, delivered by me to the P. and O. people on any one of my three cases could, in my judgement, lead to contention, to unpopularity in various quarters for the author, and conceivably even to a libel action in which the Fund would be involved. There are few subjects on which people are more touchy than the 'supernatural', as they call it. It is the measure of the importance they attach to it, even if few of them care to admit it. The delivery of such a report would hardly be construed by the Council as lying within my duties, if trouble resulted. One can but speculate upon the mass of important information which never sees the light of day for similar reasons. I have thought it best to confine the circulation of my narrative to a few selected people, binding them in advance to the strictest confidence; and to place a copy for posterity in my small archives.

The position of Special Duties Officer, of which I have so far been the only incumbent, was created when the growth of the Fund, and the number and variety of its properties, conjured up a miscellany of tasks, often urgent, but all outside the scope of any member of a staff which had been recruited almost solely for duties connected with preservation in the strictest sense – and which, as was freely admitted at the time, was often by then advanced in service. My ploys have varied from setting up a large bequest of sculpture in a once ducal park, to organising a sailing-boat harbour on an island off the Welsh coast; from a frustrating six months devoted to relaying an ornamental paving, to an even longer period spent in promoting an open-air season of fertility plays with singing and dancing. Most of my work has been done in the open air, trying to dodge the British climate, the local authority Philistines, and the Fund's own members, so many of whom have ideas of their own and think they have bought the entire staff with their own small subscriptions. Well, not *all* perhaps. Some of the members are very nice people, and eager to offer their hospitality. I have had my moments of cynicism, when I have felt that all that has mattered of the Fund's work has rested on my single shoulders, but that was mere self-pity and I really know quite well that I have done much better as a Fund officer than I could expect to do in any other job. I fell right on my feet when the Fund engaged me.

The events I am about to describe took place at Clamber Court in Bedfordshire, a seat of the Brakespear family, the family of which one branch is said to have provided the only Englishman ever to be Pope; who was also the Pope with the greatest physical strength of all the Popes. The Clamber Court branch was represented by two unmarried sisters. Their father, the last Lord St Adrian, had died years before, and their mother was said to have been a little queer ever since. At least that was the gossip around the Fund office. In the end, the girls had settled Clamber on the

Fund, but remained there themselves as Fund tenants. The same office gossip said that the girls had lived very wildly at one time, having no one to control them, and had got through a lot of money. Explanations like that might have been true in former times, but there is seldom much in them nowadays. It is far more likely that the Brakespears were orphans of the social storm like most of the Fund's clients.

My sojourn in the house had nothing to do with the building itself or the surrounding property, as I shall explain in a moment, but it so happens that I had paid Clamber one previous visit. It had not been in the course of my duties, which do not include any kind of regular round. I went there as an ordinary Fund member, without disclosing anything more. In those early days, I often found it instructive to do this and to note how my colleagues were faring in their endless struggle with the different buildings, often near to collapse even when offered to the Fund; and with the odd and recalcitrant people who lived in them. In those days, the Fund's aged President frequently described the staff as an extra-large family, and it was by no means only a cliché: one felt the presence of the Fund wherever one went, watching how one behaved, and difficult to get away from. Of course I felt much more at home in a year or two, much more sure of my ground. When it came to my going to places like Clamber Court, it should also be remembered that I had worked at one time in architecture, though I never qualified, and so had an interest in buildings for their own sake.

Naturally that is true of many of the Fund's staff.

Clamber Court proved to be a square, four-storeyed, brick pile, with, on each side, a square, two-storeyed, smaller brick pavilion. The pavilions had slate roofs coming to points, and pilasters on three sides. They were linked to the main block by lengthy one-storey passages, with big, circular-topped windows. This branch of the large Brakespear family had become rich at the time of the Hanoverian succession, and that then entered upon a new period of importance, drifting so far from the other branches that ultimately no heir could be found to the title. A conspicuous feature of the property was two very long drives. The first one led from the front of the house, dead straight down a two-mile avenue of fine old trees to a noble, ornamental gateway on the main road. The other ran, less straight, but at no less length, from a pretty lodge at the east to a related lodge at the west (also on the main road). The drives crossed at about a quarter of a mile from the house-front. At the point of intersection was a baroque fountain, with an heroic male figure about to drive a spear into a fat boar. I found it an uncomfortable group, but redeemed by the all too unusual excellence of its condition and maintenance. In modern Europe, most estate fountains are broken, sordid, and regarded with indifference even by their owners. This one shimmered, and, supreme marvel, actually spouted water, quite probably at the proper force. I had already noted that the drive down which I had driven my Mini (the transverse drive) was clean and weeded; every pane of glass in the two long corridors from the main house to the pavilions appeared to be in place, and gleaming in the spring sun. The Fund cannot always afford perfections of that kind. Almost certainly, the Brakespears must have had something left in the kitty.

The interior of the house confirmed this. Not only did it contain many objects of real excellence, but it was painted, tended, and polished. There were no sagging wallpaper and no holes in the ceiling. On the other hand, I could not say that the house was dusted. This was curious. One might have written names in the deposit on the gleaming surfaces, as Rembrandt did in Korda's film. Indeed, I did write 'Historic Structures Fund' on the top of a dining-room table, and the words stood out quite clearly in the light of a sunbeam. The odd thing was that one of the house employees, a tall, grey woman in a grey nylon wrapper, just watched me do it from the other side of the room, and said nothing at all, though she was presumably stationed to keep an eye on the behaviour of the public. I particularly noticed that she didn't even smile at what I had done. I was so surprised by the dust in the house and by the indifference shown to it that the next day I sent a memo to the Fund's Regional Representative. I suggested that there might be a cement works in the district, an idea that had occurred to me during the night; and that the Fund should possibly require all the house windows to be kept shut.

That was nine years ago. Two years later, I was required to stay in the house for (as my Diary confirms) eighteen days. The reason was the need to superintend one of the maddest schemes in which the Fund ever entangled itself – indeed, the maddest of all, as I said at the time, when anyone asked me, and as events have since confirmed, to my very sincere regret: the so-called recovery of the River Bovil. For years, there had been complaints in various quarters (none of them, of course, in full possession of the facts) that the Fund was too conservationist and backward-looking; too little prepared to enter the field and do battle. The worst consequence of this uninformed agitation was that the Fund found itself saddled with the project for cleaning out the weeds and mud from this small, local river that no one had ever heard of (not even the people who lived in the district, as I soon found), and patching up the broken-down locks. The view that I (and others) expressed was the obvious one that if there was any real demand for the river, then the proper public authorities could be depended upon to attend to it. The matter was simply nothing to do with the objectives of the Fund. But there was the usual group of hotheads, with not enough work to do in the world, as one could not but feel; and they had interested one of the local landowners in putting up a little money, though only one landowner and nothing like *enough* money. They said that most of the work could be done by volunteers, and that the public would find the rest of the finance. Needless to say, neither claim proved to be true, and the whole business committed the Fund to endless travail, by no means ended yet, nor likely to be. The Fund is simply not equipped for struggle, argument, and publicity. Nor has my own experience disposed me in favour of what are called 'voluntary workers'. In practice much more is always achieved by regular, salaried staff, keeping themselves out of the limelight. And so it has proved in the case of the Bovil project. But if I say more on that topic, I shall be suspected of disloyalty to the Fund Council, which would be quite wrong. It is more a case of loyalty being often best shown by preventing mistakes being made.

After (in my view) insufficient discussion, the Bovil project was agreed to and the hottest and most thrusting of the hotheads put in charge of the actual works, a man named Hand. I myself didn't think he was altogether an Englishman, but it was obvious that he was very young for the degree of responsibility in which he had involved himself, so I was asked to look after him during the first stages of the work, as I was twenty or more years older and had gained experience from a wide variety of different jobs. Hamish Haythorn, the National Secretary of the Fund, wrote to Miss Agnes Brakespear, reputedly the more businesslike sister, to ask if I could stay at Clamber Court while I was launching the scheme. The Fund expects people whose properties have been accepted to help in this way, as the need may arise; though sometimes Fund employees find themselves offered only an attic and very simple fare. This had by then happened to me several times, and I was quite prepared for it at Clamber Court. (Nowadays, of course, in my case it hardly ever happens, because I have learned to enter into the different foibles of the

Fund's tenants.) I remember that Miss Brakespear took a long time to answer at all, and all the while the Bovil scheme was held up; but we heard from her in the end, and off I went that very afternoon. I arrived in good time for dinner, though that, as I have just said, might not have meant very much.

There was a long tradition that the great gates on the main road were opened only for family weddings, family funerals, and visits of the Sovereign, and the smaller gate further up the same road had been padlocked by the Fund's Regional Representative, because it had proved impossible to find a tenant for the adjoining lodge, owing to the noise of the traffic; so that I wound my way in my Mini through the lanes leading to the eastern entry, as I had done two years before. It had perhaps been not quite as much as that, because now it was earlier in the spring, with not yet a leaf on any of the big, old trees: in fact, not yet officially spring at all. This time, the man at the gate was wearing a hat, which he touched when opening for me.

My spirits rose as I saw that the long, winding drive was as spruce as before. All the hedges within view had been properly laid and many of the farm gates had been renewed. The hero huntsman, when at length I reached him, was enshrined among complex traceries of water, and the doomed quarry adrip with it. The house, I thought, as I completed the finishing stretch up to the wide parterre of rectangular stones before the double staircase, looked immaculate but unfunctional, like a vast Staffordshire model. When I stopped my engine and stepped out, the complete silence contributed to the illusion. I stood for a moment looking down the slow descent to the great gates, and watching big, black rooks wheel like sheets of burnt newspaper between the bare trees, the only life there was.

'Hullo,' said a casual voice from above. 'Come in.'

Standing with her hands on the balustrade at the top of the two flights of steps was a woman; plainly one of my two hostesses, though I had never then knowingly seen either. I wavered, as one does, between ascending the right-hand steps or the left, but she said nothing and just watched me.

'I'm Olive Brakespear,' she said as I arrived, and held out her hand. I should have expected the hand to be cold, as it was one of those fine March days, which often seem the chilliest of the year. But it was not. 'You're my landlord.' In my experience, the tenants always either said something like that or, alternatively, did everything to pretend that the relationship was the other way round.

Miss Brakespear, however, was an unusual figure. She was well above average height for a woman (and six or eight inches above mine), and remarkably slender and well-shaped, though tough and wiry looking. The last impression was reinforced by the fact that she was wearing worn brown riding breeches, worn brown riding boots, and a dark-blue shirt, open at the neck and with the sleeves rolled up. Her face, neck and forearms were all tanned and brown, even though it was the end of the winter. Her face was striking because she had strong, prominent bones, large, melancholy eyes, and a big, rectangular mouth, but some might have said that her head was too long, her cheeks too sunken. She had straight reddish-brown hair, starting rather far back on the brow. It was glossy and well-kept, like the mane of a race-horse, but worn shoulder-length and curled outwards at the ends, after the fashion which prevailed during the Second World War. It was very difficult to guess how old she was. Her physical style was one which is eminently durable.

'I was watching the rooks,' she said. 'Sometimes when the trees are bare and the light beginning to go, I do it for an hour at a time.' Looking at her in her blue shirt, I am sure I must have shivered. 'Come on in, or you'll get cold,' said Miss Brakespear.

The big, oblong, pillared hall contained only formal furniture, though I was pleased to observe a heap of the Fund's official, blue-covered guidebooks to the house. The wide door had lain open while Miss Brakespear stood outside, so that the cavernous room was cold and echoey, especially as there was no fire. It was also dim, as evening was descending, and Miss Brakespear had not turned on the light.

She went before me up the dark main staircase, taking two steps at a time with her swinging stride. Impeded by my bundle, I followed her much less gracefully.

We turned leftwards along a high, wide passage which traversed the first floor of the house, with big white doors opening into silent rooms on either side. I had not previously been upstairs, because the rooms open to the public were all below. Miss Brakespear's step in her riding boots was sharp and swift, whereas I am sure that I merely shuffled. At the eastern end of the passage, Miss Brakespear opened the door of my room. At least I had not been relegated to one of those designed for occupation by the servants.

It was a big, square, dark red room, with a heavy dado, two windows looking down the long avenue, a modern double bed, and a general look of having been furnished by a good contractor in, perhaps, 1910.

'Turn on the light, if you like,' said Miss Brakespear; 'unless you prefer the dusk, as I do. There's a bathroom opposite. It's all for you, because nowadays there's never anyone else on this side of the house. My sister and I sleep at the other end. Elizabeth Craw, our housekeeper, sleeps upstairs, and the two girls in the village. You'll find the whole house quiet for your work until the open season begins at Easter. Come down for a drink when you're ready. In the music room to the left of the hall.'

She strode away down the dark passage, leaving my bedroom door open. She had a rich and liquid voice, really rather beautiful; and a casual inflection which one felt never varied, no matter what she was saying or to whom. I noticed that she had not mentioned her mother, who was supposed to live somewhere in the house also.

I shut the door and stood in the middle of the room waiting. I might well have been waiting for the twilight to become more like darkness, so that, even by Miss

Brakespear's standard, I could turn on the light with a good conscience. Then I realised how absurd this was, and pressed the switch. The result was disappointing. The only light in the room came from three rather faint bulbs attached to a brass frame which the 1910 contractor had suspended from the plaster rose in the centre of the coffered ceiling. They would effectively illumine neither a reader in bed nor a maker-up or report-writer at the heavy dressing table. I felt that from the park my room must look little more luminous than in the year the house was built.

I unpacked a few things and stowed them away. I set my book hopefully by the side of the bed (Christopher Hussey's *The Picturesque*, I see in my Diary that it was). I cased the room for heat of any kind. There was none. I wondered if I should change into something darker, but decided that I could decide while taking my drink, as it was still early enough to change after it, if that seemed appropriate. I crossed the passage to the bathroom.

Here the electric light seemed a little stronger. I looked at my hands as one does after a journey, to see how travel-stained they are. They were filthy. I was as-tonished, and as I turned the tap of the washbasin (of course, there was nothing like that in my bedroom), I worried about having shaken hands with Miss Brakespear. Then I realised that the grime had spread from darker patches at the tips of my fingers, and that I had probably picked it up in my bedroom. And only then did I remember about the dust I had noticed on my previous visit to the house. The matter had not lately been in my mind. I remembered also about the memo on the subject which I had sent to old Blantyre, the impoverished country gentleman who acted as the Fund's Regional Representative in that area. Thinking about it now, I was almost sure that Blantyre had never even sent an acknowledgement; so that, almost certainly, he had taken no action whatever. I let the water run and run, but it never ran hot.

I remembered the beautiful music room quite well. As I stood in the dark hall outside the thick, closed door, I could just hear the sound of a piano within. Real music in the music room of a British mansion is today so rare that at first I took it for granted that the wireless had been turned on, but when I opened the door and entered, I saw that Miss Brakespear was herself playing. She did not stop when I walked in, but merely indicated with a movement of her head that I should sit down. The gesture seemed quite friendly but she did not smile. I suspected that Miss Brakespear smiled seldom. In here a big log fire burnt: the supply of logs, rough and knotty, being piled high in a vast, circular bin of chased brass, itself gleaming like a yellow furnace. I know nothing about music but it seemed to me that Miss Brakespear played the piano much as she talked; beautifully, but with a casualness that was not so much indifference as the reflection of melancholy and resignation. There was no music before her, and no light by which she could have read it: quite possibly she was improvising, though she seemed to my ignorance to be doing it with depth and fluency. I daresay this was nonsense on my part, but as she played on and on, I found that I was pleased to warm myself right through at rather long last, and to listen to her and watch her dim shape by the light of the fire. I could see that she was still wearing her riding clothes, with the tips of her boots on the pedals.

I am not sure how much time passed in this way; but certainly it was quite dark outside the uncurtained windows, when the door opened and a third person stood there. It was another woman. I could not see her at all clearly, but I could see the shape of her dress and the outline of her hair. She stood for a while with the door still open behind her. Miss Brakespear went on playing, as if in a trance with herself. Then the newcomer shut the door and turned on the light: more effective lighting than in the rooms above. At once, Miss Brakespear broke off.

'Dreaming?' asked the newcomer; none too agreeably, I thought.

Miss Brakespear made no direct reply. 'Agnes,' she said, 'this is Mr Oxenhope, at once our landlord and our guest. Mr Oxenhope, let me introduce my sister, Agnes.'

The other Miss Brakespear (hereafter I must call them Olive and Agnes, though I do not find it comes very naturally) seemed little interested. 'How do you do?' she said in an offhand way from the door.

'How do you do?' I replied.

Now that the lights were on, I glanced about for dust.

'You really are a fool,' said Agnes to her sister, and walked over to the fire. One could have said she spoke in affectionate derision, as is the way within a family (the alternative commonly being silence); but I might rather have called it habitual derision, accepted derision.

Olive closed the piano and got up. At that exact distance from me, and by fairly strong artificial light, her neck, inside the open collar of her dark shirt, looked more withered and less shapely than I had thought. 'How did the meeting go?' she asked quietly.

'Exactly as expected,' replied Agnes, standing before the blaze, her feet slightly apart, her hands behind her back. She was of an entirely different physical type from her sister: a squarish, fattish woman at about my height, with a thickening face and neck, dark eyes and abundant dark hair in a style more fashionable than her sister's. She wore a plain dress in thick, purple wool, and black, high-heeled shoes. She might have been described by an enemy as too heavily made up, but that is a difficult problem for a woman of her build and period of life: even though I should not have cared to assess her exact age within a range of perhaps twenty years. As will be gathered, she seemed very much more the customary Englishwoman than her sister; and she had something of the frustration and suppressed, long-lost feeling that goes with the customary Englishwoman, however banal the customary manifestation of it. When one spends one's time going round the different properties of the Historic Structures Fund, one grows to learn the essential characteristics of the customary Englishwoman.

Olive had unlocked an ebony and ivory cabinet and was getting us drinks. There was no further reference to the meeting that had been mentioned. Indeed, there was silence. I knew that it was for me to help things along, but I could think of nothing to say. Agnes saved me the trouble.

'What are you feeling for?' she asked.

It seemed appallingly observant of her.

'I thought I'd dropped my handkerchief,' I improvised, perhaps more readily than convincingly.

'Mr Oxenhope's visit has nothing to do with the house,' said Olive conciliatingly. It was excellently intended, no doubt, but the form of words suggested that she too had cottoned on. Because I had, of course, been feeling (as Agnes had put it) for dust. And, what was more, I had been doing it without being aware of it. Needless to say, it was very discourteous of me, socially speaking.

'And his gropings have nothing to do with his handkerchief,' said Agnes drily. 'With *either* of his handkerchiefs: the one in his sleeve or the pretty one in his breast pocket. Do you carry three handkerchiefs, Mr Oxenhope?'

'No,' I replied calmly. 'We were sitting here in the dark and I thought the handkerchief had fallen out of my sleeve.'

'I believe you, Mr Oxenhope. Sitting in the dark is the only thing my sister really likes doing.'

'Not altogether,' said Olive. 'As you might guess, I like riding too. Do you ride?'

'I'm afraid I don't.' As a matter of fact, I had thought of trying to take it up when I began to realise what my work with the Fund would be like, but Hamish

Haythorn had strongly advised me against it, saying that it was a mistake to meet the tenants on their own ground. I have since wondered whether Haythorn's view was not affected by the fact that he could neither ride himself nor be conceived as capable of it. But no doubt this was mere malice on my part.

'Just as well for you,' said Agnes. 'Going riding with my sister is an act of desperation.'

'I'm sorry all the same,' I said, looking at Olive as I spoke, and trying to meet her eyes, because, self-sufficient though she seemed, I was growing sorry for her, as well as for myself.

'Sherry?' asked Olive, either avoiding my glance or being unaware of my intention. 'Or gin? Or pascado? Pascado is an aperitif that Agnes brings back from one of her committees. It is Elizabethan and based on quince juice. Or would you prefer a whisky?'

I thought that I had better make some effort to appease Agnes, so volunteered for the pascado.

'Very few people like it,' said Agnes.

The evening continued to be uneasy.

The sisters were, at the least, utterly bored with one another. Such communication as they attempted was confined to jibing and belittlement. As at the start, most of the attacking seemed to come from Agnes; but I thought this might have been partly because Olive gave the impression of having years ago said all she had to say, and of by now preferring to sit in silence. Later that evening it seemed to me, however, that Olive on several occasions struck home on her own; though Agnes each time behaved as if she were too stupid to understand. It might have been the fact of the matter, but I doubted it. The sisters had obviously been committed to this form of exercise for years, and every sentence and every small action had overtones and undertones soaring and sinking beyond the apprehension of any outsider. I, of course, attempted intermittently to make 'general conversation', but Agnes was antagonistic, and Olive, though perfectly polite, was indifferent and world-weary. One might have said that Olive knew it all already, but I doubted whether she really did. I suspected that she fought off knowing, and that it was really Agnes who knew much more. One often finds this with women of Agnes's type. I perhaps make it all sound as if I was having a dreadful time, and it is certainly true that I was not enjoying myself; but by then I was surprisingly accustomed to such family sessions in the houses I visited. I had found them to be common: perhaps as patrician standards merge with plebeian ones, and there is less opportunity for the graces of entertainment as distinct from the utilities. The new conditions take different people in different ways, but are seldom to the advantage of the guests.

There seemed to be no question of any clothes being changed for dinner. When we entered the dining room, the big, polished table was as dusty, beneath the shaded candles, as it had been when I saw it two years earlier in the sunlight; and the tall, grey woman who stood there waiting for us, was recognisably she who had watched my writing on it with my finger. Supposing that Agnes would be observing me, I tried to avoid all reaction.

Dinner was good and the wine excellent, but conversation there was almost none. The presence of the grey servant (still, by the way, in a grey nylon wrapper) seemed to prevent the sisters even from bickering. I felt that very little ever went into the house: not even ordinary news, let alone what are called ideas. It would be very difficult for the Brakespear sisters to have many friends. Apart from foodstuffs and practicalities, I felt that almost nothing and nobody entered but the public visitors in summer: by definition aloof and alien; merely staring in through the bars, and, even then, uncomprehending of everything that mattered, even when (occasionally) qualified to discriminate between Meissen and Nymphenburg.

And, as I had seen for myself, the visitors to Clamber Court, though, according to Haythorn, increasing slightly in number, were powerless to dispel the dust. On the dining-room table it was so thick it marked my cuffs. I observed circles left in it by platters or glasses that had been removed, became inconspicuous within minutes, and by the time the meal was finished, had almost vanished, though not quite, when one carried the exact spot in one's mind and looked keenly. But the fare was fine. In very few of the Fund houses, if any, had I been offered such wine (let alone anywhere else). I knew this even though I was by no means a connoisseur; little more than of music.

Back in the music room after dinner, a wry discussion started about the ethics of coursing. I could contribute little. The sisters disagreed about reafforestation, and later about the flowers that were being planted for the benefit of the summer visitors. My views were hardly sought. I imagine that Agnes would have despised them and Olive pitied them. Ultimately, Agnes said she must get on with the accounts, and sat by the fire making entries in a black book, with a pile of bills and receipts on the floor at her feet. 'You won't mind being treated as one of the family,' she had said to me before starting this labour.

Olive suggested that I might care to look for a book in the library. It was well known to be a very fine library, largely assembled by a Lord St Adrian of the early eighteenth century and hardly disturbed since. But I said that I was in the middle of a book I had brought with me, and that I might fetch it down from my bedroom in a moment. I made no further move, because I always have difficulty in reading when in the company of others, let alone the company of strangers. Instead, I turned over the pages of *Country Life* and *Field*, dusty back numbers of which lay about the room, looking almost unopened. They would have to be burnt or stacked before the public season opened.

Olive merely sat in front of the fire, with her long legs stretched towards it. Her eyes remained open, but almost expressionless; too resigned, I thought, even to look sad. I was sure that she would have returned to the piano, if Agnes had not been there. Olive was by no means in her first youth, but there was something appealing about her, and, though it may not be a suitable comment for even this confidential record, I thought, by no means for the first time in such surroundings, what an odd way it was for people of opposite sexes to spend the evening, when, after all, there was nothing ahead that any of us could be sure of but infirmity, illness, and death. It is strange that people train themselves so carefully to go to waste so prematurely.

Every now and then, Agnes wondered sharply whether I would mind adding something up or working something out for her; and surprisingly bristly some of these small tasks of hers proved to be. Olive never even sighed. In the end, the grey servant appeared (the sisters addressed her as 'Elizabeth') and brought in a large bowl of fruit.

'What time would you like breakfast?' Agnes asked me.

'What time would suit you best?' I responded politely.

'Elizabeth will bring it to your room,' said Agnes. 'We go our own ways.'

I suggested a time and the grey servant departed.

'I understand that you'll be fully occupied throughout the day?' asked Agnes.

'Very fully,' I replied, remembering what I was there for and in for.

'Then we shall see you as tonight?'

I expressed assent and gratification.

Over oranges and apples, the evening ended. Agnes ate nothing, but, as well as an apple, I accepted from Olive a whisky, and she herself consumed a noticeably stronger one. Already, on our first evening together, we were running out of generalities.

'More whisky?' asked Olive after a munching silence.

I accepted, though it was unlike me. She refilled my glass to the same strength as her own. The curious dust lay all around me in the warm light.

There was some clattering with bolts and chains, some checking of locks and hasps: all Agnes's work.

'Don't wait,' she said, but we did, and all ascended the stairs together.

The sisters turned to the right, where I turned to the left, but I had not even shut the door of my imperfectly lighted room when I heard familiar steps approaching along the passage, and Olive stood in the doorway.

'I just came to say I'm sorry we're so dull.' She spoke in her usual noncommittal voice, but softly; perhaps so that Agnes could have no chance of overhearing.

'I'm sorry I don't ride,' I said; and I still think it was clever of me to think of it so quickly.

'Yes,' said Olive. 'It's a pity. Especially when we can do so little to entertain you. The company of two middle-aged sisters who don't get on isn't much fun.'

'I don't see you as middle-aged at all,' I replied. Whether I did or not, I saw Olive as most attractive, especially at that moment, when she stood slender and poetical in my doorway, and both of us were about to go to bed.

But she made no response. She did not even smile. There was merely a moment's silence between us.

Then she said, 'I apologise for us. Goodnight,' and

walked quickly away.

I found myself thinking of her for a long time, and being kept from sleep by the thought.

My breakfast arrived at the exact moment I had named. The grey factotum woke me when she knocked. Having fallen asleep belatedly, I had then slept deeply. It seemed very cold. Without thinking about it, I swept the dust off the polished bedside table with my pyjama sleeve. Then I realised that the grey Elizabeth, who was putting down my tray on the table, might take my action as a slight.

'The dust seems to blow in again as soon as it's swept away,' I said, shivering in my unheated bedroom, and in the tone of one making an excuse for another. 'There must be some dusty new industry near the house.'

'It blows off the drives,' said Elizabeth. 'The drives are always dusty.'

'If that's what it is, I think something might be done. I'll have a word with Mr Blantyre about it. He might arrange to have the drives tarmacked – anyway, near the house. The dust is really rather terrible.' After all, I was one who had some indirect responsibility in the matter.

'Terrible, as you say,' said Elizabeth noncommittally. 'But please don't bother. There's nothing to be done about it.' She spoke with surprising authoritativeness; as if she, and not the Brakespear sisters, were the Fund's tenant – or, rather, perhaps, still the landowner.

To argue would naturally have been a mistake, so, continuing to shiver in the cold of the morning, I asserted that the coffee on the tray would suit me well and that there was no need to change it, as she had suggested, for tea.

I found it hard to accept Elizabeth's explanation of the omnipresent dust. It was true that the drives were dusty, noticeably so, quite like what I imagine country roads to have been in the early days of motoring, when veils and goggles had to be worn, and the back of the neck thickly muffled; but there was so *much* dust in the house, and with so many of the windows shut, at least during the winter. For example, I had not opened mine on going to bed the previous evening, though this was contrary to a rule of health from which I seldom depart. I drew on, over my pyjamas, the heavy sweater I had brought against the river winds; poured out excellent hot coffee with a shaking hand; chewed scrambled egg and toast; and resolved to pay Blantyre a visit, even though it meant driving more than forty miles each way, to discover why still no action seemed to have been taken on my memo of two years before.

I put on all my thickest garments, descended, looked in the cold state rooms for the sisters, failed to find them, and decided simply to depart as had been agreed the previous night. As I drove away in my Mini, I observed my wake of dust with more conscious care. There certainly was a cloud of it, a rare sight nowadays in Britain, but I still found it hard to believe that all the self-renewing, perennial dust of Clamber Court came from the two drives, long though they were.

I noticed that the water in the bowl of the huntsman

fountain was patched with ice, though the jets still spurted frigidly upwards and sideways. The immaculate fountain was a symbol of the whole property: cold but kempt, as one might say. And one could only suppose that the responsibility and burden lay upon Miss Agnes Brakespear. Nobody who lacks direct knowledge of such a task can know how heavy it is in the conditions of today. I, with my increasing professional experience in such concerns, thought I could understand how irritating Olive Brakespear's attitude might be to Agnes Brakespear. Olive still behaved, however diminished her force, as if Clamber Court maintained itself; still took the house, in however reduced a degree, at its own valuation when built. The struggle lay with Agnes; and no doubt the better part of the nation owed her a debt, and others like her. All the same, I knew which of the sisters was the one to whom my greatest debt was owed. I thought sophistically that there would be little purpose in keeping up Clamber Court unless someone had at least an inkling of the style associated with dwelling there. It was a sentiment of a kind often to be discovered in the Fund's own literature. Olive Brakespear also served. Still, it seemed hard that dedicated Agnes should be additionally encumbered with so much dust. The cold wind blew it around me. It penetrated cracks in the bodywork, however shut the windows.

I drove towards the little house which young Hand had leased beside one of the broken-down locks. It had been unoccupied for years, having neither gas nor electricity, neither water, except from the river, nor a road;

so that Hand did not have to pay very much for it, which was just as well, as the Fund was all too heavily committed in other directions on his behalf. I had to leave my car by the roadside and cross two freezing fields by a muddy path. Hand and a group of six or eight other youthful enthusiasts were frying bacon on a primus stove while the wind whistled through the broken windows. A row of Hounsfield beds, all unmade after having been slept in, was almost the only approach to furniture. The party seemed to be dressed entirely in garments from those places known as 'surplus stores'. In every way, it was an odd background for a project under the auspices of the Historic Structures Fund, though no doubt it had a certain pioneering value in its own way.

Unfortunately, I arrived considerably later than the hour we had agreed; though this did not surprise me, as I had always said that the time insisted on by Hand was far too early, especially as it was still winter – officially and in every other way. They were sarcastic about my lateness, and they were hardly of the type to appreciate my concern with the worrying problem of the dust; which, therefore, I did not even mention.

I shall say little more of the Bovil Restoration Project: partly because most of the details are already well known (at least among those likely to be interested in them), and have been the subject of an exhaustive Report, edited by Hand himself (though I myself think an independent editor would have been better); and more because it is my sojourn at Clamber Court that I am describing, upon which the Project impinged hardly at all. The two parts of my life at that time were almost in watertight compartments, to use the obvious but apt metaphor.

After that rather terrible first day on the river, freezing cold (and, later, raining as well), muddy everywhere, and spent mainly (as it now seems) in pushing through endless thickets of dead bramble and dogrose, with insufficiently defined authority over Hand's rough-mannered group, I returned to Clamber Court and a first-class dinner with much relief. The second evening with the Brakespear sisters, a replica of the first, presented the oddest contrast to my day with Hand and his noisy friends, as can easily be imagined. A really bitter wind was getting up, as it often does towards the end of March; but though it made the house creak a little, it did nothing to disturb the dust. At one point, I had proposed to mention the dust to Olive Brakespear, if I could find myself long enough alone with her; having at least made a start with the grey Elizabeth. But no possible moment seemed to arise that evening. Perhaps I was too exhausted with the river, to embark gratuitously upon new uncertainties. Probably I thought that I should wait until I knew the Brakespears better: if one ever could.

Only when back in my room for the night did it clearly strike me that Agnes might deliberately have prevented my being alone for more than a minute or two with Olive. Thinking back over the evening that had just passed, I could recall more than one moment when Agnes had obviously been about to fetch something or do something, and when, instead, she had remained. The reasons for leaving us had been tiny, and many people might have been dissuaded by mere inertia; but hardly, I felt, Agnes. She had sat on, though she had been fretful and under-occupied from the start; and was then all the more fretful, no doubt, if she felt tied by the task of never taking her eyes from two people she did not trust. Could it relate to her immediate suspicion of me concerning the dust, when first she saw me? Did she imagine that Olive and I were becoming affectionate? Was it merely that she did not believe in allowing Olive any unnecessary peace? Or had I altogether deceived myself?

One of the moments which I found to be oddest in this generally odd way of life, was the moment when I returned to the house after my day on the river. It was always evening and always I seemed quite alone in the world, or at least in the big park. There was not even a light in the house, because Olive never turned one on unless compelled, and Agnes came back an hour or so later from undertakings which were apparently demanding, apparently unsatisfying, but never quite defined (and one could hardly enquire). Everything was silent. I had to mount the curving stone steps, and disturb the silence by pressing the little bellpush at the centre of the long façade, stretching through the evening from pavilion to pavilion. The illusion of the house being a vast, empty model always returned to me at this time. That there should be any living person in the huge, dark, noiseless interior seemed either absurd or sinister.

But I never had to ring more than once. The grey Elizabeth always appeared after the same short interval and let me in. She never put on a light for me, and I never did it for myself. I suppose we both held back out of regard for Olive. I myself found Olive's day-after-day passivity as unfathomable as Agnes's day-after-day agitation. Three or four of these days passed, and I never saw Olive on a horse, though all the time she wore the same worn riding breeches and boots. It was true that I had always left fairly early and returned fairly late, and that Olive might have tended to these clothes because she looked her best in them, as many women do. All the same, I might by now have been invited to visit the stables, at least in principle. Elsewhere, it had usually happened during my first luncheon; with the time unchallengeably fixed for immediately after it: at houses where the stables still functioned, of course, and had not been let off as a mushroom farm or school of art.

Up the dark staircase I went on my fourth evening (as I see it was from my Diary), while Elizabeth trailed back across the almost empty hall to the kitchen at the rear. I walked leftwards from the landing along the dark passage to my room.

Then something absolutely unexpected took place. I opened the door and I saw the back of a man standing before one of the two windows; the window not fronted by the big dressing table. He was looking out into the dark park: dark, but not yet completely dark, and, of course, less dark than the interior of the house. I could see perhaps a little more than just his black silhouette.

I know exactly what happened next, because I wrote it down the next morning. First, I stood there for a quite perceptible time, in plain shock and uncertainty. The man must have heard me approaching and opening the door, but he made no move. I then switched on the three poor lights, though far from sure what I ought to do next. The man did then turn and I got a quite good view of him. He was taller than I was, young and handsome, with a prominent nose and a quantity of dark hair which curled effectively on his brow. This description makes his aspect sound like that of an artist, but in fact, it was more like that of an athlete, and perhaps most of all like that of a soldier. I cite these misleading popular types only to give some idea of the impression he left upon me during the seconds I looked at him. Undoubtedly, he was very well dressed in a conventional, unostentatious way. He might have been a visitor to the house, who, in the dusk, had strayed into the wrong room. What he next did, however, made an idea of that kind unlikely (though not impossible): he simply walked with a quick step towards me as I stood by the door, looked straight into my eyes (of that, naturally, I am certain), and then, without a word, strode past me into the passage outside. I do not think I was more than normally upset (I noted down the next morning that I was not), but, none the less, I could find nothing to say, even though silence made me look a fool. He departed down the passage and vanished in the darkness. I made no note of how far I could hear his steps if at all. I imagine that waiting for him to speak took all my attention.

And now, of course, I have no recollection.

From every point of view, I should, I suppose, have followed him, but instead I shut the door, and walked over to the window where he had been standing. The floor boards were thick with dust, but there was no mark of his feet. It was when I saw this that real fear began to rise in me: the explanation that the dust had already covered the marks, though not in its own way impossible, to judge by what I had noticed elsewhere in the house, was by now hardly less unsettling than the notion of there being something queer about the man himself.

I went through my drawers and I accounted for all objects that I could remember I had left lying about. Nothing seemed missing. I was almost sorry.

I returned to the window and looked out into the darkening park. And then something really frightening took place. It was now dark enough for my ill-lighted room to reflect itself in the glass and appear in even more ill-lighted reproduction outside; but not dark enough for the room to be *all* I could see beyond the window. Through the reflection of the back wall of the room, the wall behind me as I stood, I could still see the shadows of trees and the whiteness of the intersecting drives. The outline of the huntsman fountain was clear enough quite to catch my attention. As I stared at it, I saw, or thought I saw, the figure of the man I had seen, standing on the drive a short distance to my left of it. There really was *not* enough light to distinguish one person from another, and certainly not at anything like that distance; but I had no doubt that this figure was he. Moreover, I had never before looked from my window and seen anyone on the drive. It was a very isolated and, one would have thought, under-manned establishment. The moment I set eyes on the figure standing on the drive, I was carried away by ter-ror, so that I may not be completely reliable about what happened next. I did not seem to see the figure move, but within moments, instead of being on the drive, it was somehow within the four walls of the room that was reflected immediately before me. The reflection of the room was mis-shaped, as such reflections al-ways are, and the walls were still transparent, but it was impossible to doubt where the figure now stood. Star-ing out petrified, I made absolutely certain, as a child might; checking in the reflected room behind me: and among them the figure stood.

I know, as will be seen, that at this point, I cried out. Those who deem this either weak of me or incredible, are invited to find themselves in a like situation. But I did manage to turn myself round, to confront the in-truder: perhaps because it was even worse to suppose he was standing out of my sight.

I found I was alone in the room. I stared at its empti-ness to make quite sure; and then looked back at the reflected room. That was now empty also, apart from my own vaguely reflected shape in the foreground. I fell into an armchair.

There was a knock at my door; and I thought that the manner of it was familiar.

'Come in.'

It was the grey Elizabeth, who had knocked as when she brought my breakfasts.

I rose to my feet. I don't quite know why.

'Miss Brakespear says she heard something and asked me to find out whether anything was wrong.'

On the instant, I decided to plunge.

'When I came in here a few minutes ago, a man was standing by the window looking out.'

'Yes, sir,' was all the grey Elizabeth said.

'What do you mean by that? Who was he?'

'Other people have supposed they saw him.'

Annoyance rose in me to drive out fear.

'Are you saying that I've been given some kind of haunted room?'

'Certainly not, sir. People have seen him in many different rooms. But you won't see him again. No one has ever seen him more than once.'

'Have *you* seen him?'

'No, sir.'

'Who is he?'

'That's not for me to know.' She looked and spoke as if I had asked her something improper.

'Then I shall ask one of the Miss Brakespears.'

'Please don't do that, sir. The tale upsets the Miss Brakespears very much. Let's just keep it to ourselves, sir. I'll tell Miss Brakespear that you cried out because you'd cut yourself.'

It sounded utterly absurd. It reminded me of the suggestion that the dust in the house came from the drives.

'But I haven't cut myself.'

'Yes you have, sir. Look.'

It was not the least astonishing thing. There was a quite bad gash on the soft part of my left hand, the area between the little finger and the wrist. Half my hand was greasily wet with blood. I did not know how I had done it, and I never learned. Possibly it had happened while I was blundering about the room a few minutes earlier.

'Let me get the first-aid box,' said the grey Elizabeth. It was scarcely practicable to object. She departed and soon came back with it. The Fund's rules require that at least one box of this kind be kept at every property, because the public visitors manage to do the most extraordinary things to themselves.

The grey Elizabeth bound me up quite skilfully; so skilfully that I had to congratulate her.

'Miss Brakespear taught me,' she said. 'She's a qualified, trained nurse.'

It was obvious that the grey Elizabeth admired Agnes. I had noticed it before.

'And now, sir,' said Elizabeth, finishing me off, 'if I promise that you'll see nothing ever again, will you please promise me that you'll not speak about what you've seen to the Miss Brakespears?'

It seemed to me an excessive request.

'They shouldn't have people to stay in a haunted house without warning them.'

'They seldom do, sir. With respect, sir, you'll recall that you were not invited by either Miss Brakespear.'

It could hardly be denied.

36

'And therefore, sir, I'm sure you'll agree that it would be better to leave private things unspoken.'

This exceedingly plain hint brought back to me that at other properties of the Fund I had sometimes stumbled upon privacies that I should have preferred to be ignorant of; and that, occasionally, small difficulties had ensued.

'You'll know better than I do, sir, that in houses where things such as we're talking about are supposed to happen, the owners often don't care for them to be spoken of.'

That too I did know; and the Fund's Psychic and Occult Committee has since been much impeded by it.

But I was still doubtful, as was only natural.

'How can I be sure that nothing more will happen?'

'Those to whom anything happens, find that it happens only once. In this house, anyway,' replied the grey Elizabeth, with the most convincing confidence.

'I might be an exception.'

'Even if you are, sir, you wouldn't wish to do a hurt to the two ladies.'

The truth was that by now I knew in my bones that it was not a thing to talk about with the sisters. I could not even imagine how I could possibly begin.

'All right,' I said to grey Elizabeth. 'All right, if nothing more happens.'

Suddenly Agnes Brakespear appeared in the doorway, wearing one of her dark dresses.

'Whatever is going on? Elizabeth, why didn't you come back to tell me? Mr Oxenhope, are you hurt?'

'I foolishly managed to cut myself, and Elizabeth has been binding me up.'

So that evening passed like the three previous ones.

When the time came for bed, I certainly cannot say that I was easy in my mind, but I thought that I could rely upon the grey Elizabeth. I had gone through an exhausting day in the open with Hand and his intolerable gang, and I soon fell asleep.

When Elizabeth brought me breakfast, I felt that we were parties to a bargain, and took advantage of this to make some new, exploratory remark about the dust.

'Old houses are always full of dust,' she replied, calmly avoiding my eye; 'do what you will. A gentleman in your position must know that better than I do.' And she went without asking me a question, as she usually did, about the contents of the tray being to my liking.

That day was Saturday, but Hand had pointed out that so far from the weekend being a holiday, it was the time when we could expect the number of volunteers to be doubled. This was obvious enough, but I must have looked put out, because Hand had gone on to say that he was sure they could manage on their own if I cared to miss the Saturday and Sunday. But I was certain that something appalling would happen in my absence, so did not avail myself of his suggestion.

For example, friction had already begun with the riverside farmers, as anyone could have foreseen, and Hand was only waiting his chance to deal with them forcefully, so that the name of the Fund would quite probably have been dragged into the national press.

For weeks the local paper had contained little but correspondence about the scheme, and 'statements' concerning it from Mayors, Chairmen of Councils, and businessmen: the great majority adverse, as could well be understood. The editor had also published two long letters from Hand himself, but both so aggressive and so clever in the wrong way that they could only have done more harm than good. Hand was never able to understand the kind of objections that normal, reasonable people feel to operations that directly forward none of their interests. The majority like to confine any idealism they may have to approved outlets, and not let it enter their immediate environments and working lives. This may or may not be sensible and admirable, but it is a fact of life. Hand could never really grasp it.

At weekends on the river, there were even girl volunteers, or, more probably, girls who followed boys who had volunteered; so the chaos and confusion were worse than ever. Some of the volunteers showed qualities that were, doubtless, in many ways excellent, even though ill-adapted to the world of today, when everything at all serious is settled by agreement, manifestly or behind the scenes. I should not necessarily have been opposed even to the scheme itself, provided that the Fund had not been required to assist with it, let alone I personally. The central mistake was in the commitment of the Fund to anything so harebrained and explosive ... All the same, I ploughed on through a welter of mud and a continuous bitter wind; doing my best among people with whom I had little in common, if only because I was older and had seen so much more of the world than they had.

And every evening I returned to the vast, dusky, silent house; ascended to the room where I had made that strange encounter; hung my clothes out to dry; scraped the worst of the mud off my boots on to a sheet of local newspaper; lay on my bed for half an hour; and then went down to Olive playing out her endless dreams on the music-room piano. She sometimes spoke, but never stopped playing or offered me a drink until Agnes's step could be heard in the stone-paved hall. Where I left my car at the front of the house, Agnes left hers at the back, and entered through the kitchen quarters. When she came into the music room, she was always the first to speak, and seldom much more agreeably than on my first evening. It was plain that Olive's habitual silence irritated her in itself, and one could understand how this might be, when Agnes had to live with Olive year after year. Nor could I doubt that there were other things than silence about Olive that irritated Agnes. Agnes always wore one of the woollen dresses I have mentioned. I saw three or four of them in all. I imagine that, unlike Olive, she, to this extent, changed for dinner. I had not so far set eyes on her at any other time of the day. Agnes usually made some formal enquiry about the progress of the river project, to which I made a formal reply; and nothing more was ever said on the subject, somewhat to my relief. We talked about Agnes's local preoccupations, with Olive sometimes breaking her silence to be sarcastic, though only mildly and gently so.

We discussed topics in which no one of us succeeded in interesting any of the others for a moment. Agnes produced a large embroidery frame and decussated away the hours, without, to my mind, producing anything very beautiful. The work was for presentation at Christmas to the meeting place of a women's organisation in a nearby town.

One evening, I remember, we talked about the Fund itself. Agnes was not very cordial.

'Since the property was settled on the Fund,' she asserted, 'we haven't been able to call our souls our own.'

I had heard something of the kind from other tenants, so cannot say that I was exactly shocked.

'The Fund has the ungrateful task of having to meet the requirements of the State,' I replied. 'It does all it can to soften the wind to the shorn lamb.'

'By this time it could do more to stop the wind blowing,' said Agnes.

This, for me, was too much after the style of Hand. I had been listening to such tiresome talk all day.

'The Fund has to keep out of all controversy,' I said, with such deliberate firmness as I could achieve. 'If it didn't, it wouldn't be permitted to hold property, and your house might have been pulled down by now, or become an institution.'

'*Our* house!' exclaimed Agnes, with bitterness. The tenants all feel the same, and I suppose one cannot blame them.

'Since the Fund took over, we've been living here on sufferance, almost on charity. Our lives have ceased to be our own. We are unpaid curators. The nobility in Poland who have had their estates stolen, are sometimes permitted to go on curating a few rooms in their former houses. Though in England it is dressed up, that is our position, and nothing more. At least it is my position. I can't speak for Olive.'

Olive was lying back in her usual chair before the fire, her legs stretched out, her hands beneath her head.

'Oh, I agree,' she said. 'We are simply waiting. Soon it will all be gone.'

'The Fund,' I pointed out, 'likes to keep members of the family living in the house. The public doesn't take to museums, and very few of them know or care anything about architecture or pictures. What appeals to them is getting into someone else's home, and having the right to poke about inside it. It is only on that basis that the Fund keeps going. It may or may not be sensible and admirable, but it's a fact of life, and we all have to do our best to accept it, even though I quite see it's often not easy.'

'You can't *live* in a house you no longer own,' said Agnes. 'The choices, the decisions, the responsibilities are no longer yours. You are at the best a housekeeper; at the worst, a dummy. Not that people in any way cease to hate and envy you. Often they hate and envy you more, because they've seen more. The difference is that you're tied down, and deprived of any redress against them. I hope you'll agree from what you've seen that I'm an efficient housekeeper, but I spend as little time in the house as possible. I get away as much as I can, even if what goes on outside the walls is often frustrating too.'

'It won't last,' said Olive. 'It can't last. Not even in Poland.'

'My job is to see that it does last,' I said, smiling. 'Or at least it is the job of my colleagues.'

'We should have fought harder for ourselves,' said Agnes. 'We should have put up more of a struggle.' She spoke as one merely placing an opinion on record; not even attempting to convince, not expecting in the least to be agreed with. Here she differed from Hand, who would have begun to make immediate plans, however impracticable.

An irritation of our age is the collapse of the rules concerning names. My hostesses had still not begun to address me as 'Nugent', no doubt owing to my invidious position, of which, like many of the other tenants, they were so excessively conscious. And, in that same position, it was hardly for me to begin calling them 'Agnes' and 'Olive'. On the other hand, the old fashioned formalities would have seemed strained; would have caused the very embarrassments they were designed to eliminate. We never altogether reached a settlement of this problem. No doubt that was symbolical. It was a house in which the rules lingered, because a house in which it was otherwise impossible to live with decency; but the rules, like Olive Brakespear, now lacked force, let alone fire.

Often I thought about Olive; about her square mouth, her slenderness, her lovely hands, her air of poetical mystery: but though there had seemed to be

43

a certain understanding between us from the start, she took care to add not one twig to the tiny flame, one brick to the rudimentary fabric. Probably she no longer had twigs or bricks in her store.

I found Agnes was beginning to talk much more to me, even though it was most of the time *at* me. 'This whole thing about us and the Fund is grotesque,' she would exclaim. 'Don't you think so?' Or she would suddenly make a wide and difficult enquiry: 'What do you think of Dutch barns? The Fund must have more experience of them than I have'; or 'Are there any *really good people* working for the Fund? Is there even one?' Once she suddenly asked: 'What is your own candid view of my sister Olive?', and this with Olive sitting there as usual, silent and indifferent unless directly addressed.

At least it all tended to ward off sheer dullness. And the food and drink continued as good as the general maintenance. And the dust remained. By then, snatching thirty minutes here and thirty minutes there, I had prowled half across five parishes looking for a cement works, but had failed to find one.

And next came the incident of the dust-cloud at dawn.

Each night, worn with the burden of communication, we went to bed rather early. I was usually quite ready for it; so hard was my life on the river – in a way, I suppose, so healthy, albeit unenjoyable. I used to fall asleep immediately, and every night thought less of the intruder I had seen; but I found that on most mornings I awoke early. The truth was that, as in many country houses, far too long was officially set aside for slumber. I would awake, and in the cold, grey light see by the ticking French clock that it was only six, or even earlier; whereas Elizabeth could not be expected to arrive with my breakfast until half past seven. Sometimes I climbed out of bed and walked several times up and down the room in my pyjamas, deliberately chilling myself; having learned from experience elsewhere that the change from cold air to warm sheets and blankets often sends one more quickly back to sleep than anything else.

At that hour, the fountain huntsman looked both more alive and more mythological than when he stood transfixed and obsolete in the rushing world. One felt that he was the single living man in square miles of farm-haunted landscape. As I stumped about looking for new sleep, I glanced out at him, even when I had to scrub the frost off the panes to see him. On one of these early mornings, I saw something else. The park was greyly lit, lightly frosted, and, as far as I could see and hear, perfectly unpopulated and still: an excellent world, in fact, for a stone man to hunt in. As I looked out, excited, I admit, by the cold, quiet beauty of the scene, I saw a cloud of dust bowling along the white drive from among the trees on the let; a *globe* of dust might better describe it. It was possibly ten or twelve feet high, and quite dense; and though more or less spherical, dragged a dusty train behind it, like a messy comet. The dust looked almost black in the faint dawn light, but I was sure it was really grey – the perfectly ordinary grey one would expect. It rolled along quite steadily towards the fountain; and, in the apparent absence of any wind, I thought at once that it must be raised by some small, heavy vehicle – or, anyway, moving object – at the invisible centre of it. The invisibility was especially odd, however: one would expect to have seen something of such a vehicle, probably the front of it, butting out from the cloud that followed it. I was so carried away that I actually opened one of the heavy sash windows with their thick glazing bars, and listened for the noise of an engine. I could hear nothing at all: not even awakening rooks and hedgehoppers.

Leaning further out, I saw the dust-cloud roll on until it reached the intersection of drives at the fountain; and then the episode ended in total anticlimax: somehow the cloud was not there at all. It could not really have blown away, because there was no wind; and that quite apart from the question of there having presumably been some solid object to cause it, though still none was visible. I could not even say that I had seen the cloud disperse. It was more as if I had been so concentrated on the movement and character of the cloud that I had been half-asleep to the particulars of its dissolution, to a development so unanticipated. Anyway, there was now neither cloud nor cause for cloud: nothing but the cold, still morning with the stone huntsman perched half-iced at the centre of it.

I shut the window, shivered a little, and returned to bed, though not to sleep. In fact, it was this seeming freak of nature that I have described which really propelled me to Blantyre. That same morning, I drove round to

Hand's lock cottage; told the assembled volunteers that other Fund business, coming unexpectedly, would compel me to be missing from the river that day; made no reference to the rather obvious looks of relief which followed my words; and drove off to Bagglesham, where Blantyre, the Fund's Regional Representative, operated from his crumbling, half-timbered house in a side street. It had once belonged to a family of pargeters, and legend said one could still smell the dung that went into their special kind of plaster; but that was a paranormal manifestation that never came my way.

Basil Blantyre, who has since, unfortunately, died (still in harness), was already nearer to eighty than to seventy, and sensibly reluctant to leave the warm fire in March weather; but he welcomed me in most cordially, though I had not been able to tell him I was coming. There was a telephone at Clamber Court, but I had never heard it in use, and I thought that a call to the Fund's local luminary could, if overheard, cause only trouble. Blantyre most kindly made me a cup of instant coffee with his own hands. He lived quite alone, his wife having never fully recovered (as I had been given by Hamish Haythorn to understand) from the shock of the bankruptcy and the compulsion to leave the house where the Blantyre family had lived, reputedly, since the Middle Ages. To Blantyre, as to me (and others), the Fund had proved a welcome haven from life's storm.

'I want the lowdown on Clamber Court and the Brakespear sisters,' I said, pushing back the scum on the hot coffee.

'There was a lot of sadness in the family. I speak of the time before Clamber was settled on the Fund.'

'There hasn't been much happiness since, judging by what I've seen and heard.'

'What can you expect, Oxenhope? People don't like losing their houses and still living on in them. That, at least, Millicent and I were spared.'

Quite possibly this was a form of sour grapes, as the Blantyre house had been much too far gone for any decision but demolition.

'There may be more to it than that,' I said. 'What splendid coffee! There seem to me some very odd goings-on at Clamber Court.'

'So I have heard,' said Blantyre, looking away from me and into the blazing logs.

'To start with, the Brakespear girls appear to have no visitors. Apart, of course, from the public.'

'Poor old dears!' exclaimed Blantyre vaguely.

'They're not as old as that. I acknowledge that I myself find one of them quite attractive.'

'So-ho!' exclaimed Blantyre in the same vague way. It was manifest that he had long ago lost all touch with the Clamber situation.

'And then,' I said, 'the house is full of dust.'

'Yes,' said Blantyre. 'I know. That's just it.'

'That's just what?' I asked, putting down my cup. The second half of the contents was thick and muddy.

Blantyre did not answer. After a pause, he answered with another question.

'Did you see anything else? Or hear?'

'See,' I said, lowering my voice, as one does; even though it was still the middle of the morning. 'Not hear.'

'You saw *him*?' asked Blantyre.

'I think so,' I said. 'I suppose so.'

'And *it*? You perhaps saw *it* as well?'

'Yes,' I said. 'This very morning, as a matter of fact.'

'You don't say so.' Blantyre turned back towards me.

'If what I saw was the same it.'

'I have no doubt of it,' replied Blantyre.

'I first saw the dust, the ordinary dust, when I visited the house two years ago. I went incognito, you know.'

'You should never do that,' said Blantyre very seriously.

Coming from a man almost twice my age, I let the reproof go.

'At the time I sent you a memo on the dust,' I said.

'I don't wonder. Many people do.'

'You mean that there's nothing to be done about it?'

'What do *you* think about that?' asked Blantyre. 'Now that you've had more experience.'

'The servant says it blows in off the long drives.'

'So it does,' said Blantyre. 'In a way.' Here he started coughing rather alarmingly, as if the dust had entered his own lungs.

'Can't I get you something?' I asked.

'No, thank you,' Blantyre wheezed. 'Just give me a minute or two. You haven't finished your coffee.'

I swallowed a little more, and then sat looking into the fire, as Blantyre had done. Before long, his breath seemed to be coming more easily.

'Will you please tell me the story?' I asked, still staring at the logs. 'All within the four walls of the Fund, of course.'

'You mean that I shan't last long? That I ought to pass it on before I go?'

'Of course not. I never thought of such a thing. After all, the Brakespear girls must know, and almost certainly Elizabeth, and doubtless others.'

'Not many others,' said Blantyre. 'Or only village tales. If the Fund has to have official knowledge of the story, it is my successor I should tell, but I don't know who he'll be and I daresay I shall never meet him, so I'm prepared to tell you. You've been *staying* in the house, I believe? Spending nights there?'

'Yes,' I said. 'And still am. All thanks to young Mr Hand.'

'There's a good lad,' said Blantyre unexpectedly. 'It's a bad thing for England that there are not more like him.'

'Who knows if you're not right, but you can be glad you don't have to work with him.'

'Men of the best type are seldom easy to work with. Being easy to work with is a talent that often doesn't call for any other talents in support of it.'

I said nothing: again remembering Blantyre's age. This time the gulf between the generations positively yawned at my feet.

'If you're called upon to live in the house,' said Blantyre, 'you've possibly a claim to the story. Not that I've heard of actual harm coming to anyone. Not physical harm, anyway. Only to Tony Tilbury, who was killed. But he was just run over.'

'I don't follow,' I said.

'The one certain fact is that Tony Tilbury was run down and killed early one morning by a car which Agnes Brakespear was driving.'

'Oh,' I said, feeling a little sick.

'Olive Brakespear saw it happen from one of the windows. That's another fact: at least, I suppose so. There is considerable doubt as to how far her account of the details can be relied on.'

'I shouldn't have thought it was an easy place to have an accident of that kind; especially with nothing else about.'

'You're not the only person to have thought that, and, in fact, if it hadn't been for Olive's evidence, Agnes would have been in serious trouble. A manslaughter charge, at least. Even murder, perhaps.'

'Who *was* Tony Tilbury?'

'He was a fine-looking young chap; descended from one of Queen Elizabeth's admirals. I met him myself several times, when we were still in the old place. But then I think you may have seen for yourself what he looked like. If we understood one another just now. The thing was that Tilbury and Olive Brakespear were in love – very much in love, people say – and Agnes objected.'

'You mean she was in love with him herself?'

'Perhaps,' said Blantyre. 'That's one of the many things that no one knows, or can be expected to know, unless one of the sisters speaks up, and I should say that's pretty unlikely by this time. But there's no doubt at all about the rows it all caused between them. There were plenty of people who were quite prepared, or said they were, to swear to having seen Agnes setting about Olive, and even threatening to kill her.'

'That seems an unlikely thing to threaten before witnesses.'

'It's what people said. Whether they would really have taken an oath on it when it came to the point, is, needless to say, another matter. It never did come to a point of that kind, because Olive swore at the inquest that she had seen the whole thing from one of the windows and that the car had quite obviously got out of control. She swore that she saw Agnes struggling with it and doing all she could be expected to do. Even so, there were a lot of unanswered questions, when it had come to running down a solitary man in all that open space. And, apparently, Olive at one point half-admitted that she couldn't *really* see, because of all the dust which the car had stirred up. Agnes made a big thing of the dust too, in her own evidence. She put a lot of the blame on it. In the end the coroner gave Agnes the benefit of the doubt, and the jury brought in Accidental Death. I daresay the dust was pretty decisive, however you look at it. It can get into people's eyes, like smoke. That's not the only dusty verdict I've known to come from a coroner's jury. Inquests often take place in rather a rush, oddly enough; though I didn't attend the one on Tony Tilbury.'

'Why did people suppose he was standing about all by himself at that hour of a winter morning?'

'It wasn't winter,' said Blantyre. 'It was pretty near midsummer. Hence all the dust.'

'Oh,' I said. 'I hadn't realised.' Blantyre waited for me to go on. 'At Clamber there seems dust enough at any time. Even so, what was Tilbury doing?'

'Agnes and Olive told a story about Tilbury sleeping badly and often going out in the early hours to walk about the park. I daresay it was more or less true. But what people said was something different. They said that on the morning in question, Tilbury was about to elope with Olive. A far-fetched thing to do, in all the circumstances, but the two of them were said to have been driven to it by Agnes's behaviour. The idea seems to me to leave a lot of unanswered questions also. And I don't know that there's any real evidence for it at all. Tilbury's own car – a racing sort of thing – was found in the background along the drive, but there was nothing very remarkable about that. As a matter of fact, I'm not sure that the whole business, queer though it was, would have started so many tales, or at least kept the tales going for so long, had it not been for one or two other things.'

'What were they?' I asked.

'In the first place, Olive had a complete breakdown after the inquest – or so, once again, it was said: I suppose one can't be certain even of that. All that is certain is that she was missing for more than a year. And when she came back, she had changed. She had intended to be a professional pianist, as you possibly know: perhaps before she met Tony Tilbury. Even that was odd: the effect that Tilbury appears to have had on her. Tilbury was an agreeable young chap, and good-looking, of course, but perfectly ordinary, as far as I could ever see; and it was hard to imagine why a sensitive, artistic creature like Olive should be so gone on *him* in particular. Because I think she really was gone on him. I don't think there's much doubt about that. I'm told they behaved quite absurdly together, even in public. Anyway, when she came back, after more than a year, from wherever it had been, she'd given up music and gone nuts on riding; and not the usual sort of riding either, but endless treks all by herself. She still does it, or did, the last I heard. But you'll probably know more about that than I do.'

'Olive still plays the piano as well,' I said. 'Whenever Agnes lets her.'

'I see,' said Blantyre, looking me in the eye. 'Well, there you are. I mean as to the relationship between them. You've summed it up from your own observation.'

'I'd believe almost anything about their relationship. But what's the next reason why people still talk?'

'Do you have to ask? You're not the only one to have seen things and heard things – or to have *said* they've seen and heard them. Not that I wish to reflect any doubt upon you personally, you understand.'

'Elizabeth told me that no one sees anything more than once. At least, she said that no one sees what I now take to have been Tilbury's figure more than once.'

'Did she now? That's a new superstition to me. But it

follows a familiar line, of course, and when things like that are alive at all, they always grow. Also I haven't been to Clamber for some time, though that's probably something I shouldn't admit. I just don't like the place, and, between ourselves, I don't go out much more than I can help in any case, unless it happens to be set fair weather.'

'Elizabeth implied that people have seen him in many different rooms in the house.'

'I suspect,' replied Blantyre, 'that he's just *in* the whole place, and that the people who see him, do so when they happen to be in the right mood. What exactly that means, I have no idea, but none of the theories that are supposed to explain these things, goes very far, as you may have noticed. "All telepathy", people say, for example. What does it mean? Whether it's true or not? It gets one almost no distance at all, though it may perhaps just be worth saying. I claim no more for what I have just suggested about Tony Tilbury at Clamber.'

'And, from what you say, we know no more about what those three people were doing all up and about so early in the morning?'

'Not a thing. Nor ever shall, in all probability. Of course the father had died years before. As a matter of fact, he killed himself: so much seems certain, though they succeeded in hushing it up, and I've never come upon so much as a rumour as to his reasons. The older people who knew him just say he always seemed depressed or always seemed aloof, or some such word. All in all, they're not a lucky family. The mother went queer after her husband's death, though she's still alive.'

'I was told in the Fund offices that she lived in the house.'

'I don't think so,' said Blantyre, smiling a little. 'It's the sort of thing that I should be notified about officially, wouldn't you say? I suspect it's another example of the growth that takes place in the absence of facts. Or have you heard the old thing screaming in the night above your head?'

'Never,' I replied.

'Well, I hope you don't. It's not a pleasant sound, I assure you.'

Blantyre spoke as if it were one with which he was thoroughly familiar.

'And that reminds me,' he went on. 'I shouldn't be frightened of Clamber, if I were you, or let it get me down. I mention this because that might be the tendency of some of the things I've said. I think it is quite unnecessary. It's true that I don't like the place, but it's far more true that no one was ever hurt by a ghost yet, unless he made use of the ghost to hurt himself. Ghosts don't hit you over the head: you do it yourself when you're not thinking about it, and blame them for it because you can't understand yourself. A homely illustration, but all the records confirm the truth of it. It's only in fiction that there's anything *really* dangerous. And of course old houses do tend to dust up when their families no longer own them: though that's not a line of thought we are permitted to pursue. So now let me make you another cup of coffee.'

Despite Blantyre's reassurances, I was thereafter really afraid not only of Clamber Court, but of the two sisters as well. Fortunately, I had only four more nights to stay there; because my nights had become as forbidding as my days.

Driving back from seeing Blantyre, I actually came upon Olive on her horse, visibly now a rather elderly animal, though once, I had no doubt, a nice roan. Despite all the references to riding, I had never seen her mounted before, probably because I had always before driven about the countryside either too early or too late. The horse was stepping out slowly towards me, along a very minor road. The reins were quite loose in Olive's hand. There seemed little chance of the desperate galloping and charging that Agnes had implied was Olive's manner of equitation; though I could well believe that Olive was entirely capable of such things, perhaps even longed for them. Possibly it was what once she did, but did no more. The weather was as bleak as ever, with a bitter wind getting up under a cold sky, but Olive wore a sand-coloured shirt, open at the neck, and so old that, when I came up with her, I saw little tears in it. When first I saw her, she was looking up at the great, almost white, heavens while the horse found his own way. There was no reason why she should have taken any notice of my car, nowadays one of so many in the lanes, had I not slowed almost to a stop, because of the horse and because it was Olive. She met my eyes through the windscreen, even smiled a little, and raised her left hand in greeting, like a female centaur. She made no sign of stopping or speaking, but rode slowly on. I watched her for a few seconds through my rear window: noticing the small tears in her shirt, noticing and admiring the straightness of her back, the sleekness of her hair, the perfection of her posture.

Although I had stayed for a simple lunch with Blantyre, because he seemed lonely and pressed it upon me, and because it hardly seemed worth visiting the river for a short spell of failing light, I arrived back at Clamber Court much earlier than usual. Naturally, the grey Elizabeth looked surprised.

'I've been visiting Mr Blantyre, our local Representative,' I said.

It was an explanation that was unlikely to be well received, and Elizabeth's surprise duly changed to hostility and suspicion.

'Aren't we doing what they want?' she asked.

'Of course you are. I was only passing the time of day with him.'

But I cannot deny that, going along the familiar passage to my room, I felt very quavery. I even hesitated before opening my door. The room, however, was merely much lighter than it usually was when I came back to it.

An indefensible thought struck me. For the first time, I was more or less alone in the house and it was still daylight. I resolved to look about, starting with the room next to my own. Or at least to try the door. It was better, I thought, to know than not to know.

Still in my overcoat, I tiptoed back into the passage. There were little cold draughts, and I pushed back my own door as far as it would go. I did not want it to slam and bring upstairs the grey Elizabeth. I did not want it to make a noise of any kind or to shut me out.

The door of the next room was locked. It was only to be expected. I did something even more indefensible. I removed the key from the lock of my own door and tried it in the lock of the next door. My thought was that when the house had been built, an operation of this kind would have had small chance of success, but that the 1910 contractor who had plainly made big changes, might well have installed new locks that were not merely standard but identical. I was right. The lock stuck a bit, but I made the key turn. I did not just peek in, but threw the door wide open, though, at the same time, I did it as quietly as I could.

The room was entirely empty of furniture, but the air was charged with moving dust. It was almost as thick as the snow in those snowstorm glasses one used to buy from pedlars in Oxford Street. Moreover, it seemed to move in the same, slow, dreary swirl as moves the toy snow when the glass is reversed and the fall begins. There was a bitter wind outside the house, as I have said, and draughts inside it, but the room was fusty and stuffy, and I could not see how the March wind could explain everything.

Not that it mattered: at least to begin with; for through the wheeling dust I could see that at the window of the empty room a figure stood with its back to me, looking out towards the park.

It was Agnes, dressed in her day clothes; and I could

see another key of the room lying on the window sill. She had locked herself in. I had been wrong in taking it for granted that at that hour she would every day be occupied with her committees and public works.

So much time passed while I just gazed through the terrifying dust at Agnes's motionless back that I really thought I might succeed in shutting the door and getting away. But exactly as I was nerving myself to move, and to move quietly, Agnes turned and looked at me.

'I know it's no longer our house, my sister's and mine,' she said, 'but still you are our guest, Mr Oxenhope, even if only in a sense.'

'I apologise,' I said. 'I had no idea the room was not empty. I have been seeing Mr Blantyre today. Unfortunately, he's not very well, and there are one or two things I thought I should check on his behalf, before the house opens to the public.'

'Of course it is what we expect and have become accustomed to. I am not complaining. What else would you like to see? The key of your room doesn't open every door.'

'I don't think any of the other little items will involve keys,' I replied, 'though thank you very much. As for this room, I only wanted to make sure it was empty, because we should like to store a few things in it.'

'There are other empty rooms in the house,' said Agnes, 'and I am sure we can spare this one.'

'All the same, I do apologise again for not speaking to you first. It was simply that I had a little time on my hands, as today I haven't visited the river.'

'It is no longer our house,' said Agnes, 'so that, strictly speaking, there is no obligation on you to ask us about anything. Has Mr Blantyre any criticisms of my house-keeping?'

'None,' I assured her. 'We agreed that it is one of the best maintained of all the Fund's many properties.'

And, interestingly enough, the dust had by then ceased to swirl, though I am sure it still lay thick on the room floor, the floors of the other rooms, the passages, the stairs, the furniture, and all our hearts.

The Houses of the Russians

One day, when the Blessed Seraphim was
a child, his mother took him to the top of
a bell-tower which was under construction.
The child slipped and fell a hundred and
fifty feet to the cobblestones below. His
distracted mother rushed down expecting
to see his mangled body, but, to her as-
tonishment and joy, he was standing up
apparently unhurt. Later in life he was several times in mortal danger and each time
was saved by a miracle.

Prince Felix Youssoupoff

'May I buy you a drink, sir?' Dyson asked the old man
politely. 'You look as if you had seen a ghost.'

The old man was indeed very pale and he clung a
little to the bar, but he smiled slightly at Dyson's way
of putting it. 'In my mind's eye perhaps,' he replied.
'Thank you. May I make it a small whisky?'

'I'd say it's a miracle you're here at all, let alone safe
and sound,' said the man behind the bar, who had been
staring out of the window at the back, and had seen what
had happened. 'There've been many of our customers
who weren't. Most dangerous road in the west country
that is now. There's even been talk of closing the house

before some lorry knocks into it and closes it for us.'

''Bout time the whole village was redeveloped,' said Rort, 'judging by some of the places we've seen.' It was not a tactful remark, but Rort was far from consciousness of offence. He always assumed that his standards were shared by the vast majority, had they the honesty to admit it.

Before picking up the whisky Dyson had bought him, the old man did something most unexpected: one might say that he crossed himself, but he did it in a queer, backwards way that I had never seen before. He then downed the whisky in one gulp.

Not being myself a Catholic, or an authority on ritual, I might have thought that I was deceived about the old man's gesture, but Gamble, who was always the most observant among us of what was said or done, asked the old man a question: 'Does that exorcise the ghost in your mind's eye?'

'Ghosts,' said the old man quietly but amiably. 'Ghosts in the plural. But I have no wish to exorcise them, even if exorcism were possible or relevant. Whereas it is neither.'

'Tell us about exorcism,' said Dyson.

'Exorcism may only be attempted upon licence from an archbishop, and in any case is applicable only when a person is believed to be possessed by a devil. That is not my case. There was nothing diabolical about my escape, I assure you.'

'But there *was* something supernatural?' responded Gamble; often a little too much the cross-examining barrister when all the circumstances were considered.

'Yes,' said the old man in his quiet and simple way. 'At least *I* think so. It was connected with this.' He put his fingers in his bottom left waistcoat pocket and produced a coin or medal. It was dull rather than bright as it lay on his palm in the dim light of the bar; and a fraction smaller, I should say, than a penny.

The barman got in first. 'Can I hold it?'

'Certainly,' said the old man, passing it over. 'But it has no intrinsic value.'

'Just a lucky charm?' asked the barman.

'More a token. The visible symbol of an invisible grace.'

'My mother has one. Given her when she married my father, by my gran, who got it from the gypsies. I suppose these marks are the Romany?'

'No,' said the old man. 'That's Russian.'

'Have another drink,' said Gamble, 'and tell us about Russia.'

'Tell us the whole story,' said Dyson.

We were really all there to learn about fisheries: agricultural and icthyological students, prospective economists and sociologists, one or two sportsmen and aspirants to tweedy journalism, all male and all young; plus the one old man, retired, and representative of a type often to be found on such courses, often, I fear, regarded by the rest of us as more or less a nuisance. We were all boarded out on the villagers. After our substantial teas, we assembled together every evening at this battered little pub because the competitive establishment was flashy and perceptibly dearer. It was now our third night. Hitherto, the old man had spoken hardly at all. His years had cast a certain constraint upon us, but he had arrived late and left soon, and, in any case, most of us were so brimming with fish-talk and career-talk that his presence inhibited us little. I myself had supposed that he seemed genuinely pleased just to listen to us. The men who ran the course did not fraternise with us in the evenings. In any case, most of them were housed with the flashy competitor.

One reason for the old man's near-accident had been the failing light. As he went on talking, darkness fell and the night wind off the sea began to creep under the door and across the stone flags. Infrequently, a solitary villa-ger appeared, quietly ordered his drink, and settled to listening with us. One suspected that the presence of our group in the bar every evening was tending to keep out the regulars.

'Not Russia,' said the old man. 'I've never been there, though I've known Russians – in a way. It was in Finland that I knew them.' He was looking at his recovered token.

'Surely Russians are rather unpopular in Finland?' asked Gamble.

Rort was about to speak, probably in dialectical contradiction, but the old man began his story, ignoring Gamble.

'Until I retired I was an estate agent and surveyor. At the time I am talking about, I was little more than a clerk, working for a firm called Purvis and Co. I was supposed to be learning the business, and Mr Purvis was very keen that I should, because he knew my father and because he had no sons of his own. He did everything he could for me; then and for a long time afterwards. I owe Mr Purvis a great deal. When he died prematurely in 1933, I inherited most of his business. Of course, I was a qualified surveyor by then, and quite competent to handle everything that arose. Ten years earlier, I knew nothing.

'In 1923, Purvis and Co. had a client with an interest in a Finnish timber plantation. He was in the trade in a big way, with large offices down in the east end of London, but he wanted his son to have experience of all sides of the business, and for this reason proposed to lease a house in Finland for six months and actually move over there with his wife and the boy. I should mention that the wife was Finnish herself. The man's name was Danziger, so his own forebears may all have come from the Baltic also. I never set eyes on the elder Danzigers because Mr Purvis used to go to see them instead of them coming to see him, but I met the son several times. Later it struck me that he had all the wildness and toughness I saw in the Finns, but none of the steadiness and application. He might have done better as a militiaman in the Winter War than as a merchant. But of course the Winter War came much later than the time I am talking about, and as a matter of fact young Danziger was already dead before it happened.

'The nearest town to the particular timber plantation was a place called Unilinna. Mr Purvis had been asked

66

to go there himself, have a look round for a suitable house, and, if he found one, try to get hold of it. He asked me if I would like to come with him, but said that the firm could not afford to pay my fare, especially as I was such a junior. I was so pleased that I talked my father into paying for me, and, as a matter of fact, I think that this was just the main reason why Mr Purvis had chosen me. He knew that my father could manage it, where the fathers of some of the other juniors probably couldn't. Mr Purvis knew better than most that shrewd economies like that often make all the difference to the success of a business. He needed someone amenable in Finland to take notes and hold the tape. Later, it might have been different. I grew very much into Mr Purvis's confidence, and I am sure that he would have picked me anyway.

'I had never before been abroad at all. This may seem strange to you, when nowadays students spend so much of their time travelling on grants, but you may recall that the First World War was not long over, and that travelling had become enormously more difficult than it had been before the war started, when you didn't need so much as a passport. The change put off people like my father from even making the attempt. Besides, I think they were afraid of the alterations they might see.

'Mr Purvis and I took the two-funnelled Swedish-Lloyd steamer from Tilbury to Gothenburg, with him all alone in a first-class cabin, and me in with a young Swedish missioner, as he called himself, who prayed out loud for most of the two nights, wore dark grey vests and pants, and tried to convert me by catching hold of both my shoulders and speaking to me very slowly and gravely about hell and repentance. He also left a tract in English under my pillow or in my shoes every time I went outside.

'In Gothenburg, Mr Purvis took me to the beautiful amusement park called Liseberg, where I saw a different aspect of Swedish life. Oddly enough, Mr Purvis liked places like that, and would sit for hours staring at the lovely Swedish girls, and commenting to me on their points, as if they had been horseflesh. We did exactly the same in Stockholm. We went to the Gröna Lunds, where conditions were distinctly less elegant and refined than at Liseberg, but Mr Purvis didn't mind in the least. I daresay he enjoyed it all the more. I was amused to see that he was quite the Englishman abroad. I should have preferred to go off on my own a bit, but Mr Purvis seemed to like my company so much that it would obviously have been a mistake.

'After a night in Gothenburg and a night in Stockholm, we took the Finnish steamer across the Baltic from Nortälje, to Turku. We sailed through the Åland Islands, hundreds of them, mostly uninhabited, which had been captured from the Bolsheviks by the Finns marching scores of miles across the winter ice in 1918. From the harbour at Turku we went on by the boat train to Helsinki, where we spent our fifth night. We arrived very late and had to leave early the next morning, so I didn't see much of Helsinki, but it is astonishing what you can do with even an hour or two if you really want to, and I shall never forget the shape of the Great Church against the starry sky, or the view from the Kauppatori across the straits to the fortified island on the other side. There was a kind of mystery about them I have never met anywhere else. It was July or August, and in Finland never quite dark; which added to the beauty of it, even though I had no particular wish for the full midnight sun. I fancy that daylight all the time would be worse than darkness all the time. Staring out across the sea from the Kauppatori at midnight wasn't so much Mr Purvis's kind of thing, but he was very good about it all the same, recognising that I was travelling abroad for the first time, and bought us both a Finnish liqueur called Mesimarja.

'The next morning we set off for Unilinna, where we arrived about lunch-time. We passed four nights there in all. It is not a very large town and as we spent most of our time moving about it to look at various houses, I got to know it quite well. It was a beautiful place. It lay, like so many Finnish towns, on the narrows between two lakes, but it also spread over several lake islands all connected by bridges, so that it was often difficult to recollect whether you were on the mainland, so to speak, or on an island. In Finland the difference between mainland and island is often indistinct. There are supposed to be tens of thousands of lakes, many of them linked together, as at Unilinna, and there are rivers also, even canals. The sea-coast is broken up into islands in just the same way. The main impression I had of Finland was of life being mingled with the water in every direction. In between the lakes are ridges of rocky hills, mostly a hundred feet or two hundred feet high, and all covered with conifers. They look right there, of course, even if they look wrong and ugly round here. I gathered that most of the conifers I saw round Unilina belonged to the firm in which Mr Danziger had an interest. Every autumn they were floated down to the sea in rafts for export.

'Unilinna was very much a watering place for holidaymakers. It had a gay front with flags, as if it had been the seaside. The steamers lined up along it, going to different spots on the lake, some of them taking all day to reach. The steamers burnt only wood and gave off a wonderful smell, which sometimes you noticed all over the town. At one end of the front was an enormous ruined castle. It was the single proper tourist attraction I had time to see. The outside was magnificent, but I discovered that the outside was about all there was to it, as far as I was concerned. The inside was given up to open-air plays, and they weren't much use when you couldn't speak more than a few words of Finnish. Yes, I did manage to pick up just a little, but long plays in verse were something different. Nor, of course, were they right for Mr Purvis either. He liked to sit outside a café passing the girls in review. They were every bit as gorgeous as the Swedish girls, but not so elegantly dressed. Looking at them was as near as ever I got to them.

'There were gypsies too; real, opera gypsies with dark faces, flashing eyes, and brightly coloured clothes. They were to be met with all over the town, but especially in the market, which, as far as I could see, spread all the way along the waterfront every morning, but seemed to disappear almost completely after about midday. The gypsies would half come up to you and half speak, but draw quickly away, almost vanish into the air, when they realised you couldn't speak their language, any of their languages. For I was given to understand that many of them were Russian gypsies, fled since 1917 from the Bolsheviks. If this was true, they were in fact the first Russians I ever knowingly met. If, of course, gypsies can properly be described as Russians. Perhaps not. In any case, it is always a problem about Russians: when you go into it, they are so often something else; Ukrainians, Georgians, Asiatics, and, since 1939, Lithuanians, Latvians, and Estonians, in so far as any have survived. You can look out from Helsinki over the sea to Estonia, but since 1939, you haven't been able to go there, not just for the trip.'

'Of course you can go there,' muttered Rort.

Again the old man ignored him.

'All the time we were in Unilinna the sun shone by day and it was very hot, but in the evening a quite thick mist would rise, so that the temperature changed completely. The visitors would say it came off the lakes and look suspicious, but of course that wasn't the point. The mist would have been there even if there had been no lakes. It meant that next day the sun was likely to shine again. It was elementary meteorology.

'Mr Purvis had some kind of an introduction to a man in Unilinna who was the equivalent of an estate agent. We went to see him as soon as we had moved into an hotel and had lunch. His name was Mr Kirkontorni. He was quite a young man and he spoke English remarkably well. I remember wondering both how he had learnt so much and why. I couldn't believe that he met more than two or three Englishmen a year, and the Americans had not then discovered Finland at all. He knew the Danziger family quite well and he had a list of properties for us to visit, with particulars all written out in his own English, including many comments that an English estate agent would have hesitated to put in writing. Not derogatory comments, just plain-spoken and unconventional.

'We spent that afternoon looking at various places, and a large part of the following days, but all that won't interest you. Mr Kirkontorni apologised for being unable to come with us himself. He offered us a junior to go round with us, someone rather like me, but Mr Purvis refused. The lad couldn't really speak English, and Mr Purvis always disliked the company of strangers on a job like this. We found our way about on a plan of the town which Mr Kirkontorni lent to us. Mr Purvis was vain about maps and insisted on keeping this one entirely to himself, though, having other things on his mind, he would have done better to have left the path-finding to me.

'Where the lad might have helped would have been with the people who occupied the various properties. Fortunately, Mr Kirkontorni had been able to warn most of them that an English agent (as he put it) was

72

coming, but there were still some who had heard nothing, or had not grasped the message, and we had several comic experiences. But the usual trouble was that the lady of the house had cleaned the whole place up especially for us, and even laid out a large meal on the table, with a clean, white tablecloth. There was a limit to what the two of us could eat and drink, especially as the lady often just stood or sat and watched us do it, and still more of a limit to the time we had, but of course we couldn't be rude, and we fell more and more behind schedule, especially as not many of our hostesses had much English, though they all seemed to have a few phrases, like 'Sit down' and 'Help yourself and 'Very good', which they said pointing to cakes and bottles. Another difficulty was that Mr Kirkontorni had spoken of only one visitor, so that everywhere *I* came as a surprise. The main effect of that was to waste still more time. But we managed to get round most of the places on our list, even though we didn't examine all of them as well as we might have done. At the end of the first afternoon, Mr Purvis said that at least we should not have to spend much on dinner; and that couldn't be denied.'

The old man chuckled a little, and Dyson took the opportunity to buy him another drink.

'Did you discover anything suitable?' asked Jay, who had not said much earlier.

'Oh, yes,' said the old man, 'and the Danzigers moved in and everything went so well that old Danziger wrote a special letter to Mr Purvis at the end of it, and said how pleased he was. Mr Purvis even managed to get a sort of bonus out of him on top of the usual commission and expenses. A trinkgeld he called it. But, do you know, I've quite forgotten which place it was we settled on. There were so many we saw, and so many people, all perfectly charming, in so far as we could understand them. But there was one place I know it wasn't. It was a place that only I saw, and that Mr Purvis didn't.'

The old man paused; probably choosing his words, rejecting the spontaneous ones, having reached a point in his tale where persuasiveness might be required, and, therefore, artifice.

'What was Mr Purvis doing at the time?' asked Gamble, encouragingly and because someone had to say something, but still perceptibly the examining barrister.

'Mr Purvis was asleep,' said the old man, in a new tone of voice, 'or at least lying down in his room.

'It was the day after we arrived. We'd spent hours and hours walking round the town in the sun, and, as I say, we'd had a lot of mixed stuff to eat and drink. Mr Purvis said he wanted to put his feet up. I wouldn't have minded doing the same myself, but it was the first chance I'd had on the whole trip to get away on my own for a little, and I couldn't let it go. We agreed a time for me to come back and see how Mr Purvis was doing, and I wondered off to the north side of the town, where till then I had hardly been, the southern end of the northern-most of the two lakes, if you follow me. The reason why we hadn't been there much was that Mr Kirkontorni had said it was out of the sun and rather a run-down area. Of course a southern aspect does matter considerably in Finland, especially to a rich man with local connections, like Mr Danziger.

'The evening mist that I have spoken of was rising quite thickly, but in patches. In places it was really dense, but other places were still open, with the mist all round at a little distance, like clearings in a forest. Also, a breeze was getting up, so that the mist was beginning to swirl a bit. It was quite a queer effect altogether; with the sun still shining through at the same time. I felt hot and cold all at once.

'I strolled down to the waterfront of the northern lake, where I had never been before, though I had seen the water at the end of streets sloping that way. Most of the town was built on the two sides of one of the ridges I've mentioned. To go from one lake to the other, you had to go up and then down. This made the two sides of the town look different. The ridge also sloped downwards to the west, until it faded away altogether, and you came to the passage from one lake to the other. The steamers on the northern lake all went through this passage, or straits as you might say, and moored at the piers on the south side of the town. I remember all this quite clearly. Unilinna was a town of the size you could take in as a whole, at least if you were being trained in surveying. And you can get a very clear impression of a place if you are walking about it steadily for four days.

'The northern waterfront really was rather a mangy place. There was a lakeside roadway of a kind, but it was narrow and very rough. The houses were either cut up into tenements or just standing empty. There were warehouses too, but not much look of trade. There was an odd feel about the area. I thought it was mainly that there were no kids playing in the streets, as you would have expected there to be. In fact, there was hardly anyone about at all. The whole place made me remember how little I knew about foreign countries. Also I had learnt from various things that had been said, about the terrible civil war in Finland, which had ended only a few years earlier.

'But much the most interesting thing was the view out across the lake. About a third of a mile from the waterfront was a wooded island, and there was a wooden footbridge right across to it, starting from about a couple of hundred yards to the left of where I stood. I suppose the island was about half a mile long, or a little more. When I say it was a wooded island, I mean that, as far as I could see through the patches of mist, it appeared to be all thick trees from end to end. Not conifers either, but big, spreading trees that must have been planted for some particular reason. I thought at first that it might be a nature reservation, but I then noticed signs of more and more houses among the trees, chimney-stacks and ridges of roofs sticking out, and sometimes bits of the façades, where the sun caught them. There were also the remains of jetties for boats, so little left of them that you didn't notice them at first. And, as far as I could see, certainly no boats, although in most parts of Finland you see boats all along any shore where there are houses. I set off to investigate further.

'There was no one on the long footbridge, and it

was in very bad repair. It was about six feet wide, with thick transverse planks and a stout wooden double railing on either side, but, even so, it struck me as quite dangerous to cross, because many of the planks were missing and many others loose or broken, and because long sections of handrail would obviously collapse under any kind of pressure. It didn't matter much about the handrail, which would have come in only if there had been a crowd, and that seemed unlikely; but the planks really quite scared me, especially as there were patches of thick mist on the bridge, and a nasty current running underneath it towards the narrows over on my left where the ships went through. There was no question, but the way, of a ship going through where I was, because the bridge was only three or four feet above the water. When there had been boats at the little jetties, they must have been prevented by it from sailing right round the island. It struck me that the footbridge might often be under water, and that this could hardly have been good for it. The whole arrangement seemed rather inefficient, but a higher bridge would of course have cost much more and no doubt the island wasn't thought worth it. All the same, I wondered how the people got on without bridge or boats, even though they were so close to the town.

'Having dropped the nature reserve idea, I thought that the island might be a private housing estate and that at the far end of the bridge might be a locked gate or at least a notice that I shouldn't understand. But there was nothing of that kind. From the end of the bridge three rough tracks led away, one round the southern shore of the island which I had been looking at, one round the northern shore, and one up on to the usual low but steep ridge which was the island's backbone. There was no one about and no sound at all, probably because sound was muffled by the mist which seemed to be thicker now that I had reached the island, than it looked from the far shore, and very much colder. The mist had either descended on the district more heavily than on the previous evening, or else there was something about the island which made it cling there particularly. I thought it might be something to do with the thick trees. I looked back over the bridge and found that I could not see the other side, not even in patches. The mist was becoming a real fog. I even wondered whether I ought not to go back, but there seemed no sensible reason. I had left Mr Purvis only twenty or thirty minutes before, and though I did not much like crossing the bridge, I did not seriously doubt that I could do it, and by now there seemed no reason why going back at once should be any more pleasant than going back after I had walked round the island. There was no question of night coming on as soon as that.

'I picked the path which went up on to the ridge. I suppose I thought that the mist would lie heavier round the shores of the lake, and that I would get a better general idea of the island's layout from the higher ground. Not that it was all that much higher: only the usual hundred feet or less. Nor did it make any difference to the big heavy trees. They grew so thickly along the ridge that when I got there, I found I could see very little. And they were all absolutely still in the cold mist.

'I scrambled up the slope – it was only a mud-track, and it must have been terrible after rain – and when I reached the top, came almost at once upon a house, looking in the mist much bulkier than it probably was. It was built of wood, but was much more elaborate and fanciful than any of the houses I had so far seen in Finland. It was of a fanciful shape and plan, to begin with. It had been painted in several different colours. It had huge, carved bargeboards along the edges of the roof, and carvings in many other places too. Some of them struck me as rather quaint. But I didn't have time to look at them properly. The whole house was badly out of repair. I doubted if it had been painted since before the war – the *first* war, you know, and the enormous bargeboards were crumbling away, quite dangerously, I thought. The garden was completely gone to ruin.

'Normally I should have supposed the house to be empty, but that was not so. There was a fence round the garden, a heavy wooden paling, something with the weight and solidity of the wooden railing across the footbridge. Even so, there were gaps in it, and there was also a gate, which was lower than the rest of the fence. I had been creeping along the fence looking through the gaps, but it was across the top of the gate that I saw a woman sitting among the long grass and in all that mist. She was not a young girl, but she had very fair hair, tied up at the back of the head. She wore a loose brown dress and she was doing something with a machine of some kind, not spinning but possibly weaving, or possibly something quite different. I don't know what it was, but it seemed to me a very odd time and place to do it. I had only one quick look, because the woman caught my eye on the instant, as if she had been waiting for me to come into view, and stared back at me. I could see quite plainly that her eyes were a very bright blue, and that was just about all I did see with any certainty. I could have sworn that she was frightened, and I suppose it was fairly reasonable that she should be, especially if she had heard me shuffling along her fence. I wanted, above all, not to get into a scene, because of course of the language. So I got away as quickly as I could without actually running. I hesitated even to glance back, because I thought the woman might have come to the gate or be looking over it, but in the end I did, and there was nothing; only the high black paling, and the falling-down house looked huger and vaguer than ever in the mist.

'Then I came upon another house. Like the first one, it was on the south side of the ridge walk, but the trees were so thick that it could have made little difference in either case from a prospect point of view. This second house was quite different from the first, something unusual in Finland to start with, because in Finland the houses are much more alike than they are here. It is the same in many foreign countries, as you will all know. This house was a neat, classical affair, built in white stone, with a columned portico like a Greek temple.

It was all on one storey, but it occupied quite an area, and was no mere bungalow in the usual sense. The only trouble was that it was in the same state of ruin. The garden couldn't have been attended to in any way for years; some of the stones in the house walls had big splits in them, which suggested something wrong with the builder in the first place; and at least one of the portico columns had fallen right over, as if it really had been an old temple in Greece. As something to come upon in all that mist and quietness, it really was depressing.

'But there appeared to be some who did not necessarily think so. Because in several of the windows there were faint lights, so that once again the house was occupied. They had probably lighted up against the mist rather than against the night, so had not bothered to draw the curtains, as people don't at such times. If, of course, it was ever necessary to draw the curtains in that place. If, for that matter, there were curtains to be drawn, with, obviously, so little money around. I could easily have investigated further, as this time there was no wooden paling, but a low iron fence, now unpainted, rusty, and broken down, but very special and ornamental when it was first put up. But I didn't investigate further. I walked on. I daresay I should again have thought about walking back if it had not been that I feared to pass the woman who was working the machine in her garden. And it was not only because of the language difficulty that I feared it. The whole business was really very queer. So I continued ahead.

'Again there was quite a gap between the houses,

which seemed to have been dotted about the tracks in the woodland wherever the fancy struck, but before long I came to the third one. This was a tall brick affair with Italian details; rather the kind of thing you can still see in places like Sydenham and Stoke Newington – 'gentlemen's villas', they used to be called, rather handsome and often very well built. I suppose the style began in the Italian countryside, but nowadays we connect it with cities, and it seemed very out of place among all those forest trees. They were actually growing in through the upper windows. This house, I thought, really was empty. I could see no sign of life about it at all and it was even further gone than the others. As a matter of fact, I didn't care for it; looming up half-ruined in the mist, with the branches of the trees breaking through the upper windows. It made you think of squelchy, white creatures scudding about the rotten floors, and brightly coloured funguses sprouting on the walls. But I was held as well as frightened, and hung about for a bit wondering whether I dared take a closer look. The front door was at the top of a flight of steps, just like Sydenham, and I could see the remains of a paved path leading to the broken-down gate where I stood. As I shifted around outside, I realised that once again the house was not empty at all. It couldn't be, because someone had come out of the front door. There was what I might call a big, tall, black figure standing on the top step.

'I hadn't heard the door open, or heard anything else for that matter, but the mist seemed to kill all sound, as I've said, and I was growing quite accustomed to not hearing much. Nor had I *seen* the figure appear. I had been gazing around at the whole scene, noting this and that, and there was quite a lot to gaze at, and to think about. I'd seen the last of the sun when I crossed the bridge, but, all the same, there was still plenty of light in a misty sort of way, and I could see the black figure at the top of the steps really quite clearly. Properly, the dusk had hardly even begun. I call it a black figure: not only was it black from top to bottom, but it seemed to me both taller and wider than an average figure – considerably taller and considerably wider. All the same, it *was* a human figure (lest you be thinking something else): I could see the big white face.

'But that was just about all I did see. This time I took to my heels and I'm not ashamed to say so. Each one of you would have done the same, believe me.'

The old man paused. He must have been right about us too, because, rather curiously I thought, no one said a word. Even the man behind the bar leaned across it like a trick waxwork, his chin propped on his forearm. The old man continued.

'I ran on, past more houses, I don't know how many, which I didn't stop to examine, but which certainly gave no obvious sign of life. Running and walking fast, I reached the other end of the ridge and slithered down the lumpy mud slope to the lake shore at the far side of the island. At this point it struck me to wonder why the tracks through the woodland were not completely overgrown, with so few people about. This gave me a new fright. When you get into that frame of mind, almost everything in the world can seem frightening.'

Dyson interrupted. 'I expect the Finlanders went across at weekends and ploughed the place up.'

'No,' said the old man. 'The Finns didn't. I don't to this day know what the answer was.'

'Please go on, sir,' said Dyson.

'It was much the same at the end of the island as it had been at the footbridge end. There were simply the other ends of the same three tracks: the one along the ridge, and the one along each shore. By now I had more or less confirmed that there was no other way off the island than the footbridge. It was true that I hadn't seen the north shore, but I knew that it faced the open lake, whole square miles of water. There couldn't be a bridge there. I had to go back.

'I chose the southern shore. I couldn't return along the ridge, and I had lost the taste for exploration. I already had some idea what the south side of the island was like, because I had seen quite a lot of it through the mist from the mainland, and with the sun shining on it too. Mostly trees and broken-down landing places, as you'll recall. I admit that about the north shore a thought in my mind was that no one lived close opposite it on the mainland, so that no one could see at all easily what went on there. I daresay it was an absurd thing to think. I'm sure it was. But of course the island had got on my nerves.

'As I walked along the lakeside, stepping out pretty fast, I saw the same big houses continued here too, all set back among the trees, so that they hardly made the most of their position, which was really a very fine one, especially if the sun should come out. The houses were all locked up, but did not seem to be quite so neglected as the houses on the ridge. Pretty clearly, they had been designed as summer residences, and yet it was summer now, more or less, and there was no one about. Of course, it was hard to be certain, in the light of my experiences, that there was no one *inside* any of the houses, but I had no intention of trying to make sure. At the best of times, to pass by a lot of empty houses is a sad proceeding. It makes you think all the wrong thoughts. Especially when you're young, and not used to such thoughts. And most of all when the empty houses are set in a beautiful spot. That's the worst thing of all.

'Curiously enough, however, it was just about then, when I was feeling lower and lower, that the idea came to me: why might not one of these houses suit Mr Danziger? By which I mean I thought that buying the whole island for development might appeal to Mr Danziger, with a nice house for himself thrown in, a house with a lot of character, quiet, yet near the town and the timber plantation, if only the bridge was repaired, which could easily have been done, or so it seemed to me. I knew that Mr Danziger had gone in for several developments of this kind in different countries. I was quite cheered up by my own cleverness, quite carried away by the idea. I thought there might be something in it for me personally. It was my own discovery, and nothing to do with Mr Kirkontorni or Mr Purvis. The outstanding speculation ... No doubt I thought also that it would enable me to get my own back on the island. I daresay that was my real motive all the time. I am sorry that it should have been so.'

'At that stage it was rather understandable,' observed Dyson.

'At that stage perhaps it was,' acknowledged the old man. 'And yet no one and nothing on the island had done me any harm. I was no more than a raw lad trespassing; not perhaps in the full legal sense, but assuredly pushing in where I wasn't wanted. Trespassing, and not equipped to understand. What right of complaint had I?'

'What happened next?' asked Jay.

'I was striding along, all but forgetting the things that had upset me, and working out a lot of nonsense about putting up small, modern houses on the island and what I could hope to get out of it for myself, when I came upon a house where there was a crowd of folk at home, and, what was more, and to judge by the noise, giving some kind of a party. There were lights on inside the house, though they looked yellow and rather dim, as room lights always do when seen from the daylight outside, but I stared in, and could see a quite a mass of people bobbing about and enjoying themselves. I suppose they were twenty or thirty yards away, down the length of the garden in front of the house. The garden was completely gone to seed like all the others. The party looked pretty peculiar too. You know how it is when you see a lot of strangers enjoying themselves inside a room at a little distance, when they don't know you're looking in at them. And, of course, this lot were foreigners as well. They were wearing all kinds of gay clothes in very bright colours, and really seemed to be beating it up. They were too far away for me to hear very much, especially as all the windows were tight shut, as they usually are abroad. I rather imagine that they were double windows too; to keep out the winter snow and cold. That was quite the usual thing in Finland. One thing I wondered about was the light; whether gas or electricity could be laid on to the island. It might be useful to know. I craned about but couldn't see. I was too far away, and the lights themselves seemed to be out of my line of vision.

'That jolly party took a further small weight off my mind, as you may be able to imagine, but what was my surprise to find that the next house was giving a party too, and the next after that. I looked in at both of them but couldn't see any more than in the first house, in fact rather less, because these two houses were set even further back among the trees, and further away from the path I was on. Every time there seemed to be a good-sized crowd, and of all ages, including plenty of children. It was just like Christmas, especially with all that mist, and now with dusk coming down in a big way. It occurred to me that it must really be some kind of national celebration. I wouldn't have expected to know what.

'The next three or four of the houses were locked up and empty, or looked like it, and I walked down to have a closer look at the jetties I've mentioned. It was the usual story. In the first place, they had been very heavily built of wood, like the bridge and many of the fences, but all of them seemed fallen to pieces, and really pretty dangerous anyway with children around, as there were. There was nothing to stop anyone going out on to them, and there was the swift current sweeping past to the narrows. In England, the local authority would have compelled them to be cleared away and the waterside fenced. And I had been right in what I thought when I looked across from the other side: there wasn't a boat in sight, not even a sunken boat, as far as I could see. Probably the current was enough to carry away a small boat that had been neglected.

'And then I came upon a wooden house painted in faded blue, where there was still another of those parties. I was getting used to them by now, and didn't suppose there was much more I could learn by just staring in from a distance through the front windows. But I stopped and looked for a moment all the same.

'I saw at once that this time there was a face looking back at me. It was a small, round, white face, which was peeking out watching the darkness fall. At the other houses everyone had been too busy with the festivities to do a thing like that. They had all been looking inwards.

'It was a child, which had somehow detached itself from the general goings-on. And this time there were rather special goings-on. The child caught my eye and waved to me through the glass with its little white hand.

It was wearing some kind of dark tunic, buttoned right up. I waved back.

'As far as I was concerned, the things happening behind the child were very interesting. Believe it or not, in the room was another of those figures that I had seen come out of the house on the ridge above; very tall, very wide, all black, just the same; but this time I had some idea of the answer: it was an Orthodox priest, in his black robe and high black headdress. I had seen pictures of them, but I had never seen one in real life, and if you had asked me before that moment, I should have answered for sure that they had died out long ago. As I realised what it was, I felt better once more. The figure I had seen coming out of the house on the ridge had upset me badly.

'This man was occupying himself in handing something out. All the people at the party seemed to be getting one of these things. The last corners were formed up in a queue. Every time the priest handed out, the recipient, whether a man or woman, gave a kind of bob and passed on. I saw it happen about three times before the child at the window waved to me again. I presumed that he had already received his object. I imagined that the children might have come first, as there seemed to be none of them in the queue. On the other hand, there were no other children near the window either. I could not be sure whether the child who waved was a boy or a girl, but I thought it waved like a boy.

'Again I waved back, and then thought it was time to move on. I was very interested in the priest and the distribution, but it would have been rude to go on peering. When the child realised that I was going, it made the most violent gestures inviting me into the house instead. You know how vividly children can do it. In this case, it was just as well from one point of view, because we were unlikely to be able to communicate in any other way.

'All the same, I shook my head. It was hopeless to think of going in and probably being unable to speak to a soul, especially as I should have had to begin by explaining what I was doing there, with that handout going on. I might have been in real trouble and taken for a thief.

'Still I found it difficult to proceed on my way and disappoint the child so badly. There was a kind of urgency about the little lad which made one care. And there was the foreign factor too. I didn't want to make some social blunder.

'I smiled as broadly as I could manage, pointed to my watch, moved my shoulders as if I had to hurry off to an engagement, and tried to look sorry. I must have done it fairly well because the next thing that happened was that the child jumped down from whatever it was kneeling on at the window and came running out down the garden towards me. It was indeed a boy, about ten I should say, dressed not in shorts but in breeches, which little girls didn't wear in those days. He also wore boots up to his knees. I was a trifle concerned about what was likely to happen next.

'The boy somehow got through the gate, though it

looked both heavy and collapsed, and at once proceeded to offer me something. Yes, it was the medal you've seen. That was what the priest had been giving out. Blessed medals: I mean medals that had been blessed. The boy grabbed at me, but of course I couldn't understand a word. "English", I said, rather hopelessly, and of course wouldn't take his medal from him.

'He snatched hold of my hand to prevent my getting away, and went in for more dumb show. I can't tell you how good he was at it. He made me understand quite clearly the blessing that went with the medal, the luck if you like. He imitated all sorts of things going wrong, and how the medal would save me and make things go right again. The only thing I had to do was have the medal always with me and cross myself at the moment of need with it in my hand. He had let go of me because he saw that now I shouldn't just walk off. He showed me again and again. And all without a single further word. He made me feel it was a matter of life or death. Which of course it was, as you have all seen for yourselves.'

'We have that,' said the barman reverentially.

I saw a flash of impatience pass across Rort's face, but he did not comment.

'Not that I believed anything of the sort at the time,' continued the old man. 'Naturally. All the same, I was terribly struck by the boy's cleverness and his sincerity. What reason had he to care about *me*, like that?

'In the end, I took the medal, supposing that he could always get another one for himself, and did everything I could to say thank you. He just stood there with his boots close together on the mud track and smiled at me, like the boy scout on the poster who has just done his good deed. And yet more than that: the boy had his own way of smiling. I daresay it was just that he was a foreigner.

'I wondered if there was anything further. Apparently there wasn't. So I then went through the same kind of pantomime to say goodbye. I felt that just an ordinary casual goodbye would hardly do. But I didn't have to worry. Goodbye, the actual English 'goodbye', was an expression the boy knew.

'Before walking off, I looked back at the house. The priest in his high black hat and long black robe had come out and stood all by himself under the porch, looking at us down the length of the weedy garden path. I now saw that he had masses of white beard. It covered his entire face, so that you could see only his sunken eyes. As you probably know, Orthodox priests do not disfigure the image of their Maker. The priest stood quite still, and I had no idea as to whether there was something I ought to do. But I couldn't think what, so I smiled feebly and just shuffled off. The boy didn't stop to watch me. Immediately I turned, I heard him dash back into the house. I did look behind me through the mist after a minute or two, but I could see nothing of the festivities, not even the lights. Owing to the house being set back among the trees. Nor were there any more houses with parties. All the rest of them that I saw were shut up like tombs.

'Although the mist was at its thickest on the bridge,

and although it was almost night anyway, I had no trouble at all in getting across. I just walked steadily on until I reached the other side and didn't worry about the loose planks and the holes. Only when I arrived safely did it pass through my mind for a moment that I had had my medal to protect me. But the crossing was not really dangerous if you used reasonable care, as you will have gathered: so I gave no further thought to the notion.

'When I got back to our hotel I realised that I was actually ahead of the time I had settled with Mr Purvis, though so much had happened to me that this seemed incredible. When the moment came, I knocked him up (he was flat out with his boots off), and we had something to eat, despite all the eating we had done already, but I said nothing about my adventures. Mr Purvis, fine man though he was, wouldn't have taken much stock in things like that. I merely told him I'd been for a longish walk; which helped to explain how I had managed to get up another appetite.

'Inevitably, Mr Purvis asked me whether I had seen any likely houses. Young and ignorant though I was, I had by now begun to feel rather differently about the idea of Mr Danziger buying up my island, with me getting a cut. I don't think I could have said *why* I felt different about it, but I knew very well that I did. All the same, I told Mr Purvis *something* of what I had found: not laying it on at all, and not making it sound extra attractive.

'"Mr Danziger wouldn't care for a place like that," said Mr Purvis.

'He spoke to settle the matter. I can almost hear him now. He went on to say that Mr Danziger wasn't looking for an investment: that when an investment was among the things he was looking for, he never failed to indicate that fact to Mr Purvis. I felt, even then, that Mr Danziger, if he was the successful businessman everyone took him to be, would probably be glad to be put in the way of a promising investment at any time, even when he wasn't expecting it. But Mr Purvis had not brought me to Finland in order to argue with him, and, in any case, I was really relieved that the island would remain undisturbed, as far as my influence went. Nor am I saying that Mr Purvis was necessarily mistaken in his view of Mr Danziger. Probably he was quite right. In any case, he seemed pleased with me, because he ended our meal by buying me a Finnish liqueur called Lakka. They make these different liqueurs out of berries picked in the Arctic, and very good they are. I've never met with better liqueurs anywhere.'

'Can you get them in England?' asked Gamble.

'No, no. Like many good things, they don't travel,' replied the old man.

We waited for him to resume.

'Curiously enough, in view of how firm he had been with me the night before, it was Mr Purvis who raised the question of my island and the houses on it, the next morning with Mr Kirkontorni. I should not myself have mentioned the matter again, however much I thought about it.

'Mr Kirkontorni knew at once what Mr Purvis was

talking about, and didn't have to ask me for details.

"'They're the houses of the Russians," he said.

"'How's that?" asked Mr Purvis.

"'In the days before the war," said Mr Kirkontorni, "Finland was very popular with the Russians in summer. They used to build villas on the coast and on the lakes, and Unilinna was one of the places they liked best. The families spent the summer here, and a very gay time they made of it. I can remember them myself. Though I was only a child at the time, I've never seen or heard the like of their great dinners, and musical parties, and dances. Unilinna has never been quite the same place since they left; either for the money they brought or for the fun either. We had mixed thoughts about them at the time, but most of us have missed them badly since they went. All day they scattered gold and all night they sang. Not that what I've said is popular everywhere politically. And people are right there too: at politics the Russians have never been good."

"'I suppose there are none of them left now?" asked Mr Purvis. I had not told him one way or the other, but only about the island itself and the empty houses, so you can imagine how I waited for Mr Kirkontorni's answer.

"'There are supposed to be a few," said Mr Kirkontorni; "but we don't have anything to do with them any more. Politics again. Finland used to be a kind of Russian colony, as you know, and we didn't like that, though most of us had nothing against the Russians personally. And since then we've had our civil war, when we starved, and they tried to enforce Bolshevism here and would have done if we hadn't had assistance from the Germans. Today most people want to hear no more of the Russians than they can help. In fact, their houses are supposed to be unlucky, and no one goes near them. If anyone did, he wouldn't be very popular either."

"'Who owns the houses now?" asked Mr Purvis.

"'I really couldn't tell you. I should think it's a matter for international law, by this time. No one's ever bought them from the Russians: first because it wouldn't be thought right; second because there've been no Russians to buy them. Very much not, as we all know."

"'It makes you think," said Mr Purvis.

"'It's another reason why our people say the houses are unlucky."

"'You can't wonder at it," said Mr Purvis.

"'Miehen on mela Kädessä, Jumala venettä viepi," said Mr Kirkontorni. That's a Finnish proverb, meaning "man holds the paddle, but God does the steering". I heard it several times on our way home, when we idled about for a few days, and visited several Finnish townships.

'They said no more on the subject of the houses, and a little later Mr Purvis and I were tramping round Unilinna again in the full heat of the sun, eating a lot, drinking a lot, sweating a lot, and stumbling over the language, to say nothing of the map, which Mr Purvis would keep for himself. I have an idea it was on that day that we found the place Mr Purvis recommended to Mr Danziger, and that Mr Danziger liked so much. It must have been, because by the evening Mr Purvis was so done up that he kept me hanging around him, fetching the waiter up to his room and the chambermaid, and on the final day we took it very much easier. On that third evening, the one I'm speaking of, I couldn't get out at all. When Mr Purvis wasn't wanting things from the hotel staff, with me acting as intermediary, especially with the language, then he was dictating notes to me about the places we had seen, while he soaked his feet in a footbath, that had to be just the right size not to get cold, and even then had to have more hot water added to it about every five minutes, and more funny salts too, that the hotel had advised and that I'd had to scour the town to find. Mr Purvis kept changing his mind about the notes, and particularly about what was suitable for Mr Danziger to hear about. Mr Purvis always said that manner of presentation to the client was quite as important as what was presented, and often more so: and of course he was quite right. When it came to the matter of the hotel, he was a proper traveller of the old school, who knew his rights, and expected to get value for his money. Altogether I had my hands full that evening. I was not left under the impression that I was travelling only for pleasure.

'The next day, as I've said, wasn't very serious. If we'd happened to come upon Windsor Castle offered for a song, I doubt whether Mr Danziger would have heard much about it. Mr Purvis made a point of always knowing his own mind, and I'm sure he'd made it up by then. At one point, during the hot afternoon, he even suggested that I take him to have a look at the houses on the island, just for the jaunt and I suppose for the breeze off the lake, but I told him about the dangerous bridge and what a long walk it all was, and he settled for a short steamer-trip instead. We crossed to a tiny lakeside village, all set around with conifers and red rocks, and there, in the small, stone church, we saw a Finnish wedding, with the bridal couple in national dress and the dark building as full of lighted candles as a grotto. We didn't go in, but watched from outside the west door, which they'd left open, as it was so sunny, though the sun hardly entered the church at all. I noticed that the officiating pastor, who stood behind the altar rails, was not in any way like the black figures I had seen on my island. This gave me a surprise; but of course I said nothing about it to Mr Purvis.

'When we got back, Mr Purvis was all smiles, and suggested that I have a further look round on my own for a bit, while he took a rest. "You're only young once," he said, as if I'd been holding back. I arranged to call for him later, as I'd done two nights earlier.

'Of course I went down at once to have another look at my island. Mr Kirkontorni had said it was an unpopular thing to do, but I could hardly worry much about that, as I didn't live in Unilinna or even Finland. I was still frightened of the island, but I had an idea that a return visit would clear various things up, and that Mr Kirkontorni's information would enable me to look at it with new eyes, and add some queer items to my small stock of knowledge. But, given the chance, I couldn't have kept away from the island anyway. What I did hope was that I shouldn't meet one of these black priests. I had realised of course that they were probably quite the usual thing in Russia, and the thought of them was not as bad as it had been, but I still did not care for them at all.

'I had also realised that the peculiar writing on the medal I had been given must be Russian. It was only a guess, because until then I hadn't known that Russian was written in a different script. I remember taking the medal out of my pocket and looking at it as I walked down the empty street to the northern waterfront. It was not very encouraging to think that apparently people didn't like living even where they could see the island. It was a different thought from the one which had struck me on the island itself, as you may remember.

'I can't say there was anything remarkable this time about the way I crossed the bridge. I just went carefully and watched where I put my feet. I was earlier than on my previous visit, and the late afternoon mist was only beginning to rise. The island looked very beautiful, with its huge trees, and the fanciful houses sticking out here and there. From the bridge you couldn't see how badly they needed painting. The faded paint probably made them look prettier, as it often does from a distance.

'My idea was to start out along the southern path, where I'd seen those parties going on among the few Russians that Mr Kirkontorni had said were still left. I wasn't at all keen about the big houses on the ridge, and what I really wanted was to have another look at the Russians themselves, especially as I seemed to be the only person who cared about them.

'From the moment I started along the path, I felt a great sadness all about me. It was not the kind of feeling I was used to – not at that age. Naturally I put it down to the fact that now I knew about the houses, and couldn't see them any more as mere property going to waste. Not that property going to waste is ever a cheerful sight in itself. I told myself that it must be the sad story I'd heard about the Russians, even though Mr Purvis and I had been left to fill in the details, which, at that time, I knew no more about than any other ordinary English boy. Whatever I told myself, I felt worse and worse with every step I took. I felt as if a great pit was opening wider and wider, that previously I'd known nothing about; and that pretty well the whole world was sinking into it, so that soon it would be as if I were alone at the North Pole or on the moon, with no one even to cry out to. You may think that's a bit far-fetched after all these years, but it's exactly how it was. It was the feeling of being completely cut off and helpless that was the worst part; and the fact that on the face of it this was non-sense, because I could always run back across the bridge, only made it worse. I felt there was some explanation, something I didn't know about, which was the real cause of the trouble. All the same, I was determined not to run away just because I was in a blue funk.

'In the middle of it all, I remembered my medal. I pulled it out and held it clenched in my hand. Whatever I thought it might do, it didn't do. I went on feeling exactly the same. But I continued clutching hold of the medal, as I ploughed forward. And this time, the sun was shining all the while, as I've said.

'I reached the wooden house painted blue where I'd talked with the Russian lad, seen the priest giving out the medals, and all the rest of it. There was no one about and everything was quite silent, but the house was not locked up, like the houses between it and the bridge. On the contrary, the door where I had seen the priest watching me from behind his huge, fluffy beard stood wide open.

'I can't tell you how, but I knew at once that there was no one inside.

'The house had an utterly unoccupied look, but that didn't always mean much on the island, and I think it was the wide-open door itself which told me there was no one there. I thought I could risk taking a look.

'I struggled with the gate. It was even heavier and more jammed than I had supposed when I first saw it, and I couldn't think how the Russian boy had managed it so well. But I shoved it back and pushed my way up the garden path through the long grass and weeds. Believe it or not, I walked straight in. All things considered, I think it was plucky as well as cheeky, but I still didn't suppose that anything was *really* wrong. How could I? I knew nothing.'

At this point, a couple of locals who had drifted into the bar, and had been seated in the background intermittently muttering short, slow sentences to one another, drifted out again.

'There was nothing inside but blood,' said the old

man. 'Blood everywhere. Big blotches on the peeling walls, with darker centres, where the blood had started spurting. Blood splashed about the grey ceiling, as if kids had been in there with squirts that had got out of control. Blood heavy on the floorboards, dusty and rotten though they were. I could see the shapes of bodies, as they had lain there; many bodies, because it was a big room, thirty or thirty-five feet long I daresay, and perhaps twenty-five feet wide, and these shapes were right across the floor. After that, I have never doubted the marks that are said to be on the Holy Shroud at Turin: at least I have never doubted that they could have been made by a human body. The blood leaves an extraordinary definite outline. In that room, the marks suggested that several of the bodies had lain across one another. There was even blood on the windows, including the window where the little boy had waved to me. The sunshine shone through it like stained glass, and made the room redder still. It was like the Holy Grail, all glowing, and yet the room was filthy and dusty too. And the blood smelt. I can smell it now, when I think about it. At the time I all but fainted with the smell of it.

'But I didn't faint. I think it was partly because I still didn't fully understand. I got out and tore off to the bridge as fast as my young legs would carry me.

'Or rather *towards* the bridge. Because on the way I met the first person I'd seen on the island that day. He was a scruffy specimen too, dressed in little better than rags. If he hadn't been in the very middle of the mud road, I'd have run right past him.

'He said something to me in what I took to be Russian, and for some reason I stopped. His hair was going grey, and he had straggling grey wisps on his face and chin; not a proper beard, but just above the last word in neglect and untidiness. Of course I must have been looking very peculiar myself at that moment.

'I made my usual answer: "English." I imagine I was pretty well gasping.

'"What are you holding in your hand?" he said: just like that, and quite comprehensibly.

'I unfolded my hand and showed him my medal lying on the palm of it. I was past caring if he snatched it.

'"Do you know what that means?" he asked, pointing to the words.

'I shook my head.

'"The Feast of the Sheep of the Theotokos," he said. "It is a privilege to possess such a medal. Only at the Feast are they given. They bear a blessing."

'"But to participate, you have each time to cross yourself. Like this." He showed me, as the boy had done. The Greeks do it differently from the Latins, as I expect some of you know. I had forgotten that part of it until he reminded me.

'"I am a hermit," he said, "having been long a pilgrim. I am now the only Christian soul resident on this island, where once there were so many."

'I could only bow my head. Raw though I was.

'"Remember and live," he said. "Remember and live long."

'Then he passed by me without a smile, and I walked

quite slowly to and across the bridge, feeling much calmer.'

The old man stopped.

We had not expected an end just there, and were taken by surprise.

'What's the Feast of the Sheep of the whatever-it-was?' asked Gamble, somewhat ineffectively.

'It's an annual celebration in the Orthodox Church,' replied the old man, 'but the details you'll have to discover for yourself.'

'And the charm has worked ever since?' enquired the barman.

'According to my belief, it has worked on several occasions, even though I was raised in a faith which has no part in such things. Plainly I cannot expect it to work for all time.'

'In a sense perhaps you can,' said Dyson, quite quietly.

'Anyway it worked tonight right enough,' said the barman, still awed by the evidence of his own eyes.

Of course we were all shying away from the core of the experience, as people do. And it seemed inappropriate just to thank the narrator and compliment his tale, as mere courtesy suggested. We all seemed painfully short of any right things to say. This may help to excuse a certain discordancy in a question which Rort put at this point.

'The suggestion is that the people died in the civil war?'

'No,' said the old man. 'The civil war began only in 1918, and all the Russians had gone back to their own country long before that. It was in Russia that they died, not in Finland.'

Rort smiled, too polite to express doubt. One could tell from his face that he thought the tale too preposterous to be worth powder and shot. 'I expect they'd most of them done the same kind of thing to their serfs and servants in their time,' he said; entering, as he saw it, into the spirit of the narrative.

'I don't know about that,' said the old man. 'All I know is that, speaking for myself, I wouldn't have much truck with the people responsible for what I saw until they at least repudiate what they did then.'

'If we followed that line of thought, we'd have a third world war,' said Rort.

But the old man said nothing further; nor, after Dyson had thanked him (quite adroitly) on behalf of us all, did he or we return to the subject during the remainder of the course.

No Stronger than a Flower

Beauty whose action is no stronger than a
flower.

William Shakespeare

'Naturally *I* don't care, because I love you,' said Curtis.
'I'm thinking entirely of you.'

Nesta had always been given to believe that, whatever
they might say to one, it was a woman's appearance that
men really cared about; and indeed she thought that she
well understood their point of view. So understanding
had she been, in fact, that she had long regarded herself as truly resigned to the wintry consequences in her
own case. She would not, therefore, ever have accepted Curtis's proposal of marriage, had she not greatly,
though as yet briefly, loved him. She had a temperamen-
tal distaste for extreme measures.

This trait of Nesta's, and her experience of men, had
prevented her discerning that Curtis was a far more
desperate character. Having in his early twenties loved
a woman of great beauty, he considered that he had
learnt his lesson: beauty, although it had its place, was
not to be lived with. He took it for granted that there
were other values. He was horrified, therefore, to find
himself now preoccupied, almost unconsciously at the

start, with a stealthy campaign to persuade Nesta to do something about her looks. The campaign, he perceived, was being planned even before he proposed to her. This present suggestion was a climax.

'I don't really believe in it,' said Nesta.

'But, darling, how can you tell if you don't put it to the test?'

Of course this was old stuff between them.

Nesta said nothing.

'I don't see that you have anything actually to *lose*,' said Curtis.

'I suppose I might lose you.'

'Darling, please don't be silly. I keep saying it's *you* I'm thinking about.'

'I wonder how I've managed until now?'

'You've had no one to look after you.'

If she could have accepted that at anything like its face value, she would doubtless have at least tried to do what Curtis wanted. As it was (although she did not doubt that Curtis loved her in his own way), she did nothing. A date had been fixed for the marriage, and Nesta was afraid that if she took the step demanded of her, and it did not end in reasonable success, then Curtis would jilt her.

After the marriage, it became suddenly clear to Nesta that to the generally accepted rule about men Curtis was no exception. Curtis had gone about his plan cleverly enough to confuse her at a time when she so much wanted to be confused; but marriage cleared her mind like a rocket piercing a cloud and releasing a downpour. Possibly the worst symptom was that from the nuptial day Curtis had never referred to the matter. Apparently he had decided to accept her as she was. And since, having been long self-occluded, she was greatly wishful of change and adventure, she could not welcome his decision.

One trouble with Curtis's previous attitude had always been its practical vagueness. As often with men in difficult and embarrassing contexts, he had urged action upon her with a persistency which indicated, she now saw, that latterly the subject was always in the front of his thoughts about her; but never making any very precise or feasible proposition. He would generalise about the importance and efficiency of beauty culture, and even, more than once, hint at plastic surgery; but at the smallest demur by Nesta would fall back upon an aloof irritability which she took to imply that naturally the details must be left to her. There was about him a suggestion that it was the least she could contribute. Why? Because she was a woman, she supposed. It was also the reason why she loved him.

One thing which marriage did for Nesta was to stoke up a romantic sensitivity which previously she had banked down with daily loads of dust and ashes. She acquired an impersonal dissatisfaction with a way of life which a year before she would have thought ecstatic if it were not that she would then have altogether excluded it from her thoughts as impossible. Curtis's passion might be somewhat guarded, but it was neither infrequent nor frightening; his general consideration for her was admirable; and he provided her, starved as she was of affectionate outlet, with continuous opportunities to assist and look after him. Only he no longer suggested that she should seek advice about her appearance; no longer remarked that every woman did so or wasn't a woman.

Eight or nine months after she was married, Nesta for the first time gave the problem exact and business-like consideration. As commonly happens after a long period of irresolution, an apparent answer, a seeming first step, stared her in the face immediately she started seriously to look for it. She went to the library of her mother's club, where she read through the flowing advertisement columns of the fashion papers for women, papers which she would not have about the flat, lest Curtis misunderstand, and perhaps pity, her interest in them; and in one which was new to her (it was entitled *Flame*), she found a relevant intimation. Restrained, sensitive, civilised, promising nothing and alluding only to a consultation without obligation, it bespoke as much as could be hoped for, Nesta thought, in such a case, although placed somewhat unnoticeably in a corner of the penultimate page. There was an address to which enquirers were invited to write for an appointment. No telephone number was given, but it was not a matter about which Nesta would have telephoned.

The reply to Nesta's letter was elegantly typed on thick paper, bearing at the top a representation, embossed in red, of a sleek, slightly formalised head and neck (a desirable looking creature, Nesta admitted, rubbing the raised surface with her finger); but the address was in a street, and indeed a part of the town, which were outside her restricted topography. The suggested appointment was for that morning. There was no need to confirm it, stated the letter; apparently in no doubt that Nesta would hasten to attend. Nesta put the letter in her handbag. She decided in favour of a taxi.

It was a long journey and a disappointing landfall. They were high terrace houses of that kind which while apparently built for single families, and certainly very inconvenient to operate on any other basis, yet give the impression of never having been so occupied. Now, in this particular street, they appeared largely to be let out in single rooms for habitation by the elderly and disappointed. The presence of children playing on the pavement manifested both life's renascence and the street's continued social descent.

The house Nesta sought was in the middle of the row. Its knocker and letter-box flap were polished and the lace curtains at its windows clean and lusciously draped; but the general effect was somehow still so cheerless that Nesta, upon beholding it as she stepped out of the taxi, immediately decided to go home.

She hesitated for a moment, trying to assemble an explanation.

'Don't yer like the look of it?' enquired the driver.

Nesta turned to him. 'No,' she said, and regarded him seriously.

It seemed all that was needed.

"Op in. I'll soon 'ave yer back 'ome.'

Nesta nodded.

But already the moment was gone. The front door of the house was open, and a woman advancing down the short strip of garden. Nesta was unequipped with the ruthlessness which might have enabled her to act on her impulse and bolt.

'It was you who wrote to me?'

Again Nesta nodded. The woman was staring at her.

'Make up your mind,' enjoined the taxi-driver. He seemed to disapprove of the latest development. But Nesta was looking in her handbag.

'I'm Mrs de Milo. You made an appointment with me.' It was a statement of fact.

'Yes,' said Nesta. 'I think I'm in time.' She had found the fare, but the taximan still seemed doubtful.

Mrs de Milo made no reply, but stood staring at Nesta, as if minutely considering whether she for her part would take matters further. Mrs de Milo was an ageless woman with a white smooth face, Grecian nose, and large but well-shaped breasts. She wore an elegant white overall of medical aspect, gleaming with starch. Her black hair, very thick and glistening, was parted in the middle and drawn into a carefully composed bun.

'Come in,' said Mrs de Milo, her mind apparently made up. 'We can't talk in the street.'

The taxi began to move off.

The effect that evening on Curtis was interesting. His expression when Peggy let him into the flat and he first saw Nesta was one which Nesta found it difficult to decide about, wrought up though she was to observe him minutely. Then he spoke.

'Darling!'

She would not smile.

'Darling, I thought for one moment—'

Still she left him to define.

'All the same . . . You do *look* different?'

She perceived. Curtis's initial response had been nothing less than complete non-recognition. Although she had been standing in shadow it was startlingly more than she had reckoned upon.

She did not go to him, but rather drew back a step.

'I've altered my hairstyle.'

'I'll say you have.' He was almost peering at her. 'Why?'

'I wanted a change.'

His face lightened somewhat.

'Anything you want, darling.'

Peggy asked if she should bring in soup. It was amusing that Peggy had never seemed even to notice the innovation.

'Give me a minute of time to change,' said Curtis, as he always did. When alone with Nesta, he dined in one of his older suits.

Nesta turned and, full in the light, looked at herself yet again in the expensive but not very beautiful hanging glass which had been her father-in-law's wedding present.

*

Nine days later (Nesta had begun to keep a diary) Curtis, without explanation or precedent, suddenly, in the middle of dinner, began to make a scene.

They had been eating for some time in silence, when Curtis, his fish unfinished, crashed down his knife and fork and bawled out: 'What the hell's the matter with you, Nesta?'

One change in Nesta seemed to be that her nerves were growing stronger, so that she no longer trembled before the unexpected, as she had hitherto tended to do. Now she looked Curtis in the eyes. 'Nothing is the matter with me that I know of.' Her look changed as she added, 'I'm sorry the dinner isn't better. You know it's Peggy's night out.'

'You're a better cook than Peggy any day.' It was hard to believe, notwithstanding, that indifferently cooked fish was responsible for Curtis's remarkable wrath.

'I expect I didn't stick closely enough to the directions.'

'Why have you messed up your hands like that?'

It was, in fact, the first time she had worn brightly coloured nail varnish.

'Do you like it?' She stretched out her hands across the table. It was true that they now looked unlike the hands of a capable cook.

'It makes me sick.'

Nesta slowly withdrew her hands and placed them in her lap.

'It's hideous. Besides, it's vulgar. Never do it again.'

None the less, now that the cause of his fury was

exposed, the fury was ebbing, the more quickly for its violence.

'After all they're *my* hands.'

Curtis was stricken by her placidity.

'Don't do it again, there's a good girl.'

'I think it's nice.'

'Oh darling, it's not. It's horrible.'

Nesta remembered having read in some cynical book that although a woman's appearance is what a man most cares about, yet, too often, the more she does about it the less he cares for the result and for her.

Curtis had assumed that Nesta would discontinue the notion. When he was proved wrong, the thing became a small obsession with him. By bed and by board, Nesta's painted hands seemed to be deflecting him, warding him off. He had assuredly never realised that he cared so very much about carmine finger nails.

It was in his behaviour to Nesta, in acts of omission, that his distaste found expression; for after the first outburst, he seldom returned to the subject in words. He was ashamed and uncomprehending; and felt compelled secretly to agree with Nesta that her hands were her own. Also he felt that he lost status by his concern with something so unimportant. He apprehended hostility to Nesta creeping into and about him like a snake; and was dismayed.

For Nesta, in her insensitiveness to his needs and impulses, it seemed to him that the manicuring of her nails had become a main business of her life. Every evening she seemed to be plying a battery of small instruments infinitely sharp, and unpleasantly surgical in aspect; or, in the alternative, endlessly filing. The distinctive gritty sound of Nesta filing her nails became to his nerves in their emotional aspect what the dentist's drill was in their physical aspect. Once he found words to suggest that, instead of in the evening, she tend her nails during the day when he was out of the house; but later he divined that already she had been tending them by day also. Even apart from his antipathy to coloured nails, it was a disquieting revelation. It disgusted him in itself, as if Nesta had acquired a pathological obsession.

As sounds unheard can, it is said, be sweeter than those heard, so hostility unacknowledged can be bitterer than open warfare. To her preoccupation with her hands, Nesta shortly began to add the extravagant and wasteful buying of clothes. Previously she had seemed content with exactly the type and size of wardrobe favoured by other married women of her age and income level and district. Now she was buying recklessly; and, what Curtis found if possible, even more disturbing, was dressing more and more oddly. As far as he could see, her eccentric but costly garb lacked even the justification of being in the mode.

There was one evening when he arrived to escort her to a bridge party. The invitation was of long standing, and the date agreed for weeks.

'Darling, I'm sorry but you simply can't show yourself at the Foxtons' like that.'

'Does it become me?'

'That's not the point. You know what the Foxtons are like. The *Foxtons*,' he repeated with desperate emphasis.

'Should I surprise them?'

'Put on something else quickly, darling. We're forty minutes late already. More.'

'*You*'re late. I've been dressed for hours.' She picked up a tiny scalpel-like object, and began to bore with it at her nails. She brought to the task a curiously profound concentration, slowly moving her bare elbows as she made the minute movements. She resembled a subaqueous tree, gently rippling in the movement of the water.

'You're spending far too much on clothes anyway,' said Curtis, his nerves flaring, as always, at the sight of her occupation. 'I can't keep up with you.'

'Keep up with me?'

'Pay the bills,' Curtis said bitterly, although he was neither poor nor ungenerous.

'Have you been asked to pay any bills? Extra bills?' Not for a moment did she look up from her work.

'I almost wish you would ask me. I don't want them all to descend on me at once.'

She made no reply to that, but simply said, 'What about the Foxtons?'

'I'll ring up, while you change.'

'I'm not going to change for the Foxtons.'

He was sincerely shocked. The Foxtons were among their best friends.

'Darling, we'll have no friends left.'

*

It was hard not to think so; because even when Nesta did go out, he noticed that she seemed no longer to enjoy her former quiet popularity, and fancied that thereby he himself became suspect also for the shadowy change in her.

Although he had been married less than a year, Curtis came to dread his return home in the evening. Not only was Nesta apparently losing all taste for the small dinner parties and little gatherings with their friends which he so much enjoyed, but she seemed also to be losing her interest in him. It was not that the housekeeping appeared to be neglected: on the contrary, Curtis thought he now discerned a new and conscious punctiliousness over every detail. But the effect was of a household in the charge not, as is desirable, of benevolent and invisible fairies, but rather of recent graduates from a College of Domestic Science. Nesta seemed to manage her home more and more impersonally; and she carried this impression into every aspect of their joint life. Fundamentally Curtis had married neither for passion nor even for a well-kept home, but for sentiment: so that Nesta's changed behaviour particularly distressed him. She herself seemed neither happy nor unhappy; but to find an obscure contentment in sitting always by herself, impelling Peggy to correct every deviation from formal domestic perfection, wearing ornate clothes, and endlessly employing her elaborate manicure case and green taffeta-covered beauty box. From the latter, when open, rose a vapour of invisible but choking face-powder and a *mêlée* of headachy perfumes.

A very upsetting development was when Nesta began to wear hats with veils. It was now that Curtis seriously wondered what to do about her. He thought of mentioning the course of events to a doctor, but there was really nothing to be said which would not sound impossibly foolish. Nesta, although unsympathetic, was perfectly rational in her dealings with him, and was running the house more efficiently than ever. Her body was, of course, her own, to adorn as she wished. She acquired what appeared to be a large number of new hats, many of them evening hats, in the French manner, and an equally large number of veils, varying in colour, opacity, and pattern; and before long was never to be seen by Curtis without one. Because it was at this point that she began to keep strictly to her own room at nights. For reasons unacknowledged by either, they had occupied separate rooms from the start; but the rooms had a communicating door which until now had never once been locked. Nesta met Curtis's questions with simple statements that she wished to sleep alone 'for the present'; and when he became more pressing, with quiet defiance.

The new hats were all in what Curtis took to be more or less the fashion, although he did not move in circles where those fashions obtained in their full purity; and the veils were at all times elegantly, even coquettishly adjusted. Sometimes the mesh was large, and Curtis thought that he could see her face almost as well as if the veil were not there; but, on the whole, and as time passed, his idea of Nesta's features fell into steadily increasing indistinctness and even distortion. The only exception was her mouth, which she exposed in order to eat, dexterously twisting the veil above her upper lip. To Curtis, in his isolation from her, Nesta's mouth seemed newly and poignantly desirable. Its image lingered in his thoughts, growing more and more sensual as he brooded upon it. Before long he wanted merely to kiss her mouth more than once he had wanted entirely to possess her. But he considered that to kiss her would be undignified while she continued to use him so disparagingly. Even more, he doubted whether she would welcome his kiss. He held back from a conflict which might have to be final.

One day, between morning and evening, she seemed to have changed all the furniture in the flat, installing many new objects, moving into new positions most of the things which were there already, and undoubtedly casting a number of pieces away. Into the drawing room Nesta had brought a full-length looking-glass, tall and wide, stately and heavy, and bordered with a tumbling riot of gilt fauns and maenads. It might have come from a Venetian palazzo which had been redecorated in a late period. She had altered the lighting in the room, so that at night all of it bore upon the new looking-glass; which, indeed, was now almost the only object left in the room. The flat, however, was a large one, and Curtis through his inner storm of protest and bewilderment felt an intimation that Nesta had transformed something commonplace into something exciting and dramatic. Unfortunately Curtis had married neither for excitement nor for drama.

Now they dined by the light of candles stuck in writhing silver candelabra. One night Nesta was wearing a misty dress, entirely white but not in the least bridal; and over her head a silky white veil, against which her mouth as she ate showed red as a new wound. To Curtis, Nesta's mouth seemed miraculously to have changed its shape: it was impossible that it could ever have been so desirable. He forced himself to eat and to complain. He took up the theme which worried him almost as much as the change in Nesta herself.

'If you go on spending money like this, you'll compel me to disclaim responsibility for your debts.' Even the spoon with which he was eating his soup was new and sweetly chased.

'You have no responsibility for my debts.'

Nesta had a small income of her own, but Curtis well knew that it could come nowhere near to meeting her present almost daily orgies of expenditure. He considered that her implication to the contrary was insulting to his intelligence.

'I hope you'll explain that to the lawyers. The law says that a husband is responsible for his wife's debts,' said Curtis wearily and bitterly. He had no expectation of making any impression on her.

'You're paying for nothing more than you ever did.'

Curtis put down his beautiful alien soup spoon. He knew that many months had now passed since all this began, and indeed there had been no bills for any of it.

'Who is paying then?'

'I am paying. You are getting the benefit without pay-ing.'

'You can't be paying. You haven't got the money.' His need to cover her lovely mouth with kisses made him foolish. 'There's someone else. All this nonsense is for someone else.'

Nesta laughed.

'It's for someone else,' Curtis repeated.

'No. It's for me,' She spoke with a significance he was too irate to grasp.

'I should have stopped it once and for all long ago.'

'How?'

'Had you locked up, if necessary.' At this moment in-deed he would have done worse things than that.

'How could you stop it? You started it.'

Curtis changed colour in the candlelight. He re-membered the saying that what you fear is true.

'It wasn't even for your own sake. You were thinking entirely of me.'

'Nesta!' he cried. 'Tell me what is happening to you?'

But without replying, she produced a tiny shining implement and began to file her nails. The absorption which always accompanied this process was around her like a screen.

Feeling fear and shame and pity, he went to her. He pulled up a chair and put his arm round her shoulders.

'Nesta,' he said. 'Let's be as we used to be.'

He tried to kiss her. Before his lips touched hers, he was conscious of a sharp pain. He raised his other hand to his cheek. It was smeared with blood.

'Get back,' cried Nesta. 'Mind my dress.'

Now he was holding his handkerchief to his cheek with both hands. The blood seemed to be spurting out. Already Curtis felt that everything about him was discoloured with it.

Nesta had risen and was standing in the corner of the room gazing at him. He could see her eyes bright through the white silk veil.

Even with the pain of the injury and the discomfort of the blood, he also saw something else. He had supposed that Nesta, even though it seemed inconceivable, had struck at him with the small sharp file. But as she stood, the light fell on her hands, and he saw that every one of her painted nails had been sharpened to a deadly point.

'So that's what your manicuring amounts to.'

'It's time you noticed.' Nesta still spoke quietly. Curtis had seated himself at the far side of the table, on which he placed his elbows as he held his soaking handkerchief to his face. 'This is the way they grow. I keep trying to blunt them.'

Curtis looked at her.

'To file them down and to make them look socially acceptable. The way you want them.'

'It's the most horrible thing I ever head of.' Of course she was mad.

'It's getting more difficult all the time. The more I file them, the sharper they get. I don't know why I go on bothering!'

Curtis was trying to collect himself. 'Look, darling,'

he said to her across the table. 'Look, darling, you're ill. You're saying so yourself. If you'll give me a minute of time to clean up, I'll go and rout out Nicolson. I'm sure he'll come round.' Nicolson was their doctor.

'I'm not out of my mind, if that's what you mean.' She said it so calmly that Curtis, who had risen to his feet, stopped and sat down again. 'Out of my body perhaps. Not my mind. I don't suppose Nicolson can do more about the one thing than he can about the other.' She put her hands on the table, interlocking the fingers. 'Have you any further suggestions?'

'There must be something for us to do.' He thought wildly of psychiatric clinics, marriage guidance centres, and other such outposts in the jungle. The whole territory was one into which he had never thought he would have to enter.

'Perhaps what I need is an ugliness salon. You don't happen to know of one?'

'I've never seen you look so beautiful.' He had ceased to play his appointed part, and spoke his thought.

'But you don't want me all the same? Not now? Not really?'

'Of course I want you. You're my wife. If only things could be as they were. That's what I want.'

She picked up an exquisite decanter, one of their new acquisitions, and filled a delicate wineglass. 'You know, I had no idea,' she said, 'how deep it goes. Most people know nothing. Nothing. It goes to the very bottom of life.' She drained the glass. A drop of the red wine hung on her mouth. She licked her lip.

'What does? I don't understand you.'

Regarding her, and trying to puzzle out what he felt to be her insults, he was for a moment far from sure that really she looked any different from the way she had looked on the day he married her. As far as one could see: and behind her white veil. Apart from her hands, of course.

'As you don't understand me, you can't want me,' said Nesta.

'But I do want you,' cried Curtis. 'I tried to kiss you and you wouldn't let me.'

She was standing with the tips of her fingers resting on the white table cloth. Curtis was reminded of a clawed goddess with a beautiful immemorial face which he had once seen in company with that earlier woman in his life. Nesta's bright eyes were again fixed upon him. 'You say you want to kiss me,' she said. 'How long is it since you've even seen my face? Do you think you'd still recognise me?'

She began to unwind her veil. Then she picked up one of the heavy candlesticks and slowly moved it towards her face.

Except that she was now elaborately made up, Curtis was still unable to define the change in her.

'Well?' She was pressing for a response.

Curtis did not move, but sat, one hand still to his cheek, staring at her familiar face as Odysseus stared at Circe.

'I never gave you a likeness of me, but I had one taken all the same.' Putting down the candles, she opened her bag and passed a half-plate photograph across the table.

Curtis did not look at it.

'It's wonderful what make-up will do when you have a good photograph to copy,' said Nesta. 'Do you think it's like me?'

Curtis snatched at the photograph and without glancing at it, tore it into confetti.

'It doesn't matter now,' said Nesta, 'although it seems to be the only print left. It's become so difficult to make myself like it that I should have to stop trying anyway. There are limits even to make-up, you know. Besides, why should I? So look your last. There'll be only your memory left.'

She was blowing out the candles one by one. Curtis had sunk his torn face in his hands.

When the last candle was out, she spoke again.

'Kiss me goodbye.'

Curtis could hear her moving towards him through the blackness, thick with the smell of wax. He crouched into himself, but now she was beside him. Her warm lips softly and gently touched the invisible back of his neck. Her hair was newly and wonderfully fragrant.

He heard her pass onwards to the door. In the next room, the drawing room, her steps paused for many seconds, and he realised that she was looking at herself in the tall and stately glass which seemed to have come from some Italian palace. Then the steps resumed, more slowly he thought, as doubtless she drew on her furs; and soon he knew that he would never see or hear her again.

The Cicerones

John Trant entered the Cathedral of St Bavon at almost
exactly eleven-thirty.

An unexpected week's holiday having come his way,
he was spending it in Belgium, because Belgium was
near and it was late in the season, and because he had
never been there. Trant, who was unmarried (though
one day he intended to marry), was travelling alone, but
he seldom felt lonely at such times because he believed
that his solitude was optional and regarded it rather as
freedom. He was thirty-two and saw himself as quite
ordinary, except perhaps in this very matter of travel,
which he thought he took more seriously and systematically than most. The hour at which he entered the
cathedral was important, because he had been incon-
venienced in other towns by the irritating continental
habit of shutting tourist buildings between twelve and
two, even big churches. In fact, he had been in two
minds as to whether to visit the cathedral at all with so
little time in hand. One could not even count upon the
full half-hour, because the driving out of visitors usually
began well before the moment of actual closure. It was
a still morning, very still, but overcast. Men were beginning to wait, one might say, for the year finally to die.

The thing that struck Trant most as he entered the

vast building was how silent it seemed to be within; how empty. Other Belgian cathedrals had contained twenty or thirty scattered people praying, or anyway kneeling; priests importantly on the move, followed by acolytes; and, of course, Americans. There had always been dingy bustle, ritual action, and neck-craning. Here there seemed to be no one other, doubtless, than the people in the tombs. Trant again wondered whether the informed did not know that it was already too late to go in.

He leant against a column at the west end of the nave as he always did, and read the history of the cathedral in his Blue Guide. He chose this position in order that when he came to the next section to be perused, the architectural summary, he could look about him to the best advantage. He usually found, none the less, that he soon had to move if he were to follow what the guidebook had to say, as the architecture of few cathedrals can be apprehended, even in outline, by a newcomer from a single point. So it was now: Trant found that he was losing the thread, and decided he would have to take up the guidebook's trail. Before doing so, he looked around him for a moment. The cathedral seemed still to be quite empty. It was odd, but a very pleasant change. Trant set out along the south aisle of the nave, holding the guidebook like a breviary. 'Carved oak pulpit,' said the guidebook, 'with marble figures, all by Laurent Delvaux.' Trant had observed it vaguely from afar, but as, looking up from the book, he began consciously to think about it, he saw something extraordinary. Surely there was a figure in the pulpit, not standing erect, but slumped forward over the preacher's cushion? Trant could see the top of a small, bald head with a deep fringe, almost a halo, of white hair; and, on each side, widespread arms, with floppy hands. Not that it appeared to be a priest: the figure was wearing neither white nor black, but on the contrary, bright colours, several of them. Though considerably unnerved, Trant went forward, passed the next column in the arcade between the nave and the aisle, and looked again, through the next bay. He saw at once that there was nothing: at least there was only a litter of minor vestments and scripts in coloured bindings.

Trant heard a laugh. He turned. Behind him stood a slender, brown-haired young man in a grey suit.

'Excuse me,' said the young man. 'I saw it myself so don't be frightened.' He spoke quite clearly, but had a vague foreign accent.

'It was terrifying,' said Trant. 'Out of this world.'

'Yes. Out of this world, as you say. Did you notice the hair?'

'I did indeed.' The young man had picked on the very detail which had perturbed Trant the most. 'What did you make of it?'

'Holy, holy, holy,' said the young man in his foreign accent; then smiled and sauntered off westwards. Trant was *almost* sure that this was what he had said. The hair of the illusory figure in the pulpit had, at the time, reminded Trant of the way in which nimbuses are shown in certain old paintings; with wide bars or strips of light linking an outer misty ring with the sacred head. The figure's white hair had seemed to project in just such spikes.

Trant pulled himself together and reached the south transept, hung high with hatchments. He sought out *Christ among the Doctors*. 'The masterpiece of Frans Pourbus the Elder,' as the guidebook remarked, and set himself to identifying the famous people said to be depicted in it, including the Duke of Alva, Vigilius ab Ayatta, and even the Emperor Charles V himself.

In the adjoining chapel, *The Martyrdom of St Barbara* by De Crayer proved to be covered with a cloth, another irritating continental habit, as Trant had previously discovered. As there seemed to be no one about, Trant lifted a corner of the cloth, which was brown and dusty, like so many things in Belgian cathedrals, and peered beneath. It was difficult to make out very much, especially as the light was so poor.

'Let me help,' said a transatlantic voice at Trant's back. 'Let me take it right off, and then you'll see something, believe me.'

Again it was a young man, but this time a red-haired cheerful looking youth in a green windcheater.

The youth not only removed the cloth, but turned on an electric light.

'Thank you,' said Trant.

'Now have a good look.'

Trant looked. It was an extremely horrible scene. 'Oh boy.'

Trant had no desire to look any longer. 'Thank you all the same,' he said, apologising for his repulsion.

'What a circus those old saints were,' commented the transatlantic youth, as he replaced the worn cloth.

'I suppose they received their reward in heaven,' suggested Trant.

'You bet they did,' said the youth, with a fervour that Trant couldn't quite fathom. He turned off the light. 'Be seeing you.'

'I expect so,' said Trant smiling.

The youth said no more, but put his hands in his pockets, and departed whistling towards the south door. Trant himself would not have cared to whistle so loudly in a foreign church.

As all the world knows, the most important work of art in the Cathedral of St Bavon is the *Adoration* by the mysterious van Eyck or van Eycks, singular or plural. Nowadays the picture is hung in a small, curtained-off chapel leading from the south choir ambulatory; and most strangers must pay to see it. When Trant reached the chapel, he saw the notice at the door, but, hearing nothing, as elsewhere, supposed the place to be empty. Resenting wildly the demand for a fee, as Protestants do, he took the initiative and gently lifted the dark red curtain.

The chapel, though still silent, was not empty at all. On the contrary, it was so full that Trant could have gone no further inside, even had he dared.

There were two kinds of people in the chapel. In front were several rows of men in black. They knelt shoulder to shoulder, heads dropped, hip-bone against hip-bone, in what Trant took to be silent worship. Behind them, packed in even more tightly, was a group, even a small crowd, of funny old Belgian women, fat, ugly, sexless, and bossy, such as Trant had often seen in other places both devotional and secular. The old women were not kneeling, but sitting. All the same, they seemed eerily rapt. Strangest of all was their motionless silence. Trant had seen such groups everywhere in Belgium, but never, never silent, very far from it. Not a single one of this present group seemed even to be aware that he was there: something equally unusual with a people so given to curiosity.

And in this odd setting not the least strange thing was the famous picture itself, with its enigmatic monsters, sibyls, and walking allegories, and its curiously bright, other-world colours: a totality doubtless interpretable in terms of Freud, but, all the same, as dense as an oriental carpet, and older than Adam and Eve, who stand beside. Trant found the picture all too cognate to the disconcerting devotees.

He let fall the curtain and went on his way, distinctly upset.

Two chapels further round, he came upon the *Virgin Glorified* by Liemakere. Here a choir-boy in a red cassock was polishing the crucifix on the altar. Already, he had thin black hair and a grey, watchful face.

'Onze lieve Vrouw,' said the choir-boy, explaining the picture to Trant.

'Yes,' said Trant. 'Thank you.'

It occurred to him that polishing was odd work for a choir-boy. Perhaps this was not a choir-boy at all, but some other kind of young servitor. The idea of being shortly ejected from the building returned to Trant's mind. He looked at his watch. It had stopped. It still showed 11.28

Trant shook the watch against his ear, but there were no recovering ticks. He saw that the polishing boy (he was at work on the pierced feet) wore a watch also, on a narrow black strap. Trant gesticulated again. The boy only shook his head more violently. Trant could not decide whether the boy's own watch was broken, or whether, conceivably, he thought that Trant was trying to take it from him. Then, all in seconds, it struck Trant that, whatever else there was about the boy, he certainly did not appear alarmed. Far from it. He seemed as aloof as if he were already a priest, and to be refusing to tell Trant the time on principle; almost implying, as priests presume to do, that he was refusing for the other's good. Trant departed from the chapel containing Liemakere's masterpiece rather quickly.

How much time had he left?

In the next chapel was Rubens's vast altar piece of St Bavon distributing all his goods among the poor.

In the next was the terrifying *Martyrdom of St Livinus* by Seghers.

After one more chapel, Trant had reached the junction of the north transept and the choir. The choir was surrounded by a heavy and impenetrable screen of black marble, like a cage for the imperial lions. The guidebook recommended the four tombs of past bishops which were said to be inside; but Trant, peering through the stone bars, could hardly see even outlines. He shifted from end to end of the choir steps seeking a viewpoint where the light might be better. It was useless. In the end, he tried the handle of the choir gate. The gate had given every appearance of being locked, but in fact it opened at once when Trant made the attempt. He tiptoed into the dark enclosure and thought he had better shut the gate behind him. He was not sure that he was going to see very much of the four tombs, even now; but there they were, huge boxes flanking the high altar, like dens for the lions.

He stood at the steps of the altar itself leaning across the marble rails, the final barricade, trying to read one of the Latin inscriptions. In such an exercise Trant made it a matter of principle not lightly to admit defeat. He craned his neck and screwed up his eyes until he was half-dazed; capturing the antique words one at a time, and trying to construe them. The matter of the cathedral shutting withdrew temporarily to the back of his mind. Then something horrible seemed to happen; or rather two things, one after the other. Trant thought first that the stone panel he was staring at so hard seemed somehow to move; and then that a hand had appeared round one upper corner of it. It seemed to Trant a curiously small hand.

Trant decided, almost calmly, to see it out. There must obviously be an explanation, and anything like flight would make him look ridiculous, as well as leaving the mystery unsolved. An explanation there was; the stone opened further, and from within emerged a small, fair-haired child.

'Hullo,' said the child, looking at Trant across the black marble barrier and smiling.

'Hullo,' said Trant. 'You speak very good English.'

'I *am* English,' said the child. It was wearing a dark brown garment open at the neck, and dark brown trousers, but Trant could not quite decide whether it was a boy or a girl. From the escapade a boy seemed likelier, but there was something about the child which was more like a girl, Trant thought.

'Should you have been in there?'

'I always go in.'

'Aren't you afraid?'

'No one could be afraid of Bishop Triest. He gave us those candlesticks.' The child pointed to four tall copper objects; which seemed to Trant to offer no particular confirmation of the child's logic.

'Would *you* like to go in?' enquired the child politely.

'No, thank you,' said Trant.

'Then I'll just shut up.' The child heaved the big stone slab into place. It was a feat of strength all the more remarkable in that Trant noticed that the child seemed to limp.

'Do you live here?' asked Trant.

'Yes,' said the child, and, child-like, said no more.

It limped forward, climbed the altar rail, and stood beside Trant, looking up at him. Trant found it difficult to assess how old it was.

'Would you like to see one of the other bishops?'

'No thank you,' said Trant.

134

'I think you ought to see a bishop,' said the child quite gravely.

'I'd rather not,' said Trant smiling.

'There may not be another chance.'

'I expect not,' said Trant, still smiling. He felt it was best to converse with the child at its own level, and make no attempt at adult standards of flat questioning and conventionalised reference.

'Then I'll take you to the crypt,' said the child.

The crypt was the concluding item in the guidebook. Entered from just by the north-western corner of the choir, it was, like the *Adoration*, a speciality, involving payment. Trant had rather assumed that he would not get round to it.

'Shall I have time?' he asked, looking instinctively at his stopped watch, still showing 11.28.

'Yes,' said the child, as before.

The child limped ahead, opened the choir-gate and held it for Trant, his inscriptions unread, to pass through. The child closed the gate, and led the way to the crypt entry, looking over its shoulder to see that Trant was following. In the rather better light outside the choir, Trant saw that its hair was a wonderful mass of silky gold; its face almost white, with the promise of fine bones; its lips unusually red.

'This is called the crossing,' said the child informatively. Trant knew that the term was sometimes applied to the intersection of nave and transepts.

'Or the narthex, I believe,' he said, plunging in in order to show who was the grown-up.

The child, not unnaturally, looked merely puzzled.

There was still no one else visible in the cathedral.

They began to descend the crypt stairs, the child holding on to the iron handrail because of its infirmity. There was a table at the top, obviously for the collection of the fee, but deserted. Trant did not feel called upon to comment.

In the crypt, slightly to his surprise, many of the lights were on. Probably the custodian had forgotten to turn them off when he or she had hurried forth to eat.

The guidebook described the crypt as 'large', but it was much larger than Trant had expected. The stairs entered at one corner, and columns seemed to stretch away like trees into the distance. They were built in stones of different colours, maroon, purple, green, grey, gold; and they often bore remains of painting as well, which also spread over areas of the vaulted stone roof and weighty walls. In the soft patchy light, the place was mysterious and beautiful; and all the more so because the whole area could not be seen simultaneously. With the tide of centuries the stone-paved floor had become rolling and uneven, but agreeably so. There were occasional showcases and objects on pedestals, and there was a gentle perfume of incense. As Trant entered, all was silence. He even felt for a moment that there was something queer about the silence; that only sounds of another realm moved in it, and that the noises of this world, of his own arrival for example, were in a different dimension and irrelevant. He stood, a little awed, and listened for a moment to the nothingness.

The child stood too, or rather rested against a pillar. It was smiling again, though very slightly. Perhaps it smiled like this all the time, as if always happy.

Trant thought more than ever that it might be a girl. By this time it was rather absurd not to be sure, but by this time it was more than before difficult to ask.

'Bishop Triest's clothes,' said the child, pointing. They were heavy vestments, hanging, enormously embroidered, in a glass cabinet.

'St Livinus's ornament,' said the child, and crossed itself. Trant did not know quite what to make of the ornament.

'Animals,' said the child. It was an early book of natural history written by a monk, and even the opened page showed some very strange ones.

The child was now beginning positively to dart about in its eagerness, pointing out item after item.

'Shrine of St Macarius,' said the child, not crossing itself, presumably because the relic was absent.

'Abbot Hughenois's clothes.' They were vestments again, and very like Triest's vestments, Trant thought.

'What's that?' asked Trant, taking the initiative and pointing. Right on the other side of the crypt, as it seemed, and now visible to Trant for the first time through the forest of coloured columns, was something which appeared to be winking and gleaming with light.

'That's at the end,' replied the child. 'You'll be there soon.'

Soon indeed, at this hour, thought Trant: if in fact we're not thrown out first.

'Via Dolorosa,' said the child, pointing to a picture. It was a gruesome scene, painted very realistically, as if the artist had been a bystander at the time; and it was followed by another which was even more gruesome and at least equally realistic.

'Calvary,' explained the child.

They rounded a corner with the stone wall on the left, the forest of columns on the right. The two parts of a diptych came into view, of which Trant had before seen only the discoloured reverse.

'The blessed and the lost,' said the child, indicating, superfluously, which was which.

Trant thought that the pictures and frescoes were becoming more and more morbid, but supposed that this feeling was probably the result of their cumulative impact. In any case, there could not be much more.

But there were still many things to be seen. In due course they came to a group of pictures hanging together.

'The sacrifice of three blessed martyrs,' said the child. Each of the martyrs had died in a different way: by roasting on a very elaborate gridiron; by disembowelling; and by some process involving a huge wheel. The painting, unlike some of the others, was extraordinarily well preserved. The third of the martyrs was a young woman. She had been martyred naked and was of great and still living beauty. Next to her hung a further small picture, showing a saint carrying his own skin. Among the columns to the right was an enormous black cross. At a little distance, the impaled figure looked lifelike in the extreme.

The child was still skipping in front, making so light of its disability that Trant could not but be touched. They turned another corner. At the end of the ambulatory ahead was the gleaming, flashing object that Trant had noticed from the other side of the crypt. The child almost ran on, ignoring the intervening sights, and stood by the object, waiting for Trant to catch up. The child's head was sunk, but Trant could see that it was looking at him from under its fair, silky eyelashes.

This time the child said nothing, and Trant could only stare.

The object was a very elaborate, jewelled reliquary of the Renaissance. It was presumably the jewels which had seemed to give off the flashing lights, because Trant could see no lights now. At the centre of the reliquary was a transparent vertical tube or cylinder. It was only about an inch high, and probably made of crystal. Just visible inside it was a black thread, almost like the mercury in a minute thermometer; and at the bottom of the tube was, Trant noticed, a marked discoloration.

The child was still standing in the same odd position; now glancing sideways at Trant, now glancing away. It was perhaps smiling a little more broadly, but its head was sunk so low that Trant could not really see. Its whole posture and behaviour suggested that there was something about the reliquary which Trant should be able to see for himself. It was almost as if the child were timing him, to see how long he took.

Time, thought Trant, yet again; and now with a start.

The reliquary was so fascinating that he had managed somehow almost to forget about time. He looked away and along the final ambulatory, which ran to the foot of the staircase by which he had come down. While he had been examining the reliquary, someone else had appeared in the crypt. A man stood in the centre of the passage, a short distance away from Trant. Or not exactly a man: it was, Trant realised, the acolyte in the red cassock, the boy who had been polishing the brass feet. Trant had no doubt that he had come to hurry him out.

Trant bustled off, full of unreasonable guilt, without even properly thanking his child guide. But when he reached the boy in the cassock, the boy stretched out his arms to their full length and seemed, on the contrary, to bar his passage.

It was rather absurd; and especially as one could so readily turn right and weave a way out through the Gothic columns.

Trant, in fact, turned his head in that direction, simply upon instinct. But in the bay to his right, stood the youth from across the Atlantic in the green windcheater. He had the strangest of expressions (unlike the boy in the cassock, who seemed the same dull peasant as before); and as Trant caught his eye, he too raised his arms to their full extent, as the boy had done.

There was still one more free bay. Trant retreated a step or two, but then saw among the shadows within (which seemed to be deepening) the man in the grey suit with the vague foreign accent. His arms were going up even as Trant sighted him, but when their eyes met (though Trant could not see his face, very well) he did something the others had not done. He laughed.

And in the entrance to the other ambulatory, through which Trant had just come and down which the child had almost run bravely casting aside its affliction, stood that same child, now gazing upwards again and indeed looking quite radiant, as it spread its arms almost as a bird taking flight.

Trant heard the great clock of the cathedral strike twelve. In the crypt, the tone of the bell was lost: there was little more to be distinguished than twelve great thuds, almost as if cannon were being discharged. The twelve strokes of the hour took a surprisingly long time to complete.

In the meantime, and just beside the reliquary, a small door had opened, in the very angle of the crypt. Above it was a small but exquisite and well preserved alabaster keystone showing a soul being dragged away on a hook by a demon. Trant had hardly noticed the door before, as people commonly overlook the working details of a place which is on show, the same details that those who work the place look to first.

In the door, quite filling it, was the man Trant had believed himself to have seen in the pulpit soon after he had first entered the great building. The man looked much bigger now, but there was the same bald head, the same resigned hands, the same multicoloured garments. It was undoubtedly the very person, but in some way enlarged or magnified; and the curious fringe of hair seemed more luminous than ever.

'The cathedral closes now,' said the man. 'Follow me.'

The fair figures encircling Trant began to shut in on him until their extended finger-tips were almost touching.

His questions went quite unanswered, his protests quite unheard; especially after everyone started singing.

The Next Glade

'I am coming to see you,' said the man. 'Tomorrow. To-morrow afternoon.'

He looked into her eyes quite steadily, but he certainly didn't smile.

Noelle did smile. 'You don't know where I live,' she said.

'I know very well,' said the man.

Obviously, it would have been easy enough for him to have found out from Simon and Mut, whose party it was, but it seemed strange that he should have done so before even meeting Noelle, before setting eyes on her, almost certainly before being told about her. Not until that moment had he implied that he already knew anything at all about her. It would have been absurd for Noelle to ask him how he knew.

'We can't just leave it at this,' said the man, with some urgency. 'We can't.'

'Perhaps we can,' said Noelle.

'I know the district round Woking pretty well,' said the man. 'I'll call for you about three tomorrow and we'll go for a walk in the woods.'

True enough, where Noelle lived there were woods of a kind in almost every direction; but that applied to so much of residential Surrey. Specifically, there was a wood on the other side of the road, opposite her gate.

'I don't promise to be there,' said Noelle. 'I can't.'

'Then I shall have to take a chance,' said the man. 'We mustn't just leave it, and we'll get no further here.'

'What's your name anyway?' asked Noelle.

That tone was advancing upon her with the passing years. She deplored it, but one cannot expect to find people *en masse* who speak one's private language. It is bound to suffer erosion by the *lingua franca*.

But, as if to confirm the man's point that further communication was impossible, Mut at that instant turned up the record-player and Simon turned on the new strip lighting. Simon and Mut went through a party as if it were a dress rehearsal. As little as possible was left to chance. Noelle always wondered what would happen if there were ever to be an actual performance.

Still without a smile, the man had dissolved into the glare and the din. Noelle wondered if he were making an assignation with someone else; perhaps proposing the North Downs as background. Alternatively, he might well be going home. For him, the party might have fulfilled its purpose.

Only when Melvin, her husband, was on his travels, did Noelle herself go to these parties where almost everyone was younger than she. But that was quite frequently, so she realised how lucky she was that people like Simon and Mut could still be bothered with her. Not that Mut in particular was so enormously much younger. Noelle and Mut had aforetime shared an apartment. The then infant Simon had already been

Mut's lover, been it for years, but Noelle had not yet met Melvin. Indeed, when Mut had been out of the room, Simon could be depended upon for a small-scale agitation, or quick pass. It was a tradition that still lingered.

As it happened, a surprising number of men seemed still to fall fractionally in love with Noelle, and to prefer dulcet and tender talk with her to such other things as might be on offer elsewhere. Noelle could never decide whether it was merely her appearance or something less primary that drew them. She often reflected upon how little she had to complain of.

Noelle had been perfectly truthful in saying that she couldn't, as well as wouldn't, make a promise. Melvin did sometimes return before his time. As far as she could tell, there was nothing unpleasant or ulterior about this. It seemed natural that Melvin should be blown hither and thither by the trade winds, because everyone else was. Gone are the days of predictable grind in the high-stooled counting house; settled for a lifetime. Business has changed completely, as businessmen always point out.

Besides, Judith or Agnew might be sent home from school early. That often occurred. And if she was in the house when one or the other of them arrived, she had to give much time either to listening to a tale of grievance and storm, or to anxious effort in trying to discover what this time could ever have happened.

But, when the moment came, the clock she had

inherited from her father (he had been given it by his firm less than a year before his death) struck three, and the doorbell was shimmering before the last dull echo had faded.

The man was politely extending his hand. 'My name is John Morley-Wingfield. With a hyphen, I fear I must admit. Let's get that over to start with.'

His expression was serious, but not sad. His brown hair curled pleasantly, but not unduly, and was at perhaps its most impressive moment, fading in places, but not yet too seriously grey. His brown eyes were sympathetic without being sentimental. His garb was relaxed without being perfunctory.

For Noelle, hesitation would have served no purpose.

'Do come in for a little,' she said. 'My children return from school in an hour.'

'Are they doing well?'

'Not very.'

She led him into the room which Melvin called the lounge and she called nothing in particular.

'If you'll sit down, I'll bring us a cup of tea.'

'We must keep enough time for our walk.'

She looked at him. 'The wood's not all that big. None of them are round here.'

He sat on the leathery, cushiony settee, and gazed at his brightly polished brown shoes. 'I always think a wood is much the same, however big or small it is. Within reason, of course. The impact is the same. At least upon me.'

'You don't actually get lost in these particular

woods,' said Noelle. 'You can't.'

He glanced up at her. It was plain that he took all this for delay, wanted them to make a start.

'I'll hurry with the tea,' said Noelle. 'Will you be all right? Perhaps you'd care to look at this?'

She gave him the latest *Statist*. She did not remark that it was her husband who subscribed to it. The man, who had known her address, probably knew about her husband also.

'Or this might be more cheerful.'

She held out a back number of the *National Geographic* magazine. It was Melvin too who subscribed to that, though he complained that he never had time to read it, so that the numbers always lay about unsorted until Noelle gave the children an armful for use as reinforcement in and around the sandpit.

Noelle went to the kitchen.

When she came back with the tray, the man was on his feet again, and looking restlessly at the books. They were, yet again, Melvin's books. Noelle's were upstairs, not all of them even unpacked, owing to shelf shortage.

'Milk and sugar?'

'A very little milk, please. No sugar.'

'I know we *shouldn't*,' said Noelle.

He stooped over her so that she could hand him his cup. He had a faint but striking aroma, the smell of a pretty good club.

'Careful,' said Noelle.

He drifted, sipping, round the room, as if it had been full of people, or perhaps trees, and every settling place occupied, or, alternatively, gnarled and jagged.

He spoke. 'You have the most wonderful hair.' He was on the far side of the big television.

Noelle sat up a little, but said nothing.

'And eyes.'

Noelle could not prevent herself dimpling almost perceptibly.

'And figure. It would not be possible to imagine a shape more beautiful.'

One trouble was that Noelle simply did not know how true or untrue any of these statements were. She had always found it impossible to make up her mind. More precisely, she sometimes felt one thing, and sometimes almost the complete opposite. One had, if one could, to strike an average among the views expressed or implied by others; and others seemed to spend so much of their time dissimulating.

'Have a chocolate finger?' she said, extending the plate towards him at the full length of her arm. She was wearing a dress with delicate short sleeves. After all, it was August. Melvin particularly hated August in Pittsburgh, where now he was supposed to be.

'Nothing to eat, thank you.'

The man was ranging between the Astronaut's Globe and the pile of skiing journals.

'I like your dress.'

'It's very simple.'

'You have wonderful taste.'

'Stop being so civil, please.'

'You seem to me quite perfect.'

'Well, I'm not.' But she made no further reference to any specific defect.

'Have some more tea? Bring me your cup.'

He traversed the Eskimo-style carpet with measured, springy tread.

'Then we must go,' he said. 'We really must. I want to see you in your proper element.'

She handed up the refilled cup without looking at him. 'You're right about one thing,' she said. 'I do love our woods. I only wish they were larger.'

'You love all music too,' said the man, standing over her.

'Yes.'

'And the last moments before sunset in the countryside?'

'Yes.'

'And being alone in a quiet spot at noon?'

'I usually have the children's meal to prepare.'

'And wearing real silk next to your skin?'

'I am not sure that I ever have.'

He dashed the cup back on the tray quite sharply. Noelle could see that it was far from empty.

'Let's go. Let's go now.'

She walked out with him just as she was. He followed her down the crazy concrete path, mildly multicoloured. The reason why the gate groaned was that the children liked the noise. They swung backwards and forwards on it for hours, and threw fits at the idea of the hinges being oiled.

She crossed the road with the man, surprised that

there was no whizzing traffic. All life had eased off for a moment. They ascended the worn, earth slope into the wood.

'You be guide,' said the man.

'I keep telling you, it's not the New Forest.'

'It's far more attractive.'

As it happened, Noelle almost agreed with that; or at least knew what the man might have meant. Melvin and she took the children to the New Forest each year, camping at one of the official sites; and each year she found the New Forest a disappointment.

'You fill the wood with wonder,' said the man.

'We just go straight ahead, you know,' said Noelle. 'Really there's not much else. All the other paths come to nothing. They're simply beaten down by the kids.'

'And by the wild things,' said the man.

'I don't think so.'

They were walking side by side now, among the silver birches, and it was true that the voice of the world was becoming much drowsier, the voice of nature more express. It was, of course, a Tuesday: probably the best day for such an enterprise.

'Will you permit me to put my arm round your waist?' asked the man.

'I suppose so,' said Noelle.

He did it perfectly; neither limply, nor with adolescent tenacity. Noelle began to fall into sympathetic dissolution. She had a clear thirty-five minutes before her.

'The beeches begin here,' she said. 'Some of them are

supposed to be very old. Nothing will grow around their roots.'

'That clears the way for us,' said the man.

Hitherto, the path had gone gently upwards, but now it had reached the small ridge and begun to descend. Noelle knew that here the wood widened out. None the less, the broad and beaten track led nowhere, because at the far end of the wood lay private property, heavily farmed, and with the right of way long closed and lost, doubtless through insufficient public resistance at the time. Noelle, if asked, would have been very unsure who owned the wood. It seemed to exist in its own right.

'Glorious trees,' said the man. 'And you are the spirit of them.' He was looking up into the high and heavy branches. His grasp of Noelle was growing neither tighter nor looser: admirable. They walked slowly on.

'That's the end,' said Noelle, pointing ahead with her free arm.

Two or three hundred yards before them, the wood ended in a moderate-sized dell or clearing; probably no more than the work of all the people who at this point had rotated and gone back on their tracks, returned up the slope.

'I keep telling you how small the wood is,' said Noelle. 'Not much bigger than a tent.'

'Never mind,' said the man, gently. 'It doesn't matter. Nothing like that matters.'

All the way there had, of course, been strewn rubbish, but at the terminal clearing there was considerably more of it.

'How disgusting!' said Noelle. 'What a degradation!'

'Don't look at it,' said the man, as before. 'Look upwards. Look at the trees. Let's sit down for a moment.'

It could not be said that the sections of beech trunk lying about had been hollowed out by the authorities into picnic couches, but the said sections had undoubtedly been sliced and trimmed for public use, and arranged like scatter cushions in a television room. It must have taken weeks to do it, but Noelle was of course accustomed to the scene, and had long ago resolved not to let it upset her. She realised that the vast population of the world had everywhere to be accommodated. It was as if there were a war on always.

Seated, the man began to cuddle her, and she to sink into it for the time available to her. They were sitting with their backs to the wood end and the farmland beyond. But, after a few moments – precious moments, perhaps – he unexpectedly took away his arm and rose to his feet.

'Forgive me.' he said. 'I should like to explore for a little. You wait here. I'll soon be back.'

'How far are you going?'

'Just into the next glade.'

Naturally, she knew that it would be perfectly silly and embarrassing for her to say any more. Melvin often wandered off in that way for a few minutes, and had done it even when they were merely engaged. All men did it. Still, there was one thing she simply could not help pointing out.

'I must go back in six minutes at the very most now.'

The constant care of children makes for exactitude in situations of that kind.

He had taken several steps away before she had finished speaking. Now he stopped and half turned back towards her. He gazed at her for a perceptible period of time; then turned again, and resumed his course without speaking. Noelle had later to admit to herself that she had been aware at once of some difference between the man's deportment and the deportment of men in general. It was almost as if the man slid or glided, so tutored was his gait.

The man strode elegantly and effectively off into the woodland to her right. Here there was fairly dense brush and scrub, so that the man disappeared quite rapidly. Noelle could hear his brown shoes crushing the twigs and mast, no doubt scuffing the high polish. Presumably he was shoving through brushwood, but he seemed to advance very steadily, and soon there was no further sound from him.

Noelle gave him four uneasy minutes, then rose in her turn. She called out, 'I shall have to be going. I must go.'

There was no response. There was no sign or sound of him.

'Where are you?'

Not even a woodpecker signalled.

Noelle called out much more loudly. 'John! John, I have to go.'

That was the limit of possible action. She could not be expected to shout for the rest of the afternoon, to mount a one-woman search party. There could be no possible question of the man being lost, as she herself had already remarked.

So there was only one thing for her to do. She walked quickly home, much confused in mind and feeling.

When she had arrived, only a single aspiration was definable: that the man, having emerged from the wood in one way or another, would not reappear at her home when the children were having their tea.

He did not reappear. But Noelle remained in a state of jitters until she retired to her single bed.

The next morning she telephoned Mut. She had not cared to do so while the children were in the house.

'That man at your party. John Morley-Wingfield. Tell me about him.'

'John Morley was a nineteenth-century politico, darling. He wrote the life of Gladstone. It's a good book in its own way.'

'I'm sure it is. But it's a different man.'

'It always is a different man, darling.'

'I'm speaking of John Morley-Wingfield who was at your party.'

'Never heard of him, darling. I don't know half the people by name. Do you want me to ask Simon when he gets back?'

'I think I do. Something rather funny has happened. I'll tell you when I see you.'

'What's he look like?'

'Suave and competent. Like a diplomat.'

'At *our* party?'

'I got on rather well with him.'

'The trouble with you is you don't know your own strength. Never mind. I've written down the name. I'll ask Simon. But don't expect much joy. Any news of Melvin?'

In the event, there was no joy at all, because for some time nothing more was heard from Mut on the subject, and Noelle swiftly passed beyond the stage of wanting to know. She realised that one is often half picked up by men who soon think better of the idea, and for one or more of many different reasons, not all of them necessarily detrimental to oneself. Nothing in the least unusual had happened.

Indeed, the only discernible upshot was that Noelle ceased to walk in the woods: not only in the particular wood opposite her front gate, but all the other woods in the district. Some of them in any case were mere struggling strips of scrubland and thorn bush: hardly worth visiting unless one was utterly desperate.

But one Sunday, four or five months later, Melvin suggested that they go for a stroll with the children. It was because one car had been lent to a business friend, whose own had apparently been stolen; and Noelle had forgotten to licence the other. Melvin had been very forgiving, as he always was, always.

'Just give me a minute or two to get kitted out,' said Melvin.

Noelle knew what that meant, and herself changed into tan trousers and a lumber jacket. The least she could do was co-operate in those supposedly secondary matters that so often proved to be primary. The children were dressed as pioneers already.

Melvin, when he reappeared, eclipsed them all, as was natural. A casual looker-on could hardly have distinguished him from Wild Bill Hickock, especially as Melvin purchased most of his fun gear in the States or in Toronto.

There could be no question of going anywhere but into the wood, because for anything else a motor would have been needed. The children were permitted to walk to and from school, because Noelle had put her foot down and refused to tie herself to driving them so short a distance four times a day, whatever the other mothers might do and say. Melvin in turn put his foot down when the possibility arose of the mites straggling along the highway at any other time.

'Don't forget it may rain,' now said Melvin.

Of course, Noelle had felt certain qualms from the outset, and as soon as they were among the silver birches, she rejoiced that at least she was so differently arrayed, all but in disguise. Moreover, the woods always felt quite different when one entered them with one's entire family. The things that happened when one was with one's family were amazingly unlike the things that happened when one was not. It was this fact that made the transition between the one state and the other always so upsetting.

'Just wait till we meet a buffalo,' said Melvin to the children.

Agnew screamed with delight, but Judith hitched at her belt and looked cynical.

'Got your lasso ready, son?' asked Melvin.

Agnew twirled it round his head and started leaping about among the tangled tree roots. Judith also began to run about, holding her arms in front of her above her head, and bringing them together at short intervals, as if she were catching butterflies, which she was not. There were no butterflies. There never were many.

'I am dead to the world,' said Melvin softly to Noelle, when the two children were at what could be regarded as a safe distance, short though that distance really was. 'I'm fagged out.' In the home circle, Melvin expressed himself conservatively, domestically. He never used the words he used at work.

'You look a bit pale,' said Noelle, without turning to him. She had noticed it ever since his return from Johannesburg the day before yesterday. Pallor of any kind would be quite incompatible with his ranchhand rig.

'I don't know what I'm going to do, Noelle,' he went on. She had always disallowed any contraction or distortion of her Christian name, or any nickname. 'My head feels as if it will burst. I've felt sicker and sicker ever since that February bust-up in Edmonton.'

To Noelle it seemed that Melvin went to Edmonton more often than to anywhere else, and that always it led to trouble, though that last time had doubtless been the worst of all, because Melvin had spoken of it ever since, shaking with rage and bafflement. Edmonton in Alberta, of course; not John Gilpin's homely Edmonton.

'You'd better lay up,' said Noelle. 'I expect we can afford it.'

'No such thing,' said Melvin, with what Noelle deemed an unreasonable darkness in his tone. He had never permitted Noelle to look for even a part-time job. It was one of those various things about which she was never sure whether she was glad or sorry. She knew that she somewhat lacked any very specific qualifications.

'I can't let up for a single day,' said Melvin. I'd be shot out if I did. Make no mistake about that.'

She supposed that there he must probably be right. Many of her local acquaintances already had husbands who had been declared redundant, as the usage now was.

The matter was settled for the moment by Agnew falling over, his feet and legs entangled in his lariat, as if he'd been a steer.

Noelle hoicked him up. She had the readiness of experience, as with an acrobat or exhibition wrestler.

'No bones broken', she said, stroking Agnew's stylishly unbarbered locks. 'No blood spilt. No nasty bruise.' One could not really know about the last, but it was the thing one said, and very possibly the utterance terminated the danger.

Judith was still running about catching phantom moths. She was a lissom, leggy little girl, but already deep, much as Noelle herself was deep.

'You was riding the range,' said Melvin, stabbing Agnew between the shoulders with mock manliness. 'You've had a spill, but you're up again, and riding high.'

'It was the silly rope,' said Agnew.

'Ride on, cowboy,' directed Melvin, patriarchal, example-setting.

'Why should he?' enquired Judith at some distance and to no one in particular, no one short of the universe.

'Get going,' called out Melvin. 'Show 'em. Prove it.'

Agnew looked doubtful, but began once more to plunge about. Fortunately, they had now reached the beeches, where the roots, though thicker, were for that reason more noticeable. Agnew had begun to use his lasso as if it were a fishing line. All the pockets in the roots were full of fish. Some of them actually did contain a little water. It had been raining on and off for many weeks. Noelle had been going everywhere in a stylish mackintosh.

'I'm nearing the end of the line,' said Melvin to Noelle. 'Something will just have to give, or I shall break.'

The two children began running down the slope to the cleared space at the end, where everyone turned and went back up again. The relatively long-limbed Judith, relatively unencumbered with miniature ranch gear, arrived easily first. She started an Ashanti dance she had seen on colour television at school.

Noelle's heart began to sink further and to beat faster with every descending step. She had, as usual, forgotten how all courage leaves one when the peril, whatever it be, is really close in time or space or both.

'I've thought of applying for a transfer,' said Melvin. 'I haven't told you, because I didn't want to worry you.'

He was trying to struggle out of his trapper's jerkin, though the weather was no warmer than it had been, and Noelle felt chillier every minute.

They were all assembled in the clearing. The circum-ambient litter was now sodden, much of it eaten away by enormous, conjectural rats. There was no other human being visible, or even audible; doubtless owing to the unsettled forecast.

'Well, there's nothing else to do but go back,' said Noelle almost immediately.

'No!!!' At school the children had learned the trick of negating loudly in unison.

'Let's sit down for a moment,' said Melvin.

'It's all too soggy,' protested Noelle.

'I've got *The Frontiersman* from last time,' proclaimed Melvin, producing it from the rustler's pocket in his cast-off jerkin. 'I'll rip it up and we can take half each. I never have time to read it anyway.'

'We can't sit among so much litter. It's disgusting. It's degrading.'

But Melvin was settled on one of the adapted tree trunks and was chivalrously holding out the bigger portion of the bisected journal.

'Just for a moment, Noelle,' he said wistfully, all but smiling at her. 'I need to get back some part of my sanity.'

So she slumped on the trunk beside him. She tried hard to keep her bottom on the small, thin package. 'Don't go too far away,' she said to the children. 'We're only stopping here for a minute.'

Melvin had drawn his lumberjack's knife, and was running his finger along the blade. His gaze was at once concentrated and absent-minded. Fortunately, the blade was unlikely to be very sharp.

'I often dream of what it *should* have been like,' said Melvin. 'On some island. Our island. You in a grass skirt, me in a leopard skin, perhaps a snow leopard skin, sun all the time, and breadfruit to chew, and mangoes, and coconuts, and flying fish. All day and all night the throbbing of the surf on the reef, and every now and then a distant schooner to wave to. Birds of paradise sweeping from palm tree to palm tree. Monkeys chattering and swinging. Loving you on the warm sand in the darkness beneath the Southern Cross.'

'Beautiful,' said Noelle, gently taking his hand. 'I'd like that.'

Melvin looked at her doubtfully. Agnew often had just that same look, inherited or acquired.

'I mean it. Truly,' said Noelle softly. 'I'd like it too. But we have to be practical.' She could not help squirming a little on the tiny, extemporised cushion.

'Do we? Must we?' He was drawing the lumber knife across the back of his hand.

'Of course we must, darling. I'm sure we can work something out together. Something practical.'

She always said that, and she would have been sincerely pleased if it had ever proved possible. What happened every time in actuality was that she had nearly expired of combined boredom and nausea before Melvin had made any real progress in describing the full details of the particular crisis. She never doubted that Melvin's business life was truly terrible. One trouble was that a terrible life is less fulfilling to others than a happy life.

He squeezed her hand. 'If the men in white coats don't come for me first,' he said.

'I'll keep them away,' she replied softly. 'I'll distract their attention.'

Inevitably, the children, forbidden to go far, were enjoying themselves among the litter. They were investigating discarded food and drink cans, deciphering sodden letterpress, speculating about indelicate proprietary utilities. Really they were only a few feet away. All along, surreptitiousness had been enforced upon the parental intimacies.

'You'd distract anyone's attention, Noelle,' said Melvin, almost whispering.

Noelle looked away from his fatigued face and glanced for a moment towards the thicker foliage to the right of the clearing.

'I'd like you to distract mine this very moment,' said Melvin, *sotto voce*.

'We must be *practical*,' said Noelle.

Melvin threw the knife into the ground, though it failed to enter, and merely lay horizontally, adding to the litter.

'Children!' he called out. 'Run away and play for a bit.'

Noelle rose. 'No, don't,' she called to them.

Confused, the children came to a standstill before

reaching the thicket towards which they had started charging. They began to play 'Triangles' on the rough ground. It was a game that everyone was playing and involved much darting about in a small area. Preferably, there should of course have been more players, but Agnew and Judith were still young enough to improvise. The game was something like 'Rounders', an elementary version of it.

'We can't possibly,' said Noelle to Melvin. She sat down again beside him. 'We'll stay just a few more minutes, so that the children can have a run about, and I'll see if I can get them to bed a little earlier than usual.'

'I want you *now*,' said Melvin

Noelle smiled at him, but said nothing. Though she rather fancied herself as a backwoods girl, she really preferred Melvin in one of his executive suits. At the time of Watteau and Fragonard, people played in the woods wearing wigs, panniers, and flowered silk from Lyon. They carried ribboned crooks.

'*Now*,' said Melvin. He picked up the knife and re-attached it to its thong. 'Let's get lost in the forest. The kids won't even notice for a long time.'

Melvin often had whims of that kind. Noelle supposed them to be outlets for the pressure under which so much of his life was passed.

He rose to his feet and pulled Noelle to hers. 'Let's see how lost we can get.'

She had found it best at such moments to go along with him as far as was practicable. At the moment, it was quite true that the children seemed absorbed in their running and tumbling. 'Triangles' is a far more physically demanding game than, say, 'Ring-a-Ring-a-Roses'. The children seemed not even to notice their gaucho parents departing across the worn clearing; exactly as Melvin had said. And, after all, there was no real reason why Noelle should not enter those bushes.

'I don't think we shall get lost,' she said. 'It's just into the next glade.'

'Have you been there?'

'Not really.'

'Then how do you know? When we stray from the warpath, we enter the impenetrable rain forest.'

All the same, Noelle did know. She had a precise mental picture of what it was like on the other side of the bushes. She always had had. She must have been there some time, though she could not remember the circumstances.

'It's impossible to get lost in these woods,' she said. 'Or in any of the other woods round here.'

Melvin had produced the knife once more with a view to hacking and slashing a path for them.

'Truly, it's not as dense as that,' said Noelle. 'A very little pushing will do it. You could almost get through in evening dress.'

So, though the whole idea was Melvin's, it was she who went ahead, while he made a more proper job of it.

Duly, she was through the thicket in about ninety seconds, and in the next glade. As she expected, it was quiet there, reassuring; unlittered, because untracked. The trees were taller and more dignified. There was an element of natural architecture, an element of mystery. Foliage hid the sky, moss the ground.

The moss was so deep and so apparently virgin as, in the exact present circumstances, to be suggestive. Noelle paddled through it across the width of the glade. The children might be temporarily out of touch with their parents, and she was fleetingly out of touch with Melvin, left further behind than mere yards would account for. She could not even hear his woodsmanship exercises; perhaps because she was not particularly listening for them.

She entered the trees on the far side of the glade; not in the least overwhelming, all comforting to perfectly acceptable proportions. Beyond this, however, she was sure she had never penetrated; and she was very aware of it. She had no idea of what she might find, though she knew perfectly well how small was the scope. She was in momentary and diplomatic flight.

She stopped. She had reached the end of the world already; even sooner than she had expected. It was marked by a tangle of wire: several different varieties and brands of wire; stretching between rotten leaning posts, with wood lice at their feet.

There was a house, timbered but not thatched. The rather large windows were one and all filled with diamond panes. There was a squinting figure in artificial stone above the garden door. Much of the detail was monastic in style. There was a very neat, big-leafed hedge all round the rectangular garden, every item in which was perfect. The hedge was low enough for

Noelle to see across it where it ran parallel with the world's tangled boundary.

A man was digging a hole in one of the garden beds. For the purpose, a quantity of blooms had been displaced, which now lay forlorn on the grass. Indeed, one might well define the new artifact not as a hole but as a trench. The man was in his braces and wore a shirt and tie, as if he were acting upon impulse. They seemed to be an elegant silk shirt, and a handsome moiré tie. His was the only figure in sight, except for a mammal of some kind which scuffled ceaselessly up and down in a small cage near the house. The man was concentrating on his work and a minute or two passed before there was any question of his looking up.

As far as Noelle was concerned, it was unnecessary for him to look up. She knew quite well who he was. If the wires in front of her had been taut instead of tangled, she would have clutched at and clung to them.

It had at no time so much as occurred to her that John Morley-Wingfield was so near a permanent neighbour. At least it explained whither he had so casually disappeared. Furthermore, if he possessed a house of the type before her, he almost certainly possessed a wife and a family also. Everything seemed unbelievably normal and familiar. There was even the pet in its cage.

But still she could not move or look away. This it was to be turned into a pillar of salt, even if only provisionally, and even though Melvin must surely be coming up behind her, with a knife in one hand, a miniature axe in the other. Necessarily, the man before her, almost

166

certainly unaccustomed to steady manual effort, would soon be taking a short breather.

In an instant, he looked straight into Noelle's eyes.

Though his hair was hardly disarranged, his face was a confused mask, surrounding eyes filled with horror, eyes so large as to suggest that they would never again be their former size.

Noelle turned and ran. She managed, as everyone does at such times, to avoid all the roots and briars and potholes. Within seconds, she was tripping back across the tranquil and unvisited glade. Within a minute, she was making a disturbance. She was calling, 'Melvin! Melvin!'

Melvin answered. 'Here, curse it.'

Before she could find him, she was out on the other side of the thicket. The children had at that very moment stopped playing and were strolling towards her.

'What's the matter, Mummy? Has something happened?'

'I'm *here*,' roared out Melvin, from among the bushes. 'Blast it.'

'I think your father may have hurt himself,' said Noelle. 'Let's go and see if we can help, shall we?'

Melvin's left hand was streaming with blood. It had always been one of the most individual things about them that he had less than the usual differentiation between right-handedness and left-handedness. In most matters he seemed able to use both left and right with equal results. Noelle had never before met anyone else like that.

'We must just get you home as soon as possible and tie you up. You must lie down and rest, and Agnew and Judith will go to bed as quietly as mice.'

'*Why* must we?' asked Judith.

But Agnew was good and helpful all the way back.

This time Noelle remained in a state of jitters for considerably longer than on the previous occasion; and her nerviness was exacerbated by the unexpected complications that followed Melvin's mishap. He was required to remain at home and most of the time in bed, while his depleted system struggled with the toxins; and, all the time, but more and more vividly, he saw his position with the firm diminishing, receding, vanishing. The vision was so transparent to him that for much of the time Noelle could all too lucidly see it also.

'But they can't just get rid of you. It wouldn't even be legal.'

'They have ways and means. Make no mistake about that. We're going to starve, Noelle. But do come over here first. Take that dress off.'

In the end, Mut telephoned. Melvin was in bed with a particularly demanding group of complications. In the strict and immediate context, his absence from the scene downstairs was merciful.

'How's Melvin going on?'

'Not too good. He thinks the infection is poisoning his brain.'

'What do *you* think?'

'I've simply no idea. It's impossible to tell. It's just one thing after another.'

'You know that man you asked about. The one you said you met at our party?'

'I certainly do,' said Noelle. 'Has Simon anything to say about him?'

'Simon had never heard of him, but that doesn't matter. The point is that I think you just got his name out of the paper. I think you were dreaming.'

'Perhaps I really was,' said Noelle. 'But what makes you think so at this moment?'

'There was a criminal of that name, and apparently his case keeps turning up. I've come across him in the cornflakes crime book. You know, you get a copy in exchange for the backs of the boxes. Simon collected them and sent them in. It's the sort of thing you do if you're a barrister. William Morley-Westall. He lived in Kensington Square.'

'What name?' asked Noelle faintly.

'William Morley-Westall. The name you gave me.'

'It wasn't the name I gave you. It's you who are in a state of muddle, Mut.'

'I'm sure it was.'

'Well, it wasn't. What happened in the end to your man, anyway?'

'He was sent to Broadmoor. I expect he's out by this time. Ages ago, in fact. They only keep them for a matter of months nowadays. Simon says it's all wrong. But people are still arguing about the case. It's in the news the whole time. I'm sure that's where you saw it.'

'I expect so, Mut. I haven't much time to think about such things at the moment.'

But of course it was difficult to think much about anything else. Men and their dreams! One man driven to crime, obviously horrifying. The other prostrate with complications, and almost certainly dragging himself and his family to ruin.

That disaster was not immediate, because there were scattered savings that could be drawn upon, but in the end Melvin had to be taken to hospital. Probably he would have been taken sooner, had there been room for him.

Noelle began to read the jobs advertisements in the local paper, buying odd copies for the purpose, but not yet very systematically. She even found herself glancing at the offers and miniature proclamations in the window of the shop.

Week followed week, and as it became more and more necessary to be sensible, it became more and more difficult. Noelle suspected that the doctors were baffled, though of course they never said so. Certainly she herself had begun to find life as a whole baffling as never before. It was all but impossible to decide how big a step it was appropriate to take.

Judith had begun to ail in various different ways, two or three of them at a time; and had no difficulty in making plain that fundamentally the trouble lay in her anxieties about her daddy, and her doubts about her mummy. Agnew, on the other hand, had quietened down and become a quite nice little boy. It was as when a running bull calf ceases to be chivvied and goaded. Noelle began in small ways to confide in him; in trifles, positively to rely upon him. Previously she had never been able to speak to him, to endear herself, to trust him.

One night the telephone rang. It was well after eleven.

'Get up please, darling,' said Noelle to Agnew, whose unkempt head lay in her lap. 'Just for a second.'

Agnew responded quite obligingly.

'Hullo. Oh it's you, Mut.'

'Come to a party on Friday. Sorry to be so late in asking you. It'll be the usual people and the usual things.'

'I don't think I'd better, Mut.'

'It'll take you out of yourself.'

'No, not really.'

Agnew was gazing at her with big eyes, though less big than those other eyes, which she saw for so much of the time.

'Thank you very much, none the less,' said Noelle. 'It's sweet of you.'

'How *is* Melvin, anyway?'

'Worse, as far as I can tell. The doctors seem to be baffled.'

'Quite seriously, Noelle, I suggest the time has come to fetch him back home. Where he is, it's the blind leading the blind.'

Agnew had crept up to her on the floor, and was nuzzling into her thigh.

'I daresay you're right, Mut. But you know how bad I am as a nurse. You'll remember for yourself how hopeless I always was.'

'I remember,' said Mut. 'In that case, I suggest you come to the party. At least, it will take your mind off.'

'I'm not sure it will. It didn't the last time.'

Agnew took away his nose and cheek. He had very nearly suffocated himself.

'You mean the mystery man. Simon's got a new idea about *him*. From your description, he thinks he can only have been a man called John Martingale, who lives quite near you. He's supposed to have a lovely garden.'

'I don't want to talk about it,' said Noelle. 'There's been far too much of one thing leading to another from it. I'll try to tell you one day.'

'I'm sure the whole thing's a fantasy, as I said before.'

'It is, and yet it isn't,' said Noelle.

'Oh, it's like that!' said Mut. 'Then come to our party and take your mind off *two* things. I think you need a big change.'

'Thank you, Mut, but no. Really not. Please ask me next time.'

'Well, of course I shall. The best possible about Melvin. And from Simon.'

The impression made upon Noelle, as she put back the receiver, was that Agnew had drawn himself tightly together in the manner of a small soapstone idol, though a brightly coloured one. He was squatting there like a holy pussycat. Never once in previous years had she noticed anything so peculiar about him, not even

172

when he had been a baby; so equivocal also.

'Well, darling?' she said to him, a little cautiously.

He looked at her, and then crawled back to her. She caught him up, set him on her knee, and hugged him.

Almost at once, the telephone rang again. Noelle clung on to Agnew, and managed to stretch out her arm, supposing it to be renewed supplications from her best friend, Mut.

'Yes, it's me,' she said, in Mut-like tones, and giving Agnew a squeeze.

But it wasn't Mut.

'Is that Mrs Corcoran?'

'It is.'

'Mrs Melvin Corcoran?'

'Yes.'

'Then you'll remember me at the hospital. I'm sorry to say I have some bad news.'

There was a woman who lived about half a mile away named Kay Steiner. When Noelle had gone to parties in Melvin's absence, Kay Steiner had almost always taken in the children for the night. They had seemed almost to like going to her. They managed, both of them, to praise the food and they both appeared to respond to her way with them. Mrs Steiner had no children of her own, but she was not a widow, as might for much of the time have been supposed. It was merely that her husband, Franklin Steiner, was often away from home for long periods. Noelle fancied she had never been told what he did at these times, or at any other times, but he seemed nice enough in his own way when occasionally encountered. About Kay Steiner, there could be no doubt of any kind. Kay was a brick.

After the funeral, attended by several people who had not been expected, and otherwise by hardly anyone whom the bereaved knew at all, Noelle had a quiet talk with the solicitor, who had remarked that it might be useful if the position of things were roughly indicated by him as soon as possible.

He asked if their talk could be attended also by Mr Mullings, who was an executor. Noelle had several times entertained Melvin's friend, Ted Mullings, to dinner or supper, and put him up subsequently for the night, and she knew that the other executor, who was rather elderly, had been included simply for form. Ted Mullings had already played a prominent part at the funeral, to which he had driven all the way in his Jaguar from his home near Sandgate, having taken a day off from business for the purpose.

At the end of the discussion, which was quite short, the future stretching before Noelle and the two children seemed just about as open as it could possibly be. She would have to create an entirely new world for the three of them. Noelle looked white. What Americans call 'challenge' never brought out the best in her.

They had all had a first tea after the funeral itself, but, during the little talk with the legal people, Kay Steiner had been quietly preparing a small second one, for consumption before the men went their ways.

Trying to lap down her fifth or sixth cup of tea,

Noelle reflected that in less than three weeks she would be thirty-eight. Kay Steiner did not know this, though of course Mut did, who, however, would never tell, or never tell the truth. The two children knew the date, and celebrated it, naturally, but had not been told the full facts. Now, perhaps, they need not know for a long time. Noelle also reflected how strange it was to be dressed quite ordinarily for her husband's requiem.

Anyone could see that she was worn out. Kind Kay suggested that she take in Judith and Agnew for a few days, so that Noelle would have time to find her feet. The children were not in the room at the time, and Noelle accepted with hardly a demur. Judith had been weeping excessively, and was now lying down. Agnew had been looking paler and more mature every moment.

There was resistance at the time of departure, but Kay dealt with it skilfully, and Ted Mullings offered a ride to Kay's house in his gamboge Jaguar. Agnew stepped in ahead of everyone, but Judith declined furiously to go at all, and had to be dragged all the way on foot by Kay, while Agnew waited on her doorstep, as Ted Mullings had to be on his way back to his wife in Kent.

The solicitor had a quantity of work to take home, especially as he had been away from the office for so much of the day; and thereafter Noelle was alone in the house. She had declined Kay's offer to take her in also for that one night at least. She had much thinking to do, and solitude might help the process, though she was far from sure whether or not it would.

It was autumn and she threw the remains of the funeral baked meats into the fire. Melvin had always insisted upon as many open grates as possible, and today one of them had been put into use. Noelle regularly had to stand over the daily woman, Clarice, while it was done. Noelle disliked such sustained exercises in authority exceedingly.

Her father's clock struck six. Noelle felt like midnight, but at least there was a reasonable amount of time for all the thinking she would have to do; all the bricks she would have to make without straw, without the right kind of experience, or the proper temperament.

She could scarcely make herself another cup of tea; scarcely just yet even want another cup. She picked up a boomerang with which Melvin had returned from Darwin. Melvin had admitted that he had only bought it in a shop, but it had been a special shop. The boomerang was not a commercially produced plaything, he had said, but a real weapon. Ever since, it had lain on his desk. Noelle handled it wistfully. The house was of course packed with all kinds of things that would have to be disposed of somehow; and profitably, if at all possible. Not even Melvin's life assurance had proved to be of a kind best suited to the circumstances as they had turned out. Noelle realised that she really must start thinking at once. Her situation was considerably better than that in which many widows found themselves. She knew that well.

*

But the bell rang.

Noelle looked at her father's clock. It was not yet ten minutes past six. Doubtless someone had left something behind. Instantly, it occurred to Noelle that she herself had been left behind. She flushed for a second and managed to open the door.

The man from the house on the other side of the wood was standing there. Naturally, he showed no sign of the disarray in which Noelle had last seen him. His eyes were quite unstaring. This time he even wore a hat, though he swept it off as the door opened. He spoke at once.

'I was so sorry to hear of your great loss. I did not think it right to intrude upon the funeral, but I wish to say how much I should like to do anything I can which might help you. It seems to me the sort of thing that should be said as soon as possible. So here I am to say it, and to say that I really mean it. Perhaps you would permit me to think for you about the many matters that must arise?'

'There are indeed many matters,' said Noelle. She felt that she was being watched from the houses on the other side of the road, beyond the worn entrance to the wood.

'Possibly it would help if we ourselves could define our position in the light of the changed circumstances?'

Noelle glanced at him for the first time. 'All right,' she said. 'If you think so. Please come in for a few minutes.'

He followed her in. She felt that she should take his hat, but in a modern house there was nowhere in particular to put it.

'I have sent the children away,' she said.

He sat on the same sofa; the sofa on which she herself had just been scrying the opaque future.

'This is a boomerang,' he said, as if most people would not know.

'It was my husband's.'

'Yours is a terrible loss for anyone.'

Noelle nodded.

'Most of all for a woman as sensitive and highly strung as you. Your cheeks are wan and your lovely eyes are shadowed.'

'I was very fond of my husband.'

'Of course. You have a warm heart and a tender soul.'

'In some ways he was not very grown up. I think he needed me.'

'Who would not need *you*?'

Noelle hesitated. 'Would you care for a glass of sherry?'

'If you will join me.'

'Yes, I'll join you. It may be the last sherry I shall see for some time.' She filled the two glasses. 'I admit that I have been left in a difficult position, Mr Morley-Wingfield. All this will have to be sold. Everything.'

He seemed to smile. 'You do not really suppose that I can agree to be addressed by so absurd a name?' He raised his glass. 'To the best possible future!' he said very seriously.

'You told me it was your name,' said Noelle, not responding to his toast. 'Actually, you volunteered the information. What, in fact, *is* your name?'

'My name is John,' he said, now undoubtedly smiling, but smiling at her.

'Mut and Simon seem to know nothing about you.' She was sitting on one of the leather-padded brass ends to the fender.

'I can return the compliment. I know little about *them*. All I know is that I met you in their company. That matters very much. I hope to both of us. I greatly hope it.'

'I think I should tell you,' said Noelle, 'that I saw you digging in your garden. I was with my husband.'

'You are mistaken,' he replied. 'Never willingly have I held a spade in my hands since I left Harrow.'

'Do you know how my husband's illness began? His last illness?'

'I must acknowledge ashamedly that I do not.'

'We went for a walk in the wood with our children. My husband insisted on breaking through the next glade, while we left the children playing. He slashed himself quite badly, and he never really got over it. Some kind of blood poisoning, I suppose, but the doctors were baffled. In the end, he died of it.'

'It is a sad moment to say such a thing, but I admit to being baffled also. I cannot follow the story. I think there is an element of fantasy somewhere, my sweet Noelle. It is because you are so upset by everything that's happened.'

She thought it was the first time he had addressed her by her name. Indeed, she knew very well that it was.

'That is just what Mut said to me on the telephone. But it's not true. It was when we were in the next glade that we saw you digging. We saw you quite clearly.'

'So your husband saw me too?'

'No,' said Noelle, after a second. 'I don't really think he did. He was preoccupied. But I know perfectly well that *I* did.'

'How was I dressed?' asked the man. 'Seeing that I was digging. How then was I got up?' His tone was perfectly friendly, perhaps quizzical, though he was gazing straight at her.

'You had taken off your jacket.'

'My dear girl! Whatever next? Was I digging in my braces?'

'As a matter of fact, you were.'

The man looked away from her and down at the Eskimo-style carpet. He had drained his glass, as, for the matter of that, had Noelle.

'It all seems rather unlikely,' said the man, though only in a tone of mild remonstrance.

'The sincerity of your belief,' he added, 'makes you look more charming and delightful than ever. What suggestions had our mutual friend, Mut, to offer? Another delightful woman, by the way, though a daisy in a spring field, where you are the lovely lily of the world, body and soul and spirit.'

He had ceased to fondle the boomerang and was letting it lie beside him on the leathery cushion. Noelle crossed to the sofa and picked it up. She continued holding on to it.

'Would you like another glass of sherry?'

'If *you* would.'

She filled the two glasses and went back to the fender seat.

'Previously,' she said, 'I had no idea at all that you actually lived in the neighbourhood. You should have told me.'

'But I don't!' he cried. 'I merely came to know it from the time I was at Sandhurst. What days those were! The laughing and the grieving!' Then he raised his glass. 'I propose another toast. To a bright future erupting from the troubled past!'

Again Noelle did not respond.

'We must expect that it will take a little time,' said the man, soberly. 'It will be the crown of my life to see the task accomplished.'

Noelle almost emptied her glass at a swig.

'You push through into the next glade,' she said. 'You go straight across it, and beyond the trees and bushes on the far side is a half-timbered house with lots of big windows, and you live there.'

'Half-timbered houses do not usually have big windows, or they should not have them. I would not live in such a house.'

Noelle was twisting the boomerang round and round. There was nothing left of her second glass of sherry.

'I saw you,' she said.

Then she threw the boomerang down. Against the Eskimo carpet it looked like every modern painting.

'What does it matter,' cried Noelle, half to herself,

hardly at all to the man.

All the same, it did matter: the house was only ten to fifteen minutes away, even when one was walking at the pace of one's children, and then struggling through the bushes and undergrowth in a quite sedate manner.

'I came in the hope of helping with any difficulties there might be,' said the man, 'and plainly this is the first of them. The distance is very short. I suggest we go and look for this house. We both know the way quite well. Besides, the fresh air will do you good.'

'I think it is going to rain again,' said Noelle.

'We shall be back before it falls.'

The moist surface mud on the woodland path could not but remind Noelle of the funeral. She had been surprised that Melvin had not stipulated for cremation, but the Will had proved to be immaterial at almost all points.

At the funeral it had drizzled persistently, but now it was merely a matter of a penetrating moisture in the air. Noelle was wearing her stylish mackintosh, but the man was seemingly unprotected. Noelle feared that his trousers would lose their crease, even that the entire fine fabric of his suit might lose texture and buoyancy. Already his shoes were streaked and smeared. Noelle was wearing boots.

'Are you sure you want to go through with this?' she asked him.

'I mean to drive out some of the megrims,' he said.

They descended the slope to the clearing. The recurrent raininess had left nothing but a mush. One could no longer distinguish plastic bag from squashed balloon, cigarette pack from snapcorn box. Natural forces were mounting a liquidation of their own.

'Ane now for the next glade!' admonished the man jovially.

'We can't possibly,' cried Noelle. 'The bushes are soaking. You'll utterly wreck your suit. I hadn't realised.'

She made no reference to his hat, which was even more inappropriate.

'I haven't been noticing the weather very much lately,' said Noelle.

'We'll be through in an instant,' said the man. 'If you've done it already, you'll know that.'

She surmised that Melvin's fate could not but be in his mind, though of course he would never speak of it, perhaps never again.

'It's just your suit,' said Noelle. 'I know it's not very difficult.' She must not permit him the slightest doubt that she had at least once been through, had seen his house. 'You really need to dress up for a thing of this kind in weather like this.' Melvin had always overdone it, as he overdid so many things, but of course he had been basically right. She had always seen that.

'I'll take off my hat,' said the man, 'and then you'll feel better.'

And, under his lead, they were through in no time. On the other side, Noelle had to admit that she could detect no particular damage to his clothes, apart from his shoes; and that even her own elegantly flowing mackintosh seemed unscathed.

The man had been laughing for a moment, but now the two of them stood silently in the next glade. The tree structures, the pendant greens and browns, seemed to Noelle more mysteriously architectural than ever. They too brought back the funeral to her, but she realised that many things would do that for some time to come, possibly for the rest of her life, which in any case might not be a long one, as Melvin's had proved not to be.

'It has an atmosphere,' said Noelle, in the end. 'I admit that.'

'Yes,' said the man. 'But you are almost the only being who would feel it. You are a wonderful person.'

All the time there was a faint tinking and tapping which Noelle had certainly not been aware of on the previous occasion. She realised that in the then circumstances she might well not have noticed it. She said nothing about it. It reminded her of a visit she had paid with a German business party to *Das Rheingold* in English at the Coliseum. She had not understood a word or appreciated a note of it, though at the end the Germans had been very courteous and affable about it.

'They all kissed my hand,' said Noelle out loud. 'Every single one of them.'

The man looked at her.

'I *am* so sorry,' said Noelle. 'I was uttering my thoughts. I must be very tired.'

'Of course you are tired, dear, sweet Noelle,' said the man.

'You hardly know whether you are on your charming head or your pretty feet.' He looked at Noelle's boots. 'But we shall change all that. Slowly but surely.'

It would have been uncouth of Noelle not to smile, though noncommittally.

'The house you mentioned stands at the other side of the glade?' enquired the man, not too obviously humouring her. He had resumed his hat.

'Through there,' said Noelle, pointing.

'More bushes!' cried the man, in mock irony.

'Not such dense ones. Then you come to a barbed-wire fence. All of which you know perfectly well. I'm afraid your shoes will suffer in all this wet moss. But it's entirely your own fault.'

'But of course,' cried the man, as before. 'Please go ahead.'

Noelle wallowed across the river of moss without looking back. She wondered if there were small snakes and horrid insects concealed in it, which the dampness might bring out, perhaps for feeding purposes.

At the far side, the tapping and tinking were distinctly clearer. Noelle looked quickly back. She saw that the man's shoes were submerged at every pace, and that water streamed from them each time he took a new step. She knew from her own experience how wringing wet the bottoms of one's trousers become at such moments.

'Are you all right?' she enquired weakly.

'Go on, go on,' the man said. 'Go on as though I were not here.'

Noelle considered for a moment.

'All right,' she decided. 'I shall.'

But through the second belt of trees and bushes, and short though this part of the journey was, she advanced far more slowly.

The staid truth was that now there was no other sound at all but that of the tapping, the hammering, the clanking – perhaps even clanging. It seemed to Noelle that the din was rising in a degree entirely out of proportion with the distance she was covering, as presumably, she advanced towards it. It was continuing to be much as in the opera, when hurricanes of sound had at times risen almost on an instant from a seemingly peaceful and even flow. She realised perfectly well, however, that the present turmoil of noise was as nothing to that on a reasonably large modern building site; or not yet. There was always something for which to be grateful when one made the effort to see life in that way.

Furthermore, all the disfiguring barbed-wire seemed to have vanished or been taken away; at least for the limited distance in either direction that Noelle could find time to take in.

The hedge round the garden was still there, low and thin, but now sadly shredded, selectively shrivelled.

The costly looking half-timbered house seemed not to be there. Alas for so many human certainties!

Noelle compelled herself to advance in her mackintosh and boots across the line which once the barbed-wire had marked. At that moment, she realised that though barbed-wire had a bad name among her friends, yet those having recourse to it might often so do for largely benevolent reasons. Melvin's friends would take that for granted. What was happening to her now was like going over the top.

She peered downwards over the tattered hedge.

There was the most enormous hole or cavity; excessively diametered, far deeper than Noelle could discern.

All down the hole men were working constructionally – or so she assumed. Hundreds of men – thousands, she might have been forgiven for thinking. Men were doing pretty well everything the mind could think of – and not only Noelle's quiet and reasonable mind.

Sooner rather than later, she realised that women too were working down there: to start with, at typewriters, at comptometers, at computers. Noelle knew these things from the days when she had herself worked in offices, as Mut still did.

There was noise enough in all conscience, for any auditor who was fully human; but Noelle soon realised that probably the noise was nothing like enough for everything that was being actually done. The comparison with the fully modern building site of average scale recurred to her. Properly, there should have been far, far *more* noise. She was sure of it. Perhaps that was the most alarming thought of all on that day of her husband's obsequies.

Noelle turned herself right round and stood with her entire back squarely against the garden hedge. She looked in every direction for the man who had challenged her to this strange experience on such a day of threnody.

John Morley-Wingfield, like the once-tangled wire, was no longer visible. His apparition was no more finite than his name.

Of course, notwithstanding his talk, he might have failed at the last thicket; might have decided upon some care, after all, for his suit; might even have retreated before the full moss crossing, and be composedly awaiting Noelle on her own fully domestic side of the edificial glade.

His case would in some degree have been made. Noelle had seen for herself that, in the strictest construction of words, there was no half-timbered house with over-large windows. Possibly, indeed, Mr Morley-Wingfield was a property speculator who had demolished his dwelling to set up a factory more or less on the site, or an office block. Few of Melvin's friends would have seen much to criticise in that, and some would have pointed out that the transformation would give employment at many different levels, and thus contribute to progress.

The moisture in the air had begun to precipitate heavily and also to darken the sky. Right through the experience, Noelle had realised, at the back of her mind, how late in the day it was. Possibly the second most alarming thing of all was that at such an hour all these entities were still at work.

One could call this nothing but heavy rain. Noelle wondered if there was a way out of the wood by turning rightwards up the glade: a shortcut. She had no wish ever again in her life, short or long, to meet those furbelows of parched or sodden trash at the point where people turned; to behold those deftly shaped official seats, fouled with inscriptions, nicked in or encrusted.

But turning rightwards up the unknown, moss-bottomed glade would be far too much of a further new experience at this of all moments. The glade might appear comparatively indifferent to her, but, even in a suburban wood, the coming of darkness could bring unexpected risks, as poor Melvin had so often emphasised. Noelle was sure that Melvin had often been right in matters of that kind.

Indeed, while hurriedly reflecting in this way, Noelle had almost recrossed the spongy moss, which this time seemed less likely to harbour leeches and freshwater scorpions than to be in itself vaguely bottomless. Had John Morley-Wingfield simply sunk through a particularly soft spot?

She pushed into the by now almost familiar bushes. At this point the noise of the rain had become loud enough to drown the faint thumping and tip-tapping of the overtime workers.

Noelle could not hold back a cry. The briar immediately before her was still splashed and flushed with blood; exactly as when she had last seen it. The weeks and months of rain had made no difference at all.

Up the slope from where the rubbish rotted, down the gentler slope through the silver birches, Noelle, encumbered by her boots, ran for home, with half-shut eyes. She was quite surprised to find her home still there.

But she did not enter the house: partly because the man might soon be there too; partly because, after all, Melvin might still be there (it was supposed to take forty days for the dead to clear); partly, perhaps mainly, for wider reasons still.

Instead she walked to Kay Steiner's house. Though winded by her up-hill and down-dale run, she still walked briskly and unobtrusively. But surely it was by now too dark for the neighbours to continue watching her, abstaining the while from the television?

'I've changed my mind. Can I please stay the night too?'

'Of course you can, dear. I always thought it would be the best thing. I hated leaving you in that gloomy house.'

'Yes, it *was* a gloomy house, wasn't it?'

Kay Steiner looked at Noelle. 'Well,' she ventured, 'in all the circumstances—'

'No. It was not that only.'

'Really? In that case you'd better all move in here until Franklin gets back.'

'Kay. Are you in love with Franklin?'

'Of course I'm in love with Franklin. Don't ask such silly questions. Now take off your boots and your wet clothes. These smart macs never keep out the rain, do they? I'll lend you some clothes, if you like. We're exactly the same size. Perhaps I ought to tell you that Judith is a little feverish. I think it's because she fought so hard on the way here. She's been refusing anything to eat or drink, and she's been screaming. It's nothing to worry about, of course. I'll lend you a thermometer so that you can take her temperature yourself during the night.'

Noelle entered the dining room in Kay's clothes, less sophisticated than her own, but not necessarily less expensive, or less fashionable.

Kay had laid the table beautifully, and with pink lighted candles; all as if it had been a special occasion. She was hard at work in the kitchen. The many surfaces were strewn with comestibles and accessories. Kay wore an apron publicising British Airways. The *British Leyland Cook Book* lay open.

'I see no reason why we shouldn't make the best of things,' said kind Kay. 'I'm glad you like that sweater. It's my favourite. It was given me in rather romantic circumstances.'

They consumed several glasses of sherry and a whole bottle of wine. Franklin Steiner belonged to a wine club connected with a well-known firm, which made the selections: neither costly top table nor cheap plonk.

'Let's have coffee in the lounge,' said Kay ultimately.

'Tell me,' said Noelle, while Kay was filling the two cups. 'Have you ever taken a lover? Since you married Franklin, I mean.'

'Yes,' said Kay. 'I've taken, as you call it, several. But you don't take milk, do you?'

'No milk,' said Noelle. 'But you might stick in a spoonful of sugar.'

'You shouldn't, you know,' said Kay, but affection-ately, understandingly.

'I know I shouldn't,' said Noelle.

Kay passed across the cup. All the things belonged to a set which Franklin had bought somewhere upon impulse at an auction.

'Does it make any difference?' asked Noelle.

'To what, dear?'

'To your feelings for Franklin. To the nature of your marriage.'

'Most certainly not. How serious you are!'

'Yes,' said Noelle. 'I think I am serious.'

'It takes all sorts,' said Kay.

Noelle began to stir her coffee. 'Did you ever know a man calling himself John Morley-Wingfield?'

'If you mean was he one of them, the answer is no. Mine didn't have names like that.'

'He may be a neighbour,' said Noelle. 'But you never heard of him?'

'Never,' said Kay. 'And I don't believe you did either. You've just dreamed him up.'

Wearing Kay's solidly pink nightdress, Noelle lay un-sleeping in one of Kay's beds. As Kay had no children, there were no fewer than four spare rooms in the house; and as Kay was Kay, all four were always available. It was just as well at such times as this.

The door opened quietly. In the stream of light from the passage, Noelle could see Agnew's wild head.

'Mummy.'

'What is it, darling?'

'Who was that man you were walking with after I came here? Was it Daddy?'

Certainly the almost total darkness was something of an immediate relief to Noelle.

'Of course it wasn't Daddy, Agnew. It was someone quite different. But how did you see him?'

'Mrs Steiner was making a fuss about Judith, so I was bored, and just ran home. What man was he, Mummy?'

'He was a friend of Daddy's, who couldn't come earlier. There are always people like that in life. You must never let them upset you.'

'Mummy, are you going to marry him?'

'I don't think so, Agnew. I'm not proposing to marry anyone for some time yet. No one but you.'

'Really not, Mummy? Why did you go for a walk with him if he was only Daddy's friend?'

'He wanted to take me out of myself. It was kind of him. You know it's been a difficult day for me, Agnew.'

'Are you *sure* that's all, Mummy?'

'Quite sure, Agnew. Now get into bed with me for a little while, and we'll say no more about it, if you please, not even think about it.'

Agnew put his arms round her, squeezing himself tightly against her breasts; and all was peace until the morrow.

Ravissante

I had an acquaintance who had begun, before I knew him, as a painter but who took to 'compiling and editing' those costly, glossy books about art which are said to sell in surprising numbers but which no person one knows ever buys and no person one sees ever opens.

I first met this man at a party. The very modern room was illuminated only in patches by dazzling standard lamps beneath metal frames. The man stood in one of the dark corners, looking shy and out of it. He wore a light blue suit, a darker blue shirt, and a tie that was pretty well blue-black. He looked very malleable and slender. I walked towards him. I saw that he had a high, narrow head and smooth dark hair, cut off in a sharp, horizontal line at the back. I saw also that with him was a woman, previously invisible, though, as a matter of fact, and when she had come into focus, rather oddly dressed. None the less, I spoke.

It seemed that I was welcome after all. The man said something customary about knowing almost none of the guests, and introduced the nearly invisible woman to me as his wife. He proceeded to chat away eagerly but a little anxiously, as if to extenuate his presence among so many dark strangers. He told me then and there about his abandonment of painting for editorship:

'I soon realised I could not expect my pictures to sell,' he said, or words to that effect. 'Too far-fetched.' About that particular epithet of his I am certain. It stuck in my mind immediately. He offered no particulars, but talked about the terms he got for his gaudy pictorial caravanserais. I have, of course, written a little myself from time to time, and the sums he named struck me as pretty good. I avoided all comment to the effect that it is the unread book which brings in the royalty (after all, modern translations of the *Iliad* and the *Odyssey* are said to sell by the hundred thousand, and the Bible to be more decisively the best seller of all with every year that passes); and observed instead that his life must be an interesting one, with much travel, and, after all, much beauty to behold. He agreed warmly and, taking another Martini from a passing tray, described in some detail his latest business excursion, which had been to somewhere in Central America where there were strange things painted on walls, perfect for colour photography. He said he hoped he hadn't been boring me. 'Oh, no,' I said. All the time, the man's wife had said nothing. I remark on this simply as a fact. I do not imply that she was bored. She might indeed have been enthralled. Silence can, after all, mean either thing. In her case, I never found out which it meant. She was even slenderer than he was, with hair the colour (as far as I could see) of old wheat, collected into a bun low on the neck, a pale face, long like her husband's, and these slightly odd, dark garments I've mentioned. I noticed now that the man had a rather weak, undeveloped nose.

In the end, the man said would I visit their flat in Battersea and have dinner? and I gave my promise.

It will be noticed that I am being discreet with names. I think it is best because the man himself was so discreet in that way, as will be apparent later. Moreover, at no time did I become a close friend of the pair. One thing, however, must have had importance.

The Battersea flat (not quite overlooking the Park) did exhibit some of the man's paintings. I might compare them, though a little distantly, with the once controversial last works of the late Charles Sims: apparently confused on the surface, even demented, they made one doubt while one continued to gaze, as upon Sims's pictures, whether the painter had not in truth broken through to a deep and terrible order. Titles of the Sims species, 'Behold I Am Graven on the Palm of Thy Hand' or 'Am I Not the Light in the Abyss?', would have served with this man's pictures also. In fact, with him there was no question of titles, not, I thought, only out of compliance with the contemporary attitude, but more because the man did not appear to see his works as separate and possibly saleable objets d'art. 'I found that I couldn't paint what people might want to buy,' he said, smiling beneath his weak nose. His wife, seated on a hard chair and again oddly dressed, said nothing. As a matter of fact, I could imagine quite well these strange pictures being ingathered for a time by fashion's flapping feelers, though, obviously for entirely wrong reasons. I remarked to the two of them that the pictures were among the most powerful and exciting I had ever seen, and what I said was sincere, despite a certain non-professionalism in the execution. I am not sure that I should have cared to live surrounded by such pictures, as they did, but that is another matter. Perhaps I exaggerate the number: there were, I think, three of these mystical works in the living room, all quite large; four in the matrimonial bedroom, into which I was conducted to look at them; and one each in the small bedroom for visitors and in the bathroom. They were framed very casually, because the painter did not take them seriously enough; and mingled them on his walls with framed proofs from the art books, all perpetrated at the fullest stretch of modern reproductive processes.

I went there several times to dinner, perhaps six or seven times in all; and I reciprocated by entertaining the two of them at the Royal Automobile Club, which at that time I found convenient for such purposes, as I was living alone in Richmond. The Battersea dinners were very much of a pattern: my host did most of the talking; his wife, in her odd clothes, seemed to say less and less; the food, cooked by her, was perfectly good though a trifle earnest; I was treated very consciously as a guest. From this last, and from other things, I deduced that guests were infrequent. Perhaps the trouble was that the establishment lacked magic. The painter of those pictures should, one felt, have had something to say, but everything he brought out, much though there was of it, was faintly disappointing. He seemed eager to welcome me and reluctant to let me go, but entirely unable to make a hole in the wall that presumably enclosed him, however long he punched. Nor, as will be gathered, can his wife be said to have been much help. Or, at least, as far as one could see. Human relationships are so fantastically oblique that one can never be sure.

Anyway I fear that the acquaintanceship slowly died, or almost died. The near-death was slow because I made it so. I felt, almost at the beginning, that anything quicker would have meant a painfulness, conceivably even a dispute. Knowing what I was doing (within the inevitable – exceedingly narrow – limits), I fear that I very slowly strangled the connection. I was sad about it in a general sort of way, but neither the man nor his wife had truly touched anything about me or within me, and associations that are not alive are best amputated as skilfully as possible before the rot infects too much of one's total tissue and unnecessarily lowers the tone of life. If one goes to parties or meets many new people in any other way, one has to take protective action quite frequently, however much one hates oneself in the process; just as human beings are compelled to massacre animals unceasingly, because human beings are simply unable to survive, for the most part, on apples and nuts.

Total death of the connection, however, it never was. The next thing that happened was a letter from a firm of solicitors. It arrived more than four years after I had last seen the Battersea couple, as I discovered from looking through my old engagement books after I had read it; and two years, I believed, after the last Christmas card had passed between us. I had moved during that latter period from Richmond to Highgate. The letter told me that my Battersea acquaintance had died ('after a long illness,' the solicitors added) and that he had appointed me joint executor of his Will. The other executor was his wife. Needless to say, it was the first I had heard of it. There was a legacy which the testator 'hoped I would accept': the amount was £100, which, I regret to say, struck me at once as having been arrived at during an earlier period of Britain's financial history. Finally, the letter requested me to communicate as soon as possible with the writers or directly with their client's wife.

I groaned a little, but when I had reached the office where I worked before my marriage, I composed a letter of sympathy and in a postscript suggested, as tactfully as I could, that an evening be named for a first meeting of the executors. The reply came instantly. In the smallest number of words possible, it thanked me for my sympathy and proposed the evening of the next day. I put off an engagement to meet my fiancée and drove once more to Battersea.

I noticed that my co-executor had abandoned the unusual style of costume she had previously favoured, and wore an unremarkable, even commonplace, dress from a multiple store. Perhaps it was her response to the inner drive that until recently swept the bereaved into black. In no other respect could I observe a change in her.

She did not seem broken, or even ruffled, with grief, and she had little more to say than before. I did try to discover the cause of death, but could get no clear answer, and took for granted that it had been one of the usual bitter maladies. I was told that there was no need for me to put myself to trouble. She would do all there was to be done, and I could just come in at the end.

I did remark that as an executor I should have to see a copy of the Will. She at once handed the original to me in silence: it had been lying about the room. It was simple enough. The body was to be cremated, and the entire estate was left to the testator's wife, except for my £100, and except for the fact that all the testator's pictures were to be offered to the National Gallery of British Art; if refused, to a long list of other public galleries, ten or twelve of them; and if still refused, to be burnt. I saw at once why I had been brought into the settlement of the estate. I had been apprehensive ever since I had heard from the solicitors. Now I was terrified.

'Don't worry,' said my co-executor, smiling faintly. 'I dealt with that part myself while he was still alive. None of the places would touch the pictures with a bargepole.'

'But,' I said, 'as an executor I can't just leave it at that.'

'See their letters.' She produced a heap of paper and passed it over to me. 'Sit down and read them.'

She herself drew back her normal hard chair, and sat half watching me, half not; but without taking up any other occupation.

I thought that I might as well settle the matter, if it really were possible, there and then. I checked the letters against the list in the Will. Every named gallery was accounted for. All the letters were negative; some not. The correspondence covered rather more than the previous twelve months. Many public servants are slow to make up their minds and slower to commit themselves.

'Did he know?' I asked.

That was another question to which I failed to get a clear answer, because she merely smiled, and even that only slightly. It seemed difficult to persist.

'Don't worry,' she said again. 'I'll look after the bonfire.'

'But don't *you* want to keep the pictures?' I cried. 'Perhaps you've lived with them so long that they've become overfamiliar, but they really are rather remarkable.'

'Surely as executors we have to obey the Will?'

'I am certain you can keep the pictures, as far as the law is concerned.'

'Would *you* like to take them? Bearing in mind,' she added, 'that there's about a hundred more of them stored in Kingston.'

'I simply haven't room, much though I regret it.'

'Nor, in the future, shall I.'

'I'd like to take *one* of them, if I may.'

'As many as you wish. Would you like the manuscripts also? They're all in that suitcase.' It was a battered green object, standing against the wall. I think it was largely her rather unpleasant indifference that made me accept. It was quite apparent what would happen to the manuscripts if I did not take them, and one did not like to think of a man's life disappearing in a few flames, as his body.

'When's the funeral?' I asked.

'Tomorrow, but it will be quite private.'

I wondered where the body *was*. In the matrimonial bedroom? In the small room for guests? In some mortuary?

'We neither of us believed in God.' In my experience of her, it was the first time she had taken the initiative in making such a general pronouncement, negative though it had proved to be.

I looked at the pictures, including the one I had mentally selected for myself. She said nothing more. Of course, the pictures had been painted a number of years earlier: perhaps before the painter had first met her.

She offered me neither a cup of coffee nor a helping hand with the picture and the heavy suitcase down the many flights of stairs in a Battersea block of flats. Driving home, it occurred to me that for the amount of work involved, my executor's legacy was not so inadequate after all.

The picture has travelled round with me ever since. It is now in the room next to the one which used to be the nursery. I often go in and look at it for perhaps five or six minutes when the light is good.

The suitcase contained the tumbled manuscripts of the art books, apparently composed straight on to the machine. They were heavily gashed with corrections in different coloured inks, but this did not matter to me, because it had never been in my mind to read them. All the same, I have never thrown them away. They are in the attic now, still in the green suitcase, with labels stuck on it from Mussolini's Italy. To that small extent, my poor acquaintance lives still. He must presumably have felt that I, more than most, had something in common with him, or he would not have made me his executor.

But the suitcase contained something else: a shorter, more personal narrative, typed out on large sheets of undulating foreign paper, and rolled up within a thick rubber band, now rotten. It is to introduce this narrative, so strange and so intimate, to explain how it came my way and how it comes to be published, that I have written the foregoing. The sheer oddity of life seems to me of more and more importance, because more and more the pretence is that life is charted, predictable, and controllable. And for 'oddity', of course, one could well write 'mystery'.

Under the Will, a publication fee belongs to the widow, who plainly holds the copyright. I give notice that she has but to apply. Remembering that last evening, on the day before the funeral, I am not sure that she will. But we shall see. The rest I leave to the words of my poor acquaintance.

Yesterday I returned from three weeks in Belgium. While there, I had an experience which made a great impression on me. I think it may even have changed my entire way of looking at things; troubled my soul, as people say. Anyway, I feel that I am unlikely ever to forget it. On the other hand, I have learned that what one remembers is always far from what took place. So I am taking this first opportunity of writing down as many of the details as I can remember and as seem important. Only six days have passed since it happened, but I am aware that already there are certain to be gaps bridged by imagination, and unconscious distortions in the interests of consistency and effect. It is possibly unfortunate that I could not make this record while I was still in Brussels, but I found it impossible. I lacked the time, or, more probably, the application, as people always say of me. I also felt that I was under a spell. I felt that something terrible and alarming might happen as I sat by myself in my bedroom writing it all down. The English Channel proves to have loosened this spell considerably, though I can still feel all those textures on my hands and face, still see those queer creatures, and still hear Madame A.'s croaking voice. I find that, when I think about it, I am frightened still, but attracted overwhelmingly also, as at the time. This, I believe, is what is properly meant by the word fascination.

As others may read this, even if only in the distant future, I set forth a few basic facts. I am a painter, and twenty-six years old: the age when Bonnington died. I have about £300 a year of my own, so can paint what interests me; at least I can while I remain on my own. Until now I have been quite happy on my own, though this fact seems to upset almost everyone I know. So far I have had very little to do with women, mainly because I cannot see that I have anything to offer that is likely to appeal to them, and because I detest the competitive aspect of the relations between the sexes. I should hate it for a woman to pity me, and, on the other hand, I should hate to be involved with a woman whom I had to pity; a woman, in fact, who was not attractive enough to be in the full sex war, and who might therefore, be available for such as me. I should not care to be involved with a woman who was anything less than very beautiful. Perhaps that is the artist in me. I do not really know. I feel that I should want only the kind of woman who could not conceivably want me. I cannot say that the whole problem does not trouble me, but, by the standard of what I have read and heard, I am surprised that it does not trouble me more.

I find also that I have no difficulty in writing these things down. On the contrary, I find that I like it. I fancy that I could produce a quite long narrative about my own inner feelings, though this is obviously not the occasion, for I think I have already said all that is necessary. I have to strike a balance between clearing my own mind and imparting facts to strangers. I conceive of this narrative, if I finish it, as being read only by myself and by strangers. I should not care for someone intimately in my life to read it – if there ever is such a person. I doubt whether there ever will be. Sometimes this frightens me, but sometimes it reassures me.

At this point, I remember to mention, for the strangers who may read, that both my parents died seven years ago in an aeroplane accident. It was my mother who insisted on their going to Paris by air. I was present when my father argued with her. It was the usual situation between them. All the same, I loved my mother very much, even though she was as bossy towards me as she was towards my father. No doubt this has affected me too. I fear that a woman would steal my independence – perhaps even kill me. Nor, from what I have seen, do I think these particularly unreal fears.

On the whole, I do not like people. I seem incapable of approaching them, but I find that when they approach me, I am often quite successful with them – more so, indeed, than many of those who have no trouble with bustling in and making the first gesture. When once I am started, I can talk on fluently and even amusingly (though I believe inwardly that I have no sense of humour at all), and frequently, usually indeed, seem to make a strong impression. I suppose I must get some pleasure out of this, but I do not think I ever exert any real influence. It is almost as if someone else were talking through me – wound up by an outsider, my interlocutor. It is not I who talk, and certainly not I who please. I seriously suspect that I myself never speak, and I am certain that if I did, I should never please. This is, of course, another reason why I could not sensibly think of living with anyone.

Similarly with my art. My pictures are visionary and symbolical, and, from first to last, have seemed to be painted by someone other than myself. Indeed, I have the greatest difficulty in painting anything to command. I am useless at portraits, incapable of painting at all in the open air, and quite indifferent to the various kinds of abstract painting that have followed the invention of the camera. Also I am weak on drawing, which, of course, should be a hopeless handicap. I have to be alone in a room in order to paint, though then I can sometimes paint day and night, twenty hours at a stretch.

My father, who was quite sympathetic to my talent, arranged for me to attend a London school of art. It was quite pointless. I could achieve nothing, and was unhappier than at any other period of my life. It was the only time when I felt really lonely – though worse may, of course, lie ahead. I am thus almost entirely self-taught, or taught by that other within me. I am aware that my pictures lack serious technique (if there is a technique that can be distinguished from inspiration and invention). I should have given up painting them some time ago, were it not that a certain number of people have seemed to find something remarkable in them, and have thus identified me with them and made me feel mildly important. If I were to give up, I should have to give up altogether. I could not possibly paint, as so many do, just as a hobby or on Sundays only. I am sure that soon I *shall* give up – or be given up. When I read about the mediumship of Willi and Rudi Schneider, and of how the gift departed first from one brother and then from the other, and when both were quite young, I felt at once that something of the same kind will happen to me, and that I shall settle down, like Willi Schneider, as a hairdresser or other tradesman. Not that I wish to suggest any kind of mediumistic element in my works. It is simply that they contain a glory which is assuredly not in the painter, as the few who know him will confirm. It is a commonplace that there is often more than one soul in a single body.

I must admit also to certain 'influences'. This sounds pretentious, but it has to be said because it explains what

I have been doing in Belgium and how I came to visit Madame A. I find that certain works, or the works of certain painters, affect me strongly, almost agonisingly on occasion, but only *certain* pictures and *certain* painters, really very few. Art in general leaves me rather cold, I regret to say, especially when put on public display to crowds, most of them, inevitably, insensitive. I am sure that pictures should always belong to single individuals. I even believe that pictures suffer death when shared among too many. I also dislike books about art, with their dreadful 'reproductions', repellent when in colour, boring when not. On the other hand, in the painters who *do* affect me, I become almost completely absorbed; in their lives and thoughts, to the extent that I can find out about these things or divine them, as well as in their works. The look of a painter and the look of the places where he painted can, I think, be very important. I have no use for the theory that it is the picture only that matters and the way the paint has been stuck on it. That idea seems to me both lazy and soulless. Perhaps 'my' painters are my true intimates, and them only. I cannot believe I shall ever be so close to any living person as I was to Magnasco when first I sought him out. But there again, I should emphasise that these 'influences' seem to me far from direct. I can see little sign of other people's mannerisms in my own pictures. The influence is far deeper than that. The 'only-the-picture' people would not understand at all.

It has been possible for me to travel a little in search of my particular pictures because at all times I live simply and spend hardly anything. It was to look at pictures that I have been to Belgium: not, needless to say, the Memlings and Rubenses, fine though I daresay they once were, but the works of the symbolists and their kind, painters such as William Degouve de Nuncques, Fernand Khnopff, Xavier Mellery, who said (and who else has ever said it?) that he painted 'silence' and the 'soul of things'; above all, of course, James Ensor, the charming Baron. I had worked for months before I left, to equip myself with a list of addresses, many of the finest paintings of the school being happily still in private hands. Almost everyone was kind to me, though I can speak very little French, and for the first fortnight I was totally lost and absolutely happy. Not all the owners gave signs of appreciating their various properties, but, naturally, I did not expect that. At least they were prepared, most of them, to leave me alone and in peace, which was something I had seldom found among the private owners who survive in Italy. Of them many seemed to think they might sell me something; most made a great noise; and all refused me privacy.

One of the Belgian authorities with whom I exchanged letters, told me that the widow of a certain painter of the symbolist school still survived in Brussels. Not even to myself, in the light of what has happened, do I wish to write the name of this painter. I shall simply call him A., the late A. The informed may succeed in identifying him. Even if they do, it will not matter so much by the time they are likely to read this report. If strangers read sooner than I expect, it will only be because I am dead, so that the burden of discretion will be upon them and not upon me.

The Belgian authority, without comment, gave me an address in Brussels to which I wrote from England in my basic French, not seriously expecting any kind of reply. My habitual concern with the lives and personalities of 'my' painters may, however, have made me write more urgently and persuasively than I supposed. It seemed a considerable opportunity for me. Despite my great interest, I had never met one of my particular painters nor even a widow or relative. Many of the painters, in any case, had lived too long ago for such a thing. If now I received no reply, I was quite prepared to stand about outside the house, and consider in the light of what I observed, how best to get in. That proved unnecessary. Within three days, I heard from Madame A.

She wrote in a loose, curving hand, and confined herself to the centre of a large sheet of dark blue paper. Her letter looked like the springs bursting out of a watch in a nineteenth-century comic drawing. It would have been difficult to read even if it had been in English, but in the end I deciphered most of it. Madame A. said she was extremely old, had not left the house for years or received any visitors, but was enchanted that anyone should go out of his way to see her, and would receive me at six o'clock on an evening she named with exactitude. I had given her the dates of my proposed stay in Belgium, but none the less was surprised by her decisiveness, because it was without precedent. People with pictures had always left to me the time of a visit, and an embarrassing responsibility I had often found it. Madame A. ended by asking how old *I* was?

When the time came, I spent the afternoon at the Musée Wiertz, because it seemed to be in much the same part of the city as the abode of Madame A. 'Weitz's work is noted rather for the sensational character of his subjects than for artistic merit', states, in true Beckmesser fashion, the English guidebook I had borrowed from my public library. Possibly it is true in a way. It was not true for me. I was enthralled by Wiertz's living burials and imminent decapitations; by his livid gory vision of that 'real' world which surely is livid and gory, though boring and monotonous also, which Weirtz omits. Weirtz's way of painting reality seems to me most apt to the character of reality. I was delighted also by the silence and emptiness of Wiertz's enormous, exciting studio. His official lack of merit keeps out the conducted art-lover.

All the same, anxiety was rising in me about my commitment with Madame A. I had remained fairly confident through most of my visits to picture owners, even in Italy, but these had been accepted as business transactions, and I had had no difficulty in concealing that for me they were stations on a spiritual ascent. With Madame A. I might have to disclose much more of myself and find words, even French words, for comments that were not purely conventional. She might be very infirm and intractable. It was probable that she was. It is September, and I sat on a bench before *The Fight for the Body of Patroclus*, all alone in the high studio, except for the attendant, who was mumbling to himself round the corner, while evening fell and the many clocks chimed and boomed me forward to my ambiguous assignation.

The power of solitude, not least in the Musée Wiertz, delayed me, in fact, too long. I found that I had underestimated the distance from the Rue Wiertz to the street in the direction of the Boulevard de Waterloo where Madame A. lived. They are beautiful streets through which I walked, though unostentatious; quiet, well-proportioned, and warmly alive with the feel of history. I have seen no other part of Brussels that I like so much. I loved the big opening windows, filling so much of every façade and so unlike England. I even thought that this would be a perfect district in which to spend my life. One never really doubts that one will feel always what one feels at any given moment, good or bad; or, when the moment is good, at least that one *could* always feel it if one might only preserve the attendant framework and circumstances. The activity of walking through these unobtrusively beautiful streets quietened me. Also I commonly notice that for the *very* last stretch, I cease to be anxious.

Madame A. lived in just another such house: only two storeys high, white and elegant, with rococo twirls in the fanlight above the handsome front door, a properly sized front door for a house wide enough for a crinoline, tall enough for an admiral, not a mere vertical slit for little men to steal through on the way to work. The houses to left and right repeated the pattern with subtle minor variations. I am glad to have been born soon enough to see such houses before either demolition or preservation: so far all was well.

There was a light in an upper window. It was of the colour known as old gold.

There was a bell and I heard it ring. I expected some kind of retainer or relative, since I visualised Madame A. as almost bed-ridden. But the door opened, and it was obvious that this was Madame A. herself. She looked very short and very square, almost gnomelike in shape; but the outline of her was all I could see because it was now almost dark, the street lighting was dim (thank goodness), and there was no light at all in the hall.

'*Entrez,*' said Madame A. in her distinctive croak. '*Entrez, monsieur. Fermez la porte, s'il vous plaît.*' Though she croaked, she croaked as one accustomed, if she spoke at all, to speak only in terms of command. Nothing less, I felt at once, interested her in the context of human discourse.

Up from the hall led a straight, uncarpeted staircase, much wider than in an English house of that size, and with a heavy wooden baluster, just visible by a light from the landing above.

'*Suivez, monsieur.*'

Madame A. went clambering upwards. It is the only word. She was perfectly agile, but curiously uncouth in her movements. In the dim light, she went up those stairs almost like an old man of the woods, but I believe that age not infrequently has this effect on the gait of all but the tallest. I should say that Madame A.'s height was rather under than over five feet.

The light on the landing proved to hang by a thick golden chain in an art nouveau lantern of lumpy old gold glass speckled with irregular dabs of crimson. I followed Madame A. into a room which traversed the whole depth of the house, with one window on to the street and, opposite it, another at the back of the building. The door of the room was already open. Standing ahead of me in the big doorway, Madam A. looked squatter than ever.

The room was lighted by lanterns similar to that on the landing. They were larger than the lantern outside but the old gold effulgence of the room remained distinctly dim, and the crimson dabs cast irregular red splashes on the shiny, golden wallpaper. The furnishings were art nouveau also. Everything, even the common objects of use, tended to stop and start at unexpected places; to spring upwards in ecstasy, to sag in melancholia, or simply to overhang and break away. One felt that every object was in tension. The colours of the room coalesced into strikingly individual harmony. Almost as soon as I entered, it struck me that the general colouration had something in common with that of my own works. It was most curious. The golden walls bore many pictures, mostly in golden frames: mainly, I could see, the work of the late A., as was to be expected, and about which I must not further particularise; but also some esoteric drawings manifestly by Felicien Rops, and stranger than his strangest, I thought as I sat amongst them. In the substantial, art nouveau fireplace blazed a fire, making the room considerably too hot, as so often on the Continent. None the less, I again shut the door. As I did so, I saw that behind it was a life-size marble figure of a woman in the moment of maternity. I identified it at once as the work of a symbolist sculptor well known for figures of this type, but, again, I had better not name him because about this particular figure was something very odd – odd even to me who knows about childbirth only from works of art, not least the works of this particular man.

'*Mais oui,*' said Madame A., as I could not withdraw my gaze from the figure. '*C'est la naissance d'un succube.*'

But at this point I think I had better stop trying to remember what was said in French by Madame A. In the first place, I cannot succeed in doing so, though her very first words, those that I have set down, remain clearly with me. In the second place, Madame A. soon disclosed that she could speak English perfectly well – or rather, perhaps, and as I oddly felt, as well as she could speak French. There was something about her which suggested, even to an unsophisticate like me, that she was no more a native of Belgium or France than she was of Britain. I am trying to set down events and my feelings exactly as they were, or as nearly as possible, and I am not going to pretend that I did not sense something queer about Madame A. from the very start, because there is nothing in the whole story of which I am more certain than of that.

And now there she was, standing dumpily before the big, bright fire with her long bare arms extended, almost as if to embrace me.

Yes, despite the impending autumn, despite the blazing fire, her arms were bare; and not only her arms. Her hairy legs were bare also, and her dull red dress was cut startlingly low for a woman of her years, making her creased bosom all too visible. My absurd impression was that this plain red scrap of a garment was all she was wearing, apart from the golden slippers on her small, square feet.

And yet old she certainly was; very old, as she had said in her letter. Her face was deeply grooved and grained. Her neck had lost all shape. Her stance was hunched and bowed under the weight of time. Her voice, though masterful, was senile. I imagined that her black hair, somewhat scant, but wiry and upstanding, could only be dyed. Her head was like an old, brown egg.

She made me sit and sweat before the fire, constantly urging me nearer to it, and plied me with cognac and water. She herself remained on her feet, though, even so, her corrugated brown cheekbones and oddly vague black eyes were almost on a level with mine. The chair in which she had put me had wings at the level of the sitter's head, thus making me even hotter, and, every now and then, as she spoke, she leant forward, put a hand on each of these wings, and, for emphasis or to indicate a confidence, spoke right at my face, coming almost near enough to kiss me. She appeared to drink very little herself, but she made me drink far more than I wanted, praising the quality of the brandy and also (little did she know, I thought) the power and strength of my youth.

Her very first question when we had settled ourselves was: how old had I said I was? And, she continued, born in Scorpio? Yes, I replied, impressed but not astonished, because many people have this particular divination, even though the materialists say otherwise. And how do you interpret that? I went on; because different people emphasise different aspects. Secrecy and sensuality, she croaked back. Only the first, I smiled. Then I must direct myself to awakening the second, she replied rather horribly.

And yet, I thought, how hard I am, how unsympathetic, after all; and, at the same time, how weak.

She did soon begin to talk about art, and the painters she had known long, long before. Perhaps she thought that this was the topic which would awaken me. She tended to lose the way in her long, ancient chronicles, and to fill or overfill my glass while she recovered direction.

It was noticeable that she seemed neither to admire nor to have liked any of the men she spoke of, many of whom were and are objects of my particular regard. At least I hope they still are: an object of admiration is impaired by hostile criticism of any kind, however ill judged, and there is nothing the admirer can do to mend the wound, even though his full reason may tell him that the critic has no case. Madam A.'s comments were hardly reasoned at all and thus all the more upsetting. They were jeers and insinuations and flat rejections.

'X.,' she would say, 'was an absurd man, always very dapper and with a voice like a goat.' 'Y!' she exclaimed.

'I had a very close friendship with Y. – as long as I could stand him.' 'Z.'s pictures were supposed to be philosophical but really they're not even successfully pornographic.' All the time she implied that my own enthusiastic assessments were grotesquely immature, and, when I argued back, sometimes with success, because she was not much of a hand with logic and not too accurate with her facts either, she flattened me with personal reminiscences of the comic or shady circumstances in which particular works had come to be painted, or with anecdotes which, as she claimed, showed the painter in his true colours.

'J.,' she asserted, 'was madly in love with me for years, but I wouldn't have used him as a pocket handkerchief when I had the grippe, and nor would any other woman.' Madame A. had a fine turn of phrase, but as I knew (though we did not mention) that J., painter of the most exquisite oriental fantasies, had hanged himself in poverty and despair, her line of talk depressed and disconcerted me very much. I felt that in too many cases, even though, I was sure, not in all, her harsh comments were true, even though doubtless not the whole truth. I felt that, true or not by my standards, so many people (among the few interested at all) would agree with these comments as thereby to give them a kind of truth by majority vote. I felt, most sadly of all, that what I have called harshness in Madame A. was simply a blast of life's essential quality as it drags us all over the stones; artists – these selected divinities of mine among them – included.

As so often, it would have been better not to know.

'K.!' croaked Madame A. 'K. worked for three years as a police spy and it was the happiest period of his life. He told me so himself. He was drunk at the time – or perhaps drugged – but it was the truth. And you can see it in his pictures if you only look. They are the pictures of a self-abuser. Do you know why K.'s wife left him? It was because he was impotent with a real woman, and always had been. He knew it perfectly well when he married her. He did it because she had inherited a little money and he was on cocaine already and the good God knows what else. When I read about K.'s pictures being bought for the Musée Royal des Beaux-Arts, I laugh. I laugh and I spit.' And Madame A. did both. She had a habit of snatching at the neckline of her red dress as she spoke, and dragging it yet further down. It seemed by now to have become an unconscious reflex with her, or tic.

'L.,' she said, 'started as a painter of enormous landscapes. That was what he really liked to paint. He liked to spend days and weeks entirely by himself in Norway or Scotland just painting exactly what lay before him, bigger all the time. The trouble was that no one would buy such pictures. They were competent enough but dull, dull. When you saw them lined up against the walls of his studio, you could do nothing but yawn. And that's the way people saw them when he hoped they might buy them. You couldn't imagine anyone ever buying one. You wanted only to get out of the studio and forget about such dull pictures. All those pictures of

L. that you talk about, the "Salomés" and "Whores of Babylon", weren't what he liked at all. He turned to them because two things happened at once: L.'s money ran out and at about the same time he met Maeterlinck. He met Maeterlinck only once, but it did something to him. Maeterlinck seemed fashionable and successful, and L. couldn't see why he shouldn't be too. But it really wasn't in the little man, and before long he gave it all up and became a fonctionnaire, as you know, though it was a bit late in the day for that.'

'No, madame, I didn't know.'

'Why, he's alive still! He's got the jumps, some kind of disease that gives you the jumps. The "Whore of Babylon" might have given it to him, but he never got near enough to her to make it possible. L.'s alive all right – just. I used to go and see him when I still went out. He liked to borrow my old art papers. I've got hundreds of them, all from before the war. Ah, *les sales Boches*,' added Madame A. irrelevantly, but as many people do in Belgium and France from force of habit.

Despite everything, I suppose my eyes must have lighted up at the mention of the pre-war art journals. In such publications is often information not to be found anywhere else and information of just the sort that I found most valuable and absorbing.

'Ah,' croaked Madame A. almost jubilantly. That's better. You are getting accustomed to me, *hein*?' She grasped my hands.

By now, she was flowing on in English. It was a relief. At one moment, she had spoken several sentences in a language I could not even identify. She had doubtless forgotten about me, or was confusing me with someone else.

'But you look hot,' cried Madame A., releasing me. 'Why do you not remove your jacket?'

'Perhaps,' I replied, 'I could walk round the room and look at the pictures.'

'But certainly. If you wish.' She spoke as if it were a remarkably ridiculous wish, and perhaps discourteous also.

I struggled away from her, and proceeded from picture to picture. She said nothing while I promenaded, but remained standing with her back to the fire, and her short legs well apart; gnomic in more than one sense. I cannot say that her eyes followed me with ironical glances, because her eyes were too vague for such a thing. The light in the room, though picturesque was quite unsuited to the inspection of pictures. I could see hardly anything. At the end of the room away from the street and away from the fire, it was almost dark. It was absurd for me to persist, though I was exceedingly disappointed.

'It is a pity my adopted daughter is not here,' said Madame A. from the brightness. 'She could entertain you better than I can. You would prefer her to me.'

She spoke in a tone of dreadful coyness. I could think of no convincing reply. 'Where is your adopted daughter?' I asked lamely and tamely.

'Away. Abroad. With some creature, of course. Who knows where?' She cackled. 'Who knows with whom?'

'I am sorry to have missed her,' I said, not very convincingly, I am sure. I was indignant that I had not been invited for some hour when I could see the pictures by daylight.

'Come back over here, monsieur,' cried Madame A., pointing with her right forefinger to my hot armchair and then slapping her knee with the palm of her hand, all as if she were summoning a small, unruly dog. It was *exactly* like that, I thought. I have often seen it, though I have never owned a dog myself. I forbore from comment and returned reluctantly to the hot fire. Madame A., as I have said, was commanding as well as coy.

And then an extraordinary thing happened. A real dog was there in the room. At least, I suppose I am now not sure how real it was. Let me just say a dog. It was like a small black poodle, clipped, glossy, and spry. It appeared from the shadowy corner to the right of the door as one entered. It pattered perkily up to the fire, then round several times in a circle in front of Madame A., and to my right as I sat, then off into the shadow to my left and where I had just been standing. It seemed to me, as I looked at it, to have very big eyes and very long legs, perhaps more like a spider than a poodle, but no doubt this was merely an effect of the firelight.

At that moment there was much to take in fairly quickly, but one thing was that Madame A., as I clearly realised, seemed not to see the dog. She was staring ahead, her black eyes expressionless as ever. Even while I was watching the dog, I divined that she was still thinking of her adopted daughter, and was entranced by her thoughts. It did not seem particularly remarkable that she had missed the dog, because the dog had been quite silent, and she might well have been so accustomed to seeing it around the house that often she no longer noticed it. What puzzled me at that stage was where the dog had hidden itself all the time I had been in the room with the door shut.

'Nice poodle,' I said to Madame A., because I had to break the silence, and because Englishmen are supposed to be fond of dogs (though I am, comparatively, an exception).

'*Comment, monsieur?*' I can see and hear her still, exactly as she looked and spoke.

'Nicely kept poodle,' I said, firmly sticking to English.

She turned and stared at me, but came no nearer, as at such moments she usually did.

'So you have seen a poodle?'

'Yes,' I said, and still not thinking there was anything *really* wrong, 'this moment. If it's not yours, it must have got in from the darkness outside.' The darkness was still on my mind, because of the pictures, but immediately I spoke, I felt a chill, despite the blazing fire. I wanted to get up and look for the dog, which, after all, must still have been in the room; but at the same time I feared to do any such thing. I feared to move at all.

'Animals often appear in here,' said Madame A. huskily. 'Dogs, cats, toads, monkeys. And occasionally less commonplace species. I expect it will have gone by now.'

I think I only stared back at her.

'Sometimes my husband painted them.' It was the

only reference she had made to her husband, and it was one which I found difficult to follow up. She dragged down the front of her dress in her compulsive way.

'I will talk to you,' said Madame A., 'about Chrysothème, my adopted daughter. Do you know that Chrysothème is the most beautiful girl in Europe? Not like me. Oh, not at all.'

'What a pity I cannot have the pleasure of meeting her!' I said, again trying to enter into the spirit of it, but wondering how I could escape, especially in view of what had just happened. On the instant, and for the second time, I regretted what I had said.

But Madame A. merely croaked dreamily, staring straight ahead. 'She appears here. She stays quite often. For a quite long time, you understand. She cannot be expected to remain longer. After all, I am far from being her mother.'

I nodded, though it was obscure to what I was assenting.

'Chrysothème!' cried Madame A. rapturously clasping her hands. 'My Chrysothème!' She paused, her face illumined, though not her eyes. Then she turned back to me. 'If you could see her naked, monsieur, you would understand everything.'

I giggled uneasily, as one does.

'I repeat, monsieur, that you would understand everything.'

It dawned on me that in some way she meant more than one would at first have thought.

One trouble was that I most certainly did not *want* to

understand everything. I had once even told a fortune teller as much; a big-nosed but beautiful woman in a tent when I was a schoolboy.

'Would you like to see her clothes?' said Madame A., quite softly. 'She keeps some of them here, to wear when she comes to stay.'

'Yes,' I said. 'I should.' I cannot fully analyse why I said it, but I said it. Madame A. being what she was, I could claim that I was given very little voice in the matter. Perhaps I wasn't. But that time it didn't arise. I undoubtedly chose.

Madame A. took me lightly by the wrist and drew me out of the chair. I opened the big door for her, and then another big door which she indicated. There were two on the opposite side of the landing, and she pointed to the one on the right.

'I myself sleep in the next room,' said Madame A. on the threshold, making the very wall sound like an invitation. 'When I can sleep at all.'

The room within was darkly panelled, almost to the ceiling. The corner on the left behind the door was filled by a panelled bed, with a coverlet of dark red brocade. It seemed to fill more space than a single bed, but not as much space as a double bed. From the foot of it, the plain, dark panelling of the wall continued undecorated to the end of the room. In the centre of the far wall stood a red brocaded dressing table, looking very much like an altar, especially as no chair stood before it. On the right was a window, now covered by dark red curtains, of the heavy kind which my mother used to say collected the dust. Against the wall on each side of this window stood a big dark chest. There were several of the usual art nouveau lanterns hanging high on the walls, but the glass in them was so heavily obscured that the room seemed scarcely brighter than the dim landing outside. The only picture hung over the head of the bed in the corner behind the door.

'What a beautiful room!' I exclaimed politely.

But I was looking over my shoulder to see if the black dog had emerged through the open door on the other side of the landing.

'That is because many people have died in it,' said Madame A. 'The two beautiful things are love and death.'

I went right into the room.

'Shut the door,' said Madame A.

I shut it. There was still no sign of the dog. I tried to postpone further thought on the subject.

'Most of her clothes are in here,' said Madame A. She pulled at the panelling by the foot of the bed, and two doors opened; then another pair; then a third. All that part of the bedroom panelling fronted deep cupboards.

'Come and look,' said Madame A.

Feeling foolish, I went over to her. All three cupboards were filled with dresses, hanging from a central rail, as in a shop. If they had been antiquarian rags or expectant shrouds, I should hardly have been surprised, but they were quite normal women's clothes of today; as far as I could tell, of very high quality. There were garments for all purposes: winter dresses, summer dresses, and a great number of those long evening dresses which one sees less and less frequently. All the dresses appeared to be carefully looked after, as if they were waiting to be sold. It struck me that in that direction might lie the truth: that the dresses might never have been worn. Certainly the room looked extremely unoccupied. Apart from the dresses, it looked more like a chapel than a bedroom. More like a mortuary chapel, it suddenly struck me; with a sequence of corpses at rest and beflowered on the bier-like bed behind the door, as Madame A. had so depressingly hinted.

'Touch the clothes,' said Madame A., reading my mind. 'Take them out and see the marks of Chrysothème's body.'

I hesitated. Unless one is a tailor, one instinctively dislikes the touch of other people's clothes, whoever they may be; and of unknown strangers' clothes not least.

'Take them out,' repeated Madame A. in her commanding way.

I gingerly detached a random dress on its hanger. It was a workaday, woollen garment. Even in the poor light, the signs of wear were evident.

That point made silently between us, Madame A. showed impatience with my timid choice. She herself drew out an evening gown in pale satin.

'Marvellous, exquisite, incomparable,' she exclaimed stridently. I think that if she had been tall enough, she would have held the dress against her own body, as the saleswomen so curiously do in shops; but, as it was, she could only hold it out at the end of her long arms, so that most of it flowed across the dark red carpet like a train. 'Kneel down and examine it.' I hesitated. 'Kneel,' cried Madame A. more peremptorily.

I knelt and picked up the bottom hem of the dress. Now I was down on the floor, I noticed a big dark patch which the dark carpet was not dark enough to hide.

'Lift the dress to your face,' ordered Madame A. I did so. It was a wonderful sensation. I felt myself enveloped in a complex silky nebula. The owner, the wearer of that elegant garment, began, even though entirely without definition, to be much more present to me than Madame A.

Madame A. dropped the dress and on the instant was holding out another in the same way. It also was a long dress. It was made of what I believe is called georgette, and was in some kind of mottled orange and red.

The pale satin dress lay on the floor between us.

'Kneel on it. Tread on it,' directed Madame A., seeing me about to circumvent it. 'Chrysothème would approve.'

I was unable to do such a thing, and crawled round the edges of the satin dress to the georgette dress. Immediately I reached the georgette dress, Madame A. threw it adroitly over my head, so that I had a ridiculous minute or two extricating myself. I could not but notice, and more than just notice, that the georgette retained a most enchanting scent. Her scent made the wearer of the dress more real to me than ever.

Away to my left, Madame A. now extended a third

long dress; this time in dark blue taffeta, very slender and skimpy.

'You could almost wear it yourself,' cackled Madame A. 'You like wearing blue and you are thin enough.' I had, of course, not told her that I liked wearing blue, but I suppose it was obvious.

Madame A. twisted round a chair with her foot and laid the dress on it, with the low top hanging abandonedly over the back of it.

'Why don't you kiss it?' asked Madame A., jeering slightly.

Kneeling at the foot of the chair, I realised that my lips were only slightly above the edge of the seat. To refuse would be more foolish than to comply. I lowered my face and pressed my lips against the dress. Madame A. might be ridiculing me, but I felt now that my true concern was with that other who wore the dresses.

When I looked up, Madame A. was actually standing on another chair (there were only two in the room, both originally in the corners, both heavy, dark, and elaborate). She was holding up a short dress in black velvet. She said nothing, and I admit that, without bidding, I darted towards her and pressed the wonderful fabric against my face.

'The moon,' gurgled Madame A., pointing to the pale satin dress on the floor. 'And the night.' She flapped the black velvet up and down and from side to side. It too smelt adorably. I clutched at it to keep it still and found that it was quite limp, inert in my grasp.

Madame A. had leapt off the chair with one flop, like a leprechaun.

'Do you like my adopted daughter's clothes?'

'They are beautiful.'

'Chrysothème has perfect taste.' Madame A.'s tone was entirely conventional. I was still sniffing the velvet dress. 'You must see the lingerie,' Madame A. added, merely as if to confirm the claim she had just made.

She crossed to the chest at the left of the curtained window and lifted the unlocked lid. 'Come,' said Madame A.

The big chest was full of soft underclothes in various colours; not ordered like the dresses, but tangled and clinging apparently at random.

I suppose I just stood and stared. And the same scent was rising hypnotically from the chest.

'Take off your blue jacket,' said Madame A., almost with solemnity. 'Roll up your blue sleeves, and plunge in your white arms.'

Without question, I did what she said.

'Sink your face in them.'

I hardly needed to be instructed. The scent was intoxicating in itself.

'Love them, tear them, possess them,' admonished Madame A.

All of which I daresay I did to the best of my ability. Certainly time passed.

I began to shiver. After all, I had left a very over-heated room.

I found that all my muscles were stiff with kneeling;

and I supposed with concentration too. I could hardly rise to my feet in order to rescue my jacket. As I rolled down my shirt-sleeves, I became aware that the hairs on my forearms really were standing on end. They seemed quite barbed and sharp.

'Blue boy!' exclaimed Madame A., waiting for me to make the next move.

I made it. I shut the lid of the chest.

'The other chest contains souvenirs,' said Madame A., dragging at the neckline of her dress.

I shook my head. I was still shaking all over, and could no longer smell that wonderful scent. When one is very cold, the sense of smell departs.

And at that moment, for the first time, I really apprehended the one picture, which hung above the wide bed in the corner. Despite the bad light, it seemed familiar. I went over to it, and putting one knee on the bed, leant towards it. Now I was certain. The picture was by me.

But there were two especially strange things. Though I was quite certain that the picture could only be mine (my talent may be circumscribed, but it is distinctive), I could not remember ever having painted it, and there were things about it which could at no time have been put there by me. Artists, in their later years, do sometimes forget their own works, but I was, and am, sure that this could never happen in my case. My pictures are not of a kind to be forgotten by the painter. Much worse was the fact that, for example, the central figure which I might have painted as an angel, had somehow become more like a clown. It was hard to say why this was, but, as I looked at it, I felt it irresistibly.

My attack of shivering was turning to nausea, as one often finds. I felt that I was in danger of making a final fool of myself by being actually sick on the floor.

'Quite right,' said Madame A., regarding the picture with her vague eyes, and speaking as she had spoken in the other room. 'Not a painter at all. Would have done better as a sweeper out of cabinets, wouldn't you agree, or as fetcher and carrier in a horse-meat market? It is kept in here because Chrysothème has no time for pictures, no time at all.'

It would have been absurd and undignified to argue. Nor could I be sure that she was clear in her mind as to who I was.

'Thank you, madame,' I said, 'for receiving me. I must detain you no longer.'

'A souvenir,' she cried. 'At least leave me a souvenir.'

I saw that she held a quite large pair of silvery scissors.

I did not feel at all like leaving even a lock of my hair in Madame A.'s keeping.

I opened the bedroom door, and began to retreat. I was trying to think of a phrase or two that would cover my precipitancy with a glaze of convention, but then I saw that, squatted on the single golden light that hung by a golden chain from the golden ceiling of the landing, was a tiny fluffy animal; so very small that it might almost have been a dark furry insect with unusually distinct pale eyes. Moreover, the door into the big, hot room on my left was, of course, still open. I was overcome. I merely took to my heels; clattering idiotically down the bare, slippery staircase. I was lucky not to slide headlong.

'*Mais, monsieur!*'

I was struggling in the dark with the many handles, chains, and catches of the front door. It seemed likely that I should be unable to open it.

'*Mais, monsieur!*' Madame A. was lumbering down after me. But suddenly the door was open. Now that I could be sure I was not trapped, a small concession to good manners was possible.

'Goodnight, madame,' I said in English. 'And thank you again.'

She made a vague snatch in my direction with the big, silvery scissors. They positively flashed in the light from the street lamp outside. She was like a squat granny seeing off a child with a gesture of mock aggression. 'Begone,' she might have said; or, alternatively, 'Come back at once': but I did not wait to hear Madame A. say anything more. Soon I found that I was walking down the populous Chausée d'Ixelles, still vibrating, and every now and then looking over one shoulder or the other.

Within twenty-four hours I perceived clearly enough that there could have been no dog, no little animal squatted on the lantern, no picture over the bed, and probably no adopted daughter. That hardly needed saying. The trouble was, and is, that this obvious truth only makes things worse. Indeed, it is precisely where the real trouble begins. What is to become of me? What will happen to me next? What can I do? What am I?

Bind Your Hair

No one seemed able to fathom Clarinda Hartley. She had a small but fastidious flat near Church Street, Kensington; and a responsible job in a large noncommittal commercial organisation. No one who knew her now had ever known her in any other residence or any other job. She entertained a little, never more nor less over the years; went out not infrequently with men; and for her holidays simply disappeared, returning with brief references to foreign parts. No one seemed to know her really well; and in the course of time there came to be wide differences of opinion about her age, and recurrent speculation about her emotional life. The latter topic was not made less urgent by a certain distinction in her appearance, and also in her manner. She was very tall (a great handicap, of course, in the opinion of many) and well-shaped; she had very fair, very fine, very abundant hair, to which plainly she gave much attention; her face had interesting planes (for those who could appreciate them), but also soft curves, which went with her hair. She had a memorable voice: high-pitched, but gentle. She was, in fact, thirty-two. Everyone was greatly surprised when she announced her engagement to Dudley Carstairs.

Or rather it was Carstairs who announced it. He

could not keep it to himself as long as there was anyone within earshot who was ignorant of it; and well might he be elated, because his capture followed a campaign of several years' continuance, and supported by few sweeping advantages. He worked in the same office as Clarinda, and in a not unsatisfactory position for his thirty years; and was in every way a thoroughly presentable person: but even in the office there were a number of others like him, and it would have seemed possible that Clarinda could have further extended her range of choice by going outside.

The weekend after the engagement Dudley arranged for her to spend with him and his parents in Northamptonshire. Mr Carstairs, Senior, had held an important position on the administrative side of the Northampton boot and shoe industry; and when he retired upon a fair pension had settled in a small but comfortable house in one of the remote parts of a county where the remote parts are surprisingly many and extensive. Mr Carstairs had been a pioneer in this particular, because others similarly placed had tended upon retirement to emigrate to the Sussex coast or the New Forest; but his initiative, as often happens in such cases, had been imitated, until the little village in which he had settled was now largely populated by retired industrial executives and portions of their families.

Clarinda would have been grateful for more time in which to adjust herself to Dudley in the capacity of accepted lover; but Dudley somehow did not seem to see himself in that capacity, and to be reluctant in any way to defer Clarinda's full involvement with her new family position. Clarinda, having said yes to what was believed to be the major question, smiled slightly and said yes to the minor.

Mr Carstairs, Senior, met them at Roade station.

'Hullo, Dad.' The two men gazed at one another's shoes, not wanting to embrace and hesitating to shake hands. Mr Carstairs was smiling, benignly expectant. Plainly he was one who considered that life had treated him well. Almost, one believed, he was ready to accept his son's choice of a bride as, for him, joy's crown of joy.

'Dad. This is Clarinda.'

'I *say*, my boy . . .'

Outside the station was a grey Standard, in which Mr Carstairs drove them many miles to the west. Already the sun was sinking. Soon after they arrived they had settled down, with Mrs Carstairs and Dudley's sister Elizabeth, to crumpets in the long winter dusk. Elizabeth had a secretarial position in Leamington, and bicycled there and back every day. All of them were charmed with Clarinda. She exceeded their highest, and perhaps not very confident, hopes.

Clarinda responded to their happy approval of her, and smiled at Dudley's extreme pleasure at being home. An iced cake had been baked for her specially, and she wondered whether these particular gilt-edged cups were in daily use. They neither asked her questions nor talked mainly about themselves: they all made a warm-hearted, not unskilful effort to make her feel completely one with them from the outset. She and Elizabeth discovered a common interest in the theatre (shared only in a lesser degree by Dudley).

'But Leamington's so stuffy that no one's ever made a theatre pay there.'

'Not since the war,' said Mr Carstairs in affectionate qualification.

'Not since the *first* war,' said Elizabeth.

'Is Leamington the nearest town?' asked Clarinda.

'It's the nearest as the crow flies, or as Elizabeth cycles,' said Dudley, 'but it's not the quickest when you're coming from London. Narrow lanes all the way.'

'Fortunately we've got our own friends by now in the village,' said Mrs Carstairs. 'I've asked some of them in for drinks, so that you can meet them at once.'

And indeed, almost immediately the bell rang, and the first of the visitors was upon them. Mr Carstairs went round the room putting on lights and drawing the curtains. Every now and then he gave some jocular direction to Dudley, who was complementarily engaged. A domestic servant of some kind, referred to by Mrs Carstairs as 'our local woman', had removed the remains of tea; and by the time Elizabeth had borne in a tray of drinks, three more visitors had added themselves to the first two.

'Can I help?' Clarinda had said.

'No,' the Carstairs family had replied. 'Certainly not. Not *yet*.'

Altogether there were eleven visitors, only two of whom were under forty. All eleven of them Clarinda liked very much less than she liked the Carstairs family.

Then just as several of them were showing signs of departure, a twelfth arrived; who made a considerable change. A woman of medium height and in early middle age, she had a lined and sallow face, but an alert expression and large, deeply set black eyes. She had untidy, shoulder-length black hair which tended to separate itself into distinct compact strands. Her only make-up appeared to be an exceptionally vivid lipstick, abundantly applied to her large square mouth. She entered in a luxuriant fur coat, but at once cast it off, so that it lay on the floor, and appeared in a black corduroy skirt and a black silk blouse, cut low, and with long tight sleeves. On her feet were heel-less golden slippers.

'I've been so *busy*.' She seized both of Mrs Carstairs's hands. Her voice was very deep and melodious, but marred by a certain hoarseness, or uncertainty of timbre. 'Where is she?'

Mrs Carstairs was smiling amiably as ever; but all conversation in the room had stopped.

'Do go on talking.' The newcomer addressed the party at random. She had now observed Clarinda. 'Introduce me,' she said to Mrs Carstairs, as if her hostess were being a little slow with her duties. 'Or am I too late?' Her sudden quick smile was possibly artificial but certainly bewitching. For a second, various men in the room missed the thread of their resumed conversations.

'Of course you're not too late,' said Mrs Carstairs. Then she made the introduction. 'Clarinda Hartley. Mrs Pagani.'

'Nothing whatever to do with the restaurant,' said Mrs Pagani.

'How do you do?' said Clarinda.

Mrs Pagani had a firm and even but somewhat bony handshake. She was wearing several large rings, with heavy stones in them, and round her neck a big fat locket on a thick golden chain.

By now Mrs Carstairs had brought Mrs Pagani a drink. 'Here's to the future,' said Mrs Pagani, looking into Clarinda's eyes, and as soon as Mrs Carstairs had turned away, drained the glass.

'Thank you,' said Clarinda.

'Do sit down,' said Mrs Pagani, as if the house were hers.

'Thank you,' said Clarinda, falling in with the illusion.

Mrs Pagani stretched out an arm (Clarinda noticed that her arms, in their tight black sleeves, were uncommonly long) and pulled up a chair, upon which she sat. Clarinda noticed also that when she was seated, her hips too looked bony and obtrusive. Altogether Mrs Pagani gave an impression of unusual physical power, only partly concealed by her conventional clothes. It was as if suddenly she might arise and tear down the house.

'You cannot imagine,' said Mrs Pagani, 'how much it means to me to have someone new in the village, especially someone more or less my own age. Or perhaps you can?'

'But I'm not going to *live* here,' said Clarinda, clutching hold of the main point.

'Well, of course not. But there'll be frequent week-ends. Whatever else may be said for or against Dudley, he's devoted to his home.'

Clarinda nodded thoughtfully. She was aware that everyone's eyes were upon them, and realised that Mrs Pagani had so far acknowledged the presence of none of the other guests, well though she must presumably know them.

'Who would want to know any of these people?' enquired Mrs Pagani in a husky, telepathic undertone.

One trouble was that Clarinda rather agreed with her.

'Why do *you* live here?'

'I can't live in towns. And in the country people are the same wherever you go. Most people, I mean. You don't live in the country for the local society.'

Clarinda failed to ask why you did live in the country.

Elizabeth came up with more drinks.

'Hullo, Elizabeth,' said Mrs Pagani.

For some reason Elizabeth went very red.

'Hullo, Mrs Pagani.' She left two drinks with them, and hurried away on her errand of hospitality. Mrs Pagani's eyes followed her for a few seconds. Then she turned back to Clarinda, and said: 'We two will be seeing a lot of one another.'

Again Clarinda could only nod.

'I needn't tell you that you're not what I expected. Do you know where I live?'

Clarinda, still silent, shook her head.

'Have you been round the village yet?'

'No.'

'Not seen the church?'

'It was getting dark when I arrived.'

'I live in the churchyard.' Mrs Pagani suddenly shouted with laughter. 'It always surprises people.' She placed her long bony left hand on Clarinda's knee. 'There used to be a chapel in the churchyard, with a room over it. This is a thinly populated district, and they brought the corpses from the farmhouses and cottages, often a long slow journey, and left the coffin in the chapel waiting for the funeral the next day. And the mourners passed the night upstairs, watching and, of course, drinking. When all this became unnecessary, the chapel fell into ruin. The parish council was glad to sell it to me. The vicar's a hundred and one anyway. I restored it and I live in it. The ground had to be specially deconsecrated for me.' Mrs Pagani removed her hand and picked up her glass. 'Come and see me.' For the second time she toasted Clarinda. 'I call it the Charnel House. Not quite correct, of course: a charnel house is where the dead lie *after* the funeral. But I thought the name rather suited me.' Suddenly her attention was distracted. Without moving her eyes, she inclined her head slightly sideways. 'Just look at Mr Appleby. Used to be managing director of an important company. Appleby's Arterial Bootlaces.'

Clarinda could not see that Mr Appleby, with whom she had been talking before Mrs Pagani's arrival, was doing anything much out of the ordinary. He seemed simply to be telling stories to two or three other guests, who admittedly seemed less interested than he was. But

Clarinda was unaccustomed to making twelve or fifteen intimate acquaintances for life en bloc; and all coming within the, at best, uncertain category of friends' friends.

Again Mrs Pagani had drained her glass. 'I must be going. I only looked in for a minute. I have a lot to do tonight.' She rose and held out her hand. 'Tomorrow then?'

'Thank you very much, but I'm not quite sure. I expect Mr and Mrs Carstairs have some plans for me.'

Mrs Pagani looked her in the eyes, then nodded. 'Yes. You mustn't quarrel with them. That's very important. Well: come if you can.'

'Thank you, I'd like to.'

Mrs Pagani was resuming her expensive sable coat, and saying good-bye to Mrs Carstairs.

'You've nothing to worry about,' Clarinda heard her say, 'Dudley's chosen well.'

'Darling.' It was Dudley standing behind Clarinda's chair. He kissed the top of her head. 'Don't mind her. She's far round the bend, of course, but good-hearted at bottom. Anyway she's the only one of her kind in the village. Pots of money too.'

'What makes you think that, Dudley?' asked the marzipan voice of Mr Appleby. Conversation about Mrs Pagani was now general.

'Couldn't behave as she does if she hadn't, Mr Appleby,' replied Dudley.

That seemed to be the consensus of opinion.

*

When everyone had gone, they listened to the radio. Then they had supper, and Clarinda was permitted, after strenuous application, to participate in the washing up. As they retired in a warm mist of gently affectionate demonstrativeness, the thought crossed Clarinda's mind that she might like to sleep with Dudley. It was still not an urgent wish, only a thought; but in Dudley there was no evidence that it was even a thought. For him the fateful outer wall of the fortress had been successfully battered down after a long siege; the course of time would bring the later degrees of capitulation.

The next morning Clarinda had to admit to herself that she was very depressed. As she lay in bed watching wisps of late-autumn fog drift and swirl past her window, she felt that inside the house was a warm and cosy emptiness in which she was about to be lost. She saw herself, her real self, for ever suspended in blackness, howling in the lonely dark, miserable and unheard; while her other, outer self went smiling through an endless purposeless routine of love for and compliance with a family and a community of friends which, however excellent, were exceedingly unlike her, in some way that she did not fully understand. Elizabeth might bill and coo about the theatre, but it could hardly be said that any one of them had a sense of drama. They lived in the depths of the country, but had no idea of the wilderness. They were constantly together, but knew one another too well to be able to converse. Individuality had been eroded from all of them by the tides of common sentiment. Love me, said Dudley in effect, his eyes softly glowing; love mine. His London personality seemed merely a bait with which to entice her into the capacious family lobster pot. Mrs Pagani was certainly different from the rest of them; but Clarinda was far from sure that Mrs Pagani was her idea of an ally.

Then she got up, turned on the big electric heater, and felt that her thoughts had been the morbid product of lying too long abed. Moreover, the flying swathes of fog were most beautiful. She stood in her nightdress by the window looking at them; with the heater behind her sending ripples of warmth up her back. It was an old sash window with the original well-proportioned glazing bars. The new white paint covered numerous under-currents in the surface of earlier coats. Clarinda liked such details in the house; always kept neat and spruce, like an old dandy whom people still cared about.

But from breakfast onwards her spirits once more began to sink. One trouble was that the Carstairs family, in fact, had no plans for her whatever, and nor had Dudley individually. There was a half-hearted suggestion of church, which no one seemed wishful to keep alive; and after that a sequence of minor interruptions and involved jobs which Clarinda felt could be much better organised, but which everyone else seemed quietly to enjoy as they were. The whole family, Dudley included, seemed to like even the most pointless chores simply because they were being undertaken collectively. The four of them did all they could to give Clarinda a place in the various undertakings; and Clarinda hated the perverse barrier which seemed more and more to isolate her from their kindness. But when by the middle of the afternoon (Sunday luncheon was a substantial reaping of the morning's seedtime) no one had even suggested a walk, she did something precipitate. Without speaking to Dudley, who was helping his father in the garden, she went up to her bedroom, changed into a pair of trousers and a sweater, donned her mackintosh, wrote on the inside of a cigarette box 'Gone for a walk. Back soon', and quietly left the house.

The swathes of fog were still sweeping before the wind, but, though damp, it was not a cold wind nor unfriendly. Immediately she was away from the house, Clarinda felt alive again. After walking a few hundred yards rather furtively, she ascended a roadside bank from which the grass had recently been sickled, and looked about her. She was looking for the church; and when, through a break in the mist, she saw the battlemented top of the yellow stone tower, with a jutting gargoyle at each corner, she knew which way she would go. She turned her back on the church, and walked away from the few cottages which made up the village. Mrs Pagani had possibly served a purpose as serio-comic relief the previous evening, but Clarinda had no wish to enlarge the acquaintanceship.

The patches of cloud and fog drifted and lifted, making constant changes of scene. There was no hope of sunshine, but the mist was uncharged with smoke, and served to melt the sharp air of winter and to enclose Clarinda with an advancing tent of invisibility. Other than Clarinda's light, quick step on the granite chips of the old-fashioned narrow road, the only sound was the dripping of water from the trees, the hedges, the occasional gates. At the tip of every leaf was a fat pearl about to drop and vanish. Clarinda realised that her hair was becoming damp. She bundled it on to the top of her head, soaking her hands in the process; then drew a long black scarf from her mackintosh pocket, and twisted it into a tight turban. The road seemed to be lined with dripping trees, which appeared dimly one at a time, grew into a fullness of detail which had seemed impossible a minute before, and then dissolved away, even from the backward glance; but the air also was itself heavy with soft wetness. Soft and wet, but good on the face . . . 'Let there be wet,' quoted Clarinda to herself in her clear gentle voice. 'Oh let there be wet.'

She had seen no one in the village, and if there were animals in the fields, the mist cut off sight and hearing of them. Clarinda was aware that she might have some difficult personal problems almost immediately ahead of her; but she thought nothing of them as the renewal of contact with the country, the adventurous loneliness of her walk, suffused her with their first freshness. Out of the mist advanced a small square notice-board, lopsided on top of a sloping wooden pole: 'No Rite of Way,' read Clarinda. 'Persons Proceed Beyond This Point By Favour Only.'

It was perhaps an unusual announcement, and not made more convincing by the misspelling, and by the crudeness of the erection; but Clarinda had heard of landowners who close gates on one day each year in order to prevent the establishment of an easement, and there seemed to be no change whatever in the nature or surface of the road, at least in the short distance ahead which was visible. Clarinda continued her walk.

No one, however, is entirely unaffected, either towards carefulness, or towards challenge, by passing such a notice; and in due course Clarinda realised that she was walking more slowly. Then she perceived that the road itself had for some time been rising slightly but continuously. It also seemed narrower, and the hedges higher. Clarinda stopped and looked at her watch. Despite the muffling mist, she could hear its ticking with extreme clarity, so silent were the hidden pastures around her. It had been something before three o'clock when she had crept out of the house; it was now something after half past. She had possibly another hour of daylight. If she went on for a quarter of that hour, there would be as much time in which to return as she had taken upon the outward journey, and the way back was along a known road, and one which inclined downhill. Moreover, there had not been a single cross-roads or doubtful turning. And in any case Clarinda liked walking in the dark. Certainly neither her mind nor her stomach was inclined to a cosy crumpet tea with the Carstairs family, or to a further session bound, like Catherine upon her wheel, to the mark of interrogation which Dudley remained for her. Again, therefore, she continued her walk.

The gradient increased, but the trees came more quickly, imperceptibly losing, tree by tree, the moment of clear detail which had previously characterised each of them. The road had begun to wind steeply upwards through a wood. Now the hedges, lately so high, had ceased, but the road, although the antique metalling seemed more and more lost in the damp loamy soil, remained distinct. Intermittently, the going had become a little muddy, but the softness underfoot made a change from the angular granite. The trees had now become dim and uniform shapes which passed so quickly and monotonously that sometimes they seemed almost to move, as in a very early cinematograph.

Then, unmistakably, something else was moving. From among the tall, thin trees, and out of the veiling mist, came a small animal. It crossed the track ten or twelve feet in front of Clarinda, and disappeared again almost at once. It neither walked nor ran, but slowly ambled. It was not quite silent, but the atmosphere made the sound of its passage seem insufficient; it whispered and sighed its way through the undergrowth. Clarinda could not think what animal it was. Probably a dog which the mist had misshaped. She checked for a moment, then went on.

Swiftly and momentarily the mist cleared a larger area around her, as she had seen it do several times before. She could see many trees, and could now perceive also that they were beeches. Dotted about the bare earth which surrounds beech trees even in a thick wood were many more of the animals. They were pigs.

Each of the pigs seemed very intent about its business, softly snuffling after unknown sweets in the naked soil. None grunted or squeaked; but the dead, brown-paper leaves rustled slightly as the herd rooted. The pigs were on both sides of the track, and again Clarinda hesitated briefly before advancing through the midst of them.

At first they took no notice of her, perhaps, she thought, unafraid of man because little knowing him; and the tent of mist, temporarily a marquee, advanced with her on to the wooded heights ahead. Then, most unexpectedly, there came from the obscurity thirty yards away on Clarinda's right a shattering animal shriek, short but so loud and high as to pain the ear. All the pigs looked up, stood motionless for a second, then massed together in the direction the sound had come from, some of them crossing the track behind and ahead of her for the purpose. Again they stood, an indistinct agglomeration on the edge of the mist; then suddenly swept back the way they had come. The whole herd, packed tightly together, charged across the track and disappeared into the mist on the left. The pigs had passed no more than five or six feet in front of Clarinda; who was able to observe that in the very middle of the throng was a creature much larger than the rest, a bristling, long-snouted boar, with large curving bluish-white tusks. He it was, she suspected, that had cried from the enveloping mist. She had never before seen such a creature, and was slightly alarmed.

The scampering flight of the pigs could be heard for a few seconds after the fog had surrounded them. Then the wood was silent again. It was as if the pigs had been the last creatures left alive in it. The fog had now closed up again, scudding across the track on a wind which seemed colder and stronger than it had been in the village at the beginning of Clarinda's walk. But the track was now rising steeply, and the extra exertion kept her warm. The long-drawn-out winter dusk must have begun, because not until she was right upon them did Clarinda notice two figures on the path.

They were children. They did not seem to be either ascending or descending, but to be quietly waiting by the side of the track for someone to pass. They were identically dressed in one-piece waterproof garments, like small, trim diving suits, bright blue in colour, and provided with hoods. One child had its hood over its head, but the other was bareheaded and displayed a curly mass of silky flaxen hair, much the colour of Clarinda's own in childhood. The bareheaded child had blue eyes very widely spaced, and a pale skin. The face of the other child was shadowed by its hood, and from Clarinda's altitude amounted to little more than a long red mouth. Both children, Clarinda noticed, had long red mouths. She was unable to determine their sex.

'Excuse me,' said the bareheaded child, very politely. Clarinda decided it was a girl. The girl spoke well.

Clarinda stopped.

The little girl smiled charmingly. 'Have you seen the pigs?' She spoke as if the pigs were a matter of common interest to them, and automatically identifiable; as if a straggler from a hunt had asked, Had she seen the hounds?

'Yes,' said Clarinda. 'Are they your pigs?'

'How long ago?' asked the child, with a child's disregard of side issues.

'About five minutes ago.' Clarinda looked at her watch. Quarter to four. Time to go back. 'As a matter of fact, I'm afraid I frightened them.'

'Silly old pigs,' said the child, fortunately taking Clarinda's side. 'Which way did they go? *This* way? Or *that* way?' She indicated up the hill or down. Clarinda thought that she was about eight.

'That way, I'm afraid,' said Clarinda, pointing vaguely into the mist. 'I hope they'll not get lost in the fog.'

'There's always a fog,' said the child.

Clarinda let that one go.

'What happens if I get to the top?' she asked.

The hooded child, who had said nothing, suddenly made an odd movement. It raised one foot and stamped on the ground. It was as if its whole small body were swept by a spasm. The movement reminded Clarinda of an animal which had been startled and pawed the earth: a large animal, moreover. In the child seemed to be a disproportionate strength. Clarinda was really frightened by it.

'There's a lovely view some days,' said the bareheaded child helpfully.

'Not much good this evening.'

The child shook its head, smiling politely. The hooded child snatched at the bareheaded child's sleeve and pulled it sharply.

'There's a maze.' The bareheaded child was showing

off slightly but meaning to help also.

'What kind of maze? With hedges? I don't believe it.' To Clarinda a maze meant Hampton Court.

'An ordinary maze. You have to look for it though.'

'How far away?'

'Quite near.'

'Where do I look?' Clearly the child was speaking the truth, and Clarinda was interested.

'In among the bushes. There's a little path.'

Clarinda noticed that the second child had cocked up its head and was looking at her. It seemed to have sharp, sallow features, and big eyes. In its hood it was not unlike a falcon.

'Shall I get lost in the maze?'

The bareheaded child appeared unable to understand this question and looked at Clarinda disappointedly.

'Well that's up to me,' said Clarinda, coming to the rescue.

The child nodded. She had still not understood. 'Thank you for telling us about the pigs.'

'Thank you for telling me about the maze.'

The little girl smiled her pretty smile. Really I never saw such a beautiful child, thought Clarinda. The children departed quickly down the hill. In a moment they had vanished.

Clarinda again looked at her watch. Three-fifty. She decided that she would give fifteen minutes to looking for the child's maze, and that even then she would be back soon after five.

Before long she reached a gate. It was at the edge of

the wood and the end of the track. Outside the wood was short, downlike grass, mossy with moisture. Clarinda's feet sank into it, as into very soft rubber. There were frequent, irregularly placed clumps of thorny scrub, and no sign of even the sketchiest path. The wind was still growing chillier, and the mist was darkening all the time. Clarinda had not gone fifty yards from the gate when she decided to return. The question of whether or not it would be worth looking for the maze did not arise. On top of the hill it would be easy to lose oneself without entering a maze.

In the dim light she perceived that a man was leaning against the gate and facing her. He had red curly hair which had receded slightly at the sides, and a prominent nose. He wore pale-hued riding breeches and dark boots. Across his shoulders was a fur cape, which Clarinda vaguely connected with the idea of aviation. As Clarinda approached, he neither spoke nor moved. She saw that in his right hand he held a long thick shepherd's crook. It was black, and reached from the ground to his shoulder.

Clarinda put her hand on the wooden drawbar of the gate. She assumed that this action would make the man move. But he continued leaning on the gate and regarding her. If she opened the gate, he would fall.

'I want to go through.' It was not an occasion for undue politeness.

Without change of expression, the man swiftly placed his left hand on the other end of the drawbar. Clarinda pushed at it, but it would not give. Not given to panic,

Clarinda momentarily considered the situation, and began to climb the gate.

'*Hullo*,' said a voice behind her. 'Rufo! What do you suppose you're doing?' Unmistakably it was the voice of Mrs Pagani.

Clarinda stepped down. Mrs Pagani was also wearing high boots, and her head was enveloped like Clarinda's in a dark scarf; but, strangely, she was wearing the capacious and opulent fur coat in which Clarinda had first seen her. The top of her boots were hidden beneath it.

'Rufo!' Mrs Pagani spoke to the man by the gate as if she were calling off a foolish and over-demonstrative dog. The man said something in a strange language. It was so unlike any language Clarinda had heard that at first she thought he had a defect in his speech.

Mrs Pagani, however, replied to him in what was presumably the same tongue. In her mouth it sounded less unfamiliar because she lacked his oddly throaty delivery. Clarinda wondered whether this might be Romany.

The man was remonstrating against Mrs Pagani's reproof. Her reply was curious: she was fluently pantomimic, and Clarinda could not but gather that Rufo was being told that she, Clarinda, was to be admitted where others were to be denied. The man scowled, and leered, then shuffled off. Although young and apparently strong, he stumbled in his gait and leaned on his crook. There was now very little light, but after he had gone a few paces, he appeared to draw his fur cape high over the back of his head.

'What can you think of Rufo?'

Clarinda often found Mrs Pagani's remarks difficult to answer.

'Will you forgive him? And me?'

'There's nothing to forgive. I didn't know he couldn't speak English.'

'How could you?' Clarinda got the impression that the tone of this was not apologetic, but amicably ironical. Not for the first time she thought that Mrs Pagani implied some understanding between them which did not exist.

'And *will* you come back?'

It was ridiculous. But Mrs Pagani had saved her from a menacing situation, and she had to say something.

'When should I come back?'

'Tonight.' The intonation made it plain that no other time could be in question.

'Here?'

Mrs Pagani said nothing, but dropped her head to one side and smiled.

It was almost impossible after that to seek a reason.

Moreover, Mrs Pagani left no time.

'You've bound your hair very well.'

Clarinda had been noticing how carefully Mrs Pagani's own thick locks had been turbanned.

'It was getting wet.'

Mrs Pagani nodded and smiled. She was looking Clarinda over.

'*Au revoir.*'

Clarinda had not expected that either.

'Good-bye. Thank you for rescuing me.'

'My dear, we wouldn't lose *you*.' Mrs Pagani strode off. The plural was a new mystery, for Clarinda felt that it could not refer to Rufo.

Although by now it was night, Clarinda leaped and ran down the dark track. At one time she thought she heard the pigs softly rooting in the invisible undergrowth. But she did not stop to listen, and duly reached the house only a few minutes after five.

Dudley seemed to take her escapade for granted (although she provided no details). Clarinda wondered whether this suggested that already he was growing accustomed to her, or whether it was evidence that he would be a good and unexacting husband, prepared to allow her due liberty and no questions asked. She certainly valued his success in persuading his family to adopt the same attitude.

'Out at night in winter,' said Mrs Carstairs, 'when you don't have to be!' And upon her gentle mark of exclamation, the matter dropped and tea began. Clarinda wondered whether their surprising equanimity was a product of Dudley's leadership in a full discussion during her absence. She liked Dudley for not fussing, whatever his reasons.

Elizabeth had got out a quantity of clothes and ranged them round the room for inspection and comparison by Clarinda. This was a lengthy undertaking. In the end there was a knock at the door.

'Liz.' It was Dudley's voice outside.

'One moment.' Elizabeth drew on a sweater. 'Now.'

Dudley entered. 'I've been sent up to fetch you both

256

downstairs.' He smiled fraternally.

'We're ready,' said Elizabeth, looking at Clarinda as woman to woman.

On the dark landing outside, Dudley held Clarinda back for a moment and embraced her. 'Go on, Liz, you fool.' Elizabeth went on. 'You understand?' said Dudley to Clarinda. 'At least I hope you do. I've been trying to keep out of sight as far as possible so that you can get to know the family. That walk of yours. I've been wondering.'

Clarinda squeezed his hand.

'It's all right? And you do like them?'

'Of course it's all right. And I like them very much.'

Every Sunday evening, Clarinda understood, Mr Carstairs read aloud from about half past six until they had supper at eight. Tonight the start had been delayed by her walk and by the discussion in Elizabeth's bedroom; but still there was time for four chapters of *Persuasion*. Mr Carstairs read well, Clarinda thought; and the book was new to her.

Dudley, who could be convincing in such matters, had somehow contrived to arrange that both of them could arrive late at the office the next day: otherwise they would have had to return to London that same night. Soon after supper Elizabeth had disappeared upstairs, saying she had some letters to write, and that she probably would not be coming down again. She bade Clarinda goodnight, and kissed her affectionately on the cheekbone. About half an hour later, Mr and Mrs Carstairs also withdrew. Dudley went to assist his father with stoking up the boiler for the night. The clock struck half past nine. Otherwise the house was very quiet. Clarinda supposed that she and Dudley were being purposefully left to themselves.

'I wish *we* could live in the country,' said Dudley when he reappeared.

'I expect we could.'

'Not the real country. Not unless I get another job.'

'Where does the real country begin?'

'About Berkhamstead. Or perhaps Tring. Nowadays, that is.'

'The country stretches in this direction only.' Clarinda smiled at him.

'For me it does, darling.' She had not yet got into the habit of his calling her 'darling'. 'I *belong* around here.'

'But surely until recently you lived in a town? North-ampton is a town isn't it?' She really wasn't quite sure.

'Yes, but I was always out and about.'

Clarinda had observed that every normal English male believes that he wants to live in the country, and said no more.

Dudley talked for some time about the advantages of the arrangement. Then he stopped, and Clarinda perceived that he was waiting for her assent. There was a slight pause.

'Dudley,' said Clarinda. 'How well do your father and mother know Mrs Pagani?'

'Not very well,' said Dudley, faintly disappointed. 'What you would call a bare acquaintanceship. Why?'

'They asked her to the party.'

'Actually they didn't. She heard about it and just came. Not the first time she's done it, either. But you can't put on side in a small village, and she's not a bad old bird really.'

'How do you know?'

'I don't,' said Dudley, grinning at her earnestness. 'So what?'

'What does she do with herself? Live on, I mean?'

'I don't know what she lives on, darling. Little children, I expect, like Red Riding Hood's grandmother. You know she occupies an old ruin in the churchyard?'

'So she told me. I should like to go and see it.'

'What, *now*?'

'Will you come with me?'

'It's a bit late for calls in the country.'

'I'm not suggesting a call. I just want to have a look round.'

'She might think that a trifle nosey, mightn't she?'

Clarinda nodded. 'Of course, you know Mrs Pagani better than I do.' She suddenly remembered a nocturnal stroll in Marseilles with a fellow tourist, who had proved unexpectedly delightful.

'Tell you what I'll do,' said Dudley, 'I'll whistle you round before we push off to Roade tomorrow.'

'We mustn't miss the train.'

'Never missed a train in my life.'

Clarinda's second night was worse than her first, because now she couldn't sleep at all. Dudley had considered that they should go their separate ways soon after eleven, in order, as he said, not to disturb Mr and Mrs Carstairs; and when the church clock, brooding over Mrs Pagani's romantic residence, struck one, Clarinda was still tense and tumultuous in the prickly dark. Without switching on the light she got out of bed and crossed to the window. She hoped that the sudden chill would numb her writhing nerves. When, an hour and a half before, she had drawn back the curtains, and opened the window at top and bottom, she had noticed that the mist seemed at last to have vanished, although it was so black that it was hard to be sure. Now the moon was rising, low and enormous, as if at the horizon the bottom edge of it dragged against the earth, and Clarinda saw that indeed all was clear, the sky starry, and the mist withdrawn to the distant shadowy hills. In the foreground there was nothing to be seen but the silent fields and naked trees.

Swiftly a bat loomed against the night and flew smack against the outer sash. Another two feet higher or two feet lower and he would have been in. Clarinda softly shivered for a moment, then watched the bat skid into invisibility. The silver-gilt autumn night was somehow warmer and more welcoming than Clarinda's unadventurous bed; fellow-bed, twin-bed to a thousand others in a thousand well-ordered houses. The grave self-sufficiency of the night was seeping into Clarinda's bloodstream, renewing her audacity, inflaming her curiosity; and its moonlit beauty agitating her heart. By the light of the big moon she began to dress.

When, upon her return from the woods, she had

taken off her walking shoes, she had thought them very wet; but now they seemed dried, as if by the moon's rays. She opened the door of her room. Again a bat struck the window at the end of the passage outside. There was no other sound but that of disturbed breathing; which, however, seemed all around her. The other occupants of the house slept, but, as it appeared, uneasily. She descended the stairs and creaked into her mackintosh before trying the door. She expected difficulty here, but it opened at a touch. Doubtless it would be side to lock one's doors in a village.

The moon shone on the gate and on the lane beyond; but the long path from the front door was in darkness. With the moon so low the house cast a disproportionate shadow. As Clarinda walked down the narrow strip of paving, a hare scuttered across her feet. She could feel his warmth on her ankles as he nearly tripped her. The gate had a patent catch which had caused her trouble before, and she had to stand for half a minute fumbling.

As she walked along the road, passed the 'By Favour Only' notice, and began to ascend into the wood, she never doubted that at the top of the hill would be some remarkable warrant for her efforts; and she was resolved to find out what it was. Now the regular roadside trees were as clear-cut and trim as a guard of honour, and the owls seemed to be passing a message ahead of her into the thickets. Once or twice, when entering a straighter part of the road, she thought she saw a shambling figure rounding the distant corner ahead, but she decided that it was probably only a shadow.

The bats were everywhere, hurtling in and out of the dark patches, and fluting their strange cries, which Clarinda was always so glad that she was among those who are privileged to hear. There were even some surviving or revitalised moths; and a steadily rising perfume of moisture and decay.

The gate at the hilltop was shut. But as soon as Clarinda drew near, she saw the little blue girl standing by it.

'Hullo.'

'Hullo,' said Clarinda.

'You're rather late.'

'I'm very sorry. I didn't know.'

'It's important to be punctual.' The child spoke in a tone of earnest helpfulness.

'I'll try to remember,' said Clarinda humbly.

The child had opened the gate and was leaning back against the end of it, her chin stuck in her neck and her feet in the ground, holding it for Clarinda.

Clarinda passed through. The moon was now higher, and the soft grass glistened and gleamed. Even in the almost bright light there was no sign of a continuing path.

'I shall get my feet wet.'

'Yes, you will. You should wear boots.' Clarinda observed the legs of the child's blue garment were stuck into close-fitting black wellingtons. Also its hood was now over its head.

There was no sign of the other child.

The little girl had carefully shut the gate. She stood looking ruefully at Clarinda's feet. Then apparently deciding there was nothing to be done about them, she said very politely, 'Shall I show you where you change?'

'Can I change my shoes?' asked Clarinda, humouring her.

'No, I don't think you can change your shoes,' said the child very seriously. 'Only everything else.'

'I don't want to change anything else.'

The child regarded her, all at sea. Then, perhaps considering that she must have misunderstood, said, 'It's over there. Follow me. And do take care of your feet.'

It certainly was very wet, but the grass proved to be tussocky, and Clarinda did her best to keep dry by striding from tussock to tussock in the moonlight.

'Rufo's in there already,' said the child conversationally. 'You see you're the last.'

'I've said I'm sorry.'

'It doesn't matter.' This was uttered with that special magnanimity only found in the very young.

The little girl waded on, and Clarinda struggled after her. There was no sign of anyone else: indeed, the place looked a hilltop of the dead. The lumpy, saturated grass and the rank and stunted vegetation compared most unfavourably with the handsome trees behind.

There was one place where the briars and ragged bushes were particularly dense and abundant, constituting a small prickly copse. Round the outskirts of this copse, the child led the way until Clarinda saw that embedded in its perimeter was a rickety shed. Possibly constructed for some agricultural purpose but long abandoned by its maker, it drooped and sagged into the ground. From it came a penetrating and repugnant odour, like all the bad smells of nature and the stockyard merged together.

'That's it,' said the little girl pointing. They were still some yards off, but the feral odour from the shed was already making Clarinda feel sick.

'I don't think I want to go in there.'

'But you *must*. Rufo's in there. All the others changed long ago.'

Apart from other considerations, the shed seemed too small to house many; and Clarinda could now see that the approach to it was thick with mud, which added its smell to the rest. She was sure that the floor of the shed was muddy almost to the knees.

The child's face was puckered with puzzlement.

'I'm sorry,' said Clarinda, 'but you know I don't want to change at all.'

Clearly she was behaving in quite the wrong way. But the child took a grip on the situation and said, 'Wait here. I'll go and ask.'

'All right,' said Clarinda. 'But I'll wait over there, if you don't mind.' The child seemed not to notice the awful smell, but Clarinda was not going to be the first to mention it.

'*There*,' said the child, pointing to an exact spot. Clarinda took up her stance upon it. 'Mind you don't move.'

'Not if you hurry.' The smell was still very detectable.

'Quite still,' insisted the child.

'Quite still,' said Clarinda.

Swiftly the child ran three times round Clarinda in a large circle. The light was so clear that Clarinda could see the drops of water flying up from her feet.

'*Hurry*,' urged Clarinda; and, the third circle complete, the child darted away round the edge of the copse in the direction from which they had come.

Left alone in the still moonlight, Clarinda wondered whether this were not her great chance to return home to safety and certainty. Then she saw a figure emerging from the dilapidated hut.

The figure walked upright, but otherwise appeared to be a large furry animal, such as a bear or ape. From its distinctive staggering uncertainty of gait, Clarinda would have recognised Rufo, even without the statements of the little girl. Moreover, he was still leaning upon his long crook, which stuck in the mud and had to be dragged out at every step. He too was going back round the edge of the copse, the same way as the child. Although he showed no sign of intending to molest Clarinda, she found him a horrifying sight, and decided upon retreat. Then she became really frightened; because she found she could not move.

The hairy slouching figure drew slowly nearer, and with him came an intensification of the dreadful smell, sweet and putrid and commingled. The animal skin was thick and wrinkled about his neck and almost covered his face, but Clarinda saw his huge nose and expressionless eyes. Then he was past, and the child had reappeared.

'I ran all the way.' Indeed it seemed as if she had

been gone only an instant. 'You're not to bother about changing because it's too late anyway.' Clearly she was repeating words spoken by an adult. 'You're to come at once, although of course you'll have to be hidden. But it's all right,' she added reassuringly. 'There've been people before who've had to be hidden.' She spoke as if the period covered by her words were at least a generation. 'But you'd better be quick.'

Clarinda found that she could move once more. Rufo, moreover, had disappeared from sight.

'Where do I hide?'

'I'll show you. I've often done it.' Again she was showing off slightly. 'Bind your hair.'

'What?'

'Bind your hair. Do be quick.' The little girl was peremptory but not unsympathetic. She was like a mother addressing an unusually slow child she was none the less rather fond of. 'Haven't you got that thing you had before?'

'It was raining then.' But Clarinda in fact had replaced the black scarf in her mackintosh pocket after drying it before the Carstairs' kitchen fire. Now, without knowing why, she drew it out.

'Go on.' Clarinda's sluggishness was making the child frantic.

But Clarinda refused to be rattled. With careful grace she went through the moonlit ritual of twisting the scarf round her head and enveloping her abundant soft hair.

The child led her back halfway round the copse to where there was a tiny path between the bushes. This path also was exceedingly muddy; ploughed up, as Clarinda could plainly see, by innumerable hoofmarks.

'I'd better go first,' said the little girl; adding with her customary good manners, 'I'm afraid it's rather spiky.'

It was indeed. The little girl, being little, appeared to advance unscathed; but Clarinda, being tall, found that her clothes were torn to pieces, and her face and hands lacerated. The radiance of the moon had sufficed outside, but in here failed to give warning of the thick tangled briars and rank whipcord suckers. Everywhere was a vapour of ancient cobwebs, clinging and greasy, amid which strange night insects flapped and flopped.

'We're nearly there,' said the little girl. 'You'd better be rather quiet.'

It was impossible to be quiet, and Clarinda was almost in tears with the discomfort.

'*Quieter*,' said the little girl; and Clarinda did not dare to answer back.

The slender muddy trail, matted with half-unearthed roots, wriggled on for another minute or two; and then the little girl whispered, 'Under here.'

She was making a gap in the foliage of a tall round bush. Clarinda pushed in. 'Ssh,' said the little girl.

Inside it was like a small native hut. The foliage hung all round, but there was room to stand up and dry ground beneath the feet.

'Stand on this,' whispered the little girl, pointing to a round, sawn section of tree, about two feet high and four in diameter. 'I call it my fairy dinner table.'

'What about you?'

'I'm all right, thank you. I'm always here.'

Clarinda climbed on to the section of tree, and made a cautious aperture in the boscage before her.

The sight beyond was one which she would not easily forget.

Clearly, to begin with, this was the maze, although Clarinda had never seen or heard of such a maze before. It filled a clearing in the copse about twenty or thirty yards wide and consisted in a labyrinth of little ridges, all about nine inches high. The general pattern of the labyrinth was circular, with involved inner convolutions everywhere, and at some points flourishes curving beyond the main outer boundary, as if they had once erupted like boils or volcanic blow-holes. In the valleys between the ridges, grass grew, but the ridges themselves were trodden bare. At the centre of the maze was a hewn block of stone, which put Clarinda in mind of the Stone of Scone.

Little of this, however, had much immediate significance for Clarinda; because all over the maze, under the moon, writhed and slithered and sprawled the smooth white bodies of men and women. There were scores of them; all apparently well-shaped and comely; all (perhaps for that reason) weirdly impersonal; all recumbent and reptilian, as in a picture Clarinda remembered having seen; all completely and impossibly silent beneath the silent night. Clarinda saw that all round the maze were heaps of furry skins. She then noticed that the heads of all the women were bound in black fillets.

At the points where the coils of the maze surged out beyond the main perimeter were other, different figures. Still wrapped in furs, which distorted and made horrible the outlines of their bodies, they clung together as if locked in death. Down to the maze the ground fell away a few feet from Clarinda's hiding place. Immediately below her was one of these groups, silent as all the rest. By one of the shapeless figures she noticed a long thick staff. Then the figure soundlessly shifted, and the white moonlight fell upon the face of the equally shapeless figure in its arms. The eyes were blank and staring, the nostrils stretched like a running deer, and the red lips not so much parted as drawn back to the gums: but Clarinda recognised the face of Mrs Pagani.

Suddenly there was a rustling in the hiding-place. Though soft, it was the first sound of any kind since Clarinda had looked out on the maze.

'Go away, you silly little boy,' muttered the little girl.

Clarinda looked over her shoulder.

Inside the bower, the moonlight, filtered through the veil of foliage, was dim and deceitful; but she could see the big eyes and bird-of-prey mien of the other child. He was still wearing his bright blue hooded garment; but now the idea occurred to Clarinda that he might not be a child at all, but a well-proportioned dwarf. She looked at the black ground before stepping down from the tree trunk; and instantly he leapt at her. She felt a sharp, indefinite pain in her ankle and saw one of the creature's hands yellow and clawlike where a moonbeam through the hole above fell on the pale wood of the cut tree. Then in the murk the little girl did something which Clarinda could not see at all, and the hand jerked into passivity. The little girl was crying.

Clarinda touched her torn ankle, and stretched her hand into the beam of light. There was duly a mess of blood.

The little girl clutched at Clarinda's wrist. 'Don't let them see,' she whispered beseechingly through her tears. 'Oh please don't let them see.' Then she added with passionate fury, 'He always spoils *everything*. I hate him. I hate him. I hate him.'

Clarinda's ankle hurt badly, and there was palpable danger of blood poisoning, but otherwise the injury was not severe.

'Shall I be all right if I go?'

'Yes. But I think you'd better run.'

'That may not be so easy.'

The little girl seemed desolated with grief.

'Never mind,' said Clarinda. 'And thank you.'

The little girl stopped sobbing for a moment. 'You *will* come back?'

'I don't think so,' said Clarinda.

The sobbing recommenced. It was very quiet and despairing.

'Well,' said Clarinda, 'I'll see.'

'Punctually? That makes all the difference, you know.'

'Of course,' said Clarinda.

The child smiled at her in the faint moonlight. She

was being brave. She was remembering her manners.

'Shall I come with you?'

'No need,' said Clarinda rather hastily.

'I mean to the end of the little path.'

'Still no need,' said Clarinda. 'Thank you again though. Good-bye.'

'Good-bye,' said the little girl. 'Don't forget. Punctual.'

Clarinda crept along the involved muddy path: then she sped across the soft wet sward, which she spotted with her blood; through the gate where she had seen Rufo, and down the hill where she had seen the pigs; past the ill-spelled notice; and home. As she fumbled with the patent catch, the church clock which kept ward over Mrs Pagani's abode struck three. The mist was rising again everywhere; but, in what remained of the moonlight, Clarinda, before entering the house, unwound the black scarf from her head and shook her soft abundant locks.

The question of Mrs Pagani's unusual dwelling-place arose, of course, the next morning, as they hurriedly ate the generously over-large breakfast which Mrs Carstairs, convinced that London meant starvation, pressed upon them.

'Please not,' said Clarinda, her mouth full of golden syrup. She was wearing ankle socks to conceal her careful bandage. 'I just don't want to go.'

The family looked at her; but only Dudley spoke. 'Whatever you wish, darling.'

There was a pause; after which Mr Carstairs remarked that he supposed the good lady would still be in bed anyway.

But here, most unusually, Mr Carstairs was wrong. As Dudley and Clarinda drove away, they saw the back of Mrs Pagani walking towards the church and not a couple of hundred yards from their own gate. She wore high, stout boots, caked with country mud, and an enveloping fur coat against the sharpness of the morning. Her step was springy, and her thick black hair flew in the wind like a dusky gonfalon.

As they overtook her, Dudley slowed. 'Good morning,' he shouted. 'Back to the grindstone.'

Mrs Pagani smiled affectionately.

'Don't be late,' she cried, and kissed her hand to them.

The Stains

After Elizabeth ultimately died, it was inevitable that many people should come forward with counsel, and doubtless equally inevitable that the counsel be so totally diverse.

There were two broad and opposed schools.

The first considered that Stephen should 'treasure the memory' (though it was not always put like that) for an indefinite period, which, it was implied, might conveniently last him out to the end of his own life. These people attached great importance to Stephen 'not rushing anything.' The second school urged that Stephen marry again as soon as he possibly could. They said that, above all, he must not just fall into apathy and let his life slide. They said he was a man made for marriage and all it meant.

Of course, both parties were absolutely right in every way. Stephen could see that perfectly well.

It made little difference. Planning, he considered, would be absurd in any case. Until further notice, the matter would have to be left to fate. The trouble was, of course, that fate's possible options were narrowing and dissolving almost weekly, as they had already been doing throughout Elizabeth's lengthy illness. For example (the obvious and most pressing example): how many women would want to marry Stephen now? A number, perhaps; but not a number that he would want to marry. Not after Elizabeth. That in particular.

They told him he should take a holiday, and he took one. They told him he should see his doctor, and he saw him. The man who had looked after Elizabeth had wanted to emigrate, had generously held back while Elizabeth had remained alive, and had then shot off at once. The new man was half-Sudanese, and Stephen found him difficult to communicate with, at least upon a first encounter, at least on immediate topics.

In the end, Stephen applied for and obtained a spell of compassionate leave, and went, as he usually did, to stay with his elder brother, Harewood, in the north. Harewood was in orders: the Reverend Harewood Hooper, BD, MA. Their father and grandfather had been in orders too, and had been incumbents of the same small church in that same small parish for thirty-nine years and forty-two years respectively. So far, Harewood had served for only twenty-three years. The patron of the living, a private individual, conscientious and very long lived, was relieved to be able to rely upon a succession of such dedicated men. Unfortunately, Harewood's own son, his one child, had dropped out, and was now believed to have disappeared into Nepal. Harewood himself cared more for rock growths than for controversies about South Africa or for other such fashionable Church preoccupations. He had published two important books on lichens. People often came to see him on the subject. He was modestly famous.

He fostered lichens on the flagstones leading up to the rectory front door; on the splendidly living stone walls, here grey stone, there yellow; even in the seldom used larders and pantries; assuredly on the roof, which, happily, was of stone slabs also.

As always when he visited his brother, Stephen found that he was spending much of his time out of doors; mainly, being the man he was, in long, solitary walks across the heathered uplands. This had nothing to do with Harewood's speciality. Harewood suffered badly from bronchitis and catarrh, and nowadays went out as little as possible. The domestic lichens, once intro-duced, required little attention – only observation.

Rather it was on account of Harewood's wife, Harriet, that Stephen roamed; a lady in whose company Stephen had never been at ease. She had always seemed to him a restless woman; jumpy and puzzling, the very reverse of all that had seemed best about Elizabeth. A doubtful as-set, Stephen would have thought, in a diminishing rural parish; but Stephen himself, in a quiet and unobtrud-ing way, had long been something of a sceptic. Be that as it might, he always found that Harriet seemed to be baiting and fussing him, not least when her husband was present; even, unforgivably, when Elizabeth, down in London, had been battling through her last dread-ful years. On every visit, therefore, Stephen wandered about for long hours in the open, even when ice was in the air and snow on the tenuous tracks.

But Stephen did not see it as a particular hardship. Elizabeth, who might have done – though, for his sake, she could have been depended upon to conceal the fact – had seldom come on these visits at any time. She had never been a country girl, though fond of the sea. Stephen positively liked wandering unaccompanied on the moors, though he had little detailed knowledge of their flora and fauna, or even of their archaeology, largely industrial and fragmentary. By now he was familiar with most of the moorland routes from the rectory and the village, and, as commonly happens, there was one that he preferred to all the others, and nowadays found himself taking almost without having to make a decision. Sometimes even, asleep in his London flat that until just now had been *their* London flat, he found himself actually dreaming of that particular soaring trail, though he would have found it difficult to define what properties of beauty or poetry or convenience it had of which the other tracks had less. According to the map, it led to a spot named Burton's Clough.

There was a vague valley or extended hollow more or less in the place which the map indicated, but to Stephen it every time seemed too indefinite to be marked out for record. Every time he wondered whether this was indeed the place; whether there was not some more decisive declivity that he had never discovered. Or possibly the name derived from some event in local history. It was the upwards walk to the place that appealed to Stephen, and, to only slightly lesser extent, the first part of the slow descent homewards, supposing that the rectory could in any sense be called home: never the easily attainable but inconclusive supposed goal, the clough. Of course there was always R. L. Stevenson's travelling hopefully to be inwardly quoted; and on most occasions hitherto Stephen had inwardly quoted it.

Never had there been any human being at, near, or visible from the terrain around Burton's Clough, let alone in the presumptive clough itself. There was no apparent reason why there should be. Stephen seldom met anyone at all on the moors. Only organisations go any distance afoot nowadays, and this was not an approved didactic district. All the work of agriculture is for a period being done by machines. Most of the cottages are peopled by transients. Everyone is supposed to have a car.

But that morning, Stephen's first in the field since his bereavement six weeks before, there *was* someone, and down at the bottom of the shallow clough itself. The person was dressed so as to be almost lost in the hues of autumn, plainly neither tripper nor trifler. The person was engaged in some task.

Stephen was in no state for company, but that very condition, and a certain particular reluctance that morning to return to the rectory before he had to, led him to advance further, not descending into the clough but skirting along the ridge to the west of it, where, indeed, his track continued.

If he had been in the Alps, his shadow might have fallen in the early-autumn sun across the figure below, but in the circumstances that idea would have been fanciful, because, at the moment, the sun was no more than a misty bag of gleams in a confused sky. None the less, as Stephen's figure passed, comparatively high above, the figure below glanced up at him. Stephen could see that it was the figure of a girl. She was wearing a fawn shirt and pale green trousers, but the nature of her activity remained uncertain.

Stephen glanced away, then glanced back.

She seemed still to be looking up at him, and suddenly he waved to her, though it was not altogether a kind of thing he normally did. She waved back at him. Stephen even fancied she smiled at him. It seemed quite likely. She resumed her task.

He waited for an instant, but she looked up no more. He continued on his way more slowly, and feeling more alive, even if only for moments. For these moments, it had been as if he still belonged to the human race, to the mass of mankind.

Only once or twice previously had he continued beyond the top of Burton's Clough, and never for any great distance. On the map (it had been his father's map), the track wavered on across a vast area of nothing very much, merely contour lines and occasional habitations with odd, possibly evocative, names: habitations which, as Stephen knew from experience, regularly proved, when approached, to be littered ruins or not to be detectable at all. He would not necessarily have been averse to the twelve or fourteen miles' solitary walk involved, at least while Elizabeth had been secure and alive, and at home in London; but conditions at the rectory had never permitted so long an absence. Harriet often made clear that she expected her guests to be present punctually at all meals and punctually at such other particular turning points of a particular day as the day itself might define.

On the present occasion, and at the slow pace into which he had subsided, Stephen knew that he should turn back within the next ten to fifteen minutes; but he half-understood that what he was really doing was calculating the best time for a second possible communication with the girl he had seen in the clough. If he reappeared too soon, he might be thought, at such a spot, to be pestering, even menacing: if too late, the girl might be gone. In any case, there was an obvious limit to the time he could give to such approach as might be possible.

As the whole matter crystallised within him, he turned on the instant. There was a stone beside the track at the point where he did it; perhaps aforetime a milepost, at the least a waymark. Its location seemed to justify his action. He noticed that it too was patched with lichen. When staying with Harewood, he always noticed; and more and more at other times too.

One might almost have thought that the girl had been waiting for him. She was standing at much the same spot, and looking upwards abstractedly. Stephen saw that beside her on the ground was a grey receptacle. He had not noticed it before, because its vague colour sank into the landscape, as did the girl herself, costumed as she was. The receptacle seemed to be half-filled with grey contents of some kind.

As soon as he came into her line of sight, and

sometime before he stood immediately above her, the girl spoke.

'Are you lost? Are you looking for someone?'

She must have had a remarkably clear voice, because her words came floating up to Stephen like bubbles in water.

He continued along the ridge towards her while she watched him. Only when he was directly above her did he trust his own words to reach her.

'No. I'm really just filling in time. Thank you very much.'

'If you go on to the top, there's a spring.'

'I should think you have to have it pointed out to you. With all this heather.'

She looked down for a moment, then up again. 'Do you live here?'

'No. I'm staying with my brother. He's the rector. Perhaps you go to his church?'

She shook her head. 'No. We don't go to any church.'

That could not be followed up, Stephen felt, at his present distance and altitude. 'What are you doing?' he asked.

'Collecting stones for my father.'

'What does he do with them?'

'He wants the mosses and lichens.'

'Then,' cried Stephen, 'you *must* know my brother. Or your father must know him. My brother is one of the great authorities on lichens.' This unexpected link seemed to open a door; and, at least for a second, to open it surprisingly wide.

Stephen found himself bustling down the rough but not particularly steep slope towards her.

'My father's not an *authority*,' said the girl, gazing seriously at the descending figure. 'He's not an authority on anything.'

'Oh, you misunderstand,' said Stephen. 'My brother is only an amateur too. I didn't mean he was a professor or anything like that. Still, I think your father must have heard of him.'

'I don't think so,' said the girl. 'I'm almost sure not.'

Stephen had nearly reached the bottom of the shallow vale. It was completely out of the wind down there, and surprisingly torrid.

'Let me see,' he said, looking into the girl's basket, before he looked at the girl.

She lifted the basket off the ground. Her hand and forearm were brown.

'Some of the specimens are very small,' he said, smiling. It was essential to keep the conversation going, and it was initially more difficult now that he was alone with her in the valley, and close to her.

'It's been a bad year,' she said. 'Some days I've found almost nothing. Nothing that could be taken home.'

'All the same, the basket must be heavy. Please put it down.' He saw that it was reinforced with stout metal strips, mostly rusty.

'Take a piece for yourself, if you like,' said the girl. She spoke as if they were portions of iced cake, or homemade coconut fudge.

Stephen gazed full at the girl. She had a sensitive face

with grey-green eyes and short reddish hair – no, auburn. The *démodé* word came to Stephen on the instant. Both her shirt and her trousers were worn and faded: familiar, Stephen felt. She was wearing serious shoes, but little cared for. She was part of nature.

'I'll take this piece,' Stephen said. 'It's conglomerate.'

'Is it?' said the girl. Stephen was surprised that after so much ingathering, she did not know a fact so elementary.

'I might take this piece too, and show the stuff on it to my brother.'

'Help yourself,' said the girl. 'But don't take them all.'

Feeling had been building up in Stephen while he had been walking solitarily on the ridge above. For so long he had been isolated, insulated, incarcerated. Elizabeth had been everything to him, and no one could ever be like her, but 'attractive' was not a word that he had used to himself about her, not for a long time; not attractive as this girl was attractive. Elizabeth had been a part of him, perhaps the greater part of him; but not mysterious, not fascinating.

'Well, I don't know,' said Stephen. 'How far do you have to carry that burden?'

'The basket isn't full yet. I must go on searching for a bit.'

'I am sorry to say I can't offer to help. I have to go back.'

All the same, Stephen had reached a decision.

The girl simply nodded. She had not yet picked up the basket again.

'Where do you live?'

'Quite near.'

That seemed to Stephen to be almost impossible, but it was not the main point.

Stephen felt like a schoolboy; though not like himself as a schoolboy. 'If I were to be here after lunch tomorrow, say at half past two, would you show me the spring? The spring you were talking about.'

'Of course,' she said. 'If you like.'

Stephen could not manage the response so obviously needed, gently confident; if possible, even gently witty. For a moment, in fact, he could say nothing. Then – 'Look,' he said. He brought an envelope out of his pocket and in pencil on the back of it he wrote. 'Tomorrow. Here. 2.30 p.m. To visit the spring.'

He said, 'It's too big,' and tore one end off the envelope, aware that the remaining section bore his name, and that the envelope had been addressed to him care of his brother. As a matter of fact, it had contained the final communication from the undertaking firm. He wished they had omitted his equivocal and rather ridiculous OBE.

He held the envelope out. She took it and inserted it, without a word, into a pocket of her shirt, buttoning down the flap. Stephen's heart beat at the gesture.

He was not exactly sure what to make of the situation or whether the appointment was to be depended upon. But at such moments in life, one is often sure of neither thing, nor of anything much else.

He looked at her. 'What's your name?' he asked, as

casually as he could.

'Nell,' she answered.

He had not quite expected that, but then he had not particularly expected anything else either.

'I look forward to our walk, Nell,' he said. He could not help adding, 'I look forward to it very much.'

She nodded and smiled.

He fancied that they had already looked at one another for a moment.

'I must go on searching,' she said.

She picked up the heavy basket, seemingly without particular effort, and walked away from him, up the valley.

Insanely, he wondered about *her* lunch. Surely she must have some? She seemed so exceptionally healthy and strong.

His own meal was all scarlet runners, but he had lost his appetite in any case, something that had never previously happened since the funeral, as he had noticed with surprise on several occasions.

Luncheon was called lunch, but the evening meal was none the less called supper, perhaps from humility. At supper that evening, Harriet referred forcefully to Stephen's earlier abstemiousness.

'I trust you're not sickening, Stephen. It would be a bad moment. Dr Gopalachari's on holiday. Perhaps I ought to warn you.'

'Dr Who?'

'No, not Dr Who. Dr Gopalachari. He's a West

284

Bengali. We are lucky to have him.'

Stephen's brother, Harewood, coughed forlornly.

For luncheon the next day, Stephen had even less appetite, even though it was mashed turnip, cooked, or at least served, with mixed peppers. Harriet loved all things oriental.

On an almost empty stomach, he hastened up the long but not steep ascent. He had not known he could still walk so fast uphill, but for some reason the knowledge did not make him particularly happy, as doubtless it should have done.

The girl, dressed as on the day before, was seated upon a low rock at the spot from which he had first spoken to her. It was not yet twenty past. He had discerned her seated shape from afar, but she had proved to be sitting with her back to the ascending track and to him. On the whole, he was glad that she had not been watching his exertions, inevitably comical, albeit triumphant.

She did not even look up until he actually stood before her. Of course this time she had no basket.

'Oh, hullo,' she said.

He stood looking at her. 'We're both punctual.'

She nodded. He was panting quite strenuously, and glad to gain a little time.

He spoke. 'Did you find many more suitable stones?'

She shook her head, then rose to her feet.

He found it difficult not to stretch out his arms and draw her to him.

'Why is this called Burton's Clough, I wonder? It seems altogether too wide and shallow for a clough.'

'I didn't know it was,' said the girl.

'The map says it is. At least I think this is the place. Shall we go? Lead me to the magic spring.'

She smiled at him. 'Why do you call it *that*?'

'I'm sure it *is* magic. It must be.'

'It's just clear water,' said the girl, 'and very, very deep.'

Happily, the track was still wide enough for them to walk side by side, though Stephen realised that, further on, where he had not been, this might cease to be the case.

'How long are you staying here?' asked the girl.

'Perhaps for another fortnight. It depends.'

'Are you married?'

'I *was* married, Nell, but my wife unfortunately died.' It seemed unnecessary to put any date to it, and calculated only to cause stress.

'I'm sorry,' said the girl.

'She was a wonderful woman and a very good wife.'

To that the girl said nothing. What could she say.

'I am taking a period of leave from the civil service,' Stephen volunteered. 'Nothing very glamorous.'

'What's the civil service?' asked the girl.

'You ought to know *that*,' said Stephen in mock reproof: more or less mock. After all, she was not a child, or not exactly. All the same, he produced a childlike explanation. 'The civil service is what looks after the country. The country would hardly carry on without us.

286

Not nowadays. Nothing would run properly.'

'Really not?'

'No. Not run *properly*.' With her it was practicable to be lightly profane.

'Father says that all politicians are evil. I don't know anything about it.'

'Civil servants are not politicians, Nell. But perhaps this is not the best moment to go into it all.' He said that partly because he suspected she had no wish to learn.

There was a pause.

'Do you like walking?' she asked.

'Very much. I could easily walk all day. Would you come with me?'

'I *do* walk all day, or most of it. Of course I have to sleep at night. I lie in front of the fire.'

'But it's too warm for a fire at this time of year.' He said it to keep the conversation going, but, in fact, he was far from certain. He himself was not particularly warm at that very moment. He had no doubt cooled off after speeding up the ascent, but the two of them were, none the less, walking reasonably fast, and still he felt chilly, perhaps perilously so.

'Father always likes a fire,' said the girl. 'He's a cold mortal.'

They had reached the decayed milestone or waymark at which Stephen had turned on the previous day. The girl had stopped and was fingering the lichens with which it was spattered. She knelt against the stone with her left arm round the back of it.

'Can you put a name to them?' asked Stephen.

'Yes, to some of them.'

'I am sure your father has one of my brother's books on his shelf.'

'I don't think so,' said the girl. 'We have no shelves. Father can't read.'

She straightened up and glanced at Stephen.

'Oh, but surely—'

For example, and among other things, the girl herself was perfectly well spoken. As a matter of fact, hers was a noticeably beautiful voice. Stephen had noticed it, and even thrilled to it, when first he had heard it, floating up from the bottom of the so-called clough. He had thrilled to it ever since, despite the curious things the girl sometimes said.

They resumed their way.

'Father has no eyes,' said the girl.

'That is terrible,' said Stephen. 'I hadn't realised.'

The girl said nothing.

Stephen felt his first real qualm, as distinct from mere habitual self-doubt. 'Am I taking you away from him? Should you go back to him?'

'I'm never with him by day,' said the girl. 'He finds his way about.

'I know that does happen,' said Stephen guardedly. 'All the same—'

'Father doesn't need a civil service to run him,' said the girl. The way she spoke convinced Stephen that she had known all along what the civil service was and did. He had from the first supposed that to be so. Everyone knew.

'You said your dead wife was a wonderful women,' said the girl.

'Yes, she was.'

'My father is a wonderful man.'

'Yes,' said Stephen. 'I am only sorry about his affliction.'

'It's not an affliction,' said the girl.

Stephen did not know what to say to that. The last thing to be desired was an argument of any kind whatever, other perhaps than a fun argument.

'Father doesn't need to get things out of books,' said the girl.

'There are certainly other ways of learning,' said Stephen. 'I expect that was one of the things you yourself learned at school.'

He suspected she would say she had never been to school. His had been a half-fishing remark.

But all she replied was, 'Yes.'

Stephen looked around him for a moment. Already, he had gone considerably further along the track than ever before. 'It really is beautiful up here.' It seemed a complete wilderness. The track had wound among the wide folds of the hill, so that nothing but wilderness was visible in any direction.

'I should like to live here,' said Stephen. 'I should like it *now*.' He knew that he partly meant 'now that Elizabeth was dead'.

'There are empty houses everywhere,' said the girl. 'You can just move into one. It's what Father and I did, and now it's our home.'

Stephen supposed that that at least explained something. It possibly elucidated one of the earliest of her odd remarks.

'I'll help you find one, if you like,' said the girl. 'Father says that none of them have been lived in for hundreds of years. I know where all the best ones are.'

'I'll have to think about that,' said Stephen. 'I have my job, you must remember.' He wanted her to be rude about his job.

But she only said, 'We'll look now, if you like.'

'Tomorrow, perhaps. We're looking for the spring now.'

'Are you tired?' asked the girl, with apparently genuine concern, and presumably forgetting altogether what he had told her about his longing to walk all day.

'Not at all tired,' said Stephen, smiling at her.

'Then why were you looking at your watch?'

'A bad habit picked up in the civil service. We all do it.'

He had observed long before that she had no watch on her lovely brown forearm, no bracelet; only the marks of thorn scratches and the incisions of sharp stones. The light golden bloom on her arms filled him with delight and with desire.

In fact, he had omitted to time their progression, though he timed most things, so that the habit had wrecked his natural faculty. Perhaps another twenty or thirty minutes passed, while they continued to walk side by side, the track having as yet shown no particular sign of narrowing, so that one might think it still led somewhere, and that people still went there. As they advanced, they said little more of consequence for the moment; or so it seemed to Stephen. He surmised that there was now what is termed an understanding between them, even though in a sense he himself understood very little. It was more a phase for pleasant nothings, he deemed, always supposing that he could evolve a sufficient supply of them, than for meaningful questions and reasonable responses.

Suddenly, the track seemed not to narrow, but to stop, even to vanish. Hereunto it had been surprisingly well trodden. Now he could see nothing but knee-high heather.

'The spring's over there,' said the girl in a matter-of-fact way, and pointing. Such simple and natural gestures are often the most beautiful.

'How right I was in saying that I could never find it alone!' remarked Stephen.

He could not see why the main track should not lead to the spring – if there really was a spring. Why else should the track be beaten to this spot? The mystery was akin to the Burton's Clough mystery. The uplands had been settled under other conditions than ours. Stephen, on his perambulations, had always felt that, everywhere.

But the girl was standing among the heather a few yards away, and Stephen saw that there was a curious serpentine rabbit-run that he had failed to notice – except that rabbits do not run like serpents. There were several fair-sized birds flying overhead in silence.

Stephen fancied they were kites.

He wriggled his way down the rabbit path, with little dignity.

There was the most beautiful small pool imaginable: clear, deep, lustrous, gently heaving at its centre, or near its centre. It stood in a small clearing.

All the rivers in Britain might be taken as rising here, and thus flowing until the first moment of their pollution.

Stephen became aware that now the sun really *was* shining. He had not noticed before. The girl stood on the far side of the pool in her faded shirt and trousers, smiling seraphically. The pool pleased her, so that suddenly everything pleased her.

'Have you kept the note I gave you?' asked Stephen.

She put her hand lightly on her breast pocket, and therefore on her breast.

'I'm glad,' said Stephen.

If the pool had not been between them, he would have seized her, whatever the consequences.

'Just clear water,' said the girl.

The sun brought out new colours in her hair. The shape of her head was absolutely perfect.

'The track,' said Stephen, 'seems to be quite well used. Is this where the people come?'

'No,' said the girl. 'They come to and from the places where they live.'

'I thought you said all the houses were empty.'

'What I said was there are many empty houses.'

'That *is* what you said. I'm sorry. But the track seems

to come to an end. What do the people do then?'

'They find their way,' said the girl. 'Stop worrying about them.'

The water was still between them. Stephen was no longer in doubt that there was indeed something else between them. Really there was. The pool was intermittently throwing up tiny golden waves in the pure breeze, then losing them again.

'We haven't seen anybody,' said Stephen. 'I never do see anyone.'

The girl looked puzzled.

Stephen realised that the way he had put it, the statement that he never saw anyone might have been tactless. 'When I go for my long walks alone,' he added.

'Not only then,' said the girl.

Stephen's heart turned over slightly.

'Possibly,' he said. 'I daresay you are very right.'

The kites were still flapping like torn pieces of charred pasteboard in the high air, though in the lower part of it.

'You haven't even looked to the bottom of the pool yet,' said the girl.

'I suppose not.' Stephen fell on his knees, as the girl had done at the milestone or waymark, and gazed downwards through the pellucid near-nothingness beneath the shifting golden rods. There were a few polished stones round the sides, but little else that he could see, and nothing that seemed of significance. How should there be, of course? Unless the girl had put it there, as Stephen realised might have been possible.

Stephen looked up. 'It's a splendid pool,' he said.

But now his eye caught something else; something other than the girl and the pool. On the edge of the rising ground behind the girl stood a small stone house. It was something else that Stephen had not previously noticed. Indeed, he had been reasonably sure that there had been nothing and no one, not so much as a hint of mankind, not for a quite long way, a quite long time.

'Is that where one of the people lives?' he asked, and in his turn pointed. 'Or perhaps more than one?'

'It's empty,' said the girl.

'Should we go and look?'

'If you like.' said the girl. Stephen quite saw that his expressed response to the glorious little spring had been inadequate. He had lost the trick of feeling, years and years ago.

'It's a splendid pool,' he said again, a little self-consciously.

Despite what the girl had said, Stephen had thought that to reach the house above them, they would have to scramble through the high heather. But he realised at once that there was a path, which was one further thing he had not previously noticed.

The girl went before, weaving backwards and forwards up the hillside. Following her, with his thoughts more free to wander, as the exertion made talking difficult, Stephen suddenly apprehended that the need to return for Harriet's teatime had for a season passed completely from his mind.

Apprehending it now, he did not even look at his

watch. Apart from anything else, the struggle upwards was too intense for even the smallest distraction or secondary effort. The best thing might be for his watch simply to stop.

They were at the summit, with a wider horizon, but still Stephen could see no other structure than the one before him, though this time he gazed around with a certain care. From here, the pool below them seemed to catch the full sun all over its surface. It gleamed among the heathered rocks like a vast luminous sea anemone among weeds.

Stephen could see at once that the house appeared basically habitable. He had expected jagged holes in the walls, broken panes in the windows, less than half a roof, ubiquitous litter.

The door simply stood open, but it was a door, not a mere gap; a door in faded green, like the girl's trousers. Inside, the floorboards were present and there was even a certain amount of simple furniture, though, as an estate agent would at once have pointed out with apologies, no curtains and no carpets.

'Nell. Somebody lives here already,' Stephen said sharply, before they had even gone upstairs.

'Already?' queried the girl.

Stephen made the necessary correction. 'Someone lives here.'

'No,' said the girl. 'No one. Not for centuries.'

Of course that was particularly absurd and childish. Much of this furniture, Stephen thought, was of the kind offered by the furnishing department of a good

Co-op. Stephen had sometimes come upon such articles on visits paid in the course of his work. He had to admit, however, that he had little idea when such houses as this actually were built at these odd spots on the moors. Possibly as long ago as in the seventeenth century? Possibly only sixty or eighty years ago? Possibly—?

They went upstairs. There were two very low rooms, hardly as much as half lighted from one small and dirty window in each. One room was totally unfurnished. The sole content of the other was a double bed which absorbed much of the cubic capacity available. It was a quite handsome country object, with a carved head and foot. It even offered a seemingly intact mattress, badly in need of a wash.

'Someone *must* be living here,' said Stephen. 'At least sometimes. Perhaps the owners come here for the weekend. Or perhaps they're just moving in.'

As soon as he spoke, it occurred to him that the evidence was equally consistent with their moving out, but he did not continue.

'Lots of the houses are like this,' said the girl. 'No one lives in them.'

Stephen wondered vaguely whether the clear air or some factor of that kind might preserve things as if they were still in use. It was a familiar enough notion, though, in this case, somewhat unspecific. It would be simpler to disbelieve the girl, who was young and without experience, though perfectly eager. They returned downstairs.

'Shall we see some more houses?' asked the girl.

'I don't think I have the time.'

'You said you had a fortnight. I know what a fortnight is.'

'Yes.' He simply could not tell her that he had to report for Harriet's astringent teatime; nor, even now, was that in the forefront of his mind. The truth was that whereas hitherto he had been trying to paddle in deep waters, he was now floundering in them.

The girl had a suggestion. 'Why not live *here* for a fortnight?'

'I am committed to staying with my brother. He's not very fit. I should worry about him if I broke my word.' He realised that he was speaking to her in a more adult way than before. It had really begun with her speaking similarly to him.

'Does your worrying about him do him any good?'

'Not much, I'm afraid.'

'Does your worrying about everything do *you* any good?'

'None whatever, Nell. None at all.'

He turned aside and looked out of the window; the parlour window might not be too grand a term, for all its need of cleaning.

He addressed her firmly. 'Would you give me a hand with all the things that need to be done? Even for a tenancy of a fortnight?'

'If you like.'

'We should have to do a lot of shopping.'

The girl, standing behind him, remained silent. It was an unusual nonresponse.

'I should have to cook on a primus stove,' said Stephen. 'I wonder if we can buy one? I used to be quite good with them.' Rapture was beginning.

The girl said nothing.

'We might need new locks on the doors.'

The girl spoke. 'There is only one door.'

'So there is,' said Stephen. 'In towns, houses have two, a front door and a back door. When trouble comes in at one, you can do a bolt through the other.'

'People don't need a lock,' said the girl. 'Why should they?'

He turned away from the filthy window and gazed straight at her. 'Suppose I was to fall in love with you?' he said.

'Then you would not have to go back after a fortnight.'

It could hardly have been a straighter reply.

He put one arm round her shoulders, one hand on her breast, so that the note he had written her lay between them. He remembered that the first letter written to a woman is always a love letter. 'Would you promise to visit me every day?'

'I might be unable to do that.'

'I don't want to seem unkind, but you did say that your father could manage?'

'If he discovers, he will keep me at home and send my sister out instead. He has powers. He's very frightening.'

Stephen relaxed his hold a little. He had been all along well aware how sadly impracticable was the entire idea.

For example: he could hardly even drive up to this place with supplies; even had his car not been in the course of an opportune overhaul in London, a very complete overhaul after all this anxious time. And that was only one thing; one among very many.

'Well, what's the answer?' Stephen said, smiling at her in the wrong way, longing for her in a very different way.

'I can't come and go the whole time,' said the girl.

'I see,' said Stephen.

He who had missed so many opportunities, always for excellent reasons, and for one excellent reason in particular, clearly saw that this might be his last opportunity, and almost certainly was.

'How should we live?' he asked. 'I mean how should we eat and manage?'

'As the birds do,' said the girl.

Stephen did not enquire of her how she came to know Shakespeare, as people put it. He might ask her that later. In the meantime, he could see that the flat, floating birds he had taken to be kites, were indeed drifting past the dirty window, and round and round the house, as it seemed. Of course his questions had been mere routine in any case. He could well have killed himself if she had made a merely routine response.

'Let's see,' he said. He gently took her hand. He kissed her softly on the lips. He returned with her upstairs.

It would perhaps have been more suitable if he had been leading the party, but that might be a trifle. Even the damp discoloration of the mattress might be a trifle. Harriet's teatime could not, in truth, be forced from the mind, but it was provisionally overruled. One learned the trick in the course of one's work, or one would break altogether.

There were of course only the bed and the mattress; no sheets or blankets; no Spanish or Kashmiri rugs; no entangling silkiness, no singing save that of the moor. Elizabeth had never wished to make love like that. She had liked to turn on the record-player, almost always Brahms or Schumann (the Rhenish Symphony was her particular favourite), and to ascend slowly into a deep fully made bed. But the matter had not seriously arisen for years. Stephen had often wondered why not.

Nell was lying on her front. Seemingly expectant and resistant at the same time, she clung like a clam. Her body was as brown as pale chestnut, but it was a strong and well-made body. Her short hair was wavy rather than curly. Stephen was ravished by the line of it on her strong neck. He was ravished by her relaxed shoulder blade. He was ravished by her perfect waist and thighs. He was ravished by her youth and youthful smell.

'Please turn over,' he said, after tugging at her intermittently, and not very effectively.

Fortunately, he was not too displeased by his own appearance. The hair on his body was bleaching and fading, but otherwise he could, quite sincerely, see little difference from when he had been twenty-four, and had married Elizabeth. He knew, however, that at these times sincerity is not enough; nor objectivity either. When are they?

'Please,' he said softly in Nell's ear. Her ears were a slightly unusual shape, and the most beautiful he had ever beheld, or beheld so intently.

He put his hand lightly on her neck. 'Please,' he said.

She wriggled over in a single swift movement, like a light stab from an invisible knife. He saw that her eyes were neither closed nor open, neither looking at him, nor looking at anything but him.

On the skin between her right shoulder and her right breast was a curious, brownish, greyish, bluish irregular mark or patch, which had been hidden by her shirt, though Stephen could not quite see how. It was more demanding of attention than it might have been, partly because of its position, and partly, where Stephen was concerned, because of something vaguely else. In any case, it would mean that the poor girl could not re-posefully wear a low-cut dress, should the need arise. Though it was by no means a birthmark in the usual sense, Nell had probably been lying on her front through chagrin about it. Upon Stephen, however, the effect was to make him love her more deeply; perhaps love her for the first time. He did not want her or her body to be quite perfect. In a real person, it would be al-most vulgar. At this point, Harriet and Harriet's teatime came more prominently into view for a few seconds.

Nell might say something about the mark sooner or later. He would never take an initiative.

At the moment, she said nothing at all. He simply

could not make out whether she was watching him or not. Her mouth was long and generous in a marvellous degree. He could not even make out whether she was taut or relaxed. No small mystery was Nell after years and years of a perfect, but always slow-moving, relationship with Elizabeth!

He kissed her intimately. When she made no particular response, not even a grunt, he began to caress her, more or less as he had caressed his wife. He took care not to touch the peculiar blemish, or even to enter its area. There was no need to do so. It occurred to Stephen that the mark might be the consequence of an injury; and so might in due course disappear, or largely so. In the end that happened even to many of the strangest human markings. One day, as the nannies used to say.

Suddenly she made a wild plunge at him that took away his breath. The surprise was directly physical, but moral also. He had found it a little difficult to assess Nell's likely age, and enquiry was out of the question; but he had supposed it probable that she was a virgin, and had quite deliberately resolved to accept the implication. Or so he had believed of himself.

Now she was behaving as a maenad.

As an oread, rather; Stephen thought at a later hour. For surely those moors were mountains, often above the thousand-foot contour; boundless uplands peopled solely by unwedded nymphs and their monstrous progenitors? Stephen had received a proper education at a proper place: in Stephen's first days, one had not made the grade, Stephen's grade, otherwise. Stephen's parents had undertaken sacrifices so immense that no one had fully recovered from them.

The last vestige of initiative had passed from Stephen like a limb. And yet, he fancied, it was not because Nell was what Elizabeth would have called unfeminine, but merely because she was young, and perhaps because she lived with contamination, merging into the aspect and mutability of remote places. So, at least, he could only suppose.

Soon he ceased to suppose anything. He knew bliss unequalled, unprecedented, assuredly unimagined. Moreover, the wonder lasted for longer than he would have conceived of as possible. That particularly struck him.

Nell's flawed body was celestial. Nell herself was more wonderful than the dream of death. Nell could not possibly exist.

He was fondling her and feeling a trifle cold; much as Elizabeth would have felt. Not that it mattered in the very least. Nell was no maenad or oread. She was a half-frightened child, sweetly soft, responsive to his every thought, sometimes before he had fully given birth to it. She was a waif, a foundling. And it was he who had found her. And only yesterday.

'Tell me about your sister,' said Stephen. He realised that it was growing dark as well as chilly.

'She's not like *me*. You wouldn't like her.'

Stephen knew that ordinary, normal girls always

responded much like that.

He smiled at Nell. 'But what is she like?'

'She's made quite differently. You wouldn't care for her.'

'Has she a name?'

'Of a sort.'

'What do you and your father call her?'

'We call her different things at different times. You're cold.'

She was a human, after all, Stephen thought.

She herself had very little to put on. Two fairly light garments, a pair of stout socks, her solid shoes.

They went downstairs.

'Would you care to borrow my sweater?' asked Stephen. 'Until tomorrow?'

She made no reply, but simply stared at him through the dusk in the downstairs room, the living place, the parlour, the *salon*.

'Take it,' said Stephen. It was a heavy garment. Elizabeth had spent nearly four months knitting it continuously, while slowly recovering from her very first disintegration. It was in thick complex stitches and meant to last for ever. When staying with Harewood, Stephen wore it constantly.

Nell took the sweater but did not put it on. She was still staring at him. At such a moment her grey-green eyes were almost luminous.

'We'll meet again tomorrow,' said Stephen firmly. 'We'll settle down here tomorrow. I must say something to my brother and sister-in-law, and I don't care what happens after that. Not now. At least I *do* care. I care very much. As you well know.'

'It's risky,' she said.

'Yes,' he replied, because it was necessary to evade all discussion. 'Yes, but it can't be helped. You come as early as you can, and I'll arrive with some provisions for us. We really need some blankets too, and some candles. I'll see if I can borrow a Land Rover from one of the farms.' He trusted that his confidence and his firm, practical actions would override all doubts.

'I may be stopped,' she said. 'My father can't read books but he can read minds. He does it all the time.'

'You must run away from him,' said Stephen firmly. 'We'll stay here for a little, and then you can come back to London with me.'

She made no comment on that, but simply repeated, 'My father can read *my* mind. I only have to be in the same room with him. He's frightening.'

Her attitude to her father seemed to have changed considerably. It was the experience of love, Stephen supposed: first love.

'Obviously, you must try to be in a *different* room as much as possible. It's only for one more night. We've known each other now for two days.'

'There's only one room.'

Stephen had known that such would be her rejoinder.

He well knew also that his behaviour might seem unromantic and even cold-hearted. But the compulsion upon him could not be plainer: if he did not return to the rectory tonight, Harriet, weakly aided by

305

Harewood, would have the police after him; dogs would be scurrying across the moors, as if after Hercules, and perhaps searchlights sweeping also. Nothing could more fatally upset any hope of a quiet and enduring compact with such a one as Nell. He was bound for a rough scene with Harriet and Harewood as it was. It being now long past teatime, he would be lucky if Harriet had not taken action before he could reappear. Speed was vital and, furthermore, little of the situation could be explained with any candour to Nell. First, she would simply not understand what he said (even though within her range she was shrewd enough, often shrewder than he). Second, in so far as she did understand, she would panic and vanish. And he had no means of tracking her down at all. She was as shy about her abode as about the mark on her body; though doubtless with as little reason, or so Stephen hoped. He recognised that parting from her at all might be as unwise as it would be painful, but it was the lesser peril. He could not take her to London tonight, or to anywhere, because there was no accessible transport. Not nowadays. He could not take her to the rectory, where Harriet might make Harewood lay an anathema upon her. They could not stay in the moorland house without food or warmth.

'I'll walk with you to the top of the clough,' he said.

She shook her head. 'It's not there I live.'

'Where then?' he asked at once.

'Not that way at all.'

'Will you get there?'

She nodded: in exactly what spirit it was hard to say.

He refrained from enquiring how she would explain the absence of specimens for her father. Two or three stones dragged from the walls of the house they were in might serve the purpose in any case, he thought: outside and inside were almost equally mossed, lichened, adorned, encumbered.

'Goodnight, Nell. We'll meet tomorrow morning. Here.' He really had to go. Harriet was made anxious by the slightest irregularity, and when she became anxious, she became frenzied. His present irregularity was by no means slight already; assuredly not slight by Harriet's standards.

To his great relief, Nell nodded again. She had still not put on his sweater.

'In a few days' time, we'll go to London. We'll be together always.' He could hardly believe his own ears listening to his own voice saying such things. After all this time! After Elizabeth! After so much inner peace and convinced adoration and asking for nothing more! After the fearful illness!

They parted with kisses but with little drama. Nell sped off into what the map depicted as virtual void.

'All the same,' Stephen reflected, 'I must look at the map again. I'll try to borrow Harewood's dividers.'

He pushed back through the heather, rejoicing in his sense of direction, among so many other things to rejoice about, and began lumbering down the track homewards. The light was now so poor that he walked faster and faster; faster even than he had ascended. In the end, he was running uncontrollably.

Therefore, his heart was already pounding when he discovered that the rectory was in confusion; though, at the rectory, even confusion had a slightly wan quality.

During the afternoon, Harriet had had a seizure of some kind, and during the evening had been taken off in a public ambulance.

'What time did it happen?' asked Stephen. He knew from all too much experience that it was the kind of thing that people did ask.

'I don't really know, Stephen,' replied Harewood. 'I was in my specimens room reading the *Journal*, and I fear that a considerable time may have passed before I came upon her. I was too distressed to look at my watch even then. Besides, between ourselves, my watch loses rather badly.'

Though Stephen tried to help in some way, the improvised evening meal was upsetting. Harriet had planned rissoles sautéed in ghee, but neither of the men really knew how to cook with ghee. The homemade Congress Pudding was nothing less than nauseous. Very probably, some decisive final touches had been omitted.

'You see how it is, young Stephen,' said Harewood, after they had munched miserably but briefly. 'The prognosis cannot be described as hopeful. I may have to give up the living.'

'You can't possibly do that, Harewood, whatever happens. There is Father's memory to think about. I'm sure I should think about him more often myself.' Stephen's thoughts were, in fact, upon quite specially different topics.

'I don't wish to go, I assure you, Stephen. I've been very happy here.'

The statement surprised Stephen, but was of course thoroughly welcome and appropriate.

'There is always prayer, Harewood.'

'Yes, Stephen, indeed. I may well have been remiss. That might explain much.'

They had been unable to discover where Harriet hid the coffee, so sat for moments in reverent and reflective silence, one on either side of the bleak table: a gift from the nearest branch of the Free India League.

Stephen embarked upon a tentative *démarche*. 'I need hardly say that I don't want to leave you in the lurch.'

'It speaks for itself that there can be no question of that.'

Stephen drew in a quantity of air. To put it absolutely plainly, I feel that for a spell you would be better off at this time without me around to clutter up the place and make endless demands.'

For a second time within hours, Stephen recognised quite clearly that his line of procedure could well be seen as cold-blooded; but, for a second time, he was acting under extreme compulsion – compulsion more extreme than he had expected ever again to encounter, at least on the hither side of the Styx.

'I should never deem you to be doing that, young Stephen. Blood is at all times, even the most embarrass-ing times, thicker than water. It was Cardinal Newman, by the way, who first said that; a prelate of a different soteriology.'

Stephen simply did not believe it, but he said nothing. Harewood often came forward with such assertions, but they were almost invariably erroneous. Stephen sometimes doubted whether Harewood could be completely relied upon even in the context of his private speciality, the lichens.

'I think I had better leave tomorrow morning and so reduce the load for a span. I am sure Doreen will appreciate it.' Doreen was the intermittent help; a little brash, where in former days no doubt she would have been a little simple. Stephen had always supposed that brashness might make it more possible to serve Harriet. Doreen had been deserted, childless, by her young husband; but there had been a proper divorce. Harewood was supposed to be taking a keen interest in Doreen, who was no longer in her absolutely first youth.

'You will be rather more dependent upon Doreen for a time,' added Stephen.

'I suppose that may well be,' said Harewood. Stephen fancied that his brother almost smiled. He quite saw that he might have thought so because of the ideas in his own mind, at which he himself was smiling continuously.

'You must do whatever you think best for all concerned, Stephen,' said Harewood. 'Including, of course, your sister-in-law, dear Harriet.'

'I think I should go now and perhaps come back a little later.'

'As you will, Stephen. I have always recognised that you have a mind trained both academically and by your work. I am a much less co-ordinated spirit. Oh yes, I know it well. I should rely very much upon your judgement in almost any serious matter.'

Circumstanced as at the moment he was, Stephen almost blushed.

But Harewood made things all right by adding, 'Except perhaps in certain matters of the spirit which, in the nature of things, lie quite particularly between my Maker and myself alone.'

'Oh, naturally,' said Stephen.

'Otherwise,' continued Harewood, 'and now that Harriet is unavailable – for very short time only, we must hope – it is upon you, Stephen, that I propose to rely foremost, in many pressing concerns of this world.'

Beyond doubt, Harewood now was not all but smiling. He was smiling nearly at full strength. He explained this immediately.

'My catarrh seems very much better,' he said. 'I might consider setting forth in splendour one of these days. Seeking specimens, I mean.'

Stephen plunged upon impulse.

'It may seem a bit odd in the circumstances, but I should be glad to have the use of a Land Rover. There's a building up on the moors I should like to look at again before I go, and it's too far to walk in the time. There's a perfectly good track to quite near it. Is there anyone you know of in the parish who would lend me such a thing? Just for an hour or two, of course.'

Harewood responded at once. 'You might try Tom Jarrold. I regret to say that he's usually too drunk to drive. Indeed, one could never guarantee that his vehicle will even leave the ground.'

Possibly it was not exactly the right reference, but what an excellent and informed parish priest Harewood was suddenly proving to be!

Harewood had reopened the latest number of the *Journal*, which he had been sitting on in the chair all the time. His perusal had of course been interrupted by the afternoon's events.

'Don't feel called upon to stop talking,' said Harewood. 'I can read and listen at the same time perfectly well.'

Stephen reflected that the attempt had not often been made when Harriet had been in the room.

'I don't think there's anything more to say at the moment. We seem to have settled everything that *can* be settled.'

'I shall be depending upon you in many different matters, remember,' said Harewood, but without looking up from the speckled diagrams.

As soon as Stephen turned on the hanging light in his bedroom, he noticed the new patch on the wallpaper; if only because it was immediately above his bed. The wallpaper had always been lowering anyway. He was the more certain that the particular path was new because, naturally, he made his own bed each morning, which involved daily confrontation with that particular surface.

Of course there had always been the other such patches among the marks on the walls.

Still, the new arrival was undoubtedly among the reasons why Stephen slept very little that night, even though, in his own estimation, he needed sleep so badly. There again, however, few do sleep in the first phase of what is felt to be a reciprocated relationship; equally fulfilling and perilous, always deceptive, and always somewhere known to be. The mixed ingredients of the last two days churned within Stephen, as in Harriet's battered cookpot; one rising as another fell. He was treating Harewood as he himself would not wish to be treated; and who could tell what had really led to Harriet's collapse?

In the end, bliss drove out bewilderment, and seemed the one thing sure, as perhaps it was.

Later still, when daylight was all too visible through the frail curtains, Stephen half-dreamed that he was lying inert on some surface he could not define and that Nell was administering water to him from a chalice. But the chalice, doubtless a consecrated object to begin with, and certainly of fairest silver from the Spanish mines, was blotched and blemished. Stephen wanted to turn away, to close his eyes properly, to expostulate, but could do none of these things. As Nell gently kissed his brow, he awoke fully with a compelling thirst. He had heard of people waking thirsty in the night, but to himself he could not remember it ever before happening. He had never lived like that.

There was no water in the room, because the house was just sufficiently advanced to make visitors go to the bathroom. Stephen walked quietly down the passage, then hesitated. He recollected that nowadays the bathroom door opened with an appalling wrench and scream.

It would be very wrong indeed to take the risk of waking poor Harewood, in his new isolation. Stephen crept on down the stairs towards the scullery, and there *was* Harewood, sleeping like the dead, not in the least sprawling, but, on the contrary, touchingly compressed and compact in the worn chair. For a moment, he looked like a schoolboy, though of course in that curtained light.

Harewood was murmuring contentedly. 'Turn over. No, right over. You can trust me'; then, almost ecstatically, almost like a juvenile, 'It's beautiful. Oh, it's beautiful.'

Stephen stole away to the back quarters, where both the luncheon and the supper washing-up, even the washing-up after tea, all awaited the touch of a vanished hand.

The cold tap jerked and jarred as it always did, but when Stephen went back, Harewood was slumbering still. His self-converse was now so ideal that it had fallen into incoherence. The cheap figure on the mantel of Shiva or somebody, which Stephen had always detested, sneered animatedly.

But there Nell really was; really was.

In his soul, Stephen was astonished. Things do not go

like that in real life, least of all in the dreaded demesne of the heart.

However, they unloaded the Land Rover, as if everything were perfectly real; toiling up the heather paths with heavy loads. Nell always ahead, always as strong as he: which was really rather necessary.

'I must take the Rover back. Come with me.'

He had not for a moment supposed that she would, but she did, and with no demur.

'It's rough going,' he said. But she merely put her brown hand on his thigh, as she sat and bumped beside him.

They were a pair now.

'It won't take a moment while I settle with the man.'

He was determined that it should not. It must be undesirable that the two of them be seen together in the village. Probably it was undesirable that he himself, even alone, be seen there before a long time had passed. He might perhaps steal back one distant day like Enoch Arden, and take Harewood completely by surprise, both of them now bearded, shaggily or skimpily. What by then would have become of Nell?

They walked upwards hand in hand. Every now and then he said something amorous or amusing to her, but not very often because, as he had foreseen, the words did not come to him readily. He was bound to become more fluent as his heart reopened. She was now speaking more often than he was: not merely more shrewd, but more explicit.

'I'm as close to you as that,' she said, pointing with

her free hand to a patch of rocky ground with something growing on it – growing quite profusely, almost exuberantly. She had spoken in reply to one of his questions.

He returned the squeeze of the hand he was holding.

'We'll be like the holly and the ivy,' she volunteered later, 'and then we'll be like the pebble and the shard.'

He thought that both comparisons were, like Harewood's comparisons, somewhat inexact, but, in her case, all the more adorable by reason of it. He kissed her.

At first he could not see their house, though, as they neared it, his eyes seemed to wander round the entire horizon: limited in range, however, by the fact that they were mounting quite steeply. But Nell led the way through the rabbit and snake paths, first to the spring, then upwards once more; and there, needless to say, the house was. Earlier that afternoon they had already toiled up and down several times with the baggage. The earlier occupants had been sturdy folk; men and women alike; aboriginals.

It was somewhere near the spring that Nell, this time, made her possibly crucial declaration.

'I've run away,' she said, as if previously she had been afraid to speak the words. 'Take care of me.'

They entered.

When they had been lugging in the food and the blankets and the cressets and the pans, he had of policy refrained from even glancing at the walls of the house; but what could it matter now? For the glorious and overwhelming moment at least? And, judging by recent experience, the moment might even prove a noticeably long moment. Time might again stand still. Time sometimes did if one had not expected it.

Therefore, from as soon as they entered, he stared round at intervals quite brazenly, though not when Nell was looking at him, as for so much of the time she was now doing.

The upshot was anti-climax: here was not the stark, familiar bedroom in the rectory, and Stephen realised that he had not yet acquired points, or areas, of reference and comparison. He was at liberty to deem that they might never be needed.

Nell was ordering things, arranging things, even beginning to prepare things: all as if she had been a *diplomée* of a domestic college; as if she had been blessed with a dedicated mamma or aunt. After all, thought Stephen, as he watched her and intercepted her, her appearance is largely that of an ordinary modern girl.

He loved her.

He turned his back upon her earlier curious intimations. She had run away from it all; and had even stated as much, unasked and unprompted. Henceforth, an ordinary modern girl was what for him she should firmly be; though loyaller, tenderer, stronger than any other.

When, in the end, languishingly they went upstairs, this time they wrapt themselves in lovely new blankets, but Stephen was in no doubt at all that still there was only the one mark on her. Conceivably, even, it was a slightly smaller mark.

He would no longer detect, no longer speculate, no

longer be anxious, no longer imagine. No more mortal marks and corruptions. For example, he would quite possibly never sleep in that room at the rectory again.

Thus, for a week, he counted the good things only, as does a sundial. They were many and the silken sequence of them seemed to extend over a lifetime. He recollected the Christian Science teaching that evil is a mere illusion. He clung to the thesis that time is no absolute.

Nell had the knack of supplementing the food he had purchased with fauna and flora that she brought back from the moor. While, at a vague hour of the morning, he lay long among the blankets, simultaneously awake and asleep, she went forth, and never did she return empty-handed, seldom, indeed, other than laden. He was at last learning not from talk but from experience, even though from someone else's experience, how long it really was possible to live without shops, without bureaucratically and commercially modified products, without even watered cash. All that was needed was to be alone in the right place with the right person.

He even saw it as possible that the two of them might remain in the house indefinitely: were it not that his 'disappearance' would inevitably be 'reported' by someone, doubtless first by Arthur Thread in the office, so that his early exposure was inevitable. That, after all, was a main purpose of science: to make things of all kinds happen sooner than they otherwise would.

Each morning, after Nell had returned from her sorties and had set things in the house to rights, she descended naked to the spring and sank beneath its waters. She liked Stephen to linger at the rim watching her, and to him it seemed that she disappeared in the pool altogether, vanished from sight, and clear though the water was, the clearest, Stephen surmised, that he had ever lighted upon. Beyond doubt, therefore, the little pool really was peculiarly deep, as Nell had always said: it would be difficult to distinguish between the natural movements of its ever-gleaming surface, and movements that might emanate from a submerged naiad. It gave Stephen special pleasure that they drank exclusively from the pool in which Nell splashed about, but, partly for that reason, he confined his own lustrations to dabblings from the edge, like a tripper. Stephen learned by experience, a new experience, the difference between drinking natural water and drinking safeguarded water, as from a sanitised public convenience. When she emerged from the pool, Nell each day shook her short hair like one glad to be alive, and each day her hair seemed to be dry in no time.

One morning, she washed her shirt and trousers in the pool, having no replacements as far as Stephen could see. The garments took longer to dry than she did, and Nell remained unclothed for most of the day, even though there were clouds in the sky. Clouds made little difference anyway, nor quite steady rain, nor drifting mountain mist. The last named merely fortified the peace and happiness.

'Where did you get those clothes?' asked Stephen, even though as a rule he no longer asked anything.

'I found them. They're nice.'

He said nothing for a moment.

'*Aren't* they nice?' she enquired anxiously.

'Everything to do with you and in and about and around you is nice in every possible way. You are perfect. Everything concerned with you is perfect.'

She smiled gratefully and went back, still unclothed, to the house, where she was stewing up everything together in one of the new pots. The pot had already leaked, and it had been she who had mended the leak, with a preparation she had hammered and kneaded while Stephen had merely looked on in delighted receptivity, wanting her as she worked.

He had a number of books in his bag, reasonably well chosen, because he had supposed that on most evenings at the rectory he would be retiring early; but now he had no wish to read anything. He conjectured that he would care little if the capacity to read somehow faded from him. He even went so far as to think that, given only a quite short time, it might possibly do so.

At moments, they wandered together about the moor; he, as like as not, with his hand on her breast, on that breast pocket of hers which contained his original and only letter to her, and which she had carefully taken out and given to him when washing the garment, and later carefully replaced. Than these perambulations few excursions could be more uplifting, but Stephen was wary all the same, knowing that if they were to meet anyone, however blameless, the spell might break, and paradise end.

Deep happiness can but be slighted by third parties, whosoever, without exception, they be. No one is so pure as to constitute an exception.

And every night the moon shone through the small windows and fell across their bed and their bodies in wide streaks, oddly angled.

'You are like a long, sweet parsnip,' Stephen said. 'Succulent but really rather tough.'

'I know nothing at all,' she replied. 'I only know you.'

The mark below her shoulder stood out darkly, but, God be praised, in isolation. What did the rapidly deteriorating state of the walls and appurtenances matter by comparison with that?

But in due course, the moon, upon which the seeding and growth of plants and of the affections largely depend, had entered its dangerous third quarter.

Stephen had decided that the thing he had to do was take Nell back quickly and quietly to London, and return as soon as possible with his reinvigorated car, approaching as near as he could, in order to collect their possessions in the house. The machine would go there, after all, if he drove it with proper vigour; though it might be as well to do it at a carefully chosen hour, in order to evade Harewood, Doreen, and the general life of the village.

He saw no reason simply to abandon all his purchases and, besides, he felt obscurely certain that it was unlucky to do so, though he had been unable to recall the precise belief. Finally, it would seem likely that some of the varied accessories in the house might be useful in Stephen's new life with Nell. One still had to be practical at times, just as one had to be firm at times.

Nell listened to what he had to say, and then said she would do whatever he wanted. The weather was entirely fair for the moment.

When the purchased food had finally run out, and they were supposedly dependent altogether upon what Nell could bring in off the moor, they departed from the house, though not, truthfully, for that reason. They left everything behind them and walked down at dusk past Burton's Clough to the village. Stephen knew the time of the last bus which connected with a train to London. It was something he knew wherever he was. In a general way, he had of course always liked the train journey and disliked the bus journey.

It was hard to imagine what Nell would make of such experiences, and of those inevitably to come. Though she always said she knew nothing, she seemed surprised by nothing either. Always she brought back to Stephen the theories that there were two kinds of knowledge; sometimes of the same things.

All the others in the bus were old-age pensioners. They had been visiting younger people and were now returning. They sat alone, each as far from each as space allowed. In the end, Stephen counted them. There seemed to be eight, though it was hard to be sure in the bad light, and with several pensioners already slumped forward.

There were at least two kinds of bad light also; the

beautiful dim light of the house on the moor, and the depressing light in a nationalised bus. Stephen recalled Ellen Terry's detestation of all electric light. And of course there were ominous marks on the dirty ceiling of the bus and on such of the side panels as Stephen could see, including that on the far side of Nell, who sat beside him, with her head on his shoulder, more like an ordinary modern girl than ever. Where could she have learned that when one was travelling on a slow, ill-lighted bus with the man one loved, one put one's head on his shoulder?

But it was far more that she had somewhere, somehow learned. The slightest physical contact with her induced in Stephen a third dichotomy: the reasonable, rather cautious person his whole life and career surely proved him to be, was displaced by an all but criminal visionary. Everything turned upon such capacity as he might have left to change the nature of time.

The conductor crept down the dingy passage and sibilated in Stephen's ear. 'We've got to stop here. Driver must go home. Got a sick kid. There'll be a reserve bus in twenty minutes. All right?'

The conductor didn't bother to explain to the pensioners. They would hardly have understood. For them, the experience itself would be ample. A few minutes later, everyone was outside in the dark, though no one risked a roll call. The lights in the bus had been finally snuffed out, and the crew were making off, aclank with the accoutrements of their tenure, spanners, and irregular metal boxes, and enamelled mugs.

Even now, Nell seemed unsurprised and unindignant. She, at least, appeared to acknowledge that all things have an end, and to be acting on that intimation. As usual, Stephen persuaded her to don his heavy sweater.

It was very late indeed, before they were home; though Stephen could hardly use the word now that not only was Elizabeth gone, but also there was somewhere else, luminously better – or, at least, so decisively different – and, of course, a new person too.

Fortunately, the train had been very late, owing to signal trouble, so that they had caught it and been spared a whole dark night of it at the station, as in a story. Stephen and Nell had sat together in the buffet, until they had been ejected, and the striplighting quelled. Nell had never faltered. She had not commented even when the train, deprived of what railwaymen call its 'path', had fumbled its way to London, shunting backward nearly as often as running forward. In the long, almost empty, excursion-type coach had been what Stephen could by now almost complacently regard as the usual smears and blotches.

'Darling, aren't you cold?' He had other, earlier sweaters to lend.

She shook her head quite vigorously.

After that, it had been easy for Stephen to close his eyes almost all the way. The other passenger had appeared to be a fireman in uniform, though of course without helmet. It was hard to believe that he would suddenly rise and rob them, especially as he was so silently slumbering. Perhaps he was all the time a hospital porter or a special messenger or an archangel.

On the Benares table which filled the hall of the flat (a wedding present from Harewood and poor Harriet, who, having been engaged in their teens, had married long ahead of Stephen and Elizabeth), was a parcel, weighty but neat.

'Forgive me,' said Stephen. 'I never can live with unopened parcels or letters.'

He snapped the plastic string in a second and tore through the Glyptal wrapping. It was a burly tome entitled *Lichen, Moss, and Wrack. Usage and Abusage in Peace and War. A Military and Medical Abstract.* Scientific works so often have more title than imaginative works.

Stephen flung the book back on the table. It fell with a heavy clang.

'Meant for my brother. It's always happening. People don't seem to know there's a difference between us.'

He gazed at her. He wanted to see nothing else.

She looked unbelievably strange in her faded trousers and the sweater Elizabeth had made. Elizabeth would have seen a ghost and fainted. Elizabeth did tend to faint in the sudden presence of the occult.

'We are not going to take it to him. It'll have to be posted. I'll get the Department to do it tomorrow.'

He paused. She smiled at him, late though it was.

Late or early? What difference did it make? It was not what mattered.

'I told you that I should have to go to the Department tomorrow. There's a lot to explain.'

She nodded. 'And then we'll go back?' She had been anxious about that ever since they had started. He had not known what to expect.

'Yes. After a few days.'

Whatever he intended in the first place, he had never made it clear to her where they would be living in the longer run. This was partly because he did not know himself. The flat, without Elizabeth, really was rather horrible. Stephen had not forgotten Elizabeth for a moment. How could he have done? Nor could Stephen wonder that Nell did not wish to live in the flat. The flat was disfigured and puny.

Nell still smiled with her usual seeming understanding. He had feared that by now she would demur at his reference to a few days, and had therefore proclaimed it purposefully.

He smiled back at her. 'I'll buy you a dress.'

She seemed a trifle alarmed.

'It's time you owned one.'

'I don't own anything.'

'Yes, you do. You own me. Let's go to bed, shall we?'

But she spoke. 'What's this?'

As so often happens, Nell had picked up and taken an interest in the thing he would least have wished.

It was a large, lumpy shopping bag from a craft room in Burnham-on-Sea, where Elizabeth and he had spent an unwise week in their early days. What the Orient was to Harriet, the seaside had been to Elizabeth. Sisters-in-law often show affinities. The shopping bag had continued in regular use ever since, and not only for shopping, until Elizabeth had been no longer mobile.

'It's a bag made of natural fibres,' said Stephen. 'It belonged to my late wife.'

'It smells. It reminds me.'

'Many things here remind *me*,' said Stephen. 'But a new page had been turned.' He kept forgetting that Nell was unaccustomed to book metaphors.

She appeared to be holding the bag out to him. Though not altogether knowing why, he took it from her. He then regretted doing so.

It was not so much the smell of the bag. He was entirely accustomed to that. It was that, in his absence, the bag had become sodden with dark growths, outside and inside. It had changed character completely.

Certainly the bag had been perfectly strong and serviceable when last he had been in contact with it; though for the moment he could not recollect when that had been. He had made little use of the bag when not under Elizabeth's direction.

He let the fetid mass fall on top of the book on the brass table.

'Let's forget everything,' he said. 'We still have a few hours.'

'Where do I go?' she asked, smiling prettily.

'Not in there,' he cried, as she put her hand on one of the doors. He very well knew that he must seem far too excitable. He took a pull on himself. 'Try *this* room.'

When Elizabeth had become ill, the double bed had been moved into the spare room. It had been years since Stephen had slept in that bed, though, once again, he could not in the least recall how many years. The first step towards mastering time is always to make time meaningless.

It was naturally wonderful to be at long last in a fully equipped deep double bed with Nell. She had shown no expectation of being invited to borrow one of Elizabeth's expensive nightdresses. Nell was a primitive still, and it was life or death to keep her so. He had never cared much for flowing, gracious bedwear in any case; nor had the wonder that was Elizabeth seemed to him to need such embellishments.

But he could not pretend, as he lay in Nell's strong arms and she in his, that the condition of the spare room was in the least reassuring. Before he had quickly turned off the small bedside light, the new marks on the walls had seemed like huge inhuman faces; and the effect was all the more alarming in that these walls had been painted, inevitably long ago, by Elizabeth in person, and had even been her particular domestic display piece. The stained overall she had worn for the task still hung in the cupboard next door, lest the need arise again.

It was always the trouble. So long as one was far from the place once called home, one could successfully cast secondary matters from the mind, or at least from the hurting part of it; but from the moment of return, in fact from some little while before that, one simply had to recognise that, for most of one's life, secondary matters were just about all there were. Stephen had learned ages ago that secondary matters were always the menace.

Desperation, therefore, possibly made its contribution to the mutual passion that changed the few hours available to them.

Within a week, the walls might be darkened all over; and what could the development after *that* conceivably be?

Stephen strongly suspected that the mossiness, the malady, would become more conspicuously three dimensional at any moment. Only as a first move, of course.

He managed to close his mind against all secondary considerations and to give love its fullest licence yet.

Thread was in the office before Stephen, even though Stephen had risen most mortifyingly early, and almost sleepless. It was a commonplace that the higher one ascended in the service, the earlier one had to rise, in order to ascend higher still. The lamas never slept at all.

'Feeling better?' Thread could ask such questions with unique irony.

'Much better, thank you.'

'You still look a bit peaky.' Thread was keeping his finger at the place he had reached in the particular file.

'I had a tiresome journey back. I've slept very little.'

'It's always the trouble. Morag and I make sure of a few days to settle in before we return to full schedule.'

'Elizabeth and I used to do that also. It's a bit different now.'

Thread looked Stephen straight in the eyes, or very nearly.

'Let me advise, for what my advice is worth. I recommend you to lose yourself in your work for the next two or three years at the least. Lose yourself completely. Forget everything else. In my opinion, it's always the best thing at these times. Probably the only thing.'

'Work doesn't mean to me what it did.'

'Take yourself in hand, and it soon will again. After all, very real responsibilities do rest in this room. We both understand that quite well. We've reached that sort of level, Stephen. What we do nowadays *matters*. If you keep that in mind at all times, and I do mean at *all* times, the thought will see you through. I know what I'm talking about.'

Thread's eyes were now looking steadily at his finger, lest it had made some move on its own.

'Yes,' said Stephen, 'but you're talking about yourself, you know.'

Stephen was very well aware that the sudden death some years before of Arthur Thread's mother had not deflected Thread for a day from the tasks appointed. Even the funeral had taken place during the weekend; for which Thread had departed on the Friday evening with several major files in his briefcase, as usual. As for Thread's wife, Morag, she was a senior civil servant too, though of course in a very different department. The pair took very little leave in any case, and hardly any of it together. Their two girls were at an expensive boarding school on the far side of France, almost in Switzerland.

'I speak from my own experience,' corrected Thread.

'It appears to me,' said Stephen, 'that I have reached the male climacteric. It must be what's happening to me.'

'I advise you to think again,' said Thread. 'There's no such thing. Anyway you're too young for when it's supposed to be. It's not till you're sixty-three; within two years of retirement.'

Thread could keep his finger in position no longer, lest his arm fall off. 'If you'll forgive me, I'm rather in the middle of something. Put yourself absolutely at ease. I'll be very pleased to have another talk later.'

'What's that mark?' asked Stephen, pointing to the wall above Thread's rather narrow headpiece. So often the trouble seemed to begin above the head. 'Was it there before?'

'I'm sure I don't know. Never forget the whole place is going to be completely done over next year. Now do let me concentrate for a bit.'

As the time for luncheon drew near, another man, Mark Tremble, peeped in.

'Glad to see you back, Stephen. I really am.'

Thank you, Mark. I wish I could more sincerely say I was glad to *be* back.'

'Who could be? Come and swim?'

Stephen had regularly done it with Mark Tremble and a shifting group of others; usually at lunchtime on several days a week. It had been one of twenty devices for lightening momentarily the weight of Elizabeth's desperation. The bath was in the basement

331

of the building. Soon the bath was to be extended and standardised, and made available at times to additional grades.

'Very well.'

Stephen had at one time proposed to tear back; to be with Nell for a few moments; perhaps to buy that dress; but during the long morning he had decided against all of it.

His real task was to put down his foot with the establishment; to secure such modified pension as he was entitled to; to concentrate, as Thread always concentrated; to depart.

He had not so far said a word about it to anyone in the place.

The two seniors changed in the sketchy cubicles, and emerged almost at the same moment in swimming trunks. There seemed to be no one else in or around the pool that day, though the ebbing and flowing of table tennis were audible through the partition.

'I say, Stephen. What's that thing on your back?'

Stephen stopped dead on the wet tiled floor. 'What thing?'

'It's a bit peculiar. I'm sure it wasn't there before. Before you went away. I'm extremely sorry to mention it.'

'What's it look like?' asked Stephen. 'Can you describe it?'

'The best I can do is that it looks rather like the sort of thing you occasionally see on trees. I think it may simply be something stuck on to you. Would you like me to give it a tug?'

'I think not,' said Stephen. 'I am sorry it upsets you. I'll go back and dress. I think it would be better.'

'Yes,' said Mark Tremble. 'It does upset me. It's best to admit it. Either it's something that will just come off with a good rub, or you'd better see a doctor, Stephen.'

'I'll see what I can do,' said Stephen.

'I don't feel so much like a swim, after all,' said Mark Tremble. 'I'll dress too and then we'll both have a drink. I feel we could both do with one.'

'I'm very sorry about it,' said Stephen. 'I apologise.'

'What have *you* been doing all day?' asked Stephen, as soon as he was back and had changed out of the garments currently normal in the civil service, casual and characterless. 'I hope you've been happy.'

'I found this on the roof.' Nell was holding it in both her hands; which were still very brown. It was a huge lump: mineral, vegetable, who could tell? Or conceivably a proportion of each.

'Your father would be interested.'

Nell recoiled. 'Don't talk like that. It's unlucky.' Indeed, she had nearly dropped the dense mass.

It had been an idiotic response on Stephen's part; mainly the consequence of his not knowing what else to say. He was aware that it was perfectly possible to attain the roof of the building by way of the iron fire ladder, to which, by law, access had to be open to tenants at all hours.

'I could do with a drink,' said Stephen, though he had been drinking virtually the whole afternoon, without

Thread even noticing, or without sparing time to acknowledge that he had noticed. Moira, the coloured girl from the typing area, had simply winked her big left eye at Stephen. 'I've had a difficult day.'

'Oh!' Nell's cry was so sincere and eloquent that it was as if he had been mangled in a traffic accident.

'*How* difficult?' she asked.

'It's just that it's been difficult for me to make the arrangements to get away, to leave the place.'

'But we *are* going?' He knew it was what she was thinking about.

'Yes, we are going. I promised.'

He provided Nell with a token drink also. At first she had seemed to be completely new to liquor. Stephen had always found life black without it, but his need for it had become more habitual during Elizabeth's illness. He trusted that Nell and he would, with use, wont, and time, evolve a mutual equilibrium.

At the moment, he recognised that he was all but tight, though he fancied that at such times he made little external manifestation. Certainly Nell would detect nothing; if only because presumably she lacked data. Until now, he had never really been in the sitting room of the flat since his return. Here, the new tendrils on the walls and ceiling struck him as resembling a Portuguese man-o'-war's equipment; the coloured, insensate creature that can sting a swimmer to death at thirty feet distance, and had done so more than once when Elizabeth and he, being extravagant, had stayed at Cannes for a couple of weeks. It had been there that

Elizabeth told him finally she could never have a child. Really that was what they were doing there, though he had not realised it. The man-o'-war business, the two victims, had seemed to have an absurd part in their little drama. No one in the hotel had talked of anything else.

'Let's go to bed *now*,' said Stephen to Nell. 'We can get up again later to eat.'

She put her right hand in his left hand.

Her acquiescence, quiet and beautiful, made him feel compunctious.

'Or are you hungry?' he asked. 'Shall we have something to eat first? I wasn't thinking.'

She shook her head. 'I've been foraging.'

She seemed to know so many quite literary words. He gave no time to wondering where exactly the forage could have taken place. It would be unprofitable. Whatever Nell had brought in would be wholesomer, inestimably better in every way, than food from any shop.

As soon as she was naked, he tried, in the electric light, to scrutinise her. There still seemed to be only the one mark on her body, truly a quite small mark by the standards of the moment, though he could not fully convince himself that it really was contracting.

However, the examination was difficult: he could not let Nell realise what exactly he was doing; the light was not very powerful, because latterly Elizabeth had disliked a strong light anywhere, and he had felt unable to argue; most of all, he had to prevent Nell seeing whatever Mark Tremble had seen on his own person, had himself all the time to lie facing Nell or flat on his back. In any case, he wondered always how much Nell saw that he saw; how much, whatever her utterances and evidences, she analysed of the things that he analysed.

The heavy curtains, chosen and hung by Elizabeth, had it seemed, remained drawn all day; and by now the simplest thing was for Stephen to switch off what light there was.

Nell, he had thought during the last ten days or ten aeons, was at her very best when the darkness was total.

He knew that heavy drinking was said to increase desire and to diminish performance; and he also knew that it was high time in his life for him to begin worrying about such things. He had even so hinted to Arthur Thread; albeit mainly to startle Thread, and to foretoken his, Stephen's, new life course; even though any such intimation to Thread would be virtually useless. There can be very few to whom most of one's uttered remarks can count for very much.

None the less, Nell and Stephen omitted that evening to arise later; even though Stephen had fully and sincerely intended it.

The next morning, very early the next morning, Nell vouchsafed to Stephen an unusual but wonderful breakfast – if one could apply so blurred a noun to so farfetched a repast.

Stephen piled into his civil service raiment, systematically noncommittal. He was taking particular trouble not to see his own bare back in any looking-glass. Fortunately, there was no such thing in the dim bathroom.

'Goodbye, my Nell. Before the weekend we shall be free.'

He supposed that she knew what a weekend was. By now, it could hardly be clearer that she knew almost everything that mattered in the least.

But, during that one night, the whole flat seemed to have become dark green, dark grey, plain black: patched everywhere, instead of only locally, as when they had arrived. Stephen felt that the walls, floors, and ceilings were beginning to advance towards one another. The knick-knacks were dematerialising most speedily. When life once begins to move, it can scarcely be prevented from setting its own pace. The very idea of intervention becomes ridiculous.

What was Nell making of these swift and strange occurrences? All Stephen was sure of was that it would be unwise to take too much for granted. He must hew his way out; if necessary, with a bloody axe, as the man in the play put it.

Stephen kissed Nell ecstatically. She was smiling as he shut the door. She might smile, off and on, all day, he thought; smile as she foraged.

By that evening, he had drawn a curtain, thick enough even for Elizabeth to have selected, between his homebound self and the events of the daylight.

There was no technical obstacle to his retirement, and never had been. It was mainly the size of his pension that was affected; and in his new life he seemed able to thrive on very little. A hundred costly substitutes for direct experience could be rejected. An intense reality, as new as it was old, was burning down on him like clear sunlight or heavenly fire or poetry.

It was only to be expected that his colleagues should shrink back a little. None the less, Stephen had been disconcerted by how far some of them had gone. They would have been very much less concerned, he fancied, had he been an acknowledged defector, about to stand trial. Such cases were now all in the day's work: there were routines to be complied with, though not too strictly. Stephen realised that his appearance was probably against him. He was not sure what he looked like from hour to hour, and he was taking no steps to find out.

Still, the only remark that was passed, came from Toby Strand, who regularly passed remarks.

'Good God, Stephen, you're looking like death warmed up. I should go home to the wife. You don't want to pass out in this place.'

Stephen looked at him.

'Oh God, I forgot. Accept my apology.'

'That's perfectly all right, Toby,' said Stephen. 'And as for the other business, you'll be interested to learn that I've decided to retire.'

'Roll on the day for one and all,' said Toby Strand, ever the *vox populi*.

Mercifully, Stephen's car had been restored to a measure of health, so that the discreet bodywork gleamed slightly in the evening lustre as he drove into the rented parking space.

'Nell, we can leave at cockcrow!'

*

'I forgot about buying you that dress.'

He was standing in his bath gown, looking at her in the wide bed. The whole flat was narrowing and blackening, and at that early hour the electric light was even weaker than usual.

'I shan't need a dress.'

'You must want a change sometime.'

'No. I want nothing to change.'

He gazed at her. As so often, he had no commensurate words.

'We'll stop somewhere on the way,' he said.

They packed the rehabilitated car with essentials for the simple life; with things to eat and drink on the journey and after arrival. Stephen, though proposing to buy Nell a dress, because one never knew what need might arise, was resolved against dragging her into a roadside foodplace. He took all he could, including, surreptitiously, some sad souvenirs of Elizabeth, but he recognised plainly enough that there was almost everything remaining to be done with the flat, and that he would have to return one day to do it, whether or not Nell came with him. In the meantime, it was difficult to surmount what was happening to the flat, or to him. Only Nell was sweet, calm, and changeless in her simple clothes. If only the nature of time were entirely different!

'You'll be terribly cold.'

She seemed never to say it first, never to think of it.

He covered her with sweaters and rugs. He thought

339

of offering her a pair of his own warm trousers, but they would be so hopelessly too wide and long.

Islington was a misty marsh, as they flitted through; Holloway pink as a desert flamingo. The scholarly prison building was wrapped in fire. Finsbury Park was crystal as a steppe; Manor House deserted as old age.

When, swift as thoughts of love, they reached Grantham, they turned aside to buy Nell's dress. She chose a rough-textured white one, with the square neck outlined in black, and would accept nothing else, nothing else at all. She even refused to try on the dress and she refused to wear it out of the shop. Stephen concurred, not without a certain relief, and carried the dress to the car in a plastic bag. The car was so congested that a problem arose.

'I'll sit on it,' said Nell.

Thus the day went by as in a dream: though there are few such dreams in one lifetime. Stephen, for sure, had never known a journey so rapt, even though he could seldom desist from staring and squinting for uncovenanted blemishes upon and around the bright coach-work. Stephen recognised that, like everyone else, he had spent his life without living; even though he had had Elizabeth for much of the time to help him through, as she alone was able.

Northwards, they ran into a horse fair. The horses were everywhere, and, among them, burlesques of men bawling raucously, and a few excited girls.

'Oh!'cried Nell.

'Shall we stop?'

'No,' said Nell. 'Not stop.'

She was plainly upset.

'Few fairs like that one are left,' said Stephen, as he sat intimately, eternally beside her. 'The motors have been their knell.'

'Knell,' said Nell.

Always it was impossible to judge how much she knew.

'Nell,' said Stephen affectionately. But it was at about that moment he first saw a dark, juicy crack in the polished metalwork of the bonnet.

'Nell,' said Stephen again; and clasped her hand, always brown, always warm, always living and loving. The huge geometrical trucks were everywhere, and it was an uncircumspect move for Stephen to make. But it was once more too misty for the authorities to see very much, to take evidence that could be sworn to.

The mist was more like fog as they wound through Harewood's depopulated community. Harewood really should marry Doreen as soon as it becomes possible, thought Stephen, and make a completely new start in life, perhaps have a much better type of youngster, possibly and properly for the cloth.

Stephen was struck with horror to recollect that he had forgotten all about the costly book which had been almost certainly intended for Harewood, and which Harewood would be among the very few fully to appreciate and rejoice in. The book had not really been noticeable at first light in the eroding flat, but his lapse perturbed Stephen greatly.

341

'A fungus and an alga living in a mutually beneficial relationship,' he said under his breath.

'What's that?' asked Nell.

'It's the fundamental description of a lichen. You should know that.'

'Don't talk about it.'

He saw that she shuddered; she who never even quaked from the cold.

'It's unlucky,' she said.

'I'm sorry, Nell. I was thinking of the book we left behind, and the words slipped out.'

'We're better without the book.'

'It wasn't really our book.'

'We did right in leaving it.'

He realised that it had been the second time when, without thinking, he had seemed ungracious about the big step she had taken for him: the second time at least.

Therefore, he simply answered, 'I expect so.'

He remained uneasy. He had taken due care not to drive past the crumbling rectory, but nothing could prevent the non-delivery of Harewood's expensive book being an odious default, a matter of only a few hundred yards. To confirm the guilt, a middle-aged solitary woman at the end of the settlement suddenly pressed both hands to her eyes, as if to prevent herself from seeing the passing car, even in the poor light.

The ascending track was rougher and rockier than on any of Stephen's previous transits. It was only to be expected, Stephen realised. Moreover, to mist was now added dusk. At the putative Burton's Clough, he had to take care not to drive over the edge of the declivity; and thereafter he concentrated upon not colliding with the overgrown stony waymark. Shapeless creatures were beginning to emerge which may no longer appear by daylight even in so relatively remote a region. Caution was compelled upon every count.

Thus it was full night when somehow they reached the spot where the track seemed simply to end – with no good reason supplied, as Stephen had always thought. Elizabeth would have been seriously upset if somehow she had seen at such a spot the familiar car in which she had taken so many unforgettable outings, even when a virtual invalid. She might have concluded that at long last she had reached the final bourne.

The moon, still in its third quarter, managed to glimmer, like a fragrance, through the mist; but there could be no visible stars. Stephen switched on his flash, an item of official supply.

'We don't need it,' said Nell. 'Please not.'

Nell was uncaring of cold, of storm, of fog, of fatigue. Her inner strength was superb, and Stephen loved it. But her indifference to such darkness as this reminded Stephen of her father, that wonderful entity, whom it was so unlucky ever to mention, probably even to think of. None the less, Stephen turned back the switch. He had noticed before that he was doing everything she said.

As best he could, he helped her to unload the car, and followed her along the narrow paths through the damp heather. Naturally, he could not see a trace of the house, and he suddenly realised that, though they struggled in silence, he could not even hear the gently heaving spring. They were making a pile at the spot where the house must be; and Nell never put a foot wrong in finding the pile a second, third, and even fourth time. Much of the trip was steep, and Stephen was quite winded once more by his fourth climb in almost no moonlight at all, only the faint smell of moonlight; but when, that time, he followed Nell over the tangled brow, the mist fell away for a moment, as mist on mountains intermittently does, and at last Stephen could see the house quite clearly.

He looked at Nell standing there, pale and mysterious as the moonlight began to fade once more.

'Have you still got my letter?'

She put her hand on her breast pocket.

'Of course I have.'

They re-entered the house, for which no key was ever deemed necessary. It might be just as well, for none was available.

Stephen realised at once that what they were doing was moving into the house pretty finally; not, as he had so recently proposed, preparing to move out of it in a short time. It was clear that once Nell truly and finally entered one's life, one had simply to accept the consequences. Stephen could perceive well enough that Nell was at every point moved by forces in comparison with which he was moved by inauthentic fads.

Acquiescence was the only possibility. The admixture in Nell of ignorance and wisdom, sometimes even surface sophistication, was continuously fascinating. In any case, she had left familiar surroundings and completely changed her way of life for him. He must do the same for her without end; and he wished it.

The moonlight was now insufficient to show the state of the walls or the curiously assorted furnishings or the few personal traps he had omitted to bear to London. Stephen had worn gloves to drive and had not removed them to lug. He wore them still.

None the less, when he said, 'Shall we have a light now?' he spoke with some reluctance.

'Now,' said Nell. 'We're at home now.'

He fired up some of the rough cressets he had managed to lay hands on when he had borrowed the sottish Jarrold's Land Rover.

Nell threw herself against him. She kissed him again and again.

As she did so, Stephen resolved to look at nothing more. To look was not necessarily to see. He even thought he apprehended a new vein of truth in what Nell had said on that second day, still only a very short time ago, about her father.

Nell went upstairs and changed into the dress he had bought her. She had done it without a hint, and he took for granted that she had done it entirely to give pleasure. In aspect, she was no longer a part of nature, merging into it, an oread. Not surprisingly, the dress did not fit very well, but on Nell it looked like a peplos. She was a sybil. Stephen was scarcely surprised. There was no need for him to see anything other than Nell's white and black robe, intuitively selected, prophetically insisted upon; quite divine, as ordinary normal girls used to say.

When he dashed off his gloves in order to caress her, he regarded only her eyes and her raiment; but later there was eating to be done, and it is difficult, in very primitive lighting, to eat without at moments noticing one's hands. These particular hands seemed at such moments to be decorated with horrid subfuse smears, quite new. Under the circumstances, they might well have come from inside Stephen's driving gloves; warm perhaps, but, like most modern products, of no precise or very wholesome origin. If ineradicable, the marks were appalling; not to be examined for a single second.

When Nell took off her new dress, Stephen saw at once (how else but at once?) that her own small single mark had vanished. She was as totally honied as harvest home, and as luscious, and as rich.

Stephen resolved that in the morning, if there was one, he would throw away all the souvenirs of Elizabeth he had brought with him. They could be scattered on the moor as ashes in a memorial garden, but better far. The eyes that were watching from behind the marks on the walls and ceilings and utensils glinted back at him, one and all. The formless left hands were his to shake.

In the nature of things, love was *nonpareil* that night; and there was music too. Nell's inner being, when one knew her, when one really knew her, was as matchless as her unsullied body. Goodness is the most powerful aphrodisiac there is, though few have the opportunity of learning. Stephen had learned long before from the example of Elizabeth, and now he was learning again.

Time finally lost all power.

The music became endlessly more intimate.

'God!' cried Stephen suddenly. 'That's Schumann!' He had all but leapt in the air. Ridiculously.

'Where?' asked Nell. Stephen realised that he was virtually sitting on her. He dragged himself up and was standing on the floor.

'That music. It's Schumann.'

'I hear no music.'

'I don't suppose you do.'

Stephen spoke drily and unkindly, as he too often did, but he knew that everything was dissolving.

For example, he could see on the dark wall the large portrait of Elizabeth by a pupil of Philip de Laszlo which had hung in their conjugal bedroom. The simulacrum was faint and ghostly, like the music, but he could see it clearly enough for present purposes, dimly self-illuminated.

He had taken that picture down with his own hands, years and years ago; and the reason had been, as he now instantly recalled, that the light paintwork had speedily become blotched and suffused. They had naturally supposed it to be something wrong with the pigments, and had spoken between themselves of vegetable dyes and the superiorities of Giotto and Mantegna. Stephen had hidden the festering canvas in the communal basement storeroom, and had forgotten about it immediately.

Now he could see it perfectly well, not over the bed, but in front of it, as always.

'Come back,' said Nell. 'Come back to me.'

The music, which once, beyond doubt, had been the music of love, was dying away. In its place, was a persistent snuffling sound, as if the house from outside, or the room from inside, were being cased by a wolf.

'What's that noise? That noise of an animal?'

'Come back to me,' said Nell. 'Come back, Stephen.' Perhaps she was quite consciously dramatising a trifle.

He had gone to the window, but of course could see nothing save the misleading huge shapes of the flapping birds.

He went back to the bed and stretched out both his hands to Nell. He was very cold.

Though there was almost no light, Nell grasped his two hands and drew him down to her.

'You see and hear so many things, Stephen,' she said.

As she spoke, he had, for moments, a vision of a different kind.

Very lucidly, he saw Nell and himself living together, but, as it might be, in idealised form, vaguely, intensely. He knew that it was an ideal of which she was wonderfully capable, perhaps because she was still so young. All that was required of him was some kind of trust.

Held by her strong hands and arms, he leant over her and faltered.

'But whatever animal is that?' he demanded.

She released his hands and curled up like a child in distress. She had begun to sob.

348

'Oh, Nell,' he cried. He fell on her and tried to reach her. Her muscles were as iron, and he made no impression at all.

In any case, he could not stop attending to the snuffling, if that was the proper word for it. He thought it was louder now. The noise seemed quite to fill the small, low, dark, remote room; to leave no space for renewed love, however desperate the need, however urgent the case.

Suddenly, Stephen knew. A moment of insight had come to him, an instinctual happening.

He divined that outside or inside the little house was Nell's father.

It was one reason why Nell was twisted in misery and terror. Her father had his own ways of getting to the truth of things. She had said so.

Stephen sat down on the bed and put his hand on her shoulder. Though he was shivering dreadfully, he had become almost calm. The process of illumination was suggesting to him the simple truth that, for Nell too, the past must be ever present. And for her it was, in common terms, the terms after which he himself was so continuously half-aspiring, a past most absurdly recent. How could he tell what experiences were hers, parallel to, but never meeting, his own?

It would be no good even making the obvious suggestion that they should dwell far away. She could never willingly leave the moor, even if it should prove the death of her; no more than he had been able all those years to leave the flat, the job, the life, all of which he had hated, and been kept alive in only by Elizabeth.

'What's the best thing to do, Nell?' Stephen enquired of her. 'Tell me and we'll do it exactly. Tell me. I think I'm going to dress while you do so. And then perhaps you'd better dress too.'

After all, he began to think, there was little that Nell had ever said about her father or her sister which many girls might not have said when having in mind to break away. He would not have wanted a girl who had no independent judgement of her own family.

The processes of insight and illumination were serving him well, and the phantom portrait seemed to have dissipated completely. The snuffling and snorting continued. It was menacing and unfamiliar, but conceivably it was caused merely by a common or uncommon but essentially manageable creature of the moors. Stephen wished he had brought his revolver (another official issue), even though he had no experience in discharging it. He could not think how he had omitted it. Then he recollected the horrible furred-up flat, and shuddered anew, within his warm clothes.

For the first time it occurred to him that poor Elizabeth might be trying, from wherever she was, to warn him. Who could tell that Harriet had not made a miraculous recovery (she was, after all, in touch with many different faiths); and was not now ready once more to accept him for a spell into the life at the rectory?

Nell was being very silent.

Stephen went back to the bed.

'Nell.'

He saw that she was not in the bed at all, but standing by the door.

'Nell.'

'Hush,' she said. 'We must hide.'

'Where do we do that?'

'I shall show you.' He could see that she was back in her shirt and trousers; a part of the natural scene once more. Her white dress glinted on the boards of the floor.

To Stephen her proposal seemed anomalous. If it really was her father outside, he could penetrate everywhere, according to her own statement. If it was a lesser adversary, combat might be better than concealment.

Nell and Stephen went downstairs in the ever more noisy darkness, and Nell, seemingly without effort, lifted a stone slab in the kitchen floor. Stephen could not quite make out how she had done it. Even to find the right slab, under those conditions, was a feat.

'All the houses have a place like this,' Nell explained.

'Why?' enquired Stephen. Surely Nell's father was an exceptional phenomenon? Certainly the supposed motion of him was akin to no other motion Stephen had ever heard.

'To keep their treasure,' said Nell.

'You are my treasure,' said Stephen.

'You are mine,' responded Nell.

There were even a few hewn steps, or so they felt to him. Duly it was more a coffer than a room, Stephen apprehended; but in no time Nell had the stone roof down on them, almost with a flick of the elbow, weighty though the roof must have been.

Now the darkness was total; something distinctly different from the merely conventional darkness above. All the same, Stephen of all people could not be unaware that the stone sides and stone floor and stone ceiling of the apartment were lined with moss and lichen. No doubt he had developed sixth and seventh senses in that arena, but the odour could well have sufficed of itself.

'How do we breathe?'

'There is a sort of pipe. That's where the danger lies.'

'You mean it might have become blocked up?'

'No.'

He did not care next to suggest that it might now be blocked deliberately. He had already made too many tactless suggestions of that kind.

She saved him the trouble of suggesting anything. She spoke in the lowest possible voice.

'He might come through.'

It was the first time she had admitted, even by implication, who it was: outside or inside – or both. Stephen fully realised that. It was difficult for him not to give way to the shakes once more, but he clung to the vague possibilities he had tried to sort out upstairs.

'I should hardly think so,' he said. 'But how long do you suggest we wait?'

'It will be better when it's day. He has to eat so often.'

It would be utterly impossible for Stephen to enquire any further; not at the moment. He might succeed in finding his way to the bottom of it all later. He was already beginning to feel cramped, and the smell of the fungi and the algae were metaphorically choking him and the moss realistically tickling him; but he put his arm round Nell in the blackness, and could even feel his letter safe against her soft breast.

She snuggled back at him; as far as circumstances permitted. He had only a vague idea of how big or small their retreat really was.

Nell spoke again in that same lowest possible voice. She could communicate, even in the most pitchy of blackness, while hardly making a sound.

'He's directly above us. He's poised.'

Stephen mustered up from his school days a grotesque recollection of some opera: the final scene. The Carl Rosa had done it: that one scene only; after the film in a cinema near Marble Arch. Elizabeth had thought the basic opera convention too far-fetched to be taken seriously; except perhaps for Mozart, who could always be taken seriously.

'I love you,' said Stephen. No doubt the chap in the opera had said something to the like effect, but had taken more time over it.

Time: that was always the decisive factor. But time had been mastered at last.

'I love *you*,' said Nell, snuggling even closer; manifesting her feeling in every way she could.

Curiously enough, it was at the verge of the small, lustrous pool that Stephen's body was ultimately found.

A poor old man, apparently resistent to full employment and even to the full security that goes with it, found the corpse, though, after all those days or weeks, the creatures and forces of the air and of the moor had done their worst to it, or their best. There was no ordinary skin anywhere. Many people in these busy times would not even have reported the find.

There were still, however, folk who believed, or at least had been told, that the pool was bottomless; and even at the inquest a theory was developed that Stephen had been wandering about on the moor and had died of sudden shock upon realising at what brink he stood. The coroner, who was a doctor of medicine, soon disposed of that hypothesis.

None the less, the actual verdict had to be open; which satisfied nobody. In these times, people expect clear answers; whether right or wrong.

Harewood, almost his pristine self by then, enquired into the possibility of a memorial service in London, which he was perfectly prepared to come up and conduct. After all, Stephen was an OBE already, and could reasonably hope for more.

The view taken was that Stephen had been missing for so long, so entirely out of the official eye, that the proper moment for the idea was regrettably, but irreversibly, past.

The funeral took place, therefore, in Harewood's own church, where the father and the grandfather of both the deceased and the officiant had shepherded so long with their own quiet distinction. People saw that no other solution had ever really been thinkable.

Doreen had by now duly become indispensible to the

rector; in the mysterious absence of Stephen, to whom the rector had specifically allotted that function. At the funeral, she was the only person in full black. Not even the solitary young man from the Ministry emulated her there. It had not been thought appropriate to place Stephen's OBE on the coffin, but during the service, the rector noticed a scrap of lichen thereon which was different entirely, he thought, from any of the species on the walls, rafters, and floors of the church. Performing his office, Harewood could not at once put a name to the specimen. The stuff that already lined the open grave was even more peculiar; and Harewood was more than a little relieved when the whole affair was finally over, the last tributes paid, and he free to stumble back to Doreen's marmite toast, and lilac peignoir. The newest number of the *Journal* had come in only just before, but Harewood did not so much as open it that evening.

As Stephen's will had been rendered ineffective by Elizabeth's decease, Harewood, as next of kin, had to play a part, whether he felt competent of not, in winding everything up. Fortunately, Doreen had been taking typing lessons, and had bought a second-hand machine with her own money.

The flat was found to be in the most shocking state, almost indescribable. It was as if there had been no visitors for years; which, as Harewood at once pointed out, had almost certainly been more or less the case, since the onset of Elizabeth's malady, an epoch ago.

A single, very unusual book about Harewood's own speciality was found. It had been published in a limited edition: a minute one, and at a price so high that Harewood himself had not been among the subscribers.

'Poor fellow!' said Harewood. 'I never knew that he was really interested. One can make such mistakes.'

The valuable book had of course to be disposed of for the benefit of the estate.

Stephen's car was so far gone that it could be sold only for scrap; but, in the event, it never was sold at all, because no one could be bothered to drag it away. If one knows where to look, one can see the bits of it still.

Robert Aickman Remembered

by Graham and Heather Smith

GRAHAM SMITH: As others have remarked, one of Robert's idiosyncrasies was to keep the activities of his life in separate compartments. Few of his many friends knew those in other fields. Heather and I were privileged to span several aspects of his life, but could never be sure we knew them all. These words may help to bridge one large gap between his life's compartments. Robert has enchanted thousands by his 'strange stories', but how many of these readers know of the millions whose lives he enriched through his decades of dedicated work to preserve Britain's incomparable network of canal and river navigations?

Robert founded the Inland Waterways Association in 1946, and led its campaign for over thirty years. Without this work there is no doubt that all that would now remain usable of this network today would be a few isolated rivers. Occasionally, Robert's other worlds surfaced in the waterways movement. Boating rallies were augmented; they became festivals of boats and arts. A few faint traces of this other passion may also be detected by scholars in one or two of his stories. Devotees of his fiction would certainly recognise the elegance and clarity of his mandarin style in the thousands of words – amounting in length to more than fifty novels – which he wrote in the Association's *Bulletin*, of which he was the editor and principal contributor for more than three decades. As with the *Bulletin*, so with his letters: those privileged to receive them saw a quality of writing which equalled and sometimes surpassed his published work.

I was enthused and enchanted by Robert's writing in the *Bulletin* from Number 62 on, and acquired a love of this mysterious and sometimes ensorcelled world of waterways which I have never lost. I became what the late Graham Palmer (a hero of the waterways movement) dubbed 'Aickman-trained'. It was, however, many years before I met Robert, in connection with an ultimately doomed campaign to rescue one of England's most ancient and beautiful river navigations: a campaign that Robert joined and immediately empowered.

Robert fought for the whole network; but he should be celebrated also for his closer part in the rescue of individual navigations. Of these, one of the more notable was the reopening of the waterways to England's heart in Shakespeare's Stratford. While the architect and engineer of the work of restoring the Stratford-upon-Avon Canal and the Upper Avon was the unforgettable late David Hutchings, David, as he readily acknowledged, could never have started without Robert's administrative skills and, even more vital, Robert's ability to enthuse the hundreds of volunteers who laboured in the mud and those whose generosity donated the money. For, as Robert came to realise soon after the Association was founded, to appeal to those into whose care (or rather, neglect) the precious network had been entrusted was futile and likely to meet not only discouragement but, frequently, outright obstruction.

Tragically (and many would say scandalously) few of the many who enjoy the waterways today know how much they owe to Robert. He never received the recognition he deserved. Our navigations are taken for granted. But it was not always so: only some few decades ago those fighting to prevent closure had to shout, stamp and spit, and suffer the censure of grey souls. 'There is arsenic in these waters,' once declared Sir John Smith, one of Robert's friends. And thus the campaign gained Robert few friends in high places. Nor did he suffer fools gladly, and there have been those over the years, even in the ranks of the Association itself, who have tried to deflect the work. For it is not fashionable nowadays to speak so powerfully and directly, or to have and use the ability to make one's antagonists look so foolish. And it did not endear him to authority when he showed that unpaid volunteers (as on the waterways to Stratford) could do what authority never could.

But Robert's doughty spirit also encompassed a huge capacity for friendship: and Robert was outstandingly generous in his praise of the many who advanced the campaign. 'It has been a tale of prophets and heroes', he wrote, 'and if more can be found we shall succeed, but not, I think, otherwise.'

HEATHER SMITH: Graham and I first met Robert in 1974. From then until the point where he was too ill to travel he spent a weekend with us in Yorkshire almost every month, and we regularly stayed with him in London. He was a lively guest and a wonderful host.

Although part of the weekends was taken up with waterways work, the remaining time was definitely devoted to pleasure. We walked in the Dales, we went to concerts, operas and plays, and we visited stately homes. We would eat and talk late into the night – all very exhausting at a time when we had two young children. But we miss it all still.

When I think about aspects of his character that shed light on his literary genius, the first which springs to mind is – perhaps prosaically – the clarity of his thought rather than his imagination. It often came about that, in order to stay in Yorkshire an extra day, he needed to write letters before returning to London, and these I would write down at his dictation. He never made notes; he simply sat quietly with eyes closed for a minute or so and then, without warning, started to speak. He would proceed to dictate a most complicated letter, the nuance of which was subtle, or the subject needing complex detail. He dictated almost without pause, including punctuation, and rarely made an alteration after I had read back the finished script. I found this skill remarkable; and I would have loved to have been similarly involved in the process of writing his fiction. But this never happened. It was not the way he wrote literature. For this he needed silence; familiar surroundings, though not usually his own apartment; a fountain pen, and a certain paper, creamy and of an unusual size. So particular was he about the paper that when the size was reduced and the colour changed to white, he developed writer's block. A friend scoured London looking for old stock, which was eventually traced and purchased in bulk.

Robert's imagination is more difficult to illustrate. He was an excellent companion on all outings, and even a mediocre production or an outing which turned out to be disappointing could be enjoyed in his company. But the experience was only a pale shadow of what it became after the event, whereupon it acquired a patina under which the reality could just be discerned. The weather, the scenery, the music, the food, the historic houses became much better – or much worse. The river-bank picnic lost all trace of thistle and reminders of cows. But it was the people encountered who were the most altered, or, perhaps better, 'imaginatively revealed'. For instance, two women seen through a window of a bakery whilst Robert waited outside would have acquired fully fledged personalities by the time I came out of the shop. They were two sisters, one a spinster and the other unhappily married. And a young girl blackberry-picking near our house when Robert went for a short walk, and bemoaning her imminent return to school, had acquired a whole tragic background before he returned.

I am sure he remembered all these characters met by chance and made use of many of them. But, here again, in his fiction they would acquire yet an extra layer of imagination, making them difficult to spot. Perhaps he did use notebooks to record ideas, but I never saw him carry one.

As for his interest in the ghostly and strange, it was there all the time: it was part of him. He found 'the strange' everywhere: in people he encountered, places he visited. He corresponded with ghost-hunters and participated in some ghost-hunts himself (and was always rather offended that ghosts had not rewarded his interest with rather more visitations). He always said he was born into the wrong age and that this feeling of not belonging contributed to his belief in the existence of another world – one that could not be tracked by scientific means, one that could not and was not meant to be understood, but one that intruded from time to time into life as we know it.